FINAL COUNTDOWN

"Stay in formation! Hold the line. No one gets through, no matter what!"

"Alpha leader! You've got a Minbari fighter on your tail! I'm on him."

"No! Mitchell! Stay in formation! It might be a—"

The shadow of the massive Minbari fighter fell across Sinclair's Starfury. "Oh, my God. It's a trap!"

"Mitchell! Break off! Break off!"

Too late. Starfury after Starfury blown to bits, exploding like miniature suns around him. Every ship of his squadron gone. Every Earth ship in his field of view destroyed.

"Not like this! Not like this! If I'm going out, I'm taking you bastards with me. Target main cruiser. Set for full-velocity ram. Afterburners on my mark. . . Mark!"

Sinclair was thrown back in his seat, his craft hurtling toward a collision with the Minbari cruiser. Ten, nine, eight, seven . . .

Look for

VOICES, BABYLON 5, BOOK #1
ACCUSATIONS, BABYLON 5, BOOK #2
BLOOD OATH, BABYLON 5, BOOK #3
CLARK'S LAW, BABYLON 5, BOOK #4
THE TOUCH OF YOUR SHADOW, THE WHISPER OF YOUR NAME, BABYLON 5, BOOK #5
BETRAYALS, BABYLON 5, BOOK #6
THE SHADOW WITHIN, BABYLON 5, BOOK #7
PERSONAL AGENDAS, BABYLON 5, BOOK #8
THE A–Z GUIDE TO BABYLON 5

in your local bookstore

BABYLON 5:

TO DREAM IN THE CITY OF SORROWS

by

Kathryn M. Drennan

Based on the series by
J. Michael Straczynski

A Dell Book

Published by
Dell Publishing
a division of
Bantam Doubleday Dell Publishing Group, Inc.
1540 Broadway
New York, New York 10036

ISBN: 0-440-22354-7

Printed in the United States of America

Published simultaneously in Canada

July 1997

10 9 8 7 6 5 4 3 2 1

OPM

This book is dedicated with love

to

Mom and Dad

ACKNOWLEDGMENTS

First and foremost, all my love and gratitude
to Joe Straczynski:
for creating *Babylon 5* in the first place;
for suggesting I write this book and then for letting
me play the way I wanted to in the wonderful
B5 universe;
and for the innumerable suggestions and advice given
every step of the way that made this a
much better book.

My thanks to the book's editor, Jacqueline Miller, for
her unflagging good humor and saintly patience.

My thanks, also, to everyone who, along with Joe
Straczynski, has made *Babylon 5* the remarkable
television show that it is:
to the astonishingly hardworking group of talented
actors, crew, artists, designers, and production staff;
and a special thanks to actor Michael O'Hare for his
superb portrayal of "Jeffrey Sinclair."

And finally, to quote one of Sinclair's favorite
authors, Alfred, Lord Tennyson:
"More things are wrought by prayer
than this world dreams of."

INTRODUCTION

MISSING MOMENTS AND MIDNIGHT THOUGHTS

J. Michael Straczynski

MY friend Harlan Ellison has, from time to time, engaged in a bit of performance art. He will sit in a bookstore window and write a short story. As each page is finished, it's taped to the window for people to read. He can't backtrack, can't change it; it is what it is.

That trick is probably the closest available comparison to what has been done with BABYLON 5 over the last four years.

BABYLON 5 is a novel for television, with a definite beginning, middle, and end. It is also a work in progress, with its fair share of sudden turns caused when the real world impinges upon the writing process, or when better ideas are stumbled upon. Yes, one may plan to have Ivanova kick several Drazi senseless and escape from the trap they've set for her . . . but if Claudia Christian breaks her foot the day before you're to shoot that sequence, you adjust.

You keep going, and you never look back. Because unlike a print novel, where after the first draft is finished you can go back and smooth out the bumps in the road, you can't change what went before. It's *out there,* transmitted into the ether at approximately the speed of light. You cannot go back, you can only go forward, broadcasting episodes as they are finished like pages taped sequentially to a window, for all the world to see.

For the most part, this particular example of performance art—telling the BABYLON 5 story in front of fifteen million viewers in the United States and countless millions more in scores of other countries around the planet—has been very successful. Most of the bumps and subtle adjustments are barely noticeable.

But they're there. And over four years, with the real world a constant random factor in the making of BABYLON 5, there are a lot of them. Small, annoying, but there. They lurk in threads that fall by the wayside, or are mentioned but not explained in as much detail as they should be, and can thus seem like logical contradictions. It's all pretty much *there* . . . it just takes a very logical and precise mind to put the pieces together and make sense of it all.

Which makes the book you hold in your hands all the more extraordinary.

Imagine someone coming to your house with a box containing eighty-eight jigsaw puzzles, all jumbled together, and dumping the contents at your feet, saying "Here . . . all the pieces are there, all you have to do is make sense of it." That is essentially the task undertaken by Kathryn Drennan in *To Dream in the City of Sorrows*.

While all of the BABYLON 5 books operate, to one extent or another, within series continuity, this is the first real attempt to stitch together massive amounts of continuity from the series itself into one book . . . to pull together the pieces dropped here and there over eighty-eight episodes and four years, ironing out the seeming discontinuities, explaining what was not explained previously, and tying together seemingly unrelated threads into a beautifully defined tapestry, all the while telling the one story that viewers have been asking for since the first season: "What happened to Jeffrey Sinclair after he left Babylon 5 and before he returned in *War without End*?"

How difficult a task was this? Job would've packed it in, Hercules would've retired, and Orpheus would've decided that his days spent in Hades weren't really *that* bad after all.

We're talking here late-night conversations, too many to number, that began with, "Okay, now when you wrote *this* in season one, what did you *really* mean and how the heck does that tie into what happened over here in season four? You spent four years talking about the Minbari warrior and religious castes but you hardly even mention the worker caste, how do they tie in? And how the *hell* was an entire Minbari fleet able to sneak up on Sinclair's squadron at the Battle of the Line right out in open space?!"

Kathryn is not just rigorously logical, she is *relentlessly* logical. Things have to make sense, and there can't be any loose threads lying around. But there were a number of loose threads surrounding the story of Sinclair's development into Entil'Zha, the head of the Rangers . . . Marcus's months being trained for his own duties as a Ranger . . . the fate of Sinclair's fiancée Catherine Sakai . . . and the ceremonies that prepared Sinclair to take up the role of Valen, one of Minbar's greatest leaders, a Minbari not born of Minbari.

All those threads have now been tied up in this one book.

And I'm just as astonished by this as you are.

It's a remarkable achievement. A breathtaking accomplishment, if for no other reason than we both somehow came through the experience without killing each other.

Relentless. Trust me on this one. Re-fragging-lentless.

To Dream in the City of Sorrows is not simply a licensed book set in the BABYLON 5 universe. While most of the Dell books to date have contained some elements that are considered canon, this is the very first one that is considered canonical in every small detail.

What you hold in your hand is *an official, authorized chapter in the BABYLON 5 story line*. This is the definitive answer to the Sinclair question, and should be considered as authentic as any episode in the regular series.

This, you should also know, is Kathryn Drennan's first novel, though she's a Clarion graduate who has been published in *Twilight Zone* magazine and many other fine magazines. She has also written for several television series, including BABYLON 5, for which she penned the excellent episode "By Any Means Necessary." This novel marks the first time an original BABYLON 5 novel has been written by someone who has actually written for the series itself.

Trust me. You'll love it.

Would this face lie?

J. Michael Straczynski
Executive Producer/Creator
BABYLON 5
19 February 1997

PROLOGUE

MARCUS Cole still walked with a limp, a fact that did not go unnoticed by the young Minbari acolyte as Marcus entered the small temple. Marcus didn't recognize the rather chubby Minbari and briefly wondered where Sech Turval was, but as he was not in the mood for conversation, he simply made a note to seek out the venerable Minbari teacher at a later time.

This had always been his favorite place at the Ranger compound, filled with the strange melodic chittering of the *temshwee,* the odd little Minbari birdlike animals that nested in the upper arches of most Minbari temples, and the gentle clinking of the wind chimes that moved in the now cool autumn breeze that swirled through the open archways. Warm sunlight streamed through the wide crystalline windows that ringed the top portion of the temple dome, creating multicolored ribbons of light. All he wanted to do now was sit and think.

Sitting, however, was not as easy right now as it used to be. Every muscle, every bone, every inch of his body still ached from the beating he had sustained six days ago, and as he gingerly lowered himself onto one of the hard, marble benches just below the larger-than-life statue of Valen that dominated the temple, he knew the acolyte was watching him. Had he heard the story?

Probably. It seemed to be common knowledge at the Ranger compound that Marcus had been thrashed to within an inch of his life by the Minbari warrior Neroon while defending the life and honor of the new Entil'Zha against Neroon's murderous intentions.

In her gratitude, Delenn had arranged for Marcus to make this brief pilgrimage, as he thought of it, back to the Minbari city known as Tuzanor, the City of Sorrows, back to the Ranger training compound, back to the beginning of it all, to finish his recuperation and to reflect—on the past and on the future, on life and on dreams, on friends and on legends.

Marcus became aware of the young Minbari acolyte hovering just at the edge of his vision, apparently uncertain if he should leave or offer his assistance to this important Ranger. Marcus closed his eyes, took a few deep breaths and assumed the Minbari meditative pose as he had been taught such a short time and such a long time ago. After a moment, he heard the acolyte leave quietly. Marcus opened his eyes again with a silent apology to Sech Turval for not continuing the meditation the old Minbari had worked so hard to teach him, but this wasn't the time for formal meditation. He just wanted to sit here—in what he and most of the other Human Rangers affectionately thought of as The Chapel—and see if in this peaceful place he could come to a better understanding of what had been lost and what had been gained since his life had intersected with the Rangers. And he wanted to visit one more time with a friend he knew he might never see again.

Marcus looked up at the imposing statue of the great Minbari military and spiritual leader Valen, studied the stern but deliberately ambiguous features of the chiseled face, and wondered once again, could that really be his friend and mentor, the very human Jeffrey Sinclair?

It had not been that many weeks since Sinclair—former Earthforce commander of Babylon 5, former ambassador from Earth to Minbar, and former Entil'Zha of the Rangers—had taken Babylon 4 on a journey through time to live out a life he had already studied as history here on Minbar: the life of the mysterious and legendary Valen. A journey taken to save lives—in both the past and future—as was always Sinclair's primary concern. But Marcus knew it was also a journey taken for the most personal of reasons. Marcus understood those reasons far better than those who had sent Sinclair on his journey. But there was still so much he didn't know, didn't understand.

He wasn't sure he'd find the answers he was looking for by studying the life of Valen. Valen, this figure of myth that towered over him here in the temple, was a stranger to Marcus. The leader, teacher, and friend he had known and had come here to Minbar to revisit in memory was a man—a remarkable man to be sure—but very Human nonetheless. It was the life of Jeffrey Sinclair he wanted to reflect on. And as his friend, it had come to seem very important to Marcus that the man not be obscured by the myth . . .

CHAPTER 1

"ALPHA 7 to Alpha Leader, I'm hit!"

Static swallowed the rest of the frantic words. Even as he shouted his reply, Earthforce Lieutenant Jeffrey Sinclair saw Quinton Orozco's Starfury flash past overhead, trailing smoke and flames, shadowed by a Minbari fighter, "Pull out! Pull out! Alpha 7!"

"He's gone."

That was Bill Mitchell's voice in the earpiece of his helmet. Sinclair checked the scope on his instrument panel, then did a quick visual check through the cockpit windshield and canopy. How many of his squadron were left against the Minbari onslaught? How many Human ships were left at all?

"Stay in formation," Sinclair ordered as he brought his Starfury around, turning away from the sun to face what seemed to be the greater concentration of Minbari fighters. "Hold the line. No one gets through, no matter what!"

"Understood," came Mitchell's voice again, then a burst of static and "Alpha Leader! You've got a Minbari on your tail!"

But Sinclair had already seen it, and was about to initiate a defensive response within the formation when he saw Mitchell's Starfury break formation to loop up and back, over Sinclair's head and toward his pursuing attacker. Other members of the squadron followed Mitchell's lead.

"I'm on him."

"No! Mitchell! Stay in formation! It might be a—"

Sinclair's instrument panel indicated a massive jump point opening behind him, right out of the blinding glare of the sun. "Oh my God. It's a trap!"

It shouldn't have been possible. Assurances had been made that a widespread pattern of vortex frequency interference would be broadcast continuously, making it impossible for the enemy to open jump points within the Line. But a shadow fell across Sinclair's ship as a massive Minbari cruiser, larger than any he'd seen before, came out of a jump point behind him. The only chance for escape was to outrun it and regroup, but what was left of his squadron had been lured into heading full speed right at the cruiser.

"Mitchell! Break off! Break off!"

It was too late. He saw Bill Mitchell's ship blown to bits. Devorah Eisenstadt's Starfury cut in two. Jake Owasaka's ship sent tumbling wildly to smash into Alo Makya's Starfury, destroying both. Within a few seconds, every ship of his squadron and all the ships around him were destroyed.

An energy beam from the Minbari cruiser sliced through the skin of Sinclair's upper starboard engine, spinning his craft out of control. His computer gave him the bad news as he fought to regain control of his ship.

"Aft stabilizers hit. Weapons systems at zero. Defensive grid at zero. Power plant near critical mass. Minbari weapons systems locking on."

Sinclair reestablished control of his Starfury and turned it back toward the looming Minbari warship. "Not like this! Not like this!" he shouted, not caring that they didn't hear him. "If I'm going out, I'm taking you bastards with me. Target main cruiser. Set for full-velocity ram. Afterburners on my mark . . . Mark!"

Sinclair was thrown back in his seat as every last bit of fuel in his craft ignited to send him hurtling on a collision course toward the Minbari cruiser. Ten, nine, eight, seven . . .

But something was wrong, even more terribly wrong than it had been just a moment before. The Minbari cruiser was changing, undulating like a living creature, morphing before his eyes. Long tendrils grew outward from the ship, and a powerful energy surge crackled along the tendrils gathering to a sphere of destructive energy at their tips. Suddenly it wasn't a Minbari cruiser at all. It was a Vorlon warship. And there were hundreds more of them, all converging on Babylon 5, intent on destroying his space station. But what was that just beyond the outermost Vorlon ship, moving back and forth between the lights of the distant stars? Shadowy shapes, dark and spindly, difficult to see or even focus on. What was happening?

Before Sinclair could react, a blinding flash obliterated the scene—

Metal fiber ropes bit into Sinclair's wrists and legs, held him motionless, suspending him at the center of a darkened, cavernous room where one bright beam of light shone down on him. Just beyond the rim of light, he could see shadowy figures, humanoid, robed. The torture he had endured at the hands of those creatures for—what? hours? days?—had been so intense that he was now moving beyond the pain that racked his body. His consciousness seemed to be floating above the scene. One of the hooded figures approached, stood before him, held up a small triangular object that seemed to be wire and metal shaped into a triangle with a stone suspended at the center. A Triluminary. The stone began to glow.

"Who are you?" Sinclair managed to force the words out through his pain. "Why are you doing this?" He tried to look at the face under the hood—it was Minbari, clearly, but who? For a moment it could have been Neroon, but then it might be Rathenn, or perhaps it was Jenimer, the Chosen One, or—Delenn?

"We claim your soul," said the voice from under the hooded robes, "as our own."

"No!" Sinclair shouted. He struggled against the binding ropes, felt them bite into his flesh, felt the blood running down his arms and legs. "NO!"

Sinclair woke up shouting, and with a violent motion wrenched himself upright in the bed. Drenched in sweat, his heart pounding furiously, he shivered uncontrollably from the intensity of the dream. At the same time, for a short, disorienting moment, he could not figure out where he was. These were not his quarters on Babylon 5.

Slowly, he began to calm down and regain his bearings. He looked around at the small bedchamber which was dimly illuminated from one corner of the room by a small brazier filled with some type of glowing stones rather than coals. There were two doors, both shut, and no windows; the walls were unadorned, and the only furnishings were the hard, narrow bed he was sitting up on, a single low bench on which some clothes were carefully laid out, and a large metal chest, inlaid with a delicate triangular pattern of gems.

Minbar. He was on the homeworld of the Minbari Federation, former deadly enemies of the Human species, and now their most powerful ally. He was in the capital city Yedor. He was in his quarters in the exclusive residential area set aside for off-world visitors and residents such as himself. He was Earth's first ambassador to Minbar.

Sinclair realized he was now shivering more from the cold temperature in the room than the dream. He swung his legs over the side of the bed and let the feeling of the cold, stone floor against his feet wake him further, also knowing that motion would signal the automatic sensors to turn up the heat.

He wasn't in the midst of his enemies. He wasn't on Minbar as a prisoner. He had agreed to come here.

Sinclair wondered what time it was, then laughed at himself a little; he was always wondering what time it was. The Minbari day was twenty hours and forty-seven minutes long. Ever since arriving on Minbar a little under three Earth standard weeks ago, his just-under-twenty-five-hour Human body clock had been precessing through the shorter Minbari days, leaving him with what felt like a permanent case of jet lag.

With a sigh, he rose and went over to the bench where he had left his watch. It was set to count off the Minbari hours, and indicated he still had another half hour of sleep coming to him. He turned off the alarm. All he wanted now was a shower to clear his head and some time to himself before his assigned Minbari helpers showed up to bring him breakfast, straighten up the room—not that he had much for them to straighten—and scurry around and bow to him.

Sinclair shook his head as he crossed the room to the bathroom door. He could not get the Minbari helpers to look him in the eyes, or to stop bowing to him. If it were just polite social bowing, common in some cultures, it wouldn't have bothered him so much. But this too often became the bowing and scraping that he'd only seen in movies when the all-powerful ruler of some exotic, ancient land entered a room. It got to be a little embarrassing at times.

When he opened the door to the bathroom, the bright light from the early morning sun streaming through the skylights momentarily blinded him. Bedrooms did not have windows, but the bathroom was open to the sky. He checked the clothes he had washed the previous evening in the rock pool and miniature waterfall, which served as bathtub and shower and which were even now splashing cheerfully in a continuous recycling of water. It always reminded Sinclair of a hotel room in New Vegas, but somehow more spiritual.

Good, the clothes were dry. He wanted them folded and put away before his "helpers" arrived. He knew his Minbari hosts thought it odd for an ambassador to be washing his own clothes, but he had left Babylon 5 for Earth and then Earth for Minbar so abruptly he had only brought a couple of changes of clothing with him, and now that he had no idea when he might get more sent out to him, he was guarding what he did have carefully, not wanting his clothes to disappear into the helpful hands of the Minbari staff, perhaps never to reappear again.

Sinclair carried the clothes over to the metal chest and opened the heavy lid. Inside were most of the few possessions he had been able to bring along with him on the sudden, rushed transfer from Babylon 5 to Earth and then to Minbar: his few clothes; a couple of AV data crystals containing a selection of music, text, readings, and movies; two real books: *The Meditations of Marcus Aurelius* and a specially printed collection of his favorite poetry, which was a long-ago gift from his fiancée, Catherine Sakai; one bottle of the finest, most expensive, aged whiskey, a more recent gift from Catherine;

a small case that contained his badges of military rank and some of his medals; and a small framed photo of Catherine.

Sinclair stacked the clothes neatly away, then picked up the photo to say a silent good morning to the woman he had vowed to marry days before events had separated them again. Where was she now? Had she heard about his transfer? Did she know where he was? He would try again today, as he had done every day since coming to Minbar, to get an answer to those questions. Those and many other questions.

When Sinclair finished his shower and emerged from the bathroom dressed and ready to begin another day, he found the Minbari crew had already entered his quarters. He could see one of them setting out his breakfast in the sitting room. The other two had quickly and discreetly removed the towel he had wedged into the mechanism of the bed the night before to keep it horizontal instead of tilted at the forty-five-degree angle the Minbari preferred.

As Sinclair approached, they bowed expectantly, looking always down, awaiting his orders.

"I don't wish to be rude, but I've asked you not to do that. It takes a great deal of effort to get that wedged in there just right so that the bed will remain horizontal. *Please,* in the future, leave it that way."

"Yes, Ambassador," they said in unison. But that was what they said every morning. It was pretty much all they ever said to him. They seemed to be devoted to his every need, but not to doing what he asked them to do.

"You do speak English, don't you?" It was not the first time he had asked.

"Yes, Ambassador," they said in unison and then quickly scurried out to the sitting room where they and their companion then hurried out of Sinclair's quarters.

He resolved to try it again that evening in the dialect of the Minbari religious caste, which he had been studying intensively since arriving on Minbar. He had begun a study of the Minbari language after the war, but had until now focused mostly on the dialect of the military caste. The religious-caste dialect was far more difficult, with a demanding and intricate set of grammatical rules that changed from situation to situation, depending on who you were speaking to and about what. It was far too easy to say the wrong thing to the wrong person in the wrong grammatical way in the religious-caste dialect, and thereby commit a faux pas or an interstellar incident. He much preferred the straightforward, more vigorous approach of the military-caste dialect, or even the simple, unadorned style of the worker caste. But come the evening, he was resolved to try just one sentence in his best religious-caste Minbari. "Leave the bed in a horizontal position, please." Eight words in English, twenty-seven words in the most polite, precise Minbari he could muster.

Sinclair went over to the table where his breakfast had been set out. He knew there would be no bacon and eggs under that ornate, gold alloy cover. No pancakes. No toast with butter. No breakfast steak.

Oh, how he had been longing recently for just one well-cooked steak. But the meat that the military and worker castes ate on Minbar was unfit for Human consumption, and the religious caste was, in the main, vegetarian. His breakfast was what it always was, for the religious caste prized order and continuity: a custard made from the eggs of the *temshwee,* which in flavor and texture in no way resembled chicken eggs; a porridge made from local grains and fruits; spring water. It was nutritious. It was even palatable. But it was also more or less what he would get for lunch and for dinner, just in different forms, such as in cakes or casseroles. And it was beginning to drive him to an obsession with food, something he had never before experienced in his life. Until now, food had been mostly a necessity to him, to be enjoyed but not overly concerned with, even when faced with shortages during the war, or when certain foods weren't available during the early months on Babylon 5.

But on Minbar where Human food was almost impossible to obtain, he found himself longing for coffee. And steak. And maybe just a piece of chocolate cake.

Sinclair looked at the breakfast and realized he wasn't hungry, was in fact feeling a little uneasy. The nightmare, as vivid as any he had experienced since coming to Minbar, had upset him more than he wanted to admit.

The sitting room, as spartan as the bedroom, was furnished on one side with one table and three chairs, and on the other with a small Minbari altar and a meditation pillow. Sinclair threw the pillow down in the center of the room. He had a long day ahead of him, even with the shorter Minbari day, and needed to be focused and calm. He sat down, closed his eyes, and began counting backward from four with each breath.

He hadn't finished the first set of four, when the door to his quarters opened. The Minbari had different notions of privacy, and admittedly he had not locked the door. He opened his eyes to find Rathenn looking at him with an expression that was somehow both apologetic and pleased.

"Forgive me, Ambassador, for disturbing your meditation. I was just informed you had risen a little early this morning.''

''Not a problem,'' said Sinclair. He stood and kicked the pillow back to the other side of the room. ''Just a habit I picked up in my youth. Helps me focus.''

''We Minbari firmly believe in the profound benefit of daily meditation. You say you picked it up in your youth? Would that have been at the religious-caste school you spoke of yesterday, or was it part of your military training?''

Sinclair laughed. ''At school, most definitely. Our military class, for the most part, isn't as sold on the benefits of meditation as yours is.''

''But truly you were blessed to receive training in becoming both a priest and a warrior. We Minbari have always considered that the mark of the exceptional person, a goal to strive for. For instance, the great hero Branmer—''

Sinclair did not mean to tense at the name of the general who had led the Minbari forces against Humanity at the Battle of the Line, but clearly he had, for Rathenn looked stricken with the realization he had said the wrong thing.

''Well,'' Sinclair said hurriedly, trying to spare Rathenn further embarrassment, ''I didn't exactly get instruction on becoming a priest. I went to a Jesuit high school, yes, but among my people you don't have to want to be a priest to attend. It was never my intention to join the religious life. All I ever wanted was to be a fighter pilot, like my dad.''

There was an awkward pause; Rathenn seemed to be still recovering from his faux pas, and Sinclair realized he no longer wanted to talk about this, not with Rathenn, a member of the Grey Council, not still feeling as unsettled as he did from the slowly fading nightmare.

"Perhaps we should get started on the day," he said, gesturing toward the door.

Rathenn bowed and, as always, insisted Sinclair lead the way.

CHAPTER 2

THE Minbari capital city of Yedor was, by any standards, a beautiful one. Many of the old city's first dwellings, carved into the natural ice-blue crystalline outcroppings that so dominated the Minbari landscape, were still extant and being used. Great care had then been taken over the centuries to construct other buildings to resemble those sculpted out of the landscape to ensure that they would fit seamlessly into the natural aesthetic. The effect was dramatically beautiful, with towering crystal skyscrapers next to natural waterfalls, busy city streets surrounding tranquil if sparsely landscaped parks.

It was a busy center of commerce and everyday living. And yet at times it seemed to Sinclair that Yedor was pervaded by a tense stillness, like the halls of a long-forgotten museum where everything was carefully preserved in casings of ice—but for whose sake? Other times, when he was feeling less somber, it seemed like a city asleep, waiting to awaken with the dawn.

The residential quarters, where Sinclair resided, were mainly quaint Minbari-style equivalents of bungalows and resident apartments also set unobtrusively into the crystalline rock-faced terrain. From there to the vast government complex with its towering central palace was a short but pleasant walk through one of the more beautiful parks of flower beds and hedges, shrubs and small trees, a tapestry of many shades of blue, silver, and green. Every morning of the past fifteen Minbari days since Sinclair had finally been able to establish an office and try to start his work as ambassador, Rathenn had made that walk with him.

As congenial company as Rathenn was, Sinclair found this more than just a little disconcerting. Rathenn, after all, was Satai, a member of the powerful and (even to the Minbari) mysterious Grey Council, the nine-member group that ruled Minbar primarily from behind the scenes, spending most of their time between the stars on a huge Minbari war cruiser, rarely leaving the ship, even to come to Minbar.

Delenn, who Sinclair had come to think of as a friend, had been the one exception to this, assigned to Babylon 5 as the Minbari ambassador even as she retained her Grey Council membership. But Sinclair knew that had been an unusual case, and he had gradually discovered that he had been one of the main reasons for it. The Minbari had insisted on Sinclair's assignment to Babylon 5 and had then sent Delenn as their ambassador for the purpose of observing him. The Minbari religious caste were guided to an obsessive degree by prophecy and notions of destiny and predetermination. They had decided, as Delenn had told him, that he had a "great destiny" and they were determined that he fulfill it.

And now here was Rathenn, like Delenn, behaving in a way totally atypical for a member of the Grey Council. Indeed, he insisted that Sinclair not use his honorific title of Satai.

Rathenn shadowed Sinclair throughout the day, always with great politeness, seemingly at his beck and call, as if trying to anticipate his every need and giving the impression that he would move heaven and earth to do whatever Sinclair asked.

But like his attentive Minbari residential "staff," Rathenn rarely actually did anything Sinclair asked him to do, usually proclaiming the request, amid great apologies, to be "impossible to do at this time."

They walked silently for a moment under a low canopy of trees, whose branches and leaves looked exactly like delicate icicles. The triple spires of the government palace were just visible ahead.

"Has the Ambassador reconsidered my suggestion that he allow our best tailors to create for him a Minbari wardrobe more suitable to our climate and to his requirements."

Sinclair tried not to sigh. Rathenn had slipped into using the third person, his way of letting him know he knew this was a delicate subject.

"Rathenn, as always, it's a most generous offer, but it would be inappropriate for me to dress in the Minbari fashion. I am the Earth ambassador to Minbar. My job is to represent Earth and all of Humanity to the Minbari people, and to be a link back to Earth for all Humans who come to visit your world.

"When my fellow Humans come to see me here, my being dressed in the familiar clothing of Earth provides an immediate level of comfort and assurance as to who I am and who I represent. When you're a stranger in a strange land, that sort of connection to your home is very important.

"And when I meet with your fellow Minbari, my clothing immediately conveys where I come from and who I represent."

If I meet with your fellow Minbari, Sinclair thought. Every day, he saw Rathenn and perhaps a handful of religious acolytes and members of the worker caste, most of whom avoided speaking with him. But virtually no other important Minbari.

"Speaking of which, how is my request for a meeting with *F'hurs* Anoon coming along?" On his own, Sinclair had managed to find out the name of Yedor's *F'hurs*—the Minbari equivalent of *mayor*—but had not yet been able to get a meeting arranged. "It's important that I establish ties with the local government, open some communication. That is why I'm here."

"That is not possible at this time, Ambassador," Rathenn said with a little bow of his head. "Her duties make her unavailable for several more days. But soon, I assure you, you will be meeting with the appropriate officials."

It was clear to Sinclair that he was deliberately being denied access to other Minbari officials. But why? He was on Minbar as ambassador at the specific request of the Minbari government. If they didn't want him to do his job, why had they insisted upon his assignment to the job?

He wondered again if it was still just the repercussion from the incident that had occurred when he first arrived on Minbar. Almost before he'd had time to unpack he had been arrested and falsely accused of taking part in a bizarre plot to assassinate Jenimer, the recently inaugurated Minbari leader. He had seen quite a few Minbari officials then, all sitting in judgment on his life.

Though he had tried very hard to obtain it, Sinclair had never received a clear answer on exactly what had happened, or who had been behind the plot to frame him. And he knew that in the eyes of some of the higher ranking military caste, such as Neroon, who didn't like him in the first place, he had not actually been cleared of the crime—merely pardoned by the Chosen One himself, the supposed target of the plot. They couldn't argue with the Minbari leader's decision, but they didn't have to like it, and many didn't.

Rathenn, aware of this, had tried to assure Sinclair every day that most Minbari did not view Sinclair with suspicion. But Sinclair, when he allowed himself a moment of cynicism, wondered if that wasn't mainly because most Minbari had not been informed of his presence on their planet.

Sinclair and Rathenn had reached the two-story-high triangular entrance to the government palace, and as always, Rathenn accompanied Sinclair to his suite of offices.

"Stranger in a strange land," Rathenn mused. "An interesting expression."

For a moment, Sinclair didn't know what he was talking about, but then remembered what he had said. "It's a quote from the Bible, one of my people's holy books."

"Ahh," said Rathenn. He seemed pleased by this. "I have been informed that two passenger ships will be arriving, one later today and one tomorrow, both with Human passengers listed on the manifest."

"Thank you, Rathenn. I assume the manifests have been forwarded to my computer." It was the one part of his job as ambassador that Sinclair had been able to do over the past few days. By law, all alien visitors to Minbar were required to come to the government palace and register their presence. And with Sinclair's appointment, the law had been expanded to require those Humans visiting Minbar to meet with the Earth ambassador and explain their reasons for being on Minbar.

Rathenn seemed eager for Sinclair to carry out this duty, and in this matter alone was extremely helpful. There were never that many Humans on Minbar at any one time, but enough that Sinclair had been seeing a fairly steady stream of visitors. Rathenn had assigned Sinclair an aide from the Minbari religious caste to help with the paperwork involved and keep the appointments scheduled at a reasonable pace.

Rathenn bowed politely to Sinclair. "I shall leave you now, Ambassador. But if you should require anything, I am at your service."

"Thank you, Rathenn," Sinclair said, returning the bow. "There are many things I require that seem to be impossible to obtain, but I appreciate whatever efforts you are making on my behalf."

If Rathenn saw the double edge to that statement, he did not show it. "It is my pleasure, Ambassador."

"There is one other thing I'm having some difficulty with," Sinclair continued before Rathenn could leave. "Perhaps you could be of some service there. My uplink access to the StellarCom network was finally installed yesterday, but for some reason I've been unable to establish any links to Earth or to Babylon 5. And as every message I have tried to send out through your people has gotten no response, you can see how I might be concerned."

"That is most unfortunate, Ambassador," said Rathenn. "I shall, of course, look into this immediately."

"Have you been able to contact Delenn for me?" Sinclair asked, not letting the Minbari get away as he so clearly wanted to do. The last time Sinclair had seen Delenn she had been on her way back to Babylon 5, and he assumed she was still there. But she had apparently made no effort to contact him since, and he had no way of contacting her. He wanted to talk to her, to tell her of his growing concerns. She was the one Minbari he felt he could trust the most because she was the one Minbari he knew the best.

"No," said Rathenn. "I am told she is unavailable at this time."

"Is she on Babylon 5?"

"I'm afraid I have no other information to give you, Ambassador. Please excuse me, and I beg your pardon for any unintended discourtesy, but I am urgently required elsewhere at exactly this moment."

Sinclair nodded, and Rathenn hurried off, putting Sinclair suddenly in mind of the White Rabbit in *Alice in Wonderland,* a thought that only slightly amused him under the circumstances. He went into his office, as barely furnished as his living quarters, to check his schedule for the day. Venak, his Minbari aide, had not yet arrived. As best as he could determine from the nearly indecipherable scrawl on the schedule, he had almost an hour until his first appointment. With luck, that meant at least half an hour to himself before the ever-helpful Venak arrived to hover nearby.

He powered up his computer and keyed in his access to StellarCom. "Computer, I wish to contact Earth Alliance space station Babylon 5, access code on file."

The StellarCom system logo stared mutely at him from the screen while the system processed his request.

"That link will take five minutes and twenty-two seconds to process. Please stand by."

Finally. Sinclair felt a bit of hope for the first time in a long while. He had been recalled to Earth from Babylon 5 in the midst of a great crisis on Earth—the President, Luis Santiago, had died in the explosion of his personal transport ship, *Earthforce One,* just moments after Sinclair and his command staff on Babylon 5 had uncovered evidence to indicate the explosion was the result of an assassination plot, not a tragic accident. Obtaining that evidence had nearly cost the life of Babylon 5's security chief—and his friend—Michael Garibaldi.

Sinclair had tried to bring that evidence to the attention of EarthGov while still on Babylon 5 and during the short time he was on Earth. He was all but ignored both times, told the evidence was faulty, told an investigation would look into it, told not to spread dangerous rumors.

And then he was told to report to Minbar as the new Earth ambassador. *Your world needs you to go to Minbar,* President Clark, the commander-in-chief of Earthforce, had told him. *Maybe the Minbari need you as well. We've heard there is trouble between the Minbari religious caste and the military caste.*

Why send me? Sinclair had asked. He didn't want to leave Babylon 5, didn't want to abandon the important work he had been doing there, didn't want to leave behind the people who had become his friends, didn't want to leave the side of his critically wounded friend, didn't want to leave without at least trying to send word to Catherine who was somewhere on The Rim surveying new planets for the Universal Terraform Corportion.

Because, he was told, *you know the Minbari as well as any Human does. You can help keep the peace between Earth and Minbar. And because the Minbari trust you. They asked for you. They will accept only you. They think you have a Minbari soul . . .*

Sinclair was a military man; had been all his life, as his father had been before him. When a superior gave a lawful and moral order, a military man did his damnedest to carry it out to the best of his ability. He didn't have to like the order. He didn't have to agree with the reasons behind the order.

So Sinclair had come to Minbar, with assurances that they would help him get word to his fiancée, that he would be kept informed of Garibaldi's condition, that he would be kept informed of the continuing investigation into Santiago's death, and that he would be given all the support he needed to carry out his orders and establish an embassy on Minbar to the benefit of both worlds.

But since his arrival, nothing.

He'd only been imprisoned by the Minbari for the first week of his stay here, but he might as well still be in prison given the isolation he had found himself in.

Was he at last going to break out of that isolation?

The StellarCom logo suddenly began to blink. "Sorry, communication with that link cannot be established at this time. Please try later."

Sinclair fought back a surge of disappointment. "Computer, I wish to contact EarthDome, Geneva, Planet Earth, access code on file." Again the system processed the request, but this time it returned its smooth refusal within only a few moments. His disappointment was starting to turn into exasperation.

He hadn't had any contact with his only brother since Christmas, and knew he might be worried, not having heard from him, knowing only what he might be reading in the papers.

"Computer, I wish to contact Malcolm Sinclair, Australian continent, Earth, access code on file."

Again, the short time to process, again refusal.

He couldn't get through to his superiors or his family on Earth, and couldn't reach his friends on Babylon 5. There had to be a reason, but what was it? Who didn't want him making contact with anyone outside of Minbar? The Minbari? His own government?

One last shot. And a long shot at best.

"Computer, I wish to contact Universal Terraform headquarters, Hong Kong, Earth. Standard search for the access number."

The system processed the request far too quickly.

"Sorry, but communication with that link cannot be established at this time. Please try later."

Angry and frustrated, Sinclair pushed away from his desk and stood, accidentally tipping his chair over and to the floor with a clatter. Venak hurried in to see what was wrong. The startled look on the Minbari as he hurriedly backed out of the room, cooled Sinclair's anger considerably. He couldn't allow himself to get that angry. It was a luxury he could not afford right now. But he vowed that Rathenn would get him a link to Earth or to Babylon 5 by the next day at the latest, or he would damn well know the reason why.

When Sinclair got back to his quarters that evening, he was exhausted. The arriving passenger ship had brought twelve Humans from its run through the outer colony worlds. Though most would not be staying on Minbar for long, Rathenn had pushed Sinclair to see as many of them that day as he could, giving him no time to pause.

His three Minbari house helpers were setting out his dinner. Sinclair carefully enunciated his request in the Minbari religious dialect that they leave his bed from now on in a horizontal position, and was rewarded with wide-eyed looks of apparent delight at his effort. At least that's what it appeared from what he could see of their downturned faces as they bobbed up and down, bowing before hurriedly leaving.

He managed only a few bites of the dinner. Wearily, he went to the bathroom, grabbed a towel and went into the bedroom to wrestle the bed back to a horizontal position and then wedged the towel into the bed's mechanism to steady it and keep it from tilting forward or backward. As he did so, he once again regretted that the draft that came through his quarters made sleeping on the floor next to impossible.

He went to bed and found, as usual, that as tired as he was, he could not fall asleep. In fact, he was now wide awake. He sat back up, but the motion jostled the bed enough that the towel slipped from the mechanism. The bed slowly clicked up to a forty-five-degree angle and Sinclair slid off to his feet. He pushed the bed back to the horizontal position. He bent down, stuck his hand under the bed, grabbed the towel and tried to yank it back into the right place. He had tried many different objects for securing the mechanism into the right position, but the towel worked best. Usually.

He tugged and pulled on the towel, reaching further in. Without warning, the towel slipped and with a *click, click, click* the metal gears began to grind over his hand. Sinclair yanked his hand back and let out a creative stream of invective. Then with clenched teeth, he shook off the pain and tried once more, this time with success.

That battle over, hopefully for the night, but now more awake then ever, he went over to the chest, opened it, took out the bottle of whiskey, and poured himself one shot.

He was not a big drinker, but neither did he begrudge himself the occasional drink, and on a planet of aliens for whom alcohol was near poison, this small bottle contained a nearly irreplaceable Human luxury, one he guarded carefully.

And most importantly, it was a gift from Catherine. Where was she right now? What would she think of where he was now? In the darkness, he lifted the shot glass in a silent toast to their love, and drank down the burnt-gold liquid. That was all he would allow himself tonight. He was determined to make it last until he saw her again. He put the bottle away, closed the chest, and went back to bed.

He slept fitfully that night, and though the nightmares didn't return, he dreamed of trying to find Catherine, but always just missing her, always arriving a few moments too late.

CHAPTER 3

SINCLAIR overslept the next morning and awoke feeling more groggy then usual. When he finally emerged from the bathroom, his Minbari helpers had already come and gone, leaving his breakfast . . . and his bed back at a forty-five-degree angle.

He didn't know whether to laugh or cry. Take into account, he reminded himself, that the Minbari believed sleeping in the horizontal was tempting death. It had to do with their physiology, although it had been more of a danger in the past than it was now. His helpers obviously believed they were doing this stubborn Human a favor by saving him from his own folly.

Should he talk to Rathenn about it? No. He wanted Rathenn to spend his energy on more important matters, like getting him in contact with Earth and Babylon 5. Somehow he'd deal with these more trivial matters on his own.

On the walk over to the government palace, Rathenn gave him the good news.

"I think the Ambassador will find that the uplink to EarthDome has finally been established for his office."

"That's wonderful, Rathenn. Thank you. Any idea what the problem was?"

"I am not an engineer, Ambassador."

And that was not an answer, thought Sinclair. "What about other links to Earth locations?"

"I was only told of EarthDome."

"How about to Babylon 5?"

"I'm sorry, Ambassador, I was—"

"—only told of EarthDome," Sinclair finished for him. "All right. Well, thanks."

On arriving, Sinclair went immediately to his computer and called up StellarCom; within moments he was connected to EarthDome Communications. He entered the code for President Clark's office. And waited. After several more moments, an unctuous young man appeared on the screen.

"Ah, Sinclair. We've been wondering why there's been no communication from you since your arrival. The Minbari say you were having some difficulty getting through. Alien technology can be rather unreliable at times, no?"

Sinclair didn't know this man and didn't like his unwarranted and patronizing tone of familiarity, but he answered in a neutral tone. "I wish to speak to the President."

"I'm afraid that isn't possible right now. I've been instructed to help you in any way I can. Think of me as your liaison."

"And just who are you?"

"Peverell Meugnot. I am President Clark's personal aide."

"Well, Mr. Meugnot, I am the Earth ambassador to the Minbari Federation, an assignment that was given to me by President Clark, who told me that any communication I made with EarthGov was to be with him personally. Was he informed I was calling?''

''Yes, *Ambassador,*'' said Meugnot, with a subtle stress on the title, ''and the President asked me to deal with it personally. I am fully briefed on your situation. Now how can I help you?''

Sinclair took a deep breath. ''Mr. Meugnot, I have been on Minbar for almost a month. I haven't been sent a staff from Earth, and I've not been allocated a budget to establish and maintain a working embassy. I can't continue to rely solely on Minbari resources to do my job.''

''Well, we certainly appreciate your patience to this point, Ambassador. But all I can do is ask you to give it time. Things are still unsettled in the aftermath of President Santiago's tragic death. We'll raise the subject of your assignment to Minbar at the reconvening of Congress in March. Nothing can be done until then, I'm afraid.''

''That's completely unacceptable—''

''I'm afraid you have no choice but to accept it, Ambassador. How lucky for you the Minbari are so eager to help you, and that you can so obviously rely on their goodwill. Now, I fear I have a very busy schedule today, so if there's nothing else I can help you with . . .''

''There is another matter. I had been assured by your office that my personal effects, which had been sent to Earth from Babylon 5, would be forwarded to me here, but I have not yet received anything. When might I expect them?''

This seemed to take the aide by surprise. ''Your personal effects? A moment please.'' He put Sinclair on hold. After a long moment, he returned. ''I am afraid there has been something of a mix-up regarding your belongings. I'm informed that it was all forwarded to your family here on Earth. A brother, I believe? Perhaps you should take it up with him. Now if you will excuse me. Good day."

Meugnot's image was replaced by the StellarCom logo. Sinclair sat back perplexed. What was Clark's game? He had been so eager to send him to Minbar, so full of platitudes about how important the job was and how only he could do it.

Sinclair had a working relationship with at least three current senators, all of them with a good deal of influence. If the link was still up—

"Computer, reestablish link with EarthDome."

To Sinclair's relief, it was instantly reestablished. It proved a short-lived victory. Three calls to three senators. Three senatorial aides telling Sinclair the senator was unavailable, but would be informed he had called.

Then Sinclair's link to StellarCom went down altogether, and on the screen appeared an advisory message written in concise worker-caste Minbari indicating there was a problem with the main transmission station on Minbar's second moon.

He was seething. He needed to take a walk. Now.

Venak looked up in surprise as Sinclair strode briskly toward the door.

"Ambassador, you have a full schedule for the day—"

"I'll be back in an hour," Sinclair said.

A stiff breeze was blowing through the streets of Yedor, causing Sinclair to regret leaving his overcoat behind, but he was in no mood to go back now. He turned his collar up, and quickened his pace.

He needed a plan of action. He needed options. He had come to Minbar with what he had believed to be a clear mandate, but now nothing was clear. Neither EarthGov nor the Minbari government seemed to want him to function as an ambassador, and yet both had nearly fallen over themselves to get him sent here. Why? Though both Clark and Rathenn had implied a friendly cooperation between the two governments, Sinclair's deepest instincts told him they had very different reasons for wanting him on Minbar. But what were they?

Sinclair found he had walked to the central fountain of the government sector, an elaborate display of rock, crystal, precious gems, mirrored metal, waterfalls, pools, and fountain sprays, all engineered to be pleasing to the eye and soothing to the ear. He found himself face-to-face with his own reflection in a narrow strip of mirror on one wall. He still found it disconcerting to see himself in civilian clothes rather than an Earthforce uniform. He recalled Catherine saying something similar to him back on Babylon 5. Only she hadn't meant it quite the same way. An old argument over his devotion to duty always taking precedence over his personal life.

A quick movement in the mirrored surface told Sinclair there was someone behind him. He turned to find a worker-caste Minbari standing there, holding a welding torch and mask, his head tilted down in the familiar pose of courtesy. But unlike most of the Minbari workers and acolytes he encountered, this Minbari's eyes continually darted up to look at him.

Sinclair searched for the proper phrase in the worker dialect, of which he knew even less than the religious dialect. It wasn't necessary, he knew. All Minbari could understand the dialects of all three castes, at least in their pure, official form untainted by regional differences. In spite of all the differences in syntax and word use, they were essentially the same language. Indeed, members of the worker caste had to be absolutely fluent in both religious- and warrior-caste dialects, since the members of those castes would never speak worker dialect, even to a worker. But Sinclair, out of courtesy, wanted to give it a try.

"Am I keeping you from your work?" he said, or at least *hoped* he said, in the worker dialect.

The Minbari did a most unexpected thing: he tilted his head up and looked Sinclair in the eyes. And smiled.

"I am happy to wait until you are ready to go, Ambassador," he said in flawless English. "I didn't mean to disturb you. We worker caste are usually invisible to members of the other castes."

"You know who I am?" Sinclair responded, genuinely surprised.

"Oh, yes, Ambassador Sinclair. Your presence here is known."

"Well, then you have me at a disadvantage. You know my name and I don't know yours."

"Inesval, of the F'tach Islands."

"And where did you learn to speak English, Inesval? You speak it far better than I can speak your language."

"You honored me with your attempt, Ambassador," the Minbari replied with a bow. "I spent three years on Earth with my father, after the war. He was a merchant. I very much like your world."

Sinclair's watch chimed at him, telling him it was time to head back. For the first time since coming to Minbar, Sinclair was having a real conversation with a Minbari other than a Grey Council member, and he had to break it off, had to get back to his duties. What would Catherine say? He knew only too well.

But he was also keeping the Minbari from his work,

and had no idea what the worker might suffer as a consequence.

"It's been a pleasure talking with you, Inesval, but I had better let you get back to your work, and—" Sinclair stopped in mid-sentence. The Minbari had a welder's torch!

"Is it possible," Sinclair asked slowly, "and please tell me if this violates any rules or customs I'm not aware of, but could you perhaps do a job for me?"

Inesval looked amazed.

"I'm afraid I won't be able to pay you for a while, but I assure you that you will be compensated."

"Ambassador, it would be my great pleasure to be of service to you in any way I can, and I do not wish compensation."

Sinclair bowed in delighted gratitude, then explained the job he wanted done.

Sinclair returned to the government palace to find an ashen-faced Rathenn anxiously waiting for him in his office.

"Forgive me, but it is only out of concern when I say that the Ambassador shouldn't just walk off like that."

"Afraid I'll get mugged, Rathenn?"

"Mugged? I don't understand—"

"I just took a walk," said Sinclair, "and don't even think of reprimanding Venak. There was nothing he could've done to stop me. Now it looks to me like there's a waiting room full of people to talk to and register as visitors. That is what you want me doing, isn't it?"

Rathenn bowed and left without another word.

When Sinclair returned to his quarters that evening, he went straight to the bedroom. A faint smell of ozone told him Inesval had been there and gone already. The Minbari had done a first-rate job. The mechanism of the bed was now permanently welded into the horizontal position.

At last, Sinclair thought, he just might get a good night's sleep.

CHAPTER 4

"STAY in formation! Hold the line. No one gets through, no matter what!"

"Alpha Leader! You've got a Minbari fighter on your tail! I'm on him."

"No! Mitchell! Stay in formation! It might be a—"

The shadow of the massive Minbari fighter fell across Sinclair's Starfury. "Oh my God. It's a trap!"

"Mitchell! Break off! Break off!"

Too late. Starfury after Starfury blown to bits, exploding like miniature suns around him. Every ship of his squadron gone. Every Earth ship in his field of view destroyed.

"Not like this! Not like this! If I'm going out, I'm taking you bastards with me. Target main cruiser. Set for full-velocity ram. Afterburners on my mark . . . Mark!"

Sinclair was thrown back in his seat, his craft hurtling toward a collision with the Minbari cruiser. Ten, nine, eight, seven . . .

Metal fiber ropes bit into Sinclair's wrists and legs. He was racked with almost unbearable pain. Just beyond the rim of light, he could see moving shadowy shapes, humanoid, robed. Minbari.

"Who are you?" Sinclair could barely force the words out. "Why are you doing this?"

Neroon stepped out of the shadows. "You stand accused of the death of thirty-three Minbari warriors. How do you plead? Answer the court!"

"It was your war," Sinclair tried to shout, but again could barely croak out a whisper. "I was defending my planet. Defending the survival of Humanity. It was combat—"

"You stand accused," Neroon thundered, "of killing our leader Dukhat. How do you plead?"

"I wasn't even there when our two peoples met for the first time. It was a tragic misunderstanding that caused Dukhat's death. And for that you tried to exterminate an entire species of sentient beings!"

"And was it a *misunderstanding,*" Neroon shouted over him, "when you conspired to assassinate the new Chosen One? How do you plead?"

"I had nothing to do with that!"

Neroon turned away. "The council will render its verdict."

Out of the shadows stepped other Minbari. He recognized some of them. Jenimer. Rathenn. Delenn.

"Sentence him as he would be sentenced on Earth," said a voice that Sinclair did not recognize. "Death of personality."

Sinclair was no longer bound. He was standing in the center of the area of light. Rathenn walked over to him, held up the Triluminary. The stone at its center glowed. There was a mirror to his right. Sinclair looked into the mirror—and a Minbari stared back at him from out of the mirror.

He turned back around, intent on grabbing Rathenn and throttling him if necessary to find out what was happening. But the Minbari were gone. Every member of his squadron was standing there, looking at him accusingly. Bill Mitchell stepped forward.

"Why are you doing this?"

Sinclair shot upright in his bed, drenched in sweat, his heart pounding furiously, his breathing labored. He sat there, a long time it seemed, until his heartbeat and breathing returned to normal.

Damn it, he thought. The dreams shouldn't still shake him that much. He had been reliving the Battle of the Line in his nightmares for eleven years now. True, they had been changing in the last year, but they were still only dreams, weren't they?

For the first ten years, the battle itself dominated the nightmares. The events following his attempt to ram the Minbari cruiser with his Starfury, the forty-eight hours he could not remember, appeared in his dreams only as vague but sinister flashes of light, shadow, and sound, images he could not completely recall upon waking.

Then two men had come to Babylon 5, agents perhaps of his own government, or from some independent group with connections in the government. He was never able to determine which it was. They had come to try to prove his loss of memory was a sham, and that he was in fact colluding with the Minbari. They had hooked him up to a machine that had forced memories of the missing forty-eight hours back into his conscious awareness; memories of the capture, torture, interrogation, and mind-wipe he had suffered at the hands of the Minbari. These memories had afterward joined his repertoire of nightmares, slowly gaining equal prominence with his dreams of the battle.

When he had been recalled from Babylon 5 to Earth and summoned to President Clark's office, to meet with

Rathenn and be offered the position of Earth's ambassador to Minbar, Rathenn had produced a Triluminary and claimed it would restore the rest of Sinclair's memory about those forty-eight hours. The tiny alien device seemed to confirm Rathenn's claim that the Minbari surrendered even though winning the war because they had discovered some Humans possessed Minbari souls. That he, Sinclair, had a Minbari soul.

Sinclair hadn't known what to believe. Certainly, he rejected the notion that he had a Minbari soul, or even that the Minbari could be capable of determining such a thing with any kind of machine or device. So what could he trust of the memories the Triluminary had produced? He wasn't sure.

But since then, new versions of his nightmare had emerged out of his subconscious with a violent fury, dreams different from what he had endured before, even more intense and disorienting. Now his experiences at the Battle of the Line and while prisoner of the Minbari mixed freely with other experiences and with bizarre nightmare images, reality and nightmare logic jumbling together chaotically.

Sinclair didn't know what time it was, but it didn't matter. He wouldn't be getting any more sleep this night. He got up to get ready for another day.

"Forgive me for saying so, Ambassador, but you look rather tired. Are you not sleeping well?"

Sinclair looked at Rathenn, and felt a ridiculous urge to laugh. "No. Not particularly."

"That is unfortunate. Is there anything I can do?"

This time Sinclair did laugh, clearly puzzling the Minbari. This had been the first morning Rathenn had not walked him to the government palace, but had sent his aide, instead, who had walked silently one pace behind Sinclair the entire way. Rathenn was there to greet him, however, as he walked into his offices.

"Yes, you can tell me my uplink to StellarCom has been restored. Or have I been kidnapped and just don't know it?"

"Kidnapped?" Rathenn looked puzzled. "I'm afraid I don't understand."

"Neither do I. The uplink, Rathenn. Has it been restored? Do you know?"

"I will look into it." And the Minbari hurried off.

That wasn't a good sign. Sinclair went to his computer and quickly confirmed the worst. He wouldn't be contacting Earth, Babylon 5, or anyplace else, at least not this morning.

Sinclair was slowly coming to a difficult decision. Aside from acting as a glorified official greeter, what was he doing here? Wasting his time, as far as he could see.

Venak came in, bowing. "Your first appointment is here, Ambassador."

Apparently they weren't going to leave him any time on his own today. The second passenger ship they had been expecting, the one arriving from Earth, had finally docked during the night, and twenty-three new visitors needed to be greeted by their ambassador on Minbar. It was the first ship to arrive from Earth since Sinclair had himself arrived, and he was looking forward to finally getting some news as to how things were going on Earth. And, perhaps, someone might even know some news from Babylon 5.

"All right," Sinclair said. "Send 'em in."

A young man in his twenties walked in, almost bouncing with every step, a look of pure delight on his face. He was slightly built, with a pale complexion offset by a shock of dark black hair, and radiating enthusiasm and energy. He carried a satchel over his shoulder that Sinclair suspected was the sum total of his luggage—especially as he seemed to be wearing, in a great many layers, what was probably half of the clothing he possessed. An old trick to save space when traveling that Sinclair himself had used when he spent the two years before entering the Earthforce Academy to travel, work, and "find" himself.

Sinclair got up and came from around his desk to shake hands.

"It is an honor to meet you, Ambassador," said the young man stepping up quickly to shake hands. "You're a genuine hero, sir, if I may say so."

Sinclair had never gotten used to being called that, had never figured out what to say in response. He had certainly never felt like a hero. He was just a soldier doing his duty, just a man doing his best. But somehow it sounded corny to say those things, so he usually just smiled and said:

"Thank you. It's a pleasure to meet you, Mr. . . . ?" Sinclair motioned for the young man to sit down and then returned to behind his desk.

"Cole. William Cole. And believe me, the pleasure's all mine. I mean, I've read all about you. The best fighter pilot Earthforce ever had. The first commander of Babylon 5. The first ambassador to Minbar. And I've never before met anyone who actually fought on the Line. I mean, my brother was in Earthforce during the war, but he didn't fight in the Battle of the Line."

"Is your brother still in the military, Mr. Cole?" Sinclair wanted to change the subject.

"No," William replied. "He didn't much like the military. Got out as soon as the Minbari turned tail and ran. No offense intended. I mean, I like the Minbari. Really interesting people. That's why I'm here. I want to study the language, learn more about their customs, their martial arts, their history, everything!''

''So how long do you plan to be here, Mr. Cole?''

''Until they throw me out, I guess. That's about three months, right?''

''Approximately,'' said Sinclair. ''Well, if you run into any difficulties while you're here, this embassy is open to help. Before you leave, my aide will give you a packet of information that should prove useful to you. I assume you've already filled out all the required forms for the Minbari government?''

''A stack of them. Jeez, these people like their paperwork, don't they?''

Sinclair laughed in assent. He liked this young man, but he wondered how some of the more stuffy Minbari would react to him.

''Tell me, how are things back on Earth? I've had a little trouble getting news in the last couple of weeks.''

William shrugged. ''I'm not really all that up on the latest. I've been traveling around—spent a lot of time seeing the outer planets, then Mars, and then, of course, the Moon—saw the Apollo 11 museum, and did the whole tourist bit. I was born on a mining colony, and spent most of my life on one out-of-the-way colony or another, so I'd always wanted to see the sights of the Solar System, as the ads say. But I ended up only having about a day to spend on Earth, just long enough to catch the flight here.''

He paused and rummaged around in his satchel.

''I got *Universe Today* in here. It's only a couple of days old.'' He pulled the creased and tattered paper out and handed it to Sinclair. ''I've read everything I want to. You can have it.''

"Thanks." Sinclair took the paper and was stopped cold by the headline:

EARTHFORCE ONE EXPLOSION AN ACCIDENT.
INVESTIGATION CLOSED AS EA WORLDS CONTINUE TO MOURN.

"Anything else?"

Sinclair looked up from the paper. "Oh, sorry. No, that's it. It was good meeting you."

The young man stood up. "Hope to see you again. Really an honor, sir. Really an honor." And he left.

Sinclair sat back down, and began to read. The Commission on the Assassination had swiftly completed its investigation and concluded beyond doubt that a faulty power core in the main engine had caused a chain reaction, resulting in the explosion of *Earthforce One*. Other theories, including assassination, were dismissed in one line as either "fantasies, self-serving lies, or deliberate attempts to undermine the government." There was nothing about the evidence they had uncovered on Babylon 5.

The other main article on the front page covered President Clark's speech before the Industrial Assembly, in which he assailed "the undue influence of alien representatives" on Earth, hinting that the unrest on Mars might be linked to such influence, and castigating Minbar for its "seeming policy of duplicity and aggression toward the interests of the Earth Alliance throughout the galaxy."

"Ambassador?" It was Venak. "Your next appointment is here."

"Tell them to wait," he said without looking up.

He continued to read the lengthy article, growing steadily more uneasy at the tone of hysteria, bigotry, and isolationism that pervaded both the President's speech and the article itself. But he was totally unprepared for what he found when he turned to the back page to finish, and saw a sidebar article regarding himself.

" 'AMBASSADOR' OR CARPETBAGGER?" read the headline. What followed was an interview with Senator Balakirov in which the opposition leader launched a vitriolic attack on Sinclair, variously implying and stating that he had gone to Minbar under dubious authority, sent by President Clark only on the insistence of the Minbari, to function solely as a "goodwill Ambassador and fact-finder" to precede *possibly* setting up an official embassy. Now Balakirov questioned if Sinclair had "gone native and perhaps even turned traitor" and was attempting to "build a power base or reap some financial gain" perhaps with the "collusion" of the Minbari government. These charges were ambiguously and lukewarmly denied by presidential aides in explanations that only served to further confuse the issue. In "defending" his character as a war hero, the aides were careful to underscore the time he spent as a Minbari prisoner.

Sinclair crumpled the paper and tossed it aside. He had agreed, against his deepest instincts as a soldier, to accept this diplomatic post in the hope he might be able to help turn Earth and Minbar away from a dangerous militarism and xenophobia he had perceived growing on both worlds, attitudes that could threaten the cooperation between them that until now had kept the peace among many different worlds.

But now there was no denying that his appointment as ambassador was a sham, designed by Earth Central both to discredit the Minbari and keep him from pursuing any further investigation into the assassination of President Santiago.

What the Minbari had in mind with his appointment, he still didn't know. But it no longer really mattered. He couldn't do any good here without support from Earth, and he couldn't just sit here and do nothing while his planet slid into hysteria, authoritarianism, or worse. He would go to Babylon 5 first. He needed to talk with Delenn, and he knew the new commander, Captain Sheridan, and believed he could trust him.

Sinclair canceled all the rest of his appointments for the day, wrote up a resignation letter, sealed it, gave it to Venak to give to Rathenn, then returned to his quarters.

Sinclair went immediately into the bedroom to start packing the few things he had been able to bring with him. Preoccupied as he was, it took a minute for him to realize that his bed was back to a forty-five-degree angle. In spite of everything, he went over to it and stared. He looked under the bed and examined the mechanism. They had replaced his bed, probably deciding the old one had been broken.

Sinclair shook his head and went back to packing. It didn't matter. He wasn't going to be there much longer anyway.

CHAPTER 5

EARTH survey ship *Skydancer* skimmed swiftly through the upper troposphere of Planet UTC43-02C, code name Fensalir. Its onboard surveying instruments sampled the thick radioactive atmosphere that blanketed the remote, desolate world. Then its pilot, Catherine Sakai, brought the small craft into a higher orbit.

''Computer. Launch UTC Mineralogical probe 02C-2 and UTC Environmental probe 02C-2 on my mark. Mark launch.''

Skydancer shuddered slightly as the lander probe blasted toward the planet surface, then again twenty seconds later as the atmospheric satellite launched into its own preset orbit.

''Receiving data stream from 02C-2,'' the computer announced. ''Nominal functioning.'' It would be an hour before she would hear if her second ground probe was functioning as it should, but Sakai felt certain it would only confirm the data from the first lander probe she had launched several hours earlier to a different site. She could mark this one down in her logbook as an FGP, a Fool's Gold Planet. Looked good on first glance, but on closer examination, worthless.

Oh, there was plenty of diridium gas in the atmosphere, often a sign there was Quantium 40 in the planet's crust. But what little Q-40 was present seemed to consist mostly of improperly formed crystalline structures, or was too tainted by other minerals to make extraction economical, let alone profitable in the way a megacorporation like Universal Terraform would insist upon.

She would have the probes bring back some carefully selected core drills and rock samples to be examined later by the corporation scientists for other things, known and unknown, although she didn't want to waste too much energy or cargo space that could be better used for samples from a more likely planetary prospect. And she would still carefully survey and map the planet.

But for now, she had an hour to kill. Sakai took off her headset, yawned and stretched. Oh, the glamorous life of the professional planetary surveyor, she thought. Travel to distant, exotic worlds! Be your own boss! Discover untold riches! That had been the promise when she had embarked upon this career after the war ended and she had finished her hitch in Earthforce.

And it had proved to be true—partially.

The work did pay well in fees and in commissions *when* a planet proved rich with Quantium 40—the rare substance that made interstellar travel possible—or contained other valuable resources. But the bulk of the "untold riches" belonged to the corporations she contracted out to.

And she was her own boss, as much as any independent contractor was, though as more and more of the smaller surveying companies were being elbowed out by the megacorporations—a move encouraged by EarthGov in the interest of "science, safety, and efficiency"—she had begun to feel at times like just another corporate employee, but without the medical benefits or retirement plan.

And she had certainly traveled to many distant worlds. True, most Class 4 planets, the type that usually contained Q-40, looked pretty much alike, but she had seen some beautiful and amazing sights on those planets and on the few potentially habitable planets she had been hired to survey. Unbroken rings of massive volcanoes continually erupting fire on one hellish planet. A beautiful blue-ocean planet swirled with continent-size swaths of orange-and-green colony organisms that glowed with an eerie but beautiful silver light when the planet's face turned toward the night.

All from orbit, though. By the nature of her job, she never landed, merely observed and recorded from above. Landfall surveys, which were large, expensive, and highly specialized operations, were only undertaken after she had returned and the data she brought back had been scrutinized for months. Which meant, in reality, she spent months at a time in the cramped confines of her survey ship.

She loved her ship; it was dependable, maneuverable, and efficient. It didn't have a jump-point generator, but most survey ships didn't. Only Earthforce and some of the larger corporations could afford to build ships large enough to generate the power necessary for one of those.

And it wasn't luxurious. The cockpit looked like the refitted cockpit of the old freighter that it was: one chair, a console, and a jumble of instruments, vents, pipes and wiring, metal and plastic. Just behind the cockpit was her narrow bunk area; some fold-down, compact exercise equipment, necessary for long stints in zero-g such as this; storage containers for her condensed, freeze-dried food supplies; a small toilet area; and a decontamination chamber, which doubled as a shower. The rest of the ship was taken up with the air and water processors and other life-support systems, the fuel tanks, the engines, her survey equipment, the satellite launch bays, and the sample bay.

A good surveying ship had to have a first-class sample bay, and she had skimped a little on living amenities to install the best in *Skydancer*. It boasted a changeable system of sample compartments that she could configure by computer to be a large number of very small compartments, or a smaller number of larger compartments, depending on the planets she surveyed, how much soil and rock she had her sampler robots bring back, and what those samples contained. Although even large amounts of unrefined Q-40 samples could not reach critical mass and start a chain reaction, too large an aggregate could generate enough radiation and heat to pose a risk to the ship and her health, so it was better to keep it in smaller amounts in the fully shielded compartments, all of which could be emptied into space one at a time or all at once in an emergency. This last safety feature had also cost her plenty, even though she hoped never to have to use it. Coming back with an empty sample bay did not make the paying customer happy.

If only she'd be lucky enough this mission to find even one planet rich enough to make the risk of gathering that much Q-40-saturated soil and rock necessary.

What to do with the free hour she had coming up? Take a nap? Have a snack? Get some extra exercise? She leaned to her right, still strapped in her chair, and flipped on the small entertainment console screen, scrolling through the extensive index of music, movies, and books. Nothing looked good there either. What time was it? She checked the ship's chronometer. In a half hour she would be receiving a scheduled tight-beam tachyon transmission from the UTC Operations ship, giving her the top-secret location and jump coordinates for her next stop. And, maybe, some word from Jeffrey Sinclair.

Personal messages while on survey missions such as this were frowned upon, and usually only sent in emergency situations. There were many corporate reasons for this, most dealing with the issue of cost and the obsessive attention to secrecy these missions entailed. The corporations wanted to keep their target planets a secret from the competition for as long as possible. But she also suspected they wanted their pilots to keep their minds on the job, and not worry about what was happening at home.

But Jeff had said he would try to pull a few strings if he could as the commander of a space station. And as she absolutely could not send any messages to him, all she could do was wait. It was something one did quite a bit of in the glamorous profession of planetary surveyor.

So what should she do while she waited? She knew what Jeff what do in this situation. The same thing she was probably going to do yet again. It was one of the first things they discovered they had in common.

"Computer," she said, "lower the lights."

She released herself from the chair, pushed herself up gently in the microgravity, just above the console, and settled in to watch the surface of Fensalir moving broadly past the bow of her ship and to float with the incredible swarm of stars beyond the planet, all shining in the particularly intense way seen only in the deep night of space.

And she thought of Jeff, who always tried to do the same thing at least once a day: simply look out at the stars from whatever spot on Babylon 5 he could, be it a temporarily empty Command and Control, or one of the observation domes, or even walking along the outside surface of the station in a space suit, having cobbled up some plausible reason for taking a space walk. Best way to meditate and think, he would say. And to help keep everything in perspective.

What was he doing right now? She had left him on Babylon 5, on New Year's Day, Earth time, two days after he had asked her to marry him. Even though they had lived together once for a short period of time, it had taken her fifteen years to say yes to that question.

So much had changed in the years since they had first met at Earthforce Academy where she had been the second-year cadet, and he had been the incredibly handsome and dashing lieutenant and flight instructor.

He had literally taken her breath away on their first meeting, by executing a hairpin backward loop followed by a spinning barrel roll on her first instruction flight with him that had nearly blacked her out. She had accused him of being a dangerous show-off, although she had to admit to herself later that her anger had come more from embarrassment at almost losing it than at anything he had done. He told her she wasn't tough enough to make it as a pilot and said she was treading very close to insubordination. It was, embarrassingly enough, love at first sight.

What followed was war and separation and reunion and separation again, fifteen years of fighting with him, breaking up and getting back together, breaking up again and seeing other people. But always, always loving each other. As he put it, that just never went away, even if they sometimes didn't know why.

But they had spent far too much time apart during those years, and for what reason? Her job, his job, his stubbornness—her stubbornness. It didn't make any sense to her now, and yet here she was again, many light-years away, orbiting a godforsaken planet, having left just two days after agreeing to marry him to carry out a five-month stint on the rim of explored space.

The irony of the situation hadn't been lost on either of them as one of their longest-running arguments had been that Jeff never allowed himself a real life, a personal life because of work and duty and honor and orders. That he was never off-duty and never would be and what kind of life could they have together if that were so?

She tried only once to get him to quit and go into business with her, but he had refused, and the resulting argument had ended in yet another one of their breakups.

She had found it particularly difficult to understand his devotion to Earthforce service since it had treated him so badly after the war. He had been the fighter pilot with the greatest number of craft-to-craft combat victories, one of the heroes of the Battle of the Line who saw virtually all of his friends and comrades killed—and had emerged from the experience so emotionally scarred she had barely recognized him the first time she saw him after the war. But in spite of his heroism, he had been treated with suspicion and harassment by his superiors, shunted aside when he refused to resign, and then assigned to the worst postings.

But now he was commander of Babylon 5, so maybe his steadfast devotion to duty had finally paid off. On Babylon 5 he at last had been given a job that was both important and worthy of his abilities. It had helped him become a man more at ease with himself and his world. He laughed more easily now than he had in years. He no longer automatically tried so hard to keep others at a safe, emotional distance, a tendency he had developed after losing so many people dear to him both before and during the war (a trait not unknown to Sakai herself, as she knew he would be gently reminding her right about now). He had made some important new friends and deepened some old friendships. The true Jeffrey Sinclair had finally reemerged from the hard shell the war had put around him.

The computer broke into her reverie. "Incoming transmission from Universal Terraform tachyon transmission channel four zero eight zero seven six."

"Receive and record. Oh, and restore the lights."

Sakai swam back to her seat and strapped in, eagerly watching the data log scroll by on the communications monitor: new planetary and jump gate coordinates, jump gate codes, updated mission instructions—but no personal transmissions.

Oh, well, she thought. It had been a nice hope. There was always next time—four more months of "next times." For now, it was time to get back to work.

CHAPTER 6

MARCUS Cole checked his instrument readings, took another visual check through the murky atmosphere of Arisia 3, brought up the nose of his XO-Sphere Personal Flyer, banked right just a touch, and saw his target—the massive natural rock formation known as Perdition Bridge. There was just enough width under the rock bridge for the wing span of his flyer to pass through, if his heading was straight and true. And it always was.

Marcus eased to full throttle and as his flyer hit maximum speed, he shot under the bridge and began his climb, eased into his backward loop to follow the 360-degree path that would bring him back down and under the bridge again. Just as he came out of the last part of the curve back in front of the bridge, the planet, perhaps displeased at seeing this daredevil display one time too many, shook the small craft with an unexpectedly violent gust of wind, causing it to slip right.

Marcus had only seconds to fight the craft into a controlled slip left or he would lose the right wing of his craft—and everything else. The flyer swooped through the opening and shuddered as the right wing tip scraped the rock face in a shower of sparks, then emerged with a violent yaw to the left that was quickly becoming an uncontrolled tumble.

Marcus fought for control of the craft as it flashed through his mind that this would be a particularly stupid way to die. He had to risk activating the computer and the automatic stabilizers without shutting off manual control. He hit the sequence of buttons, causing the whole craft to lurch violently, but within a few seconds Marcus had the flyer back under control and on its original heading.

He quickly disabled the manual override and let the autopilot take sole control as he concentrated on getting his heart to stop thumping quite so wildly, then: "Computer. Damage report."

"Nonterminal damage to wing tip. Compensating for additional drag. Flight plan may proceed with caution, but fuel reserves at minimum."

Marcus took back the controls and continued toward Mining and Refinery Site 7 to do the routine inspection for which he had come planetside in the first place.

Arisia 3 was a bleak, violent, and uninhabitable world, orbiting an unremarkable F5 star on the far edge of explored space. Twice the size of Earth with three times the density, the massive planet, with its 2-G gravity, its poisonous, radioactive atmosphere, the scorching winds, and high degree of tectonic and volcanic activity, was not a place where Humans could linger for long. It might have been simply dismissed as a tiny, forgettable piece of Hell, if it hadn't been rich in the most valuable substance in the known galaxy: Quantium 40, the stuff that made jump gates, and thus interstellar travel, possible. It could be very profitable to mine, but cost-intensive and dangerous.

It was the rarest of minerals, naturally radioactive, chemically complex, and possessing an extremely unusual, naturally occurring quasi-crystalline structure. In its raw form, Q-40 could only be found in small amounts in other rock, mostly on Class 4 worlds like Arisia 3.

Mobile robot mining machines, directed from the colony in orbit, dug out the rock and delivered it to the squat, cumbersome but mobile automated refineries, which resembled, to Marcus's mind, nothing so much as giant, steam-belching beetles. There the first crude processing took place, separating the Q-40 from the other rock.

This automation meant workers only went planetside to conduct inspections, carry out repairs, and pick up the crudely refined Q-40 for transfer to the Orbital Refinery Platform, where usable Q-40 was separated from tainted and improperly formed amounts.

Extreme care had to be taken during every phase of this process, as the resulting purified form of Quantium 40 was so radioactive two grams of it would kill a man within fifteen feet, and so extremely unstable, one mistake might cause an uncontrolled chain reaction that could result in massive irradiation or even an explosion.

Marcus nosed his flyer down to begin his aerial inspection of Site 7. He knew that Central Control on the orbiting colony had monitored his previous little escapade, but he also knew they wouldn't say anything to him. It was one of the perks of being the boss.

In fact, it was the only perk Marcus could think of, but he hadn't taken over running the Arisia Mining Colony for perks or excitement or fun, he thought grimly. The Arisia Mining Colony was the last chance to save his family's mining company, one of the few family-owned, independent mining companies left.

Marcus had been born on a mining colony, and then been raised on a succession of colony worlds and mining colonies, rugged frontier places where Earth was only a remote irritant in the inhabitants lives that was resented for its high-handed treatment of colony worlds, particularly during the Minbari war.

Marcus had resented being just the boss's son, and didn't care much for the mining profession in general. He had been determined not to make it his life, dreaming of greater things.

But the war nearly bankrupted the company, and Marcus found that family duty was too powerful to ignore. He agreed to temporarily help his father, just until the company got back on sounder financial ground. But he found himself taking on ever-increasing amounts of responsibility as his father's health began to fail and the months turned into years. When his father died, Marcus was already almost fully in charge of the company. His mother died two years later, leaving Marcus determined to preserve his parents' legacy, even if he had to do it alone.

Marcus completed the perfunctory inspection and entered the proper log notes. Knowing he didn't have enough fuel for any further practice of maximum-performance maneuvers, he reluctantly turned his craft back toward space and the colony.

The orbiting Arisia Mining Colony consisted of two main structures: the Orbital Refinery Platform and, in a parallel orbit at a safe distance, the Inhabitants' Platform that housed one hundred and fifty workers. Marcus maneuvered his ship into the I.P. docking bay and was met immediately by his chief of maintenance, who whistled at the sight of the XO-Sphere's damaged right wing tip.

"Boy, you were lucky," the older man said. "That could have been a lot worse."

"I don't believe in luck," Marcus replied. "I expect

the worst to happen at all times, so I'm always prepared for it. That's how you walk away unscathed.''

''And what exactly did you walk away from this time, Chief?''

''Just make sure it gets repaired immediately, Hank. I'll be expecting to take it out again tomorrow.''

Marcus left the docking bay and started down the narrow corridors leading to his office. It was night on the colony's time schedule, so, thankfully, he saw very few people on the way, and they knew enough just to nod and keep moving.

He entered his office, the lights coming on automatically. He went to his desk, gathered up the stack of papers he had instructed his secretary to leave out for him, and stuffed them in a briefcase to take to his living quarters. He had a lot of work ahead of him that night.

Marcus stepped back into the muted light of the corridor and turned to lock the door. From behind him, someone called out.

''Marcus. I was hoping to catch you.''

It was Hasina Mandisa, the chief of Planetary Forecasting. It was the task of her department to keep track of the weather, earthquakes, and volcanic activity and issue hazard warnings so that the mining machines and planetary processors could be moved out of harm's way.

''I've got that report—*with* the modifications you requested. I just finished it and thought I should get it to you immediately.'' She handed him a thick sheaf of papers with an attached computer disk. ''I had it printed because I thought you might want to discuss some of the points.''

Marcus smiled. ''That's very good of you. I'll look at it tonight and if I have any questions I'll contact you first thing tomorrow.''

"Actually," she said. "I'd be happy to discuss it right now."

"I couldn't ask that," Marcus replied. "You've obviously put in your overtime for the day. Tomorrow will be fine." He turned to go, but she stopped him.

"Well, I thought, heck, I haven't eaten yet, and I was betting you hadn't had the chance to get anything yet, so I thought we could discuss it over dinner, you know, get it out of the way. In the last shipment we got from Earth, my mother sent me a stasis package with a fully cooked traditional West African beef stew, with all the trimmings—I mean the mangoes, broiled bananas, chutney, the works. She's the best cook in all of Lesotho City. Her restaurant is *the* place to eat. Anyway, I thought I could share it with you—and we could get some work done at the same time."

For a moment, Marcus considered it. And it wasn't just because of the offer of real food instead of another commissary meal. He genuinely liked Hasina—she was intelligent, capable, warm, attractive.

"No," he said, shaking his head. "It's very kind of you to offer, but I can't. I've got this fiscal report to finish, all the department reports . . ." It sounded lame to his own ears, but damn it, it was true. He couldn't take the time. Shouldn't take the time. Couldn't afford personal entanglements right now. It wouldn't be fair.

"That's all right," she said. "I understand. But listen, I haven't opened it yet. Maybe a little later. It'll keep almost indefinitely."

"Sure," he said. "Maybe later. Thanks."

He watched her retreat down the hall until he could no longer see her in the dim light, and then turned to go the other way, toward the commissary where his dinner, as always, would be waiting for him.

The commissary was on the other side of the rec room and bar. The smell of alcohol and the sounds of loud talk, laughter, music, and the electronic cacophony of a variety of 3-D games assaulted him as he approached.

He didn't like to go in there, wasn't comfortable around his employees and coworkers when they were drinking. The intake of alcohol was strictly regulated on the colony. It had to be in a work situation like theirs where one mistake could prove lethal. But his workers were employed in a dangerous profession and living in a drab environment, and many wanted that outlet on their days off.

Above the general din, Marcus heard one inebriated patron singing, very off-key, a moronic song that had been inexplicably popular on Earth a couple of years back.

"Oh, be a fine girl and kiss me right now! *Smack! Smack! Smack!"*, he sang, making appropriately annoying kissing sounds. "Oh, be a fine girl and kiss me right now! *Smack! Smack! Smack!* Oh, be a—"

"I'll smack you all right if you don't shut up!" somebody else suddenly roared.

By the time Marcus reached the two men at the far side of the bar, they were rolling on the floor, throwing punches, while the others in the bar scampered out of the way.

"That's it!" Marcus shouted. He motioned for some of the other men to help him separate the two combatants. Neither man would look Marcus in the eye.

"Your drinking day is over, both of you. Now get back to your quarters and stay there until you can pass the blood-alcohol test. Do I make myself clear?"

They nodded wordlessly, appropriately chastened,

and Marcus turned them over to the custody of their friends.

His appetite was gone now, but he went to the commissary and picked up his meal anyway, then returned, at last, to his quarters.

The incoming message light was blinking on his computer console. He put everything down and called up the list. Just one recorded message, originating from Earth, dated a month ago, which was typical as getting mail to the outer colonies wasn't a high priority with StellarCom. What wasn't typical was that the recording was from his only brother William. They hadn't seen each other since their mother's funeral, barely speaking to each other then.

Young Willie, immature and irresponsible, jumping from this job to that, working just long enough to get the money to travel aimlessly around, leaving Marcus to try to hold everything together on his own.

"He probably wants money," Marcus muttered angrily. He considered simply erasing the message, not even listening to it, but in the end, he called it up.

His brother's face smiled nervously at him from the screen. "Hello, Marcus. This is *expensive* so I'll make it short, especially since I know you'll probably just hit the erase button and not even hear this. Well, hello if you're there. I've been on a real tour of the Solar System since I saw you last—saw all those sights we used to talk about wanting to see, remember? I'll tell you all about it when I see you next. But I just wanted to let you know where I'm going next, in case you need to contact me." He paused, then broke into a big grin. "Minbar! I've always wanted to go there, and I've been learning the languages. Well, I'm running out of time here. I'll try to write you, or better yet, I hope somehow I'll see you soon. Bye."

Marcus stared dumbly at the blank screen for a moment. Minbar! He half suspected his brother was going there just to irritate him. As far as Marcus was concerned, the Minbari had a lot to answer for. Their bloody, pointless war had dragged him into military service unwillingly, killed several of his best friends, and had nearly destroyed his parents' company.

He counted it a certain measure of payback that the Minbari were among his best customers, sending freighters for regular Q-40 shipments. He always made sure they were charged the allowable maximum—nothing illegal or unethical, mind you, but no breaks, no bargains, no discounts, ever. It rather bothered him that they didn't seem to mind.

Minbar. Marcus shook his head. In a strange sort of way, he finally thought, it might do his brother some good. After all, the one thing he knew about the Minbari was their devotion to service, to putting the needs of the community and the *family* above one's own selfish interest. Might do him some good at that.

Marcus looked at the stack of paperwork that he knew would keep him up into the small hours of the night, looked at the meal that didn't look in the least bit appetizing, and then went over to his desk and reached up to the shelf of real, bound books above it. He pulled down a novel.

"Just a half hour," he said to himself, and sat down to read.

CHAPTER 7

A FULL Minbari day had passed since Sinclair had resigned as ambassador, and he had not yet heard from Rathenn or any other Minbari. No protests, no inquiries, not even a "here's your hat what's your hurry?" Perhaps he had committed so serious a transgression against the famed Minbari obsession with serving society above all else that he was now deemed persona non grata.

He didn't know and at the moment it didn't matter as long as they didn't try to interfere with his plans for leaving. For the first time since being recalled to Earth and then sent to Minbar, he was feeling genuinely hopeful. He had managed to book passage on a Narn transport ship which was departing the next day for Babylon 5—for what he had come to consider as home.

As the son of a military man, and then as a career officer himself, home had always been a transient thing, the place you stayed for just a short while until the next assignment. He had lived in numerous places on both Mars and Earth while growing up, and then had hung his hat in a hundred more locales throughout the solar system and explored space since he had himself joined Earthforce.

Odd that the one place he had truly come to think of

as home was Babylon 5. He had been there only a little over two years, and had been other places just as long. But Babylon 5 represented something more to him than all the other places because of what he had accomplished and the people he had become close to there. A great deal of hope had returned to his life there.

He was looking forward to seeing the station again, all two million, five hundred thousand metric tons of it. He wasn't returning as its commander, but that didn't matter. It would always be his station because he was the one who had brought Babylon 5 to life. In return, it had become for him the one place he called home.

A knock came on his door. He opened it to find Rathenn.

"Ambassador, I am here to request that you accompany me to the palace of the Chosen One."

This is it, thought Sinclair. "Rathenn, I doubt your leader can say anything to change my mind about leaving. My problem isn't with your government or your people, but with my own government."

"The Chosen One spared your life," Rathenn replied. "Would you refuse him an audience before you leave?"

Rathenn had him there. Jenimer had indeed spared his life by pardoning him, despite ferocious opposition from the military caste when the sham trial over his accused involvement in the assassination conspiracy had ended in a guilty verdict. Sinclair supposed he owed him one.

Rathenn had a flyer waiting to take them to the Chosen One's palace outside the city limits of Yedor in the foothills of the Tchok'an mountains. From a distance, the surrounding mountains gave a misleading impression of the palace's size, though its breathtaking beauty was evident from miles away, sparkling in the sunlight like a multifaceted jewel.

But it was only as the flyer began its final approach to the palace, that Sinclair could truly appreciate the staggering achievement of the ancient Minbari engineers, builders, craftsmen, and artisans who had over a century's time chiseled, carved, and sculpted a monumental palace out of a towering crystalline mountain. Every inch of its surface was so highly polished, reflecting the sunshine with dazzling rainbows of light, that it grew increasingly difficult to look at. Only as the flyer passed directly over the three natural crystalline pinnacles and began its descent to the landing area, could Sinclair see that every inch of its surface was intricately and beautifully carved with scenes from Minbar's history.

"It is good to have the palace occupied again," Rathenn said, almost to himself, then at Sinclair's look explained further. "From the moment of Dukhat's tragic death all who had lived and worked in the palace departed, as our Chosen One's soul had departed. The palace was left empty and untouched for ten cycles as a symbol of our mourning. Now with the inauguration of Jenimer as our new Chosen One, the palace is once again a living symbol of Minbar."

And in all that time, thought Sinclair, almost fourteen Earth years, the Grey Council had ruled Minbar—and conducted a highly successful war against Earth—without anyone occupying the office of Chosen One. That might seem to indicate that the so-called Minbari leader was only a titular head of government without power, not unlike kings and queens had become on Earth by the twentieth century. Except that Dukhat had clearly been a powerful figure, the unquestioned leader of Minbar. Jenimer's position was not as clear.

"I thought Dukhat remained in space with the Grey

Council on their warship,'' Sinclair said, ''that he spent little, if any time here.''

''True,'' Rathenn said. ''But his presence was always here.''

''What about Jenimer? Will he leave to travel with the Grey Council?''

''The Chosen One has indicated he will remain here, at the palace.''

The flyer landed with a gentle bump, and Rathenn led Sinclair into the ancient palace and through a bewildering maze of dark, polished hallways, ending in a stark, high-ceilinged room, as dimly lit as the hallways had been. Rathenn asked him to wait, then disappeared through a set of doors that Sinclair had not even noticed before Rathenn opened them, so seamlessly were they set into the walls.

Sinclair looked around for a place to sit, but it was an empty room with the same dark, polished and featureless walls as the hallways, illuminated by only one spot of light shining down from above. It was uncomfortably reminiscent of—

No, Sinclair thought. It was pointless to go there. His dreams were merely dreams now, and the past was the past. He closed his eyes and tried to quell the uneasy feeling in the pit of his stomach. He would pay his respects to Jenimer, express due gratitude, and get the hell out of here.

The doors opened and Rathenn reappeared. ''This way, Ambassador.''

Sinclair walked slowly across the room, his muffled footsteps sounding strange to his ears in the oppressive atmosphere of the palace, and stepped through the doors into another antechamber. Rathenn closed the doors behind them, and for a moment it was pitch dark. Then a set of double doors opened in front of them and Sinclair was momentarily blinded by the bright sunlight that streamed in. He took a couple of steps forward, and when he could see again, he found himself in an unexpectedly pleasant, well-furnished room with floor-to-ceiling windows looking out on a spectacular view of the distant skyline of Yedor, and the Tchok'an mountains beyond.

In front of those windows sat Jenimer, the Chosen One, a rather frail-looking, elderly Minbari male. Flanking Jenimer, to Sinclair's astonishment, were Delenn; Kosh, the Vorlon ambassador to Babylon 5; a second Vorlon he did not know; and another older Minbari male. Rathenn took his place with that group.

Sinclair smiled a greeting to Delenn. It was still a shock to see his friend with her new half-Minbari, half-Human appearance. Delenn smiled in return and then looked down.

"Ambassador Sinclair," Jenimer said in a voice far more robust than his frail appearance. "I thank you for coming."

Obviously this meeting was going to take place with everyone standing but Jenimer.

"May I please start by apologizing," Jenimer continued, "for the way you have been treated since coming to Minbar. I assure you that Minbari hospitality is usually far more generous and gentle to visitors. But then this is not the first time that you have been mistreated while within Minbari jurisdiction, is it? That you do not despise us, but indeed came here willing to work with us, is truly something of a miracle."

"You are most gracious, Chosen One," Sinclair said. "I have the greatest respect for the Minbari people, and if I may say so, a certain fondness as well."

Jenimer smiled. "I hope you continue to feel that

way when you find out that you have not been told everything about why we asked you to be assigned here.''

''And why I've been kept in virtual isolation since coming here?''

Jenimer looked a little surprised at Sinclair's directness. ''That also,'' he said apologetically, ''though I must say in our defense that not all of that was our fault. Your own government seems to have its own reasons for keeping you out of contact with your world—though I won't deny we were quick to take advantage of it.''

Sinclair folded his arms. ''Toward what end, Chosen One?'' He hoped such direct questioning didn't break some Minbari rule of etiquette for addressing the Minbari leader, but he had a lot to do before leaving, and wanted to accelerate the pace of the meeting if he could. He *was* curious, however, and hoped he could get some answers without hours of meandering Minbari pleasantries first. Sinclair had a feeling that such directness was totally acceptable to this particular Minbari.

He decided he had called it right when Jenimer responded with a laugh. ''I hope you will allow me to introduce everyone here first. You, of course, know Rathenn, and Delenn, and Kosh.''

Sinclair nodded to each of these in turn.

''So let me also introduce you to the Vorlon ambassador to Minbar, Ulkesh Naranek.''

Sinclair turned to the other Vorlon, and after a good look, simply nodded. Somehow saying ''a pleasure to meet you'' seemed wildly inappropriate, for Sinclair was not too sure he liked this Vorlon. Then he chastised himself. Talk about judging the proverbial book by its cover, he thought.

Since one never saw what a Vorlon truly looked like, but only saw the environment suits they wore, Sinclair had to admit his impression might just be a reaction to the stark, somehow ominous lines of the massive, gleaming headpiece Ulkesh wore, in contrast to that worn by Kosh.

No—it was something more. He just got a feeling of, well, *darkness* from this Vorlon that made him uneasy. This was only the second Vorlon he had ever met. He wondered if he was being unfair. He wondered which, if either, was more representative of its species.

"It is important to remember: every door has two sides."

That was Kosh, suddenly and apropos of nothing. Everyone in the room, including the other Vorlon, turned toward Kosh. The Minbari all nodded their heads as if Kosh had said something of great profundity.

Sinclair saw the Vorlons apparently exchange looks, some sort of a silent exchange. Was it some sort of disagreement? Sinclair had no way of knowing.

"This is Turval," Jenimer continued, "from the 8th Fane of Tredomo, now of the Anla'shok."

Sinclair knew that though Minbari were born into their castes, if an individual, at least among the religious and military castes, felt "called" to service in another caste, they were allowed to change castes. Jenimer's words indicated that Turval had been born into the religious caste, and was now military. Sinclair had never before heard of a military clan called the *anla'shok,* although the word sounded familiar.

"And now, we must tell you of Minbari history," said Jenimer. "I understand that you are something of a student of our history."

"I have tried," said Sinclair, "but there's not much written in any of the Human languages, at least very little of value. I've had to rely on my Minbari language skills to read your texts. It's a little difficult for me when the texts are in one of the archaic forms of your language.''

''Then perhaps you will find this of interest,'' said Jenimer, nodding to Delenn.

As Delenn stepped forward, the windows behind Jenimer gradually became opaque, the room darkened, and a glowing light formed in the middle of the room between Sinclair and the others. It slowly coalesced into a montage of moving shapes, a three-dimensional projection of scenes from Minbar's past that began to illustrate the words of Delenn.

''The ambassador will be familiar with some of what I tell him,'' Delenn said, ''but there is much he has not heard before. Over a thousand years ago, the Minbari people first reached out into interstellar space. Almost immediately, we found ourselves in conflict with an extremely ancient intelligent alien species that seemed to be pursuing a course of destruction wherever they went throughout the galaxy. It is not known whether one of our exploring ships accidentally woke them up from some long slumber, or if our activity attracted their interest from afar. All we know is that suddenly they seemed to be everywhere. At first we knew them only by the aftermath of their destruction, never glimpsing them directly. Perhaps that is why our ancestors named them the Shadows. But when we did see their ships for the first time, the name seemed apt.''

Sinclair watched as the images formed scenes of massive destruction dealt by powerful spiderlike ships that seemed to absorb any light that fell on their glistening surfaces, making them at times almost indistinguishable from the dark between the stars.

He was stunned to realize he had seen those ships before.

''These are among the only visual records we have

from that time. Much was lost and destroyed in the chaos of war.''

The projection of images ceased, and the windows gradually cleared, letting in the late afternoon light.

Delenn gazed steadily at Sinclair. ''You recognize them, do you not, Ambassador?'' Delenn asked.

Sinclair hesitated. He didn't like to give too much away when he didn't know the full situation, but it was clear Delenn knew something. ''Yeah,'' he said. ''I've seen ships like that before—at least two of them, six years ago, on Mars. Garibaldi and I were in a crash in the Martian desert when we stumbled across them.'' He paused again, but seeing Delenn's expression wordlessly urging him to continue, he did. ''I'd been sent to investigate some reports of possible unknown alien sightings. I found a lot more than I had bargained for. It looked like elements of the Psi Corps were conducting some sort of experiments with these aliens.''

''And did you report this to your government?'' asked Jenimer.

''Yes, we did. But when we returned to the site, there was nothing to be found, not a trace, not a scrap of evidence, and though I know some of my superiors believed me, my report was ultimately just filed away and I never heard anything more about it. I never forgot about it, though.''

''A thousand years ago, the Shadows threatened all life in the known galaxy,'' Jenimer said. ''Minbar led the fight against them. But we were fairly new to space flight and our technology was no match for theirs. We would have lost had not help arrived—''

''Valen,'' Sinclair said simply. This part he knew, at least some of it.

''Valen,'' agreed Jenimer, who looked to Delenn.

''Valen arrived with another race of aliens new to us,

the Vorlons. They brought a powerful battle station with them, and something even more powerful—they brought hope, and with that hope the promise the war could be won. Valen became the first Chosen One, reorganized Minbari society, formed the Grey Council—and established an elite fighting force to lead the battle against the Shadows."

Suddenly the pieces fell into place for Sinclair. "The Anla'shok."

A visibly pleased Jenimer nodded in agreement. "Yes. Loosely translated into your language as the Rangers." He motioned for Delenn to continue.

"Slowly the tide of battle turned in our favor. Eventually the Shadows were driven out of all of their places and into hiding, into what we believe is a form of hibernation. But after a thousand years of silence we now know what you discovered yourself: the Shadows have been awakened and are once again following their course of destruction. We believe that the growing Narn-Centauri conflict is part of their plan. We have tried to warn the governments of both planets that they are merely pawns in a much larger conflict, but their passions run too high to listen to any voices outside their own anger and hatred. And so they willingly march into a war that will eventually destroy us all."

"Who are these Shadows?" Sinclair asked. He had been told everything but what seemed the most important thing. "Where do they come from? What do they want?"

All the Minbari in the room, including Delenn, froze with displeasure, as if he had just asked the most impertinent question imaginable.

"We do not know," said Delenn, "and do not believe it is wise to follow that line of thought. We know only that the Shadows bring destruction wherever they go and must be stopped."

"Now wait a minute," said Sinclair, wondering briefly why he was pursuing this. He still wasn't sure what any of this had to with him being on Minbar. But he was a military man, first, last, and always, and the first thing the wise soldier finds out is who the enemy is and what the enemy wants, for that will dictate what the enemy does.

Which meant at least part of him already saw these Shadows as the enemy, Sinclair realized.

"They have to have a reason for what they do," he persisted. "Do they destroy simply to destroy, or do they want something? Power? Worship? A universe empty of all creatures but themselves? And they didn't just suddenly spin themselves out of the vacuum of space a thousand years ago. They have to have a history, a culture, perhaps even conflict among themselves about what they are doing or why. What do you know about them?"

"Only what we have told you," said Jenimer. "That they are an ancient race, and that they are the enemy of all life."

"And who told you that?"

None of the Minbari answered, but it wasn't hard to guess. The Vorlons. Of whom Sinclair, and probably the Minbari, knew no more than they knew of the Shadows. Even Kosh, who had been on Babylon 5 for most of the time Sinclair had been there, was as enigmatic now as he had been on their first meeting. Kosh, who came to Babylon 5 as an ambassador, had always gone through the motions of attending council meetings and making his presence felt, but almost always saying nothing, almost always refusing to participate in any action the council would decide on. When Kosh did act, it was usually unilaterally. And when he did speak it was usually in obscure phrases that required interpretation, so that it ended up being half what the Vorlon said, and half what the listener *thought* he said.

Sinclair had made an effort to break through that wall of detachment, an effort Kosh seemed to welcome, encouraging Sinclair's efforts to speak with him, even allowing Sinclair to visit his quarters anytime he wished. Even so, Kosh had rigorously revealed nothing of himself or what he thought.

Interesting that the Vorlons seemed to want to keep the Shadows as much a mystery as they kept themselves.

"Okay," Sinclair said at last. "I'll admit that just one encounter with these Shadows was enough to convince me they pose a potential threat. And I'm willing to grant you there is evidence that points to involvement by these Shadows in certain recent events. But why are you telling me this? To warn EarthGov? You should be having this conversation with President Clark, or the Senate, not with me. I'm just a fighter pilot and a former space station commander and now an ambassador without portfolio, it would seem. I'm not part of the upper echelons, and not exactly in favor with my government at the moment."

"We have tried to warn your government," said Jenimer. "It proved to be as unproductive as our attempts to warn the Narn and the Centauri. No, we tell you this, we brought you to Minbar, and before this had you named commander of Babylon 5 because we believe that you, Jeffrey Sinclair, are the fulfillment of prophecy."

"Now wait a minute," he began. "I know you have this idea that I somehow possess a Minbari soul, but—"

"Jeffrey, please," said Delenn gently. "Hear us out first."

Reluctantly, Sinclair waited.

"The threat the Shadows pose is not a potential threat," Jenimer said. "It is real and present. Ten thousand Narns were killed in only a few minutes when the Shadows attacked their military outpost in Quadrant 37 at what we can only assume was the request of the Centauri. I assure you, Ambassador, that was only the opening salvo. There will be millions upon millions of more lives lost to the Shadows unless something is done—if even now it is not too late. But the leaders of the military caste refuse to believe it. Perhaps they have lost the will to fight. Perhaps their anger and their hurt pride at being ordered by the religious caste to surrender to Earth has blinded their judgment. Perhaps they truly believe Minbar can only survive if it stays neutral this time, as if such a thing were possible. We do not know. We only know they refuse to act on their own, and through their representatives keep the Grey Council from taking action."

"Forgive me if I have misunderstood something here," said Sinclair, "but my reading of your history tells me that the Chosen One has the power to make certain decisions and even proclaim some policy without the approval of the Grey Council if—"

"If he can demonstrate to the satisfaction of the Council of Caste Elders that the action is justified," said Jenimer. "Yes, that is the law, and it has been invoked in our past, though only a few times, and never to declare a war. And much has changed since the time of Dukhat." He smiled a little sadly at Delenn.

"Some on the Grey Council," said Delenn, "have grown to like leading our people without a Chosen One to counter their authority. It caused much dissension over who should be selected to follow the honored Dukhat.''

''I was chosen,'' said Jenimer, ''to be only—what's the Human expression?''

''A figurehead,'' said Delenn.

''Yes, yes. A figurehead by the Grey Council, an old religious-caste scholar in failing health who they assumed would be quiet and malleable to their purposes. I'm afraid I shocked a number of people when I spared your life, even if it was unquestionably within my authority to do so.''

''For which I am grateful, Chosen One,'' said Sinclair, aware that this was the second time today he had been pointedly reminded of that action.

Jenimer simply smiled and continued. ''My office no longer carries the authority to persuade the Council of Elders on my word alone. Many of the worker-caste leaders tend to agree with the military caste in this matter, if for different reasons. And opinion is not undivided among the religious caste. But there is a way—and we believe it is the only way—to convince enough of the Grey Council, enough of the Minbari-caste leaders, and enough of the Minbari people that the great battle is upon us once again and that we must meet the challenge immediately. Our people hold prophecy in high regard, so we must show them that prophecy has foretold this moment in time and the events unfolding now, and that this prophecy must be fulfilled.''

Perhaps Jenimer wanted his pronouncement to sink in, or perhaps he wanted Sinclair to respond, for he simply paused and studied Sinclair—who waited, keeping his expression as polite as he could.

At last, Jenimer nodded to the Minbari he had earlier introduced as Turval.

''Ambassador.'' Turval bowed politely to Sinclair.

"As I believe you know through your studies of our history, when Valen first came to us, we were losing our fight against the Shadows—as much from fighting among ourselves as from the superior weapons of the enemy. Valen's first task was to unify us—first forming the Grey Council to unify our government. Then forming the Rangers to unify our military. This last was essential because before Valen, each of the military clans had its own fighting force. They argued over tactics and strategy and who was best qualified to lead the battle. Tensions escalated until, tragically and shamefully, soldiers from two of the clans clashed in anger, and some were killed.

"Valen created the Rangers to be a fighting force made up of warriors from all of the military clans. They were trained in customs and traditions that were drawn from all of the clans, but recast into a form unique to the Rangers. Most importantly each Anla'shok would no longer swear allegiance to his clan or fight on its behalf, but swear allegiance only to the Entil'Zha and fight only on his behalf."

"The Entil'Zha?" asked Sinclair.

"The meaning of the word is unknown," said Turval. "It is thought to be of Vorlon derivation."

Sinclair couldn't help a small look of disbelief. They had two Vorlons in the room. Just like the Minbari to refuse to ask out of politeness. Though, given what he knew of the Vorlons, the Minbari could have been asking that question for a thousand years and not been given an answer.

"Okay, I take it then that Valen was the first Entil'Zha?"

"Yes," said Turval. "He personally led the Rangers and all the forces of light against the Shadows and defeated them. Under his leadership, the Anla'shok were the most efficient and deadly fighting force the galaxy has ever seen. But Valen also recognized a danger in this. He knew that without an enemy to fight, such a group could become restless and dissatisfied, and should the wrong person become Entil'Zha under such circumstances, he could use that dissatisfaction to turn the Rangers into an army for conquest and power.

"But neither would he disband the Rangers, for Valen believed that without the unifying symbol of the Anla'shok, the Minbari military might once again become a collection of warring clan factions. And Valen believed the Shadows would return again some day and would succeed this time if there were not a unified Minbari to fight them, and a living Ranger tradition to lead that fight. So before Valen traveled beyond—"

Sinclair noted the strange phrase, often used with Valen, but with no one else. It was not a euphemism for death, and the Minbari never spoke of Valen actually dying.

"—he gave a new mission to the Rangers. They were not to be a fighting force anymore, but were to become sentries and watchers, collecting information quietly here on Minbar from returning travelers and friendly sources on other worlds. They would keep alive the traditions of the Rangers while they kept watch for any sign of the return of the Shadows. Their leader would be known by one of the same titles Valen himself carried—Anla'shok Na, or in your language, Ranger One—but he would not be Entil'Zha. And over the centuries, we have carried out our orders from our Entil'Zha. We are at present few in number, and we are as many old warriors as young, but entrusted with the title of Anla'shok Na, I have done my best to keep the Rangers ready for this day. I am honored and overjoyed to meet the new Entil'Zha." And he bowed to Sinclair.

CHAPTER 8

"ME?" said Sinclair, genuinely startled. He looked to Jenimer. "Listen, you think you have trouble with the military caste now, wait until you tell them you want me to be Entil'Zha. I don't think they'll go for it. And I'm not sure I want the job."

Rathenn stepped forward, speaking for the first time since they had entered the presence of the Chosen One. "You are the fulfillment of a prophecy which was precisely written and specific in its vision. There is no doubt, for it was written in the time of Valen that a time would come in the distant future when the Shadows would awaken and once again threaten all life. And it has come to pass."

"No offense intended, but as prophecies go, that probably seemed like a pretty safe bet back then," Sinclair said. "Even I could have made such a prophecy."

Rathenn continued as if Sinclair hadn't spoken. "But prophecy also says that out of the darkness, hope would emerge in the form of one who comes from outside the three castes, yet is of the three castes; a Minbari not born of Minbari who shall become Entil'Zha and awaken the Anla'shok, as the Shadows have been awakened, and lead them in the battle to defeat the Shadows."

And that, Sinclair thought, is just a reworking of the description of Valen, projected into the future.

"It is also believed," Rathenn continued, "that the prophesied one may even carry a part of Valen's soul itself."

That seemed like a massive contradiction to Sinclair since the Minbari believed absolutely that Valen himself, in the flesh, not just his soul or part of his soul, would be coming back. He decided not to press the point, fearing a theological argument would get them off the track. After all, he'd never come across any religion on Earth that didn't have its own share of contradictions.

They were waiting for him to respond. He knew what they *wanted* him to say. But he wasn't sure at all that he wanted any part of this, not on the terms they were implying. They were going to have to spell it out. He let the silence continue for a moment more, then said: "I'm sorry, but I still don't see how this prophecy applies to me."

He was rewarded with a look of slight exasperation on Rathenn's face. "Prophecy has been fulfilled in you. Consider the prophecy: You are outside the three castes, but of the three castes. You told me yourself that you trained for a religious life—"

"I went to a religious school," Sinclair protested, "but I didn't train to enter the religious life."

"And did you not then work for two years as a common laborer?" Rathenn continued.

"Well, yes, before I entered the Academy I spent two years traveling around, working construction and other odd jobs, but—"

"And then you entered the military," Rathenn continued triumphantly. "Outside the three castes, but of the three castes. And then you are Minbari not born of

Minbari because you have a Minbari soul. You are the prophesied one."

"Look, you can believe whatever you want," said Sinclair, "but let's get this straight. Whatever else you may think of me, good or bad, I'm just a man, not some fulfillment of prophecy. And a Human. Not a Minbari."

Delenn stepped in, perhaps sensing Sinclair's own growing exasperation, and said gently, "Jeffrey, we did not come to this conclusion quickly or lightly. We have studied this since—" She hesitated, looking slightly embarrassed, and the unspoken words *since you were captured and tortured and then scanned by the Triluminary* rang in the silence. "Since the war ended. We are certain this conclusion is based on rigorous logic—"

"The priest who taught my first class in logic had a favorite saying: 'Logic is a systematic method of coming to the wrong conclusion with confidence.' "

"There is no error in our conclusion. You are Minbari," Rathenn persisted. "You have a Minbari soul. Perhaps even part of Valen's soul. But certainly a more evolved soul. A Minbari not born of Minbari."

Sinclair saw absolute certainty on the face of each Minbari in the room, even Delenn. God only knew what the Vorlons were thinking.

He began to shake his head. "No, no, no," he said quietly but firmly. "Don't play word games with my soul to suit your own purposes. My Humanity isn't just some old coat to be replaced by something you deem better. You don't flatter me by trying to convince me that I am somehow different and therefore better or more evolved or special in some way that you can then exploit. Tyrants and hatemongers on my planet have tried to do that sort of thing throughout our history, proclaiming that those born on Mars are not *quite* as

Human as those born on Earth, or that if you had the wrong color skin or ethnic background or religion you weren't really Human at all. This has always been a prelude to discrimination, oppression, enslavement, and murder."

"We did not mean to offend you, Jeffrey," said Delenn. "We knew that at least some Humans hold to the concept of what you call reincarnation, so we did not think you would find what we are saying so difficult to accept—or distasteful."

"It isn't that at all," Sinclair said urgently, fearful that he had accidentally insulted and hurt his friend. "I'm just trying to say that my Humanity is not unimportant to me. And also that I don't believe *any* race is intrinsically or spiritually superior to another. As for reincarnation, I'm not sure whether I believe in it or not. I am sure of only one thing: the life that is important is the life we're living *now*. So even if I thought your Triluminary really had the power to somehow determine that reincarnation is a fact, and that I was a Minbari in a past life, or even all of my past lives, I wouldn't be offended. But it wouldn't change a thing. Because whatever physical form my soul might have been in before, I am Human now. I was born into a Human body and possess a Human mind."

"We do not deny that," said Rathenn. "But the individual soul and the individual personality are merely illusions. After death, what you call the individual soul melts into the greater species soul form, losing its individual identity in any meaningful way, but adding its knowledge to the greater soul form, which then produces new souls to be born. That is how the soul form of our species evolves, and how the Minbari people evolve and grow. Therefore, it is of great significance to the evolution of both species that Minbari soul forms are being born into Human bodies."

"But what is that significance?" Sinclair asked. "Isn't it just as possible, by that logic, that Minbari souls are being born into Human bodies because they want to be Human now and not Minbari? How do you know you're not doing me a disservice by asking me to accept a Minbari role?"

"That is not how we interpret these events," said Rathenn.

"That's my point," Sinclair replied. "This is all about our different interpretations of matters that have no sure answers. We interpret many things differently. You prize above all else a life of service to Minbari society, and look with disfavor on the growing trend among your people to want to live more for themselves because you believe the individual doesn't really exist, just the species soul form, which itself is only one of many species soul forms that are all just fragments of the greater Universal soul form. The only true individual consciousness, you believe, is that of the Universe, which somehow became sentient out of nonsentient matter and is in essence what could be called God, but a God whose existence *is* the Universe. When the Universe fades into the cold, eternal darkness of entropy, everything, including God, will die."

At Rathenn's surprised look that he would know all this, Sinclair smiled. "I've studied Minbari culture. But you have to understand, I don't agree. If there is a God, I believe He has always existed and that He created this Universe, not the other way around, and that He 'will be, when all the stars are dead,' as the poet Rilke once wrote.

"Just as we will, because I also believe the soul to be immortal, and that we retain our individuality and essential personality after death. I don't believe there are distinct soul forms, or that a soul *belongs* to any species. The particular form a soul is born into is chosen to move that soul along the path of spiritual evolution or salvation, whatever you want to call it. The individual soul does not exist only to serve society or the evolution of any one species. So I find your people's growing wish to live more individual lives to be a positive sign, not a negative one."

For the first time, Jenimer looked astonished. "You truly believe that the individual's needs are supreme to that of society? That would cause anarchy!"

"It's something of a paradox, actually. I was taught that we are in this life to achieve our own individual salvation or evolution, depending on your belief, but that we can only do so by also serving our fellow creatures. In other words, the trick is to find the proper balance between the two."

Sinclair paused. He suddenly remembered how Garibaldi used to kid him that there were times he thought and argued like a Jesuit lawyer, the worst combination Garibaldi could think of. Given the situation, the thought now amused him greatly.

"I want to be sure we are absolutely clear with each other," said Sinclair. "If I take on this job, we'll need to understand each other."

For the first time, Rathenn looked hopeful. "Then you will join with us and accept leadership of the Anla'shok?"

Was that in fact what he was saying? Sinclair was a little surprised to realize that it just might be. He looked at each of the Minbari in turn: Rathenn, Delenn, Jenimer, and Turval.

"If I do, you will have to trust me, and I have to be able to trust you. But you've been less than completely truthful with me from the moment I was taken aboard your cruiser. First, you wiped my memories of what happened. Then you secretly arranged to have me assigned to Babylon 5 for the sole purpose of ascertaining whether or not I really was the fulfillment of your prophecy. You wanted to take your time with it, but when the Shadows attacked the Narns, you had to step up your timetable. So you had me assigned to Minbar and isolated me from all contact with Earth or Babylon 5 so that you could introduce me to the Minbari way of doing things and slowly get me used to the idea that I am indeed the fulfillment of your prophecy. Have I got it right so far?''

''We feared it was a great deal to absorb all at once,'' said Jenimer quietly. ''What we ask of you will be difficult. We thought it best to reveal it to you bit by bit, as you became ready to accept it.''

''Did you?'' Sinclair said evenly. ''It was only when I threw a monkey wrench into your plans by resigning that you finally decided to lay your cards on the table. Now my cards are down as well. You know exactly what I do and don't believe in, and that I don't believe in prophecies, yours or anybody else's. Are you still sure I'm the one who is supposed to lead the Anla'shok?''

''Yes,'' said Jenimer. ''There is no other. There are many more prophecies that you will *not* believe in that must be fulfilled.''

Sinclair laughed. It was an unexpected bit of humor that made him like the Minbari leader even more.

''The most important prophecy says that the species that holds the other half of our soul will join with us in this fight. We are among those who believe that Humanity is that other half. Because of that the newly awakened Anla'shok must recruit Humans as well as Minbari to join its ranks."

Once again, the Minbari had managed to utterly astound Sinclair. He was sure that the normally insular and chauvinistic Minbari had never attempted quite so cooperative a venture with any other species—other than the enigmatic Vorlons, who seemed to dictate rather than cooperate anyway—and certainly never involving an institution like the Rangers, so central to the heart and soul of Minbari history and tradition.

"You are the only one who can make this possible," Jenimer insisted softly. "You fulfill all the requirements of the prophecy for the new Entil'Zha. You are first and foremost a warrior, a proven military leader who commands great respect among both Humans and Minbari. Even those among our military caste who hate you nevertheless respect you. You also have the mind of a scholar and priest, as you have demonstrated once again here today. This has earned you the respect of many in the religious caste. Your unpretentious air and common touch has earned you the respect of many in our worker caste. Finally, you have proven your skill at diplomacy, a trait necessary if you are to reach out to Minbari of all three castes and to Humanity and bring them all together to work for the common goal—defeat of the Shadows and the restoration of peace and justice throughout the galaxy. There is simply no one else who has all of these attributes. You alone can bridge our two worlds.

"If you cannot believe prophecy, then we ask you to join with us to defeat a proven, ruthless enemy who will massacre whole populations and lay waste entire star systems if not stopped."

How much did the Minbari believe their own rhetoric, and how much was said for the purpose of manipulation? It was difficult to know what to trust, especially with the Vorlons glowering over the scene like silent alien watchtowers. He looked to Delenn, who was watching him with an expression of such expectant hope that he knew he could not distrust her motives. She clearly believed in what Jenimer had said, and had she not already put herself on the line for him?

Maybe he would have to wait just a little while longer before going home.

"If I say yes, how will the Rangers be selected?"

They had said it themselves. He was a military man. He wanted some practical questions answered first. Exactly what kind of army did they want to put together? How much control would he have in the selection process and the training?

Suddenly there was movement, a release of held breaths, even smiles. Rathenn spoke a few soft words to Delenn, Jenimer asked something quietly of Turval, to which he received a one-word reply.

"The Anla'shok have traditionally allowed only Minbari of the military caste to join, those either born to the caste or called to it," said Jenimer, "But we fear that opposition from the military-caste leaders will make it too difficult to recruit enough candidates from their ranks, so we have studied prophecy and history and determined that it is now the proper time to open up membership more freely to the religious caste as well."

"What about the worker caste?" Sinclair asked.

"As members of the Anla'shok?" Jenimer responded almost incredulously.

Sinclair nodded.

"That would be unacceptable to the military caste," Jenimer replied.

"It is believed by some," said Delenn quietly, "that Valen did not find it unacceptable."

"There is no absolute proof of that," rejoined Rathenn.

"If I accept your request to become head of the Rangers," Sinclair said, "those worker caste who qualify will be allowed to join on a completely equal basis with all other Minbari and Humans—even if that royally knots the shorts of the military caste."

"Jeffrey I know that you have always had a deep concern for the rights of workers," said Delenn, "but it will be difficult to persuade the military caste. Is it wise to risk the reinstitution of the Rangers on this issue at this time? Perhaps later—"

"I can't take on this task," Sinclair replied, "unless I'm free to find the very *best* candidates your people have to offer regardless of caste. I'm afraid this has to be nonnegotiable."

Jenimer looked extremely conflicted. Sinclair waited patiently.

"Perhaps it can be done," Jenimer said at last.

"What about the Human candidates?" Sinclair asked.

"That is a delicate question," said Jenimer. "We do not wish to attract undue attention from your government on this matter. In fact, we would like to keep the knowledge of the Rangers' existence to as few people as possible."

"So much for putting an ad in *Universe Today,*" said Sinclair. "How then do we attract Human candidates?"

"We will start with those Humans who are already on Minbar," said Rathenn. "We have complete information on all of them, and you have already met a good many of them."

"Ah," said Sinclair with understanding. "That's why you had me personally interview as many Humans as you could fit into my schedule, so I would have a leg up on who might be a likely candidate to become a Ranger and who wouldn't."

Rathenn nodded. "You can continue to contact all visitors here from Earth without attracting unwanted attention for as long as you continue to function as the Earth's ambassador here. From those you select will come others, as they recruit other candidates from among those they know."

"Then we are agreed?" Jenimer asked. "You will join the battle and lead the Rangers?"

Sinclair took a deep breath. "Under one other condition. That if you accept me as Entil'Zha, accept me as a fully Human Entil'Zha, for that is what I am, Human, no more and no less than any other Human. If you'll agree to that, then . . . yes."

What was he getting himself into? And what was Catherine going to say about all of this?

"Our beliefs are as firm as yours," said Jenimer, "but we can accept your terms and conduct ourselves toward you as you request. It is just as well for the present, as the subject of the transference of souls is a most sensitive one. It is best not spoken of outside these walls or the chambers of the Grey Council."

Yes, that's what Rathenn had said—was it only a few weeks ago?—in the meeting with President Clark in which they had persuaded Sinclair to accept the position of ambassador. Can't tell the Minbari or Humanity about this soul business, both had said. Might upset them. Best to keep it to ourselves.

For a people who claimed they never lied, the Minbari were the masters of the art of the concealed truth.

For the first time, Jenimer stood. He walked over to Sinclair. "I understand there is a custom among your people when reaching such an agreement."

He extended his hand to Sinclair. The unexpected

gesture delighted Sinclair, and the Chosen One and the Entil'Zha-to-be shook hands.

"It is wise for the arrow to remember it does not choose the target."

Sinclair looked sharply over at the Vorlons, whom he had momentarily forgotten about. That sounded far too much like a challenge or perhaps even a threat, and it had come from Ulkesh, Sinclair realized, judging from the slight difference in the tone of the synthesized voice, and the fact that while Kosh was looking at Ulkesh, Ulkesh was looking at Sinclair.

The Vorlon abruptly moved to depart, gliding past Sinclair, apparently deciding the meeting was concluded. He had said his little piece, and would now leave the mere non-Vorlon mortals to ponder his wise words.

Like hell, thought Sinclair. He didn't like this Vorlon at all. He waited until Ulkesh was almost to the door, then said in a clear voice: "That depends entirely upon which arrow you choose. The wise archer remembers that."

Ulkesh hesitated at the door for just a moment, but did not turn around, then left without another word. A moment later Kosh also left.

Officially, the meeting was over. Sinclair was told that nothing else could be done until the joint convocation of the Grey Council and the Council of Caste Elders at which Rathenn would plead the case for the reinstitution of the Rangers and the installation of Sinclair as Entil'Zha.

Delenn escorted Sinclair and Rathenn out into the hall, then asked Rathenn if he would go on ahead so that she could have a few moments to speak to Sinclair alone.

As they walked slowly through the empty halls of the great palace, Delenn began by saying good-bye.

"I have to leave for Babylon 5 immediately," she said. "My work is still there and I cannot be away any longer."

It struck Sinclair that the Universe had suddenly been turned upside down; now it was Delenn who had to return to Babylon 5, and he was the one that had to stay on Minbar. He felt a wave of regret wash over him that he had come so close to returning to his beloved station, only to have his sense of duty once again pull him in a different direction.

"I will not be able to attend the council meeting," Delenn was saying, "But Rathenn will carry my vote, and will speak as I would have."

"I'll just be sorry not to see you there," said Sinclair. "You're the one friendly face I know I can count on when things start getting a little thick, as I'm sure they will. But it has been good to see you again. So tell me, how are things on the station? How is Garibaldi doing?"

"He is fine," said Delenn. "Well enough to return to duty." And they talked about everyone and everything that was dear to Sinclair on Babylon 5.

Delenn saw Sinclair to the portal leading out into the Minbari night and the waiting flyer, then disappeared back into the palace.

Sinclair boarded the flyer where Rathenn was waiting for him. The small craft lifted up toward the night sky.

"That was quite a contribution the Vorlons made to the meeting," Sinclair said. He had been wondering what the Minbari made of such pronouncements.

"Yes," said Rathenn. "I have been trying to comprehend the wisdom of their words. They speak so rarely, so when they do each word carries great weight."

"Maybe," said Sinclair, "but I sometimes think the Vorlons just make up nonsense to amuse themselves at our expense."

Rathenn seemed nonplussed. "Why would the Vorlon deliberately speak nonsense, Ambassador? Please forgive me for asking, but how would that constitute amusement? Surely, that would not be proper behavior in any case."

Sinclair grinned at the puzzled Minbari. "I thought the Minbari placed a high value on humor, Rathenn. What was the phrase Delenn told me—that all Minbari are trained in humor, delight, and laughter?"

"That is true, Ambassador," Rathenn quickly acknowledged, "But the Vorlons are not like the Minbari, and I had always assumed they had evolved beyond such simple emotions as humor."

"That could very well be a big part of the problem," Sinclair said.

Rathenn clearly did not know how to respond to that.

"I suspect," said Sinclair, "that the Minbari sense of humor and the Human sense of humor are quite different in many respects."

Rathenn nodded, perhaps a little too vigorously. "In that we are in complete agreement, Ambassador."

"Well, if I'm going to lead the Rangers, I guess I'm going to have to start my training in Minbari humor, delight, and laughter. Perhaps you could start by telling me the best joke you know."

"A joke, Ambassador?"

"A joke. A humorous story."

"Ah, you mean some humorous event from my life, or that has been related to me by someone else."

"Well, that's good, too," said Sinclair, "but I was

thinking more along the lines of a very short fictional anecdote with a punch line?"

"A punch line?"

Sinclair laughed again. "You don't have any idea what I'm talking about, do you?"

Rathenn bowed his head, acutely embarrassed now. "I apologize, Ambassador."

"No, no, Rathenn. No need to apologize. It seems we both still have a lot to learn about each other. And from each other. You know, I've never actually thanked you for the help you have extended to me since I've been here."

"It has been my great honor," Rathenn said, clearly now more at ease. "And I will look into this notion of 'joke' to see if we have anything similar in Minbari culture and report to you what I find."

Sinclair grinned again and sat back to enjoy the beautiful lights of Yedor sparkling in profusion below them.

CHAPTER 9

CATHERINE Sakai did not like hyperspace travel. The crackling energy discharges and the cascades of constantly shifting, eerily colored and glowing plasma clouds were beautiful, but only in the way incandescent streams of molten rock flowing from a volcano could be said to be beautiful, or the roaring, red-orange walls of flame and showering sparks of a raging forest fire. They were all humbling displays of Nature's unfathomable power and destructive potential, and were best appreciated in very short doses, preferably from a good distance away.

Sakai had been in hyperspace for five and half days now, and was suffering as bad a case of hyperspace travel syndrome as she had ever endured. HST syndrome was caused by the conditions of hyperspace in which the apparent motion of a craft as a person's eyes perceived it outside the cockpit windows was not the true motion of the craft as the craft's instrument panels would confirm it to be. This, coupled with the constantly flickering patterns of light outside, began to play tricks on the brain, scrambling notions of up and down, forward and backward, causing nausea, vertigo, and panic attacks, including an overwhelming feeling that one was caught motionless in hyperspace and not moving at all. It was like being caught in a dream or nightmare from which one could not awaken.

Because of HST syndrome, passenger ships did not have windows in the passenger compartments, or darkened them during hyperspace travel. But a pilot could not afford the luxury of flying blind. Hyperspace travel was tricky and always potentially dangerous and a ship's pilot or crew had to learn to live with the side effects, see past the optical illusions, and trust their instrument readings.

No, she wasn't at all fond of hyperspace travel. Perhaps some thought that odd for a professional space pilot, but she saw no contradiction at all. *Space* travel she liked, traveling through the deep blackness that served as the perfect backdrop for the thick swirls of brilliantly shining stars that surrounded her ship, visiting as many of those stars as she could, one by one resolving distant points of light into suns with planets of their own.

This was all she had ever wanted to do since her earliest childhood, when her father would take her outside into the cold Alaska spring nights to show her the constellations and explain the stories behind each one, then name as many of the stars for her as he could, making each one not just a distant light, but a friend that she might actually visit someday.

How important those friends in the night sky had become to her during those first painful and confusing months after her parents' divorce and she had moved with her mother to Hong Kong. She would sneak outside late at night, spread a blanket out in their little backyard, and lie down to watch the stars wheel by overhead and think about how they were still her friends even though they were trillions upon trillions of miles away. It made the few thousand miles that separated her from her father seem like a relatively short distance by comparison, and thus made her feel closer to him.

Once she had fallen asleep while under that canopy of stars, and her mother, panicked to find her daughter missing from her room in the predawn hours, had discovered her out there just as the horizon began to lighten. Instead of rushing outside to scold her daughter, she had fixed a pot of tea and brought it out on a tray, had sat down beside her and gently wakened her, and together they drank the tea and watched the sun come up and for the first time talked about the divorce and her father without rancor or bitterness, and remembered as many happy memories as they could. Her mother had assured her that she was not responsible for her parents breaking up, and that, although they had decided they could not live together anymore, her mother and father still loved one another in some way, so it was okay for her to still love both of them.

Years later, after her mother had died and she had gone to live with her father for a while, they sat outside one evening to look at the stars and she had told him about that morning. And as his eyes had filled with tears, he had reached out and taken her hand, and for a moment, in the glow of those same unchanging stars, it felt as if her family had been reunited.

Though her father was now also gone, any time she looked at the stars, she could feel the presence and love of both her parents, and the palpable sense of longing she had felt to someday travel among those stars.

The rude blaring of her computer's early warning system interrupted her reverie.

"Approaching jump gate quadrant one hundred zero two, coordinates zero seven by four eight by one six in ten minutes," intoned the ship's computer.

"Acknowledged."

Sakai initiated her ship's hyperspace departure sequence and instructed her computer to establish contact with the jump gate. She began the routine exit procedures with more than usual care. She would be exiting hyperspace into normal space through one of the oldest jump gates ever found. Universal Terraform had estimated it at some six thousand years old. Though all the original jump gates had been built to last for millennia, they could be quirky and unpredictable in operation and she was poised to be the first Human ever to go through this particular one. She had seen the data from the original robot exploration vessel that had discovered this gate and the mineral-rich planet it opened on to, and while it had indicated no unusual functionings, Sakai knew from experience not to rely on that. Each jump through these ancient gates was a unique experience and nothing could prepare a pilot for it completely.

Nobody knew anything about the alien species who had built the original network of jump gates other than what the gates themselves revealed. The aliens had been highly advanced, and were extraordinary engineers. They had built the first gates maybe as early as seven thousand years before, and had apparently flourished as an interstellar civilization for some four to five thousand years after that—then vanished, leaving only their gates behind. No trace of their civilization beyond the gates had ever been found.

Some contemporary alien civilizations such as the Minbari and the Centauri had stumbled across gates at the outer edges of their own solar systems while exploring in their first early sublightspeed ships. Once having unlocked the complex codes required to activate the jump gates, they set out to explore hyperspace in an attempt to map the jump-gate network.

But hyperspace proved to be so exceedingly difficult

and dangerous to navigate through that many of the early ships were destroyed. Those that did manage to survive discovered that finding their way out of hyperspace was an extremely difficult task. A uniform series of beacons was developed to help ships locate the gates within the chaotic nightmare of hyperspace. No one knew how the original aliens had navigated through their network of gates, but they didn't seem to use homing beacons, so it became clear that finding all the original gates would be a process that might take as many millennia as the gates had been in existence, since there was no sure method for doing so other than blind luck.

The next step then had been to determine how the gates worked so new ones could be built. That started the race to find Quantium 40 in order to build and control as many jump gates as possible. Eager for new customers, the Centauri started searching out worlds such as Earth, which hadn't been as lucky to have one of the ancient gates conveniently in the area, and sold them access to their jump gates. But Humanity soon figured out how to construct their own gates and ships with jump-point generators, and eventually joined the interstellar party as equal participants.

"Approaching gate entry point," intoned the ship's computer. "Prepare for jump to normal space."

"Acknowledged," Sakai replied, letting the computer run the controls through the standard program, but readying herself to take over on manual if need be.

"Entering gate."

For just an instant, the cockpit seemed to spin around her at a dizzying speed, then for an even briefer moment the Universe elongated—both she and her ship seemed to be stretched into a smear of atoms infinitely long—then snapped back into place, as *Skydancer* began to shake. Two seconds later she saw the stars through the cockpit canopy and *Skydancer* sailed smoothly out into normal space.

"Pretty slick," she said as she took over manual controls. Not a bad jump gate. Maybe they could do a little fine tuning on the transition-point boosters, but overall it had been a smooth ride.

"All right," she said, warming to the task ahead. The blue-white star UTC45 was shining brightly down through the top of the cockpit. This gate was closer to the center of this system than many of the ancient gates. She adjusted her heading and banked sharply to bring *Skydancer* in line with the orbital plane of Planet UTC45-03A, code named Ymir.

"Computer, let's get a fix on the target."

Skydancer adjusted course again, and Ymir swung into view. It should have been just a typical Class 4 planet, a rocky, terrestrial world, brown and red with no surface water, just lots of craggy mountain ranges and long, deep canyons and crevices, covered by a thick but basically transparent atmosphere. Nothing very interesting except for the occasional volcanic eruption—and of course the hoped-for Quantium 40. That's what it should have been.

But there was something wrong with Planet UTC45-03A. What she saw was a smooth dark brown globe—no surface features at all. There was something wrong with the atmosphere. There was something very wrong.

"Computer, report on long-range scan of planet. Check for any signs of sentient life on the planet surface or in orbit." Don't rush in where unknown aliens may be treading. She had learned her lesson on that one.

"Negative result. No energy signatures, structures, or characteristic movement consistent with sentient life."

"Increase speed to safe maximum and change preset orbital coordinates to the next standard higher orbit."

"Acknowledged."

Skydancer's engines hummed at higher pitch and Sakai was pressed back in her seat as the tiny ship increased its velocity toward the planet.

"Computer, report on atmospheric conditions—specify anomalous conditions, summarize and report."

"Unusually high level of particulate matter suspended in atmosphere planetwide. Surface temperatures one point four three of normal planetwide caused by greenhouse effect."

This was not the world described in the Universal Terraform report, not the planet the initial robot probe ship had visited eight months before. With growing disbelief, Sakai built a new profile of Ymir from the incoming data.

"Computer, show chemical composition of particulate matter." But she suspected the answer even before the data scrolled by on the screen—it was dust, a thick, choking cloud of dust that reached as high as the stratosphere and apparently covered the entire planet pole to pole. What could cause this to happen?

"Computer, check for any signs of a recent extreme extraplanetary object impact with planet."

The computer worked for a moment. "Negative result on visible limb of planet. Total negative result projected from data, ninety-five percent certainty."

So an asteroid or meteor hadn't smashed into the planet. What had happened?

"Computer, go to continuous monitoring for sentient life activity, top priority."

Skydancer's sensors would continue to report back data as the ship approached closer to the planet, but Sakai knew she wasn't likely to get any closer to an answer until she could launch the sensor satellites and probes, so it wouldn't hurt to redirect some of the sensors. She had a very bad feeling about the whole thing.

She suddenly thought about Sinclair. He always said he didn't like surprises—the result of a life spent in the military. She remembered him lecturing at the Academy: Surprises in the military could cause disaster or death. That's why one trained and prepared over and over to eliminate as much of the element of surprise as humanly possible. That was the catch, of course, Jeff would say, since there were always going to be surprises springing from outside the sphere of Human influence that no amount of training and preparation could eliminate. But just keeping that in mind would help reduce the impact of those kinds of surprises.

For all his stern lecturing, however, she had quickly learned something else about him: he appreciated a good mystery and was rather proud of his abilities at solving them.

"What would you think of this one, Jeff?" she wondered.

Skydancer reached orbital distance and assumed its preset orbit. Sakai initiated launch sequence on the satellites and sensor probes. She knew what question Universal Terraform would want her to ask first, and when data began beaming back from the probes, she asked it:

"Computer. Report on initial findings regarding presence of Quantium 40 on the planet."

"Initial data indicates trace elements suspended in atmosphere only. No Quantium 40 on planet surface."

This made no sense. How could there be trace elements in the air, but none in the rock below?

"Computer, analyze chemical composition of

ground material at initial target area and report to screen."

Sakai read with growing amazement as the unexpectedly short list of minerals scrolled by, outlining a completely unexpected, relatively simple composition composed of far more iron-magnesium minerals than would be expected outside of—

"Oh, my God!" she muttered, a chilling implication suggesting itself. "Computer, is the composition of matter at the initial target site consistent with the general composition of a Class 4 planet's upper mantle?"

"Affirmative," said the computer.

"And is the composition of the particulate matter in the planet's atmosphere consistent with the general composition of a Class 4 planet's outer crust?"

"Affirmative," said the computer.

"What the hell is going on?" she demanded aloud. "Computer, correlate data to present and answer question: Are there areas of the planet that appear to be missing the normal outer crust of rock, thus exposing what appears to be the planet's upper mantle?"

"Affirmative."

"Project, over what percentage of the planet surface does this condition exist?"

The computer worked for a moment. "Projection to twenty-eight percent of the planet surface."

Sakai could hardly believe what she was hearing, as the terrifying implications sank in. What could blast away the outer surface of a planet to a depth of from ten to thirty-five miles deep over twenty-eight percent of the planet's surface in a time frame of eight months or less?

What . . . or who?

CHAPTER 10

"WHICH is the greater outrage? It is hard to decide, is it not?" Neroon of the Star Riders Clan gazed out over the assembled members of the Council of Caste Elders—the nine members from the religious caste, the nine members from the worker caste, and the other eight members of his own military caste. "Is it a greater outrage that a few members of the religious caste have misled our beloved Chosen One into participating in a potentially illegal attempt to subvert the majority will of the Grey Council? Or is the greater outrage that they have willfully misinterpreted sacred prophecy, twisting it beyond recognition in their obscene attempt to make us all believe it could possibly refer to a *Human*?"

Sinclair was impressed with the amount of venom Neroon had managed to put into that last word. The Great Hall of the Caste Elders echoed with the intensity of the Minbari's hatred.

Sinclair had felt that anger firsthand on three occasions in the past. The first had been at the Battle of the Line, and though he had not actually met Neroon personally, the Minbari had been *alyt* (second in command) to Branmer, one of the leaders of the Minbari attack.

The next time he and Neroon crossed paths—or was the better word "swords"—Neroon had brought the body of the recently deceased Branmer to Babylon 5, ostensibly to allow all the Minbari onboard the opportunity to pay their respects. But it had been clear to Sinclair that Neroon's intent was to try to provoke the Humans on Babylon 5. As events had escalated, Neroon had even attempted—unsuccessfully—to ambush Sinclair in his own quarters. They had eventually parted on what Sinclair had hoped was better terms, but in retrospect he realized that Neroon's display of reconciliation was only a temporary reaction brought on by a severe reprimand from Grey Council member Delenn—and the embarrassment of having been beaten in a fight by Sinclair, a mere *Human*.

Because in their third meeting, Neroon had done his enthusiastic best to have Sinclair convicted and executed on the phony assassination charges.

"I mean no disrespect to Satai Rathenn or the Grey Council," Neroon continued, bowing to the section of the hall where Rathenn, after having finished his lengthy presentation regarding the Shadow threat and the Rangers, had taken his place with the other members of the Grey Council, sitting hooded and partly in shadow. One empty chair out of nine attested to Delenn's absence. "In fact, I think I respect the Grey Council even more than Satai Rathenn and certainly more than Satai Delenn—who, I will note, could not find the time to break away from her dealings with Humans on Babylon 5 to honor us with her presence here."

That brought a bit of grumbling from the Caste Elders. The Grey Council sat unmoving and silent, as they had throughout the prolonged proceedings of this extraordinary convocation of the Chosen One, the Grey Council, and the Council of Caste Elders. Jenimer sat quietly in a section that with the Grey Council and the Caste Elders completed a circle of chairs.

Sinclair, arms folded, shifted uncomfortably where he stood behind and to the right of the Minbari leader. He'd been standing there for far too many hours without a break. So had Ulkesh, who was to the left of Jenimer, but of course that sort of thing never seemed to bother a Vorlon. They were the only others present.

Neroon was too obviously aware of the singular nature of this meeting, and was doing his best to take advantage of this uncommon chance to speak before members of the Grey Council, who so rarely visited Minbar. He spoke in both the religious and military dialects, switching between them with ease to make different points. Though Sinclair had been supplied with an earpiece hooked to a translating computer, he was able to follow most of what was being said on his own, and thanked God one more time for the gift he'd been born with for learning other languages.

"But Satai Rathenn seeks to overturn the decision of a majority of the Grey Council who say that the time is not yet right to restore the Anla'shok to full military status. And he dishonors all of us by alleging that the ancient prophecy could ever be interpreted to mean that a Human," and for the first time Neroon acknowledged Sinclair's presence, pointing at him with disdain, "should be the Entil'Zha, should succeed *Valen,* because, Rathenn says, the archaic text refers to 'a Minbari not born of Minbari.' He would have you believe this refers to an alien who adopts Minbari ways. But I invite you to look at the ancient text yourselves, and listen to the majority of our scholars who interpret that phrase in the ancient language *not* as 'a Minbari not born *of Minbari'* but as 'a Minbari not born *on Minbar,'* perhaps on a colony world or a ship. But a Minbari nonetheless, not an alien, and certainly not a Human."

Sinclair shook his head slightly. He had seen this sort

of thing on Earth, far too many times, when people sought to base their actions solely on the literal dictates of an ancient text written in an archaic language. The questions of what were the right things, and the moral things, and the sensible things to do too often were lost in the debate over text interpretation.

"Look at him," Neroon said suddenly. "Standing there with smug insolence in this consecrated hall that no Human should ever have been allowed to defile. How many insults are we expected to endure at the hands of these Humans? How many more outrages can we expect you and your kind to heap upon us?" Neroon was now standing just to the side of Jenimer so that he could direct his tirade squarely at Sinclair. "In less than a lunar cycle you have promoted the most hated and dishonorable of Humans to the command of Babylon 5, attempted to kill our new Chosen One, and now wish to usurp the sacred title of Entil'Zha and defile the names of Valen and the Anla'shok." Neroon spun on his heel and walked back to the Caste Elders. "I say he should be removed from our presence and deported back to the depraved world from which he came."

Sinclair saw that Neroon's words, spoken with confidence and eloquence, had made an obvious impact on his audience, in contrast to the excruciatingly thorough, but dry and complicated presentation Rathenn had made. Neroon turned once more toward Sinclair, this time to gloat.

It was only then that Jenimer finally spoke. "A moment ago you asked Ambassador Sinclair a question, Neroon. It is his right to answer."

It was a toss-up as to who was more astounded by this, Neroon or Sinclair. Sinclair had been specifically told by the rules of the meeting he would not be allowed to speak.

"Great Leader," said Neroon, trying to sound shocked but humble, "I beg your forgiveness, but he is an off-worlder, and an observer here only. By the rules governing this great convocation, he cannot speak."

"Unless he is asked a direct question by a participant," said Jenimer pleasantly. "This is not an obscure rule, Neroon, but one used all the time in the council meetings of the Caste Elders, as you well know."

"But certainly that does not apply to an off-worlder!"

"It is not written anywhere that the rules of assembly apply only to Minbari." Jenimer turned his head slightly toward Sinclair and gestured him forward with his right hand. "Ambassador, you are granted time to respond to the Elder's question."

Had Jenimer been waiting for an opportunity such as this, hoping Neroon would slip and direct comments his way, planning all along to have Sinclair speak? Or had the Minbari leader decided that they were losing the battle anyway, so he might as well try a desperate gamble that Sinclair might be able to convince a roomful of Minbari that their great warrior Neroon was wrong, and he, a Human and their former enemy, was right.

Neroon backed away, hiding his scowl in his obeisance, but did not sit down; instead he watched from in front of the Caste Elder's section as Sinclair walked slowly to the center of the circle, gathering his thoughts.

Sinclair directed his attention to the Caste Elders. There was no need to give any attention to the Grey Council as they would probably vote again as they had before—the three members of the religious caste and one member of the worker caste would vote for Jenimer's position, and the three members of the military caste and the other two members of the worker caste would vote against.

"If I may," said Sinclair at last, speaking slowly and deliberately in warrior-caste Minbari, the dialect he knew best. He had no way of knowing how many in the hall could speak fluent English. "I would like to start by agreeing with *Alyt* Neroon on at least one thing: the attempt on the life of the Chosen One was indeed an outrage, and I share his anger at those who were involved. But," he said, switching momentarily to the religious-caste dialect, *"I was not among their contemptible number, as the Chosen One himself has so graciously discerned and decreed."*

He paused, and was gratified to see his attempt at their languages had the desired positive effect. He switched back to warrior caste, struggling more than a little to find the proper phrases. "And if indeed there were some Humans involved, then I am ashamed on behalf of Humanity. But should I be held personally accountable for the actions of any and all other Humans, any more than any of you should be held personally accountable for the actions of any and all of your fellow Minbari? Should the entire Human race be held accountable for the misdeeds of the few, any more than the entire Minbari race should be held accountable for the misdeeds of individual Minbari? How many millions of lives have already been lost to that sort of tragic thinking?"

Sinclair knew all too well that the Minbari had launched their war against Earth precisely because they had held all of Humanity responsible for the mistaken actions of a few. Once that anger wore off, many Minbari felt regret and even shame at their actions. He was counting on that, particularly as the next point was a little more tricky.

"As for the man who was chosen to replace me on Babylon 5," Sinclair said, "I can claim an acquaintance with Captain John Sheridan and can assure you he is an honorable man who will do his best to be fair. He is not the warmonger that so many believe him to be."

But the last of his words was almost lost to Neroon's outrage. "An honorable man!" Neroon shouted in English. He came to the center of the circle to confront Sinclair directly. "You can stand in front of this assembly and use our language to say such a thing? Humans must have a very different definition of the word honorable that you could use it to describe such a treacherous and contemptible person. You add further insult by defending his appointment, made over our objections, to Babylon 5. And do not assault our ears any longer with your foul attempt at our language. There is no one in this hall who does not understand your language—or your lies."

Sinclair met Neroon's look of contempt, and abruptly decided to go for broke. There was no way to win this battle with subtle diplomacy against Neroon's loud and persuasive indignation, and Sinclair felt a surge of liberation in deciding to just lay out the unvarnished truth and hope the shock of such a frontal attack would force open some minds. "Then I will ask you, in my own language, what did Sheridan do to earn such hatred? He did only what was necessary to prevent the destruction of his ship and the death of his shipmates. He fought to prevent the annihilation of his world and his people, as all of us did who fought for Humanity during the war. You talk of honor. Where is the honor in your willingness to commit genocide over a single death mistakenly inflicted?"

"The course of our holy war was not determined solely by that one grievous incident," Neroon replied in a booming voice, "even as abhorrent as that crime was. No, our anger grew and grew, and our actions were justified, because of the universal tactics of dishonor, cowardice, and murder that we saw used by Humans in almost every encounter during the war, including the actions of Sheridan."

"The destruction of the *BlackStar* owed as much to the arrogance of her captain as it did to Sheridan's tactics," Sinclair said. "You know that as well as I do. But it's much easier to blame the enemy instead of your own failings."

Sinclair turned to the Caste Elders. "I won't defend everything done by every Human during that tragic war, but we faced annihilation in a war we never wanted or meant to start against a virtually unknown but clearly superior enemy. Even the most honorable Minbari under such extreme circumstances might find fear and desperation momentarily obliterating their reason and moral judgment. But the majority of Humans fought with honor, and since the war we have enthusiastically pursued peace and even friendship with the Minbari people."

Again Sinclair paused. He wanted to say the next phrase in the worker dialect, and wanted it to be correct. *"I came to Minbar,* he enunciated carefully, *"in that spirit of peace and friendship, to work with all Minbari."* Sinclair was pleased with the reaction from the worker elders. He knew they held the swing votes and he believed they were the most likely to base their decision less on theology or historical grievances, and more on what was said here.

"I came here only with the intention of functioning as Earth's ambassador to your world. I am as surprised as most of you that I have been asked to take over the reins of the venerable Anla'shok, or in my language, the

Rangers—which, I might add, is a name with a long and honorable history on my world, used for a number of different organizations dedicated to preserving life and freedom."

Sinclair stole a quick glance over at the Grey Council. It seemed that he had a greater portion of their attention than he had started with. He silently asked a quick forgiveness from Delenn, Rathenn, and Jenimer for what he was about to say.

"And once again, I would like to agree with *Alyt* Neroon."

That retrieved Neroon's full attention.

"At the risk of disagreeing with my friends among the Grey Council and the Minbari leader, I also do not believe I am the fulfillment of any prophecy, Minbari or otherwise. I am just a simple fighter pilot. A soldier. Over the last few years I have been asked to do some extraordinary jobs. To take on the command of Babylon 5 and try to maintain the peace in our section of the galaxy. To come to Minbar as an ambassador. And now to take over as leader of the Rangers. In none of these cases have I sought out the job. And in none of these cases have I agreed to do the job out of any other motive than a sense of duty.

"And it is to duty to which you should turn your attention now. The duty of the Rangers over these past one thousand years has been to watch for the return of the Shadows and warn Minbar should that occur. The current Ranger One and his fellow Rangers have carried out their orders faithfully and are now attempting to warn you, as Valen himself ordered them to do so long ago. If you believe in the purpose of the Rangers, and in Valen's wisdom, then why won't you listen to them?

"The issue is not so much *who* should lead the Rangers as it is whether or not the Shadows' threat will be met or ignored. You have been provided with the evidence that they have returned. Now you must decide what will be done.

"This is not a matter of religion. It is a matter of survival. You know what the Shadows are capable of because you bore the brunt of the last war against them. I represent all Humans who would be willing to help this time, to stand side by side with you. Because it is the right thing to do. But you must decide if you will accept that help, from me or any other Human.

"Believe me, part of me hopes you'll decide to send me home, so that I don't have to take on this responsibility. It's tempting to stick our heads in the sand and pretend nothing is wrong. Let someone else deal with it. But I can't do that. So I'm offering my help. Not as a religious leader, not as the fulfillment of prophecy, not even as a politician or diplomat, but as a soldier whose whole life has been dedicated to fighting where necessary, and preserving life and peace where possible.

"Believe me, I do have an ulterior motive. I once stood with all Humanity before the abyss of utter annihilation, and saw how precarious is the survival of any species, more precarious than we would ever want to believe. That experience has given me a responsibility to Humanity and to all life. And if you entrust me with this responsibility, my first allegiance will be to the preservation of life. If you decide you need someone who is only interested in total war, meeting destruction with destruction and death with death at every turn, look elsewhere. I've seen too much of that already.

"I will train the Rangers to fight with extreme efficiency, but I will do my best to prevent an all-out war if possible. If fighting such a war becomes necessary, it will be fought with the purpose of saving life. All life, Minbari and Human, Centauri and Narn, Vorlon and even Shadow. Frankly, I can't think of a higher purpose. And I believe that is what Valen intended.

"So now you are left with these two questions to answer: Will you allow the Anla'shok to perform their duty as ordained by Valen to actively engage the Shadow threat now, before it is too late? And will you allow me, and the rest of Humanity, to help you in that task?"

Sinclair fell silent, worried briefly that he said more than he should have. On a little more reflection, he decided he'd only said what had to be said.

He looked to the Minbari leader, but saw nothing in the Chosen One's carefully composed expression that gave away his thoughts.

Then he heard Neroon applauding slowly in mockery. "Quite a little speech, Ambassador," he said acidly. "Smoothly spoken. And so much talk of Valen—one could almost believe you mean what you say. Except that you demonstrate so little respect or understanding for Minbari culture and customs. Perhaps some case can be made to allow the Anla'shok an expanded role in light of certain recent developments. But we will not allow sacred tradition to be flouted in that process. I am glad to hear you agree that you are no fulfillment of prophecy. But then you made that quite clear with this outrageous insistence that Humans and members of the worker caste be allowed to join the ranks of the Anla'shok. Do you care nothing of Minbari sensibilities? Do you know nothing of Minbari society? This insensitivity alone makes you, and by extension all Humans, unfit to have anything to do with the Rangers."

Sinclair glanced over at the stony faces of the worker-caste elders. Were these Minbari workers mostly coopted fronts for the status quo, as so clearly two of the worker-caste Satai were? Or were there enough worker elders ready to break ranks, like their one renegade Satai had already done? He decided to find out.

"On the contrary, *Alyt* Neroon, I have the greatest respect for your culture and customs, even if you do not return that respect. If I am to work with the Anla'shok, I will gladly learn as much about Minbari traditions and ways as you and your people are willing to teach me. But I will not be bound by tradition where it interferes with carrying out the work itself."

Sinclair turned back to the assembled elders. "If Humanity is equally at risk from the Shadows, why should we not bear some of the burden of opposing them, especially as it seems the Rangers may have few volunteers from the military caste. As for the worker caste, they are your commercial pilots, your engineers, your construction workers, your mapmakers, your miners, your manufacturers. How many skills needed by the Rangers are to be found among those jobs? In those jobs they learned the languages and the customs of many different planets and cultures, invaluable assets to the Rangers. Can that be said of as many military or religious caste? Valen proclaimed the workers to be an equal caste."

"Equal, but different in their responsibilities to Minbari society," said Neroon. "Who will do the work, if all the workers suddenly fancy themselves warriors or priests? Even Valen did not let the workers join the Anla'shok."

"Not at the very beginning, true," said Sinclair. "But toward the end of the war, he did indeed allow the worker caste to join. It was only after he traveled beyond that the worker caste was once again forbidden to join."

"That is a myth," said Neroon, "and not accepted by any reputable scholars."

"Perhaps you only accept myth when it serves your own purposes," Sinclair replied.

As they glared at each other, an unexpected thought occurred to Sinclair: he had a grudging respect for Neroon, in spite of everything, because at least Neroon said plainly what he meant, no subterfuge, no half truths.

"I believe," said Jenimer pleasantly, "that it is time to deliberate and decide."

A door opened at the far end of the hall, and two acolytes of the Chosen One hurried in. Sinclair would not be allowed to remain in the hall for the deliberations, and was escorted out to a courtyard. Gladly sitting down for the first time in hours, he waited. He did not know where the Vorlon was, but suspected Ulkesh had been allowed to remain in the hall.

Sinclair watched Minbar's sun disappear beneath the horizon and her moons rising higher and higher, then the welcome sight of the stars appearing one by one. He wished he knew which of those stars held Catherine in its gravitational embrace. He wished there were some way to get word to her.

He wished the Minbari would hurry it up.

Strangely enough, it was the Vorlon who finally came to fetch Sinclair back to the hall.

"It is time," said Ulkesh. "It begins now. Forget all but that. Come."

The Vorlon turned and walked away, leading the way back to the Great Hall. When Sinclair entered, it looked much as he had left it, with everyone back in their seats except Neroon, who again stood within the circle. But the expression on the warrior's face was quite different this time, haughty disdain replaced by angry disappointment.

"Ambassador," said Jenimer. "If you will take your place before the assembled councils."

Sinclair walked to the center of the circle, and stood facing Neroon.

"The elders of the military caste," said Neroon with undisguised animosity, "have joined with the honored Satai of the military caste to agree to the proposal to recommission the Anla'shok to full military readiness, to allow both the religious caste and the worker caste to join, *if* they can qualify . . ."

There was a long pause. This was clearly difficult for Neroon. "And to allow Humans to join also—as long as certain conditions are met. First, it must be understood that while we give permission for the Anla'shok to be trained to once again take on the role they had in the last Shadow war, they are not to be used to *start* a war where none yet exists. They will continue to observe and to gather intelligence, give aid to our friends and allies among the other worlds where such help serves the common good, and to defend themselves when necessary. But they will take no action that will attract unwanted attention from the Shadows to Minbar."

Neroon turned to Jenimer, expecting him to answer. But the Minbari leader nodded to Sinclair to respond.

"Agreed," Sinclair said.

Neroon turned to face Sinclair. "You may assume the title and function as Ranger One, but not the designation of Entil'Zha until you can prove yourself worthy of that title."

"To that also, I agree fully."

Neroon bowed to Jenimer and left the hall as doors all along the back walls opened. Without further ceremony, the Caste Elders filed out in silence after him.

Sinclair stayed where he was, not quite sure what to do. The Grey Council had not yet moved, nor had Jenimer, and no acolytes appeared to escort the new Ranger One out.

After what seemed like several minutes, the Grey Council stood as one, and filed out in silence. This left only Sinclair, Jenimer, and Ulkesh in the Great Hall. There was another minute of silence, and then Jenimer spoke.

"Your presentation, though most effective, was not . . . quite the display of gentle diplomacy I had been led to expect from your record of achievements on Babylon 5."

"There is a time for gentle diplomacy, Chosen One, and a time for clear, straightforward, no-holds-barred truth," Sinclair said. "It seemed to me a little plain talk now would save us a lot of misunderstanding down the road."

"I learned a wonderful expression from Delenn," said Jenimer. "She said you taught it to her on Babylon 5. I believe the correct phrase is 'It will be a pleasure doing business with you.' "

Sinclair laughed and then nodded. "Maybe so."

CHAPTER 11

"MITCHELL! Break off! Break off!"

Too late. Starfury after Starfury blown to bits, exploding like miniature suns around him. Every ship of his squadron gone. Every Earth ship in his field of view destroyed.

"Not like this! Not like this! If I'm going out, I'm taking you bastards with me . . ."

. . . Sinclair stood in a circle of light, surrounded by moving shadowy shapes.

"Who are you?" Sinclair could barely force the words out. "Why are you doing this?"

The Grey Council, hooded and silent, stepped out of the shadows. A voice reverberated through the oppressive stillness. "The council will render its verdict."

One by one, the Minbari pulled back the hoods of their cloaks. Delenn. Rathenn. Racine. Jenimer. Neroon. Turval. No one spoke.

Jenimer walked over to him, held up the Triluminary, its center stone glowing. Sinclair turned, and the mirror to his right revealed him transformed into a Minbari, dressed in brown robes. In the background he saw Kosh. Sinclair whirled around.

"Kosh!"

But it wasn't Kosh. It was Ulkesh, standing alone

outside the circle of light, all the Minbari having vanished.

"You are what we say," said the Vorlon.

Sinclair turned back to the mirror, and again he saw Kosh. Peering at his own reflection, he reached up hesitantly and touched the Minbari horn crest on top of his skull.

This time it was Kosh who spoke. "Do not forget who you are, Jeffrey Sinclair."

Sinclair grabbed hold of the crest and began ripping the horn from his flesh and bones, as intense pain washed over him . . .

Sinclair's head snapped forward, and the computer notebook and loose papers he had been reading when he drifted off to sleep fell from his lap. He bent to pick them up from the sitting room floor, which was a mistake; when he straightened again, a sharp stab of pain went from his temples through the crown of his head.

"Damn!" he said, disgusted with himself. He went to the bathroom and splashed cold water on his face. It was morning already and he had spent his last night in Yedor asleep on the hard, angular chair in his sitting room. Only absolute exhaustion had made that possible. Every muscle in his body ached, and his head throbbed with pain.

After years of patiently waiting to get to this point, the Minbari were now in a frenzied hurry. He had returned to his quarters after the convocation to find a stack of files on prospective Human candidates for the Rangers. He had read late into the night, making notes and recommendations, only to be awakened the next morning by a knock on his door several hours earlier than usual. He was taken to a medical facility where a group of Minbari physicians ran every conceivable test on him and took what felt to Sinclair like several dozen gallons of his blood. After he nearly passed out, the physicians apologized profusely, explaining that they still didn't know much about human physiology. These tests would help them learn how to keep him and the other Human Rangers healthy in the time ahead.

Then he had been taken back to his quarters to pack and continue reading as many of the files as he could—which he had done to the point of exhaustion, falling asleep where he sat.

How much time did he have before Rathenn would arrive to escort him to the transport ship taking them all to the historic Ranger compound in Tuzanor?

The knock on his door answered the question—it was Rathenn and a couple of acolytes. Sinclair knew it wasn't good protocol to keep the Chosen One waiting, but neither was showing up disheveled and unshaven.

"Just give me a couple of minutes to at least shave and change clothes," he said to Rathenn.

"An excellent idea," Rathenn agreed, a little too enthusiastically.

When Sinclair emerged from the bathroom again, he found Rathenn holding a set of Minbari clothing draped over one arm, a pair of boots on the floor next to him. "Today you officially assume your role as Ranger One," he said. "I am honored to present this to you, the traditional uniform of the Anla'shok Na."

Rathenn was at last getting his wish to have Sinclair dressed in traditional Minbari clothing, and this time Sinclair couldn't argue, having previously lectured Rathenn on the importance of dressing in a manner appropriate for the job. He took the garments from Rathenn who bowed and left.

Sinclair examined and then donned the clothes, recognizing them to be similar to what Turval had been wearing: a pair of fitted trousers and a shirt with a cowl neck, over which went a belted waistcoat, all made from a sturdy charcoal-gray material. In contrast was the final piece, a brown-patterned, floor-length coat with full sleeves and hood, which was made from a cloth that felt similar to silk and flowed about the uniform like a cape. It seemed a little impractical for a soldier's uniform, but Sinclair assumed this was more a dress uniform than fighting garb. He pulled on the boots and stood up, feeling a little awkward in the unfamiliar clothing.

In for a penny, in for a pound, his father had been fond of saying. With a small twinge of regret, Sinclair packed away his clothes from Earth and left his quarters in Yedor for the last time.

"The name Tuzanor," Jenimer said as the transport ship sped high over Minbar's landscape, "comes from a phrase in the ancient Na'sen dialect of the religious caste that means the City of Sorrows. It is said to have been Valen's favorite place on all of Minbar."

Sinclair was sitting with Jenimer and Rathenn in a forward cabin above the cockpit. Turval had gone ahead to Tuzanor, as apparently had Ulkesh.

"Why does it have such a somber name?" Sinclair asked.

"In the Dark Time," said Jenimer, "when Minbari still fought Minbari, and bloody wars raged continually across our planet, the most terrible battle of our history was fought on that site. More than a million Minbari soldiers died in one long day of savage fighting. The brutality and utter futility of that battle so shocked Minbari on both sides of the war that they finally sought a peaceful solution to their problems. Together they decreed that the battlefield site would forever more be dedicated to peace, healing, and prophecy. Which is why it is said that to dream in the City of Sorrows, is to dream of a better future."

"That is . . . an agreeable notion," Sinclair said.

"Most Minbari think so," said Jenimer. "It is common for the young to make at least one pilgrimage there for that purpose."

"It seems an unusual place for a military base, however," said Sinclair.

"Valen chose the ancient city for the first gathering of the Rangers and constructed their base nearby because he wanted them to train for battle where they would also be able to see the sacred city, and therefore never forget they were fighting for one purpose only, to restore peace and freedom for all."

"It's a good thought," Sinclair said. "But what did the people of Tuzanor think? Did they object to having soldiers training for war so near their city?"

"Not the people of Tuzanor. Only some elements of the military caste. They were afraid good soldiers couldn't be created in a place of peace. But Valen prevailed, and today the Anla'shok have the strongest support among the people of Tuzanor than anywhere else on Minbar."

Upon arriving, Sinclair was struck by how different the City of Sorrows was from the teeming capital city Yedor. While most definitely Minbari in its character, Yedor nonetheless had reminded Sinclair of many large cities he had seen, with its skyscrapers, traffic, bustling commerce, busy citizens, even the occasional touches of off-world influence.

But there was a far more tranquil atmosphere to the sacred city of Tuzanor. Nestled in a high valley between two spectacular ranges of snow-capped mountains, it seemed more singularly Minbari. There were no modern buildings made of high-tech materials to resemble the ancient style; every building was an ancient one carved into the crystalline outcroppings, none more than a few stories high. Each was set in its own little park or—in the case of the temples—its own large and elaborate park. While there were many temples, there were many more waterfalls and fountains, far more than even Yedor, which Sinclair had thought contained more waterfalls and fountains per square mile than anyplace he had ever seen. And all of it, Rathenn had explained, except for the most private living quarters, was open for the use and appreciation of all. When Minbari made their pilgrimages here, they did not stay in the equivalent of hotels, for there were none. Visitors stayed and were welcomed by whomever had a free room or spare bed.

Not surprisingly, Sinclair found the Minbari here to be somewhat different from Yedor; less hurried, more leisurely, and certainly friendlier. Though he supposed his Ranger uniform might have had some bearing on that. Certainly, no one seemed surprised to see him wearing it.

After their short walk through the streets of Tuzanor, the purpose of which seemed to be to introduce Sinclair to the city, and the city to Sinclair, they continued by flyer to the Ranger compound, situated in the foothills of the northern mountain range on a wide plateau that overlooked the city. It afforded a spectacular view from above, but relative seclusion and privacy from below.

They were greeted on arrival by Turval. Sinclair noted that the former Ranger One was now wearing a slightly different Ranger uniform of the same basic design, but with an overcoat made of the same type of material as the uniform beneath and cut to fall straight and narrow to the body. Sinclair decided it would be a lot easier to fight an opponent in that coat than in the one he was wearing.

He asked Turval for a tour of the facilities; to his surprise, Jenimer and Rathenn accompanied them. He was shown every inch of the large but efficiently laid-out base. As with all the architecture he had seen on Minbar, the buildings were built to fit unobtrusively and pleasingly into the natural landscape. There were comfortable barracks for upward of nine thousand Rangers—although only one of the nine buildings was currently in use, and that only partially. There were three temples; three training fields that included an elaborate obstacle course; wilderness survival and surveillance training courses; a weapons training area contained three buildings for martial arts training, and three outdoor fields for various types of target practice. There was a large airfield with nine hangars, also all closed but one. And there was a large central complex of classrooms and administrative offices that was arranged, to no surprise of Sinclair's, in groups of three and nine. The Minbari, he knew, had a remarkable obsession with those numbers.

Only one building stood by itself, and Sinclair was shown this last: a small but comfortable structure that was to be Sinclair's residence.

"I apologize for throwing you out of your home," said Sinclair to Turval as the tour of his new home finished. The old Minbari Ranger seemed puzzled, then his eyes widened slightly.

"Oh, no," said Turval. "I have never lived here, nor has any other Anla'shok Na since Valen. Only an Entil'Zha may live here."

Sinclair shook his head. They had kept this place in repair and waiting for a thousand years. If the Minbari had one outstanding trait, it was patience. "But I thought we had agreed that the title of Entil'Zha . . ."

"The military caste said only that you may not yet assume the title," responded Jenimer, before Sinclair could finish the question. "But they did not forbid you to live here, and you are what you are regardless of what a few closed minds among the military may believe."

They left him to settle in, his few belongings having been previously delivered here. Once he was settled in, he would try again to get the rest of his things sent from Earth.

He unpacked, putting his own clothes away next to another full uniform set and some other selected Minbari clothes that he found already hanging in the closet.

He took his two well-read books and placed them in the small room that seemed to be his private office, containing a computer console and a selection of books in Minbari mostly concerning the Rangers and Valen. He assumed they had been recently placed there for his benefit, and were not the great Legend's own books.

He returned to the bedroom and examined the wide Minbari bed and the tilt mechanism under it. He would have to have a talk with someone about that as well.

Finally, he put Catherine's picture on the small table next to the bed. She could have no way of imagining where he was now, what he was doing. She still thought he was on Babylon 5, that their wedding would take place on the station in July, and that she would be marrying an Earthforce officer, the commander of a space station. How would she react to the abrupt and overwhelming change in his life? After everything they'd been through, after finally putting the pieces of their relationship together, and accepting that they were meant to be together, would it all be broken apart again, this time for good, on the hard, crystalline rock of Minbar? Would she want to have her life swept up in a clandestine fight against a mysterious and destructive alien power? Would she want to marry a man under so much pressure to assume the mantle of another world's legends and leave his old life behind?

It was because of all this that he needed her, more than ever before. But what would she say? And how could he blame her if it proved to be just too much . . .

He pushed the thought down. It did no good to think about that now. It would be months before he could even talk to her about this. Concentrate on the job at hand.

He decided to take one more walk around his new residence. He liked the fact that he would have much more privacy here than in Yedor. A kitchen wing connected to the house through a small dining area where his meals would be left, leaving him undisturbed in the rest of the house.

As he finished this second inspection, it hit him again how odd it was to take up residence in a building last occupied a thousand years ago by Valen himself, the greatest personage in Minbari history, venerated almost to the point of deification. It was as if he'd been told, oh, yeah, the last person to live here was King Arthur, but now it's yours.

He resolved to intensify his already extensive reading about the mythic leader. It was the least he could do if he was going to put his feet up on the Legend's furniture and assume his job.

"Hope you don't mind," he said to Valen aloud.

Although he was no longer in Yedor, when a knock sounded on the door, he naturally assumed it was

Rathenn, come to take him someplace else. He answered the door and found his assumption was correct.

"The Chosen One requests your presence."

As they walked across the compound, Rathenn gave Sinclair what the Minbari clearly considered disastrous news. "I fear I must inform you that Sech Durhan steadfastly refuses to sanction the Human ownership of the *denn'bok.*"

Sinclair knew what a *denn'bok* was: a Minbari fighting pike. It was a retractable metal-alloy staff, about five feet at full extension. He also recalled that this traditional Minbari weapon was something of a signature symbol for the Rangers.

"Who is Durhan?" he asked.

"He is the *F'hursna* Sech, the master teacher of the fighting pike. He oversees the forging of the few new pikes made each year, and has total authority over the transfer of ownership of all other pikes, usually handed down from parent to child. No one may own a true fighting pike without his sanction," Rathenn emphasized. "He has also been teacher to the Rangers in the use of the pike, but he is now threatening to cease this work because of Human recruitment."

"It's unfortunate," Sinclair said. "But I don't see it as one of our more important problems right now."

"Rangers *must* be trained in the pike as they have always been."

"I know it's tradition, and I agree that training in the use of a pike or staff is worthwhile. So does Earthforce. I was taught how to fight with the *bo*—a wooden staff a little bit longer than the Minbari pike. The practice is excellent for improving physical conditioning and agility, and building self-confidence. We could do that here just as well with wooden staffs as with your traditional pike."

Rathenn was adamant. "It is crucial to the honor of the Rangers that they be sanctioned to own a true fighting pike. This is a matter of utmost importance."

Sinclair was getting a little exasperated. "I told you I'm not going to let tradition get in the way of doing our job here. In the real world of PPGs and weapons of mass destruction, let alone that of the destructive power possessed by the Shadows, owning or not owning a pike will hardly be a deciding factor in whether or not a Ranger can do his job."

"Forgive me for upsetting the Anla'shok Na," said Rathenn contritely. "But he must be informed immediately of all problems as per his order. Please be assured that the Chosen One is working to resolve this matter."

Sinclair saw that Rathenn was leading him to one of the temples. "I'm sure that you both are," he said, wondering what was in store for him next. In the future, he would insist on being informed ahead of time about his daily schedule.

"Does the Ambassador maintain his training with the—" Rathenn hesitated slightly to recall the word, "—the *bo*?"

"Not consistently. Off and on over the years. Or with somewhat similar weapons. The *bokken,* the *jo*. When I can."

This seemed to please Rathenn, who merely nodded as they entered the temple. It was the largest of the three temples, and was situated at the center of the compound. Sinclair was immediately struck by its beauty. Built from the native crystalline stone, it rose to a crystalline dome with open arches and crystalline windows. Below, its deliberately asymmetrical archways led to an interior adorned by hard stone seats that faced the temple's only other feature, an impressive statue of Valen.

This was clearly a later addition to the temple, not

only from the clearly different stone used in the statue, but also because Sinclair knew that during his lifetime, Valen had never allowed his likeness to be created or displayed in any form. Sinclair assumed he wanted to avoid the very cult of personality that arose anyway after he "traveled beyond." Even this statue was not a realistic portrayal, but a highly stylized one, designed to suggest but not define his appearance.

Beneath the statue stood Jenimer and Ulkesh.

"Chosen One," Sinclair said, then acknowledged the Vorlon with a nod. The sound of wind chimes filled the silence for a moment.

Jenimer spoke: "When an initiate becomes a Ranger, there is a welcoming ceremony that is performed by the Rangers. But when a new Anla'shok Na is installed, that ceremony is performed privately at the statue of the original Ranger One and Entil'Zha. This must be done before he can greet his assembled Rangers.

"From the beginning, the badge of the Rangers has been this: a perfect Isil'Zha jewel set in gold and silver fashioned to resemble the hands of a Ranger holding it. It was passed through a white-hot flame, then cooled first in two bowls of sacred water and then in the blood of the Ranger.

"But a new age has come upon us, and the badge of the Ranger must now reflect that. Jeffrey Sinclair, receive the new badge of the Rangers. It remains a perfect Isil'Zha jewel, but now the setting of gold and silver is fashioned to resemble a Minbari on one side, a Human on the other. It has been passed through a white-hot flame, then cooled first in a bowl of sacred water, then in a bowl of Minbari blood, and lastly in a bowl of your own Human blood. In Valen's name, I proclaim you Anla'shok Na. Ranger One."

And Jenimer pinned the newly designed badge to Sinclair's uniform.

That's why they took so much blood during the examination, Sinclair thought.

He was never big on ceremony, being much more interested in just getting the job done, but he knew the Minbari took their ceremonies very seriously. He bowed slightly.

"I am honored," he said. "But let us move forward with the work."

It was apparently the right thing to say. Jenimer and Rathenn both practically beamed. Ulkesh said nothing.

"The full complement of Rangers have been assembled for your inspection, Ranger One," Rathenn announced, and led him out of the temple, leaving the Minbari leader and the Vorlon behind.

At the first sight of the few Minbari standing rigidly in formation on one of the training fields, Sinclair paused to look for the others he assumed must be somewhere out of his view. Only thirty-four Rangers plus Turval were there to greet him. Thirty-four Minbari, some young and eager-looking, some quite a bit older. Thirty-four out of the seventy-eight that had been active Rangers until the day his appointment was confirmed.

"The military clan leaders put out an immediate order for their members to resign," Turval explained. "I fear some followed that order quickly and willingly. Others were agonized, but found it too difficult to turn their backs on their families and clan loyalties by repudiating the order."

Well, thirty-four was better than nothing, Sinclair thought. But clearly the overriding first priority was an immediate and aggressive search for new recruits.

"At ease," he told the assembled Rangers. It didn't seem to be an order they were familiar with, at least not in English, and he certainly didn't know any Minbari word for it. He'd been assured these Rangers knew English very well, but they continued to stand at ironclad attention, staring at a distant point somewhere over his head. It was like trying to speak to a collection of statues.

"At ease means you may relax a little and should look at me when I speak to you."

Again, none of them moved, but a few eyes darted left or right, as if unsure what to do exactly and thus were looking to see if their comrades were moving or doing anything differently.

"That's an order," said Sinclair.

The assembled Minbari relaxed just a little, and hesitantly brought their gazes down from the sky to take a look at him.

"Thank you," he said with a smile. "I am Jeffrey Sinclair, and it is my honor to have been asked to serve as your Anla'shok Na, or in my language, Ranger One. I thank you for the loyalty and trust you have demonstrated by choosing to stay here and work with me. I will do my best to live up to that trust."

Sinclair paused. There was really nothing else to say. He had Turval dismiss the assemblage.

The sun was already setting when Rathenn walked back with him to his quarters, where his dinner and more files on prospective Rangers awaited him. Much later that night he finally went to bed, hoping that his dreams would be, as Jenimer said, of a better future, not the bitter past.

But the next morning when he awoke, though he knew he had dreamed, he could not remember any of them.

CHAPTER 12

"I'M pleased with the initial response," Sinclair said, receiving nods of assent from both Jenimer and Rathenn. Ulkesh, as usual, stood silent and unmoving behind and to the left of Jenimer, who was in an ornate high-backed chair. Sinclair sat facing them in an only slightly less opulent chair. Rathenn chose to stand. Sinclair wondered if he could insist on installing a simple conference table for future meetings.

This was the first meeting with the Minbari leader and the Vorlon since Sinclair had arrived at the Ranger compound two weeks before. Jenimer had returned to Yedor within two days to attend to other business, leaving Rathenn to work with Sinclair on establishing the training schedule and a system for getting the word out to prospective Ranger candidates and bringing them to Tuzanor for a final screening. Sinclair had officially moved his embassy office to the City of Sorrows, where the interviews took place. Only after they were accepted, were the candidates brought to the Ranger base.

During this time, Sinclair had caught a few glimpses of Ulkesh, but that was all.

As things began coming to together, Sinclair was troubled by what he considered unnecessary delays and hindrances, and had insisted on a meeting with both Jenimer and Ulkesh.

"The quality of those expressing an interest in joining the Rangers, both Minbari and Human, has been quite remarkable," Sinclair continued, "The first group of twenty Minbari and thirty-five Humans are ready to begin formal training, and another group of at least twenty-five more Humans and maybe ten or twelve more Minbari will be ready soon after that. That's all to the good. But if we're going to fulfill our new mandate, we need to start sending Rangers on active patrol to gather information firsthand and return to report directly to us. We need to begin scouting locations for additional bases of operation and training centers. And we need to start gathering additional weapons and munitions.

"To do all this, we will need fully trained Rangers. At the moment we have only thirty-four, and most of those are needed here to start training new Rangers and keep this base operating. Since a new Ranger can't be commissioned until receiving three months of training, we can't afford to delay starting that training another day. But the others refuse to start training the new recruits until Durhan consents. Everything else is in place. Something must be done about this problem with Durhan immediately."

Jenimer nodded. "I have persuaded Sech Durhan to meet with us here today."

"Good," Sinclair said. "Then let's talk about the second thing we need. A fleet of ships. There are a few ships and training aircraft on this base, but not nearly as many as we need. We can arrange to purchase some commercial ships through friendly contacts in the worker caste, but we need military ships, and the military caste absolutely refuses to provide them. We can start buying ships from off world, but it'll be extremely expensive and will have to be done carefully to avoid attracting unwanted attention. This is a major problem."

"It is being taken care of by the religious caste," Jenimer said unexpectedly, "with help from our Vorlon friends. We have been privately developing and building a new type of warship, the Whitestar ships, incorporating Vorlon and Minbari technology. Some smaller experimental prototypes are being tested now. You will receive a full report on this within a few days."

"That's welcome news," Sinclair said. "But it doesn't totally solve our problem." This was an unexpected but welcome opportunity to address another issue that had been troubling him greatly. "I'm glad to hear the Vorlons are at last willing to share some of their technology. How much more can we expect you to share with us in this effort, Ambassador?"

The Vorlon stirred only slightly. "What is needed."

"What we need are ships, right now, not just in six months or a year. You have ships you could deliver to us now."

"Impossible," said the Vorlon.

"Why?"

"We can only make ships that are Vorlon. They would be of no use to you."

Sinclair was almost willing to believe this. He had seen Vorlon ships and was convinced what was said about them was true—that they were as much or more living entity as inanimate machine. But he doubted that was the whole story, because it wasn't the only thing that they were holding back.

"All right. Assuming that's true, what other kind of support can we expect from you, aside from moral support and the Whitestar ships? Logistical support, for instance—access to Vorlon space would make our job a lot easier.''

''No.''

''Why not?''

''It would not be safe.''

''Who wouldn't be safe, our pilots or you?''

''Yes.''

''That isn't an answer.''

''Permission will not be granted. It will not be necessary.''

''Not necessary?'' Sinclair asked. ''On what basis do you make that decision?''

Sinclair could see that Jenimer and Rathenn were growing increasingly uneasy at this exchange, but they seemed unwilling to intervene. Had they ever asked any of these questions before? The Minbari had the closest relationship to the Vorlons of any known sentient species and continually deferred to them, and yet they seemed to know very little about the Vorlons, almost as if they didn't care.

Ulkesh remained silent, so Sinclair tried again. ''Do you have information on the Shadows you haven't given us yet? You must know a lot more about them than you've told us so far. This would be a good time to start sharing some of that information. The less you know about your enemy, the stronger he is.''

''It is important to select information; too much information can be harmful,'' replied Ulkesh.

Sinclair seized upon that immediately. ''So you admit that you have more information than you're giving us.''

''This discussion serves no further useful purpose.''

Sinclair regarded the Vorlon for a long moment. It was clear he wasn't going to get anything more out of him, but maybe he'd gotten enough. At least now he had a better idea of what to expect from Ulkesh.

"Then let's move on," Sinclair said finally, turning back to Rathenn and Jenimer. "I'm still waiting for that comprehensive report detailing everything known to date regarding the movements of the Shadows since their return."

Rathenn was apologetic and distressed. "There was a—problem." Did he glance over at the Vorlon just then? "But it will be ready soon."

Sinclair sighed. For one brief moment, he indulged himself in the wish to be far away from Minbar, in space, in a Starfury, leading a squadron of pilots he could rely on, with a clearly defined mission to carry out, and a clean target in front of him . . .

"Then I have one last item that needs to be addressed. With more Humans arriving here, we need to set up a reliable supply line of food and medicine for the Human Rangers."

Jenimer seemed puzzled. "The traditional diet of the Anla'shok—"

"Is fine for Minbari Rangers," said Sinclair, "but is not enough for Human Rangers."

"We have determined what is and isn't appropriate for Human consumption among the traditional foods," said Rathenn.

"Which, again, is fine, and where appropriate will be used. But these men and women aren't coming here to train as monks, they're coming here to form an army. You can't expect them to train as soldiers and prepare themselves to die, if necessary, for a cause without being fed properly. It's one of the oldest truths in the Human military. I propose to send two Minbari Rangers and two Human trainees to Babylon 5 as soon as they've completed at least one week of training. Delenn will help them quietly set up accounts to begin sending shipments of food and medicine here. Afterward, the two Minbari Rangers will stay to be our temporary liaisons and observers, and the Human Rangers will return to finish their training."

"No," said Ulkesh.

"They will contact no one but Delenn."

"It is too soon."

Sinclair took a deep breath. It was time to draw a line. "Your opinion is noted," he said, "but this is my decision, not yours, and it will be done unless you can give me a far more specific and coherent reason why it shouldn't."

"I believe," said Jenimer quickly, "that the ambassador's plan can be carried without arousing unwanted attention. Perhaps we should defer to his judgment regarding the needs of the Human Rangers."

Ulkesh didn't answer right away. "With caution then," he said at last.

"Of course," said the Minbari leader. "Thank you."

Sinclair wasn't about to offer any thanks for being allowed to do what was supposed to be within his authority to do in the first place. He merely stood up and said, "Then I think that covers everything for now."

Jenimer stood as well. "Then will you take a walk with me, Ambassador?"

"Certainly, Chosen One."

They left Rathenn and Ulkesh in the room, and made their way out of the administrative complex. As they walked across the open grounds toward the weapons training area, Jenimer looked up at the deep blue Minbari sky and smiled.

"I love to walk under the open sky," he said, "and to feel the living soil of Minbar beneath my feet. I do not understand how those who choose to live in space bear it for long, living within boxes of metal.''

Sinclair laughed. ''Well, if by that you include Babylon 5, it isn't quite as bad as a metal box.''

''Did you never miss Earth?''

''Oh, yeah,'' said Sinclair. ''I miss Earth right now.''

''But you weren't born there?''

''No, I was born on Mars, but I spent as much of my youth on Earth as I did on Mars. I've a great fondness for Mars and her people, but when I feel that longing to walk under an open sky and feel the living soil beneath me, as you so beautifully put it, it's Earth I think about.''

''A connection to the land is important,'' said Jenimer. ''I worry about the Grey Council, isolated on their ship, cut off from the land, cut off from the people. It was never Valen's intention that the leaders of our people live in such a self-imposed cocoon. But much was changed when Valen traveled beyond. I suppose that is the way of things.''

They entered the largest of the three buildings used for weapons and martial arts training and proceeded to a large gymnasium.

In the middle of the room stood the most imposing Minbari Sinclair had ever seen. He was a little taller than Sinclair, and had a regal bearing that belied the simple, almost drab clothing he wore, so uncharacteristic of Minbari who usually preferred layers of beautifully embroidered garments. When he turned and bowed to Jenimer, it reminded Sinclair of the languid but powerful movements of a lion.

Sinclair had no doubt as to who he was about to be introduced to.

"Ambassador Jeffrey Sinclair, Anla'shok Na—this is *F'hursna* Sech Durhan."

Durhan did not bow, so neither did Sinclair, simply returning his steady gaze. A long silence ensued, in which they stood just looking at each other. Like a cobra and a mongoose. *Now what?* Sinclair wondered.

Abruptly, Durhan turned and walked a few paces away. From the folds of his clothing he produced two black metal tubes, each about a foot long and perhaps an inch and a half in diameter. Sinclair recognized them to be unextended Minbari fighting pikes.

"The Chosen One reminds me," Durhan said in clipped military-caste Minbari, "that Valen proclaimed that all Anla'shok must be instructed in the use and philosophy of the *denn'bok* under the supervision of the current *F'hursna* Sech. But a Sech of the *denn'bok* must also swear to uphold the honor of the ancient art. Any Sech would rather resign from his position and give up the ancient art forever than teach its ways to the unworthy."

Suddenly, a military-caste proverb Sinclair had read recently came to mind. Sinclair hoped he remembered it right, and spoke in the military dialect. "Do not proclaim a soldier worthy or unworthy before his first battle."

Durhan nodded slowly, his eyes narrowing in appraisal. "As you say," he answered in English. With a flourish he opened one of the pikes, then threw the other unopened one at Sinclair.

Instinctively, he knew he had only a second to open that pike, and he imitated Durhan's motion. The pike snapped open, and Sinclair grabbed either end and raised the five-foot weapon in front of him just as Durhan was upon him, bringing his pike down in an overhead strike. Sinclair blocked it just in time, shocked at the force with which Durhan's pike struck his own, but managed to hang on. Pure survival instinct took over as he sidestepped and blocked Durhan's downward strike at his groin. Durhan then whirled and threw a straight thrust at Sinclair's upper body. Sinclair parried as best he could, falling back another step. Relentless, Durhan continued, his pike a blur. Sinclair blocked and parried with a desperate effort even as he was being forced back against the wall by the furious assault, the sheer force of every blow draining his strength.

Sinclair decided if he was going to lose this fight anyway, he'd rather it be with him on the attack. He summoned up all his remaining strength and, when he saw an opening, threw a straight thrust. Durhan sidestepped and struck Sinclair full across the chest with the length of the pike, then brought it up under Sinclair's arms. With one hand Durhan grabbed Sinclair's left arm, and with the other used his pike as a lever to lift Sinclair up and then, crashing, hard to the floor. He landed in what, on later reflection, was certainly not the most dignified manner for a Ranger One. At that moment, though, Sinclair thought only of defending himself, and leapt back to his feet, tensing for a further attack.

But Durhan was standing placidly, leaning on his extended pike, contemplating Sinclair. The whole fight hadn't lasted more than a few minutes, and Sinclair knew quite well that it wouldn't have lasted even half of that if Durhan had not wanted it to. His Earthforce training with the *bo* in no way made him a match for such an expert. Durhan could have had him on the ground or seriously injured him within seconds if he had chosen to do so. But clearly he had wanted to test Sinclair.

"And what did we prove with that demonstration?"

Sinclair began, doing his best to ignore several painful bruises.

Durhan interrupted him with a wave of his hand. "Valen said all Rangers are to be trained in the use of the *denn'bok.* So they shall, Human and Minbari. But Valen did not say they must *own* a fighting pike, and tradition says only Minbari should own them. So it will continue to be. Human Rangers will be trained. That should be sufficient. I will train you personally, starting tomorrow."

Sinclair looked to Jenimer, who seemed to have no response at all to this. Sinclair, however, was not satisfied. He wondered if Durhan was still testing him, seeing how far he would push the issue. Sinclair bowed slightly to Durhan. "The Master honors me, but respectfully I must decline."

Durhan's serene expression did not flicker. "Why?"

"Why study to be an artist," said Sinclair, "if one is to be forbidden to practice that art afterward? And why waste the time of the Master that way?"

Durhan closed his pike and returned it to the folds of his clothing. "You will be sanctioned to own a pike."

"If I prove worthy."

"There is no doubt that you will."

"And what about the other Human Rangers?"

Durhan paused only a moment. "I will monitor the training of the Humans. If I see any who are worthy, I will instruct them further myself, and only those will be certified."

"And will any of them prove worthy enough for you?" Sinclair made the question as pointed as he could. He wasn't exactly calling Durhan a liar, but Sinclair had too much experience with the Minbari penchant for the half truth to accept that statement at face value.

For the first time, Durhan smiled, just a little. "As not all Minbari prove worthy, neither will all Humans. But there will be some, I now believe."

Sinclair returned the smile. "Then I am honored to be your student."

He turned to Jenimer, who now looked quite pleased indeed. "I am—" Jenimer began to say, then stopped in mid-sentence, as if startled by something, and crumpled to the floor. Durhan was at his side instantly. Sinclair raced to the communications console on the far wall. He had just gotten through to the Ranger physician when Jenimer's voice stopped him.

"Ambassador. No."

Sinclair turned around. Durhan was helping Jenimer to his feet. "Chosen One, the doctor—"

"Is not needed." Jenimer attempted a smile, but he was pale and still obviously shaken.

"You need medical attention."

"I simply need rest," said Jenimer. "Please, it is best if we do not make too much of this. My own doctor can attend to me later."

As much as Sinclair didn't want to add to Jenimer's distress, he knew he couldn't leave it at that. The Minbari penchant for parceling out information to him as they saw fit could jeopardize everything. "Chosen One," he said, quietly but firmly. "Is there more that I need to know?"

Jenimer smiled again. "The Grey Council did not choose me for my robust health."

An understated Minbari reply, but Sinclair understood, and was saddened to have his fears about Jenimer's failing health confirmed.

After being assured that Jenimer was all right for now, Sinclair returned to his quarters, leaving Jenimer and Durhan to confer privately for a while.

He was headed for the bathroom, his only thought being to get into the spa and start jets of hot water flowing over his painfully bruised muscles, when he heard the message tone on his computer console. There was a document waiting for his perusal. He quickly called it up, and was rewarded with the report he'd been waiting for, detailing in full the movements of the Shadows to date. He read straight through it with a growing sense of alarm. It was more than he had expected. Far more than he had been led to believe.

Within moments of finishing, he arranged to have Rathenn meet him back in the conference room, informing him that Jenimer was not feeling well this evening and need not attend. He then hurried across the compound as the sundowner winds swept over the plateau and the day slowly faded into evening.

He arrived to find Rathenn had summoned Ulkesh as well. He had wanted to talk to Rathenn first, before speaking to the Vorlon, but he would deal with it.

"I won't even ask why I wasn't told earlier," Sinclair said without preamble. "That isn't important now. What's important is to find out who you have told. Who else knows the contents of that report, how widespread Shadow activity has been for the last couple of years, how many lives have already been lost? You didn't tell the Council of Caste Elders all of this."

"We told them enough to convince them," said Rathenn, "but not so much as to panic them or the people."

"But that's the point. You almost didn't convince them. Would you have told them the rest if they hadn't finally agreed to go along with your plans?"

"But they did," said Rathenn, "so the question is merely hypothetical."

"I suppose that's what you told the governments of

Earth, Centauri, and Narn, as well. Not so much as to panic them, right? But what you did tell them didn't convince them, did it?''

''The Shadows must not know how much we know,'' said Rathenn. ''And they must not know the Vorlons are assisting us. Or they will strike before we are ready. We must be careful what we say and to whom.''

''And how many people will die needlessly in the meantime because they weren't warned?'' Sinclair asked.

''Fewer than will die if the Shadows launch an all-out war before we are ready.''

''You say that so easily,'' Sinclair said with some anger, ''as if it were fact instead of just supposition. And based on what? Horror stories from a thousand years ago? Or uncritical acceptance of everything the Vorlons tell you? My fiancée is exploring on the Rim, sent there by a corporation that knows nothing at all about the Shadows, let alone that Shadow activity has been thick in that area and is almost certainly responsible for most of the ships that have been lost there.''

''Your own government has enough information to warn them if they choose. They have chosen not to. Would such corporations listen to Minbari warnings?''

''You could have at least tried. And what about Babylon 5? How much have they been told? How much has Delenn told Sheridan?''

For the first time, Ulkesh spoke. ''He is not yet ready.''

''The Vorlons aren't the only ones who are hesitant to tell everything to Sheridan,'' said Rathenn. ''There are still those on the Grey Council who do not trust him and fear he would act precipitously if told too much too soon. Some even fear he might be allied with those elements on Earth who might be sympathetic to the Shadows."

"There are members of the Grey Council, as well as most of the military caste, who still think that about me," Sinclair said. "If I were still in command on the station, you'd be saying the same thing. You'd say it about anyone who was there, because it isn't about who's in command of Babylon 5, or who's president on Earth, or anything other than the Vorlons' need to control this information for their own purposes. Isn't that right, Ambassador Ulkesh?"

But it was the voice of Jenimer, from behind him, that answered. "Would you forgive an old Minbari religious scholar for agreeing with the Vorlons in this instance?"

Sinclair turned in surprise.

"Too much has been kept from you," Jenimer said, coming into the room, "and for that I do apologize. But we Minbari are a cautious people; I fear we move too slowly to suit the faster pace of most Humans." He sat slowly and carefully, clearly in a great deal of pain. "Now I am only religious caste, but is it not a military truth that it is best if you can make your enemy assume you know less than you really do?"

"Yes, it is," replied Sinclair.

"Then in that we are agreed with the Vorlons, whatever their reasons."

"But it's also bad policy to keep your allies in the dark," said Sinclair. "It could very well leave you with no allies at all."

"Agreed," said Jenimer. "So together we will work out a plan for better informing those who should have a fuller understanding of the situation. Sheridan, for instance, has been told more than Rathenn has unintentionally led you to believe. Please do not give up on us yet, Ambassador Sinclair. We are trying to do what is right and we do need your help."

"I know that," said Sinclair. "And I've made my commitment to seeing this work through, but I need to be kept fully informed, not in the dark."

"Agreed," said Jenimer.

Sinclair hesitated only briefly. "And I wish to get a message through to my fiancée."

Once again, unexpectedly, Ulkesh spoke: "You must forget what is personal. Concentrate on the cause."

"You can never forget the personal," said Sinclair. "Or else what are you fighting *for*? The person who fights only for the cause is always in danger of becoming a fanatic, or of losing any reason for fighting at all. But the person who fights for his family and his home fights just long enough and just hard enough to win, without losing himself to the violence or the cause. Every Ranger under my command will learn that alongside the Ranger credo."

Sinclair turned back to Jenimer. "I can word a message that will not tell the Shadows anything, but will put Catherine just enough on alert to help keep her alive. Will you allow me to do that?"

Jenimer looked to Ulkesh, but the Vorlon had nothing further to say. "We will try."

CHAPTER 13

CATHERINE Sakai was satisfied with the data she was collecting on Planet UTC 51-03B, code name Glasir. A pretty nice little place it had turned out to be. Rich in Quantium 40, it would definitely please her employers at Universal Terraform. As an added bonus, it was also proving to be a mineralogical storehouse.

Sakai studied the planet surface on an overhead monitor as she worked through her daily exercises on the training apparatus. Even from orbit, this planet was more attractive than most Class 4 planets. The usual drab red and brown had a bit more variation in shade, including some areas of pink and jet black, and wide swaths along the equator of yellow and orange. Surface images sent back by the planetary probe had revealed a landscape of amazing beauty. The howling winds had carved out geological features of lacelike delicacy in some cases, and gravity-defying balancing acts in others. It was a welcome and somewhat calming contrast to the planetary devastation she had encountered on her previous stop.

That undoubtedly was fueling the regret she now felt at the thought of UTC robot miners someday smashing through those natural wonders to get to the mineral resources deep beneath them. She had made a point of programming her sampler robots to avoid some of the more spectacular formations, and to dig carefully. It would take longer, but she had the time. She planned to fill quite a lot of the sample bay from this planet alone, more than enough to please everyone.

Part of her hoped the scientists and preservationists would find something in the data and samples she brought back to warrant a less destructive approach, but that was out of her control. She gathered the information and handed it over for others to decide the fate of these planets.

Which brought her thoughts once again to her previous stop at Ymir. In fact, she couldn't stop thinking about it. What had caused that planet to meet such a destructive fate? It had disturbed her enough that she had sent a preliminary report in an emergency-coded transmission to the coordinates where the Operations ship was scheduled to be. It wasn't standard operating procedure; all data was usually delivered directly to the corporation reps on the Ops ship at the end of the mission. Perhaps they hadn't seen it as quite the serious matter she did, and that was why, now three weeks later, she had still not heard a word in response.

That had given her three weeks on her own to speculate about the planet's condition. Perhaps the original robot probe had been malfunctioning, had sent back garbled data. Perhaps someone had misread the data. Perhaps it was a geological oddity. Perhaps some sort of natural disaster had occurred, of a type never encountered before.

She was having a hard time completely buying the rationalizations she had managed to cobble up. The truth was, something devastating had happened to that planet, and she simply had no idea of what caused it. And she could not dismiss what seemed more and more like the most probable explanation: that it was the deliberate act of some alien species. There were many aliens in the galaxy as yet not contacted by Humanity. Ymir could well have been on the edge of some alien federation that used the planet as their main Q-40 source.

Of course, this allowed her to come back to the comforting possibility that the first robot probe had malfunctioned and somehow reported the data incorrectly. Maybe the planet had been like that for a long time, the result of years, if not centuries, of mining.

Maybe. She was taking extra precautions, keeping more than the usual number of sensors turned outward as well as planetward, but she couldn't allow her gnawing unease to prevent her from doing her job. She couldn't allow her imagination to run away with her. The chances of her encountering anyone at all out here, let alone anything like that again, had to be infinitesimal.

The trouble with long solo missions to the Rim was that it left far too much time for the mind to engage in such speculation and imagination. Just stay focused on the job. The mission was nearing completion—just two more stops. Soon, she'd be back at Babylon 5. Planning a wedding. That ought to be a scary enough thought to drive all other concerns from her mind, she decided with a laugh. Getting married. Something she had always sworn she would never do. How things change.

She was folding away the exercise equipment when the computer announced an incoming transmission. *At last,* she thought, as she maneuvered over to the cockpit and strapped into her console chair.

"Incoming transmission from Universal Terraform tachyon transmission channel four zero five zero zero seven."

"Receive and record."

The data log scrolled by on the communications monitor with the usual mission coordinates and technical instructions, nothing regarding her transmission to them.

Her disappointment was transformed to delight, though, when she saw the last header at the end of the scroll—a coded personal transmission, only a few bytes long. It had to be from Jeff, she thought. He'd actually managed it somehow. She eagerly punched in the decode command, waited for the computer to reconstruct the message. It was very short.

Catherine, Remember Sigma 957?
Your current situation is different—but similar.
Be careful. All my love,
Jeff

Sakai sat back, puzzled. She hadn't known what message to expect; in truth had never really expected him to be able to cut through the red tape and send her a message at all, as much as she enjoyed hoping he might. But this was—odd. It almost read like a joke. Sigma 957? She was nowhere in the vicinity of that planet, nor was she going to be, not on this mission, and not ever again if she had her way. But he had gone to what must have been extraordinary lengths to send her this message. A little joke? Not likely.

A warning. That's what it seemed to be. He had always worried about her—too much she told him. But he wouldn't go to such an effort just to send a general warning to be careful. No, this had to be a specific warning, probably worded in a way he hoped she would understand, but would seem innocuous if intercepted by others. By whom?

Figure the message out first, and then the rest will be

clear. What happened on Sigma 957? She had gone there on a surveying mission, just as now, but the results had been very different. She had not come back with any data whatsoever. Instead, she had almost died there. Out of nowhere a massive alien ship had appeared, so technologically advanced and powerful compared to her own tiny little ship that its electromagnetic and radiation wake had nearly destroyed *Skydancer*. Most likely the aliens hadn't even noticed she was there. She had survived only because the Narn ambassador G'Kar knew she was putting herself in danger from the movements of these unknown aliens, and had sent rescue ships after her.

So what was Jeff telling her? It wasn't likely that he was sending any ships out after her.

There was only one answer that made any sense: As G'Kar had warned her about Sigma 957, Jeff was trying to warn her that there was a dangerous alien presence on the Rim. Not the same species she'd encountered on Sigma 957, he seemed to be saying, but every bit as powerful. Certainly she had proof of that if what she had seen on Ymir had any connection to these aliens.

For some reason, Jeff had felt he couldn't be more specific. Had he been afraid of somehow accidentally letting *them* know he was warning her? The chilling possibility suddenly occurred to her that these aliens could be listening in to all her transmissions.

"Oh, Jeff, thank you," she said as she began calling up her automated jump gate and orbital procedures programs to make a few changes. "You have no idea how careful I'm going to be."

Only two more missions to go.

CHAPTER 14

THE Minbari cherished their ceremonies, Sinclair thought again as he walked away from the temple dedicated to Valen—or The Chapel, as the Human Rangers had taken to calling it. He strolled silently across the compound with Jenimer and Rathenn, lost in his thoughts as they were in theirs. This had been a landmark day—the induction of the first group of trainees as full Rangers.

The Minbari had a ceremony or ritual for everything, it seemed, all performed in leisurely detail. Even a simple meal could be turned into an excruciating ordeal in the name of ceremony. Sometimes Sinclair found it an admirable trait; it was a way of slowing down and noticing things, investing importance and continuity in all aspects of life, rather than letting events rush by in a hurried jumble.

Other times it was just a pain in the ass.

Still, he understood the importance of ceremony in the military. And this day's initiation of the first new Rangers represented the culmination of three months hard work. Sinclair was proud of his young recruits, Human and Minbari. For them, it was one of the most important days they would ever know, something they would remember in great detail for the rest of their lives. And as Minbari ceremonies went, this one was relatively brief and straightforward.

So Sinclair had found himself conducting the ceremony with as much intensity and delight as the young recruits themselves, taking particular joy in presenting each one with their badge, and then shaking their hand. The latter was not part of the traditional ceremony, but was clearly expected and welcomed by the Human Rangers, and quickly adopted by the Minbari recruits as well, to only a few scandalized looks from some of the older Minbari.

One part of the ceremony, however, had bothered him a little. That was the traditional Ranger credo. The voices of the new Rangers reciting those words at the end of the ceremony still rang in his ears:

> *I am a Ranger. We walk in the dark places no others will enter. We stand on the bridge and no one may pass. We live for the One. We die for the One.*

It bothered him for two reasons. He had not been able to get a straight answer out of any of the Minbari as to exactly who or what was the One. Not that he was surprised by this after all his time on Minbar, but at times it seemed that some of the Minbari didn't know themselves. Those, like Jenimer, who probably did know, indicated (always indirectly) that it referred to the leader of the Rangers, specifically the Entil'Zha. As there currently was no Entil'Zha, and hadn't been for over a thousand years, they were pledging to the memory of Valen as invested in whoever was the current Ranger One.

That roundabout explanation still made him uneasy. He didn't believe an army should pledge itself only to one person, whether it be a king or a general or an Entil'Zha. He was uncomfortable with even the suggestion of a cult of personality. Pledge yourself to your responsibility for preserving life, and your duty to do what is right, he had told the new Rangers. But they were still required by tradition to also pledge themselves to "the One."

And then there was the other thing that bothered Sinclair. He'd heard that phrase before.

"We live for the One. We would die for the One." A rather strange alien, identified only by the name Zathras, had said that to Sinclair on Babylon 4, just before that ill-fated station went through the time rift in Sector 14 to an unknown fate. But Zathras couldn't have been a Ranger, at least not as things stood now, since the Minbari had insisted only Humans and Minbari could join. So why had he used that exact phrase, so close to the Ranger credo?

"Did the Anla'shok Na say he had some urgent business to discuss?" Jenimer asked. Both he and Rathenn seemed hesitant to break in on Sinclair's thoughts.

It was still strange for Sinclair to hear himself referred to in this way, since even Jenimer and Rathenn still usually called him ambassador. "Yes, we need to discuss our next move concerning Babylon 5."

Jenimer simply nodded.

Sinclair was growing ever more concerned about the ailing Minbari leader's health. Jenimer had clearly been pushing himself too hard over the past three months, having set himself up as the buffer between Sinclair and those in the Grey Council and military caste who still opposed what the Rangers were doing. And though he never complained or referred to it, it had taken a noticeable toll on Jenimer.

"It is time to step up our activity on Babylon 5,"

Sinclair continued. "It's crucial to us as a source of supplies and information. Now that we have Human Rangers to send there on a full-time basis, I want to increase the flow of both those commodities. It's time to inform Sheridan of our activities."

Jenimer shook his head. "The Vorlons say it is not yet time."

Even though Ulkesh wasn't walking with them, he was there, as always, needlessly putting obstacles in their way. But the Minbari, including Delenn apparently, joined the Vorlons in believing that Sheridan wasn't ready to be told everything. They had a timetable and they would not budge from it.

"I had a feeling you'd say that, but if we're going to intensify our activities on Babylon 5, we're going to attract attention. If we get the wrong sort of attention from the station's security chief, it will be impossible to do our work there, I can guarantee you that. If nothing else, we need to at least inform Chief Garibaldi of what's going on. Just him, no one else. I'll ask him to give the Rangers his cooperation, and, where necessary, turn a blind eye."

"But he will inform Sheridan immediately if you do that," said Rathenn.

"Not if I ask him not to."

"You are not his commanding officer anymore," said Jenimer.

"No, but we're still friends. And he owes me. He'll do this if I ask him to, and he'll prove an invaluable ally, I promise you. There's no other way."

Jenimer considered it. "Perhaps you're right. But the security chief only. And the message you send must be carefully worded."

"It will be," said Sinclair, then silently adding, *it'll have to be if it's going to tell Garibaldi what he needs to know and still get by Ulkesh.* "I'll instruct one of the Rangers to deliver it personally. A copy of the message should also go to Delenn, to keep her informed." Whether she would get the entire message he sent to Garibaldi, he had yet to decide. One thing at a time.

"I'm sure Ulkesh will agree to this."

"Wonderful," Sinclair said as neutrally as he could, and left it at that.

As soon as he got back to his quarters, he sat down to compose the message. He would make a visual recording, but first he wanted to carefully work out what he would say. He wrote the first words.

Hello, old friend. It's been a while.

Best to keep it simple. Garibaldi wasn't one for sentiment.

I'm trusting this message to an associate of mine who is sworn to bring it to you at any cost—including his own life.

That should help convince him of the life-and-death seriousness of what Sinclair was about to say.

My job on the Minbari homeworld is more than just representing Earth. Even the President doesn't know about that part yet, and I don't think it would be wise of you to tell him.

Be careful about what you say and who you speak to from Earth. Garibaldi would almost certainly understand that part of the message.

There's a great darkness coming. Some of the Minbari have been waiting for it a long time.

He hoped that was vague enough for the Vorlon. The next part could be, and had to be, stated directly.

I have to ask and trust that you will tell no one, not even Sheridan, what I'm about to say. The bearer of this message is one of my Rangers. Some are Minbari. Most are Humans. They have been drawn here to work to-

gether and prepare for the fight ahead. Their job, for now, is to patrol the frontier, to listen, to watch, and to return with reports too sensitive to trust to regular channels. They are my eyes and ears. Where you see them, you see me.

In the name of our friendship, I ask that you give them every courtesy and cooperation.

Sinclair paused. That was the heart of the matter. He thought for a moment, and then decided to continue the direct approach.

I wish I could tell you more. I wish I could warn you. But the others don't think it's time yet.

It still wasn't enough. He had to say something more specific. He owed Garibaldi and Babylon 5 itself at least that much. What did he really want to say to his old friend? He wanted to warn him about the Shadows. By now, he must have heard something, seen some of the reports, heard some of the rumors.

But Sinclair wanted to warn him about more than the Shadows. He also wanted to warn Garibaldi about the Vorlons. He was a little surprised when he realized how strongly he felt about this, since he wasn't really sure what exactly he wanted to warn Garibaldi against. That they were evasive? That they knew far more than they were willing to say? It was more than that. Garibaldi already knew those things. He knew Kosh. And maybe that was the point. Those on Babylon 5 only knew Kosh, knew only that one Vorlon, knew only the one side of the Vorlons Kosh represented. Mysterious but seeming benign. Sinclair had believed that image himself, until he finally met another Vorlon. Ulkesh represented another side of the Vorlons, and Sinclair believed that to be a much darker side. Perhaps the more influential side.

Sinclair remembered that Garibaldi was fond of saying "the enemy of my enemy is my friend." Sinclair was finding it increasingly hard to see the Vorlons as anyone's friends, but they were clearly enemies of the Shadows, who appeared to be enemy to all. So it was essential to cooperate with the Vorlons. And equally essential not to trust them too far. How would he get *that* across to Garibaldi without letting the Vorlon know he was doing so?

He thought about his friend for a moment. Although almost completely uninhibited when off duty, Garibaldi took his job as security chief very seriously, and was thorough and cautious on the job. Garibaldi once told him he had a motto as security chief. It came from an old, old movie he'd seen once; he had a fascination for late twentieth and early twenty-first century popular culture. "There's a line in this film," Garibaldi had told him. " 'Keep your friends close, and your enemies closer.' And if I don't know which a person is, I stay really close."

That was it, Sinclair suddenly thought. He would use that. "Stay close to the Vorlon" might just resonate with Garibaldi in the right way.

Now, what about the Shadows? He couldn't call them by name—or could he? It was, after all, a perfectly common word, one often used to denote danger in a general sense. Link that with the Vorlons in the same sentence, and maybe the point would be clear enough.

Stay close to the Vorlon and watch out for shadows. They move when you're not looking.

They. Would Garibaldi discern he meant that *both* the Shadows and the Vorlons had a tendency to "move when you're not looking"? Sinclair would just have to trust Garibaldi's instincts.

He reread the message. A bit melodramatic, perhaps, but it should do the job. Satisfied, he walked over to the computer to make the visual recording. As he sat down, he thought of his old friend and of all his friends on Babylon 5, and felt the familiar surge of conflicting emotions. The strong feelings carried through as he began.

"Hello, old friend. It's been a while . . ."

The young Ranger stood at attention, but was clearly eager for his first mission. Sinclair was at his desk in his official embassy office in Tuzanor. In a few hours, a group of Rangers would depart for Babylon 5, and Sinclair had left the assignment of the final and most important part of their mission there to the last possible moment. He also carefully decided that the instructions would best be given in the greater privacy of this small office, rather than at any of the offices in the administrative buildings or even in his quarters on the Ranger compound.

"At ease," said Sinclair. "I understand you've been to Babylon 5 before?"

"Yes, sir, a couple of times."

"Good." Sinclair handed the Ranger two small computer data crystals containing the message he had recorded that had been duly approved by Jenimer and Ulkesh. "You are to personally deliver these messages to Babylon 5's Security Chief Michael Garibaldi and to Ambassador Delenn. No one else. You must not divulge to anyone else that you carry these messages, simply insist that you must speak privately to the chief and to the ambassador, no matter what. Is that clear?"

"Yes, sir."

Sinclair hesitated briefly. "I also have a second assignment for you, which you are to discuss with no one but Mr. Garibaldi, and that only after you have delivered the first message.''

Sinclair handed the Ranger a third data crystal, containing a message that had not been approved by anyone, nor did anyone else know about it. Maybe it wasn't necessary at all, but Sinclair wanted to be sure.

''Tell Mr. Garibaldi that I request he store this message in the Babcom system without speaking of it to anyone else. Is that clear?''

''Yes, sir.''

Sinclair stood. ''Then good luck.''

''Entil'Zha veni,'' the young man said earnestly. ''In Valen's name.''

Sinclair smiled at the two oaths that the Minbari insisted the Rangers be taught. It was the unwritten rule that the first one was used only at the most solemn and important of occasions. Sinclair supposed a new Ranger's first assignment qualified as such. The second oath was almost as common on Minbar as ''please'' and ''thank you.''

''Godspeed,'' Sinclair replied.

When the Ranger left, Sinclair went to the window that looked out upon the quiet, ancient streets of the City of Sorrows. The third message, sent without the knowledge or approval of the Minbari or the Vorlons was for Catherine. He hadn't dared to do an image recording; it was a written message, encoded and unsigned, that would be placed in her mail file and tagged as originating on Babylon 5.

He had no idea what she would find when she returned to the station from her mission, no way of knowing what she would be told by EarthGov or the Minbari, but he suspected elements of both might try to convince her to stay away from Minbar and simply forget about him. Since he wasn't able to ask Garibaldi or Delenn to tell her the truth, he had to try and leave her word to come to Minbar so he could explain everything in person.

Would she want this kind of life? Married to—what? A guerrilla leader? A figure of Minbari prophecy? If she had been unhappy with the constraints of Earthforce service, what would she think of the all-encompassing lifestyle that came with being the Anla'shok Na and, at least in the eyes of Jenimer, Rathenn, and apparently the Rangers themselves, the Entil'Zha-to-be?

Forget the personal, Ulkesh had said. The Vorlons wanted automatons totally devoted to carrying out their agenda, moving only as they suggested, opposing the Shadows only as they instructed. How frustrating it must be for the Vorlons when Jenimer and Delenn and some of the other Minbari kept insisting on having ideas and wills of their own.

How annoying for everyone that their handpicked but stubborn fulfillment of prophecy kept insisting on his right to a personal, Human life, as well. The truth was he was feeling very much alone. A particular line from the one book of collected poetry he had been able to bring with him kept reverberating through his thoughts. It was from Rilke: "But how alien, alas, are the streets of the city of grief."

A stranger in a strange land, he had told Rathenn, so very long ago it seemed now. Even with new Human recruits arriving at the Ranger compound every day, he felt very much the stranger in this alien city and on this alien planet. Actually, he was the alien here, and he longed for even a small fragment of the life he had once led.

Catherine was far more than that. He knew what she meant to him, how much he wanted her to say yes, she would still marry him, in spite of everything. He would not hold her to her prior agreement, if it wasn't what she wanted. But he did want her to come to Minbar and see for herself before she made her decision. He wanted her to see the importance of the work he was doing here and why he had agreed to it in spite of certain misgivings. He wanted her to see that they could still build a life together. In both of their lives, "home" had never been defined so much by the place where they lived as by the people they were with. With Catherine, Sinclair would have a home, wherever he was.

He wanted her to see that his love for her had not changed, even if everything else in his life had changed absolutely. Only then should she make up her mind; only then would he be able to accept completely whichever decision she made.

But she could only come to Minbar if she made it back safely to Babylon 5. He had just entrusted one of his Rangers with another message for her, but he still didn't know if she had received the first one he had sent so many weeks ago. Nor did he know if she would be able to make any sense of it at all. That message had been composed and sent with the "help" of the others. He could only hope she had understood what he was trying to say, and was now taking every precaution.

There was a knock on his door. "Ambassador," came the voice of the ever-faithful Venak, still his embassy aide. "Your first appointment is here."

Sinclair pushed the button to release the lock on the door and open it. More potential Ranger candidates to screen. He had a lot of work to do this day, as every day.

Just do what you can, one of his teachers had told him a long time ago, *and let God take care of the rest.*

"Send them in," he said.

CHAPTER 15

THE arrival of a ship at the Arisia Mining Colony was usually an eagerly anticipated event. Ships from Earth or other parts of the solar system, ships from the various Earth Colonies, and even the occasional ship from Narn or the Drazi homeworld brought a welcome infusion of mail, fresh supplies, news, and gossip—along with cold cash to be paid for Quantium 40, which translated into salaries, wages, and bonuses.

But the arrival of a Minbari ship excited a bit less interest than most because the insular Minbari rarely brought anything other than their empty cargo bays and their cash. While unfailingly polite, they did not engage in small talk, speculation, or gossip, and only rarely passed along any news worth hearing.

In fact, Marcus didn't really expect to see any of the Minbari at all except the ship's captain when it was time to sign papers and make payment. He watched the monitors in his office as the newly arrived Minbari cargo ship slowly maneuvered for docking with the Orbital Refinery Platform's cargo loading bay.

Marcus had to concede that their cargo ships, like their transport ships and even their most lethal warships, were beautiful vessels. This one was a graceful-looking, brightly colored concoction sporting long tapering wings, yet still managed to convey a sense of muscular power. It was like the Minbari themselves, a deceptively frail-looking appearance that belied the true strength beneath.

He'd been a very young draftee during the war and had never seen combat, but he'd seen enough that even now the Minbari ships, for all their aesthetic appeal, put a chill down his spine.

That didn't matter. Business was business, and the Minbari were good customers. Besides, the captain and crew of these vessels tended to be worker caste, not military caste, and though hardly gregarious, they were usually pleasant enough. He returned to his paperwork and didn't give it another thought until several hours later when his secretary buzzed him to announce the arrival of the Minbari captain.

Marcus remained seated at his desk. The Minbari didn't shake hands, and didn't expect him to stand. In fact, wishing to finish a particular report, he didn't even look up from his computer screen when the Minbari entered the room.

"Just one moment, please," he said, entering a couple more keystrokes. Then he looked up—not into the face of a Minbari, but of his brother William, grinning broadly at him. For a moment his brain wouldn't process what he was seeing, and he froze, half turned from his computer, just staring at the familiar face.

"Well, are you going to say hi, or are you just going to sit there like a dead fish gaping at me?"

Marcus stood. "William, what—" but nothing else came out. Looking around for some explanation, he finally noticed that the Minbari captain was in the room, standing rather deferentially, it seemed, near the door. "How—where—"

"Who and why," his brother finished for him,

laughing. "Geez, it's good to see you, Marcus. Sorry to surprise you like this. Not that I didn't get a kick out of it. But listen, I'll explain everything to you in a while. I believe you have some business to attend to first."

William turned to the Minbari captain and spoke to him in what Marcus recognized as the military-caste dialect. The captain bowed slightly to him and approached. A now even more astonished Marcus could hardly concentrate on the business at hand as he hurried the Minbari through all the necessary paperwork. William watched silently, grinning with delight all the while, until the Minbari captain concluded his business with Marcus. The captain then turned to William and again they spoke in the military dialect. This time Marcus made a point to concentrate to see if he could catch what they were saying.

It seemed his little brother was instructing the Minbari to wait on the ship. The Minbari bowed and left. William then turned his attention to appraising the cluttered office, its plain metal desk and office chair, two angular chairs for visitors, computer console, battered filing cabinets, and bare walls.

"Uncomfortable, but at least it's messy," William said, teasing. "You know if you just removed that one photo on your desk, you could purge this room totally of all personality."

Marcus was still too stunned to really be aware what expression was on his face, but whatever it was, it caused his little brother to smile even more broadly. "We have a lot to talk about. Is there any place a little more comfortable, and a little more private, we could go to?"

Marcus nodded. He informed his secretary he'd be unavailable for at least the next few hours, and led his brother through the maze of corridors. Any question he attempted was met with a "let's wait until we get to your quarters," so they walked in silence most of the way. It was only then that he had a chance to wonder about the strange outfit his brother was wearing, complete with some sort of jeweled pin near his right shoulder. By the time they reached his quarters, it was the first thing Marcus wanted to ask about.

"What are you wearing, anyway?" he inquired, as he closed the door behind them. "Is that Minbari clothing?"

"In a sense, yes," said William. "It's the uniform of the organization I belong to."

"Uniform? Oh, God, Willie, what have you gotten yourself into now?"

For the first time, William's relentless good cheer faltered, just a little. He hated being called Willie, as Marcus well knew.

"Something very important, big brother," he said seriously. "It's the reason I'm here." He took a seat on the battered couch and waited. Marcus pulled over the only armchair and also sat down.

"Okay," Marcus said. "So what are you doing here? And just what the bloody hell *have* you been doing on Minbar? Or perhaps I should ask, what have they done to you?"

William's grin returned. "Aren't you at least a little happy to see me?"

"I'd be a lot happier if I thought you'd come here for some useful purpose, like finally taking up your share of the burden around here, helping out with the family business."

"Burden." William repeated back at him. "Interesting choice of words.

"Oh, I forgot," Marcus shot back. "Life is just supposed to be a round of endless fun. Isn't that your philosophy, if we can dignify your irresponsibility with that word?''

''Responsibility is exactly why I'm here.''

''Yeah? Responsibility to your family? Are you here to finally live up to that? It was nice of you to attend the funeral. Or is that the end of your responsibility?''

William was clearly taken aback by Marcus's vehemence, and for the first time no longer seemed so sure of what he wanted to say. His expression clouded, and when he spoke, it was in a low, intense voice.

''I loved Mother and Father every bit as much as you did.''

''You had a rather peculiar way of showing it.''

''No, you do!'' William stood up angrily. ''They wanted us to have lives of our own. You wanted to take up the family business, and that was fine. I know it made Father happy. But I wanted something else, and that was fine with him too. Mother, also. After all, she wanted Father to ease up a little himself, not to work himself to—''

''To death?'' Marcus said, standing to look his brother in the eyes.

''Yes, like you're doing now, for no reason. Mother couldn't convince Father to ease up, and she couldn't convince you, though I know she tried. She didn't want this for you, not if it made you unhappy. She didn't even want it for herself. She tried to tell you it was okay to let it go after Father died. And I know Father wouldn't want you making yourself miserable over this.''

''Just where do you think you know *anything*!'' Marcus said angrily. ''I have a responsibility. This is his legacy, to both of us.''

''God knows I don't know *you* anymore,'' replied William in a quiet voice. ''Our parents' legacy was how they raised us. To think for ourselves and be ourselves. You always hated life on a mining colony. You wanted to travel, maybe be a pilot. I remember how you used to tell me of all the adventures you were going to have when you were grown up."

"Well, I did grow up, and discovered life isn't an adolescent fantasy," replied Marcus, "which brings us to that—costume you're wearing."

"That's what I came here to talk to you about," said William, suddenly laughing. "But some things never change. 'Hi, brother,' I said, and the next thing I know we're screaming at each other."

Marcus didn't smile. But neither was he angry anymore, just weary. "Why did you come here?"

"To present you with an offer," William said solemnly, "and an opportunity."

He sat back down, and after a moment so did Marcus.

"I'm listening," said Marcus.

His brother began to spin what seemed to him a wild tale of the awakening of an ancient alien species called the Shadows that threatened all life in the known galaxy, and how a legendary Minbari military organization called—of all things, thought Marcus—the Rangers had been called once again into existence by one Jeffrey Sinclair to combat that threat. And how Humans and Minbari were now equally allowed to be a part of this honored group.

"I only went to Minbar because I've always been fascinated by Minbari culture," William was saying. "But on the very first day, I actually met Ambassador Sinclair and we talked. I was sure I'd made an idiot of myself I was so overwhelmed at meeting him. But then a few weeks later he summoned me back to his office to offer me the chance to train with the Rangers. He said he saw something in me from the start, and wanted me to be among the very first group. I could hardly believe it.''

''Well, that makes two of us,'' said Marcus. Had his brother taken leave of his senses altogether? ''You haven't said one thing that makes any sense. Minbari mumbo jumbo and mysterious aliens that are somehow wreaking widespread destruction with only a few people actually knowing about it. What game are you playing at?''

''It's not a game at all,'' said William. ''The Shadows are a real threat. Certainly you've heard the stories, ships in hyperspace and on the Rim that have encountered unknown alien ships that are as black as the darkness between the stars. There have been some very narrow escapes.''

''Yes, and people used to talk with the same straight-faced seriousness about the abominable snowman, the Loch Ness monster, ghost ships, and the Bermuda Triangle. They're all folktales, Willie, like your Shadows. It's all preposterous. Now you said you had an offer and an opportunity to put before me. I haven't heard either one yet, though I'm not sure I really want to.''

''All right, the offer,'' said William. ''The Rangers need reliable sources of Q-40. I told Ranger One that you might be willing to strike a deal with us.''

''That's the first sensible thing you've said since arriving. I'm always happy to consider a paying customer.''

''We also want to ask you to consider letting the Rangers have a permanent presence here—a very discreet presence. Not only to ensure the supply of Q-40, but to set up a listening post to watch for Shadow activity in this area.''

"I suppose there's been just a beehive of Shadow activity out here," Marcus said skeptically.

"Actually, no. At least none that's been reported to us. But then we have no reliable way of gathering information in this area yet. We need to establish observation bases out here. We're asking for your cooperation."

"I will not disrupt this colony's business so you and your friends can come here and play soldier. Was *that* the opportunity?" Marcus asked.

"No," William said, looking steadily at Marcus. "The Rangers had to start almost from zero. We're growing fast, but we need a lot more recruits. It's the responsibility of every Ranger to talk to those few people we know who could make it as Rangers and tell them what we're all about."

"You want to come here and recruit among my workers?" Marcus asked incredulously. "It's hard enough to find and keep good workers in this business, without you—"

"No, you don't understand. Not your workers. Just you. Marcus, I want you to join with us. You have all the skills. You're a superb pilot, you have military training and a working knowledge of Minbari from your service in Earthforce during the war. You've always been good at learning languages. During the war you were assigned to Earthforce Intelligence Gathering, which is primarily what we do at the moment."

Marcus looked at his little brother in disbelief. "Do I have to remind you I was drafted unwillingly into Earthforce and that I hated every moment of it?"

"The Rangers are different. We aren't just a military organization. We're more than that."

"Sounds like some kind of a cult, if you ask me. And I detest those even more than the military."

"No, it isn't. It's just that being a Ranger is more

than just being a soldier. It's a calling to serve. Ranger One impresses upon all of us that our primary duty is to preserve Life. That's what we're about."

"This *is* the Minbari, we're talking about, isn't it? And a Minbari military organization has to be run by the Minbari military caste. Well, I know a little something about them," Marcus said. "They're not particularly fond of Humans, and I don't exactly trust them. Will, don't you think it's possible you're being misled by them for reasons of their own?"

"The Rangers aren't run by the military caste, and it's not even primarily a Minbari organization anymore. Ranger One is Human and most of the other Rangers right now are Humans. Ranger One says that's because Earth is as much in danger from these Shadows as Minbar, so we have a responsibility to join in the fight. Ranger One says—"

" 'Ranger One says' quite a bit, doesn't he?" said Marcus in a mocking tone. "Sounds like a cult leader to me."

"Jeffrey Sinclair is a remarkable man, but he's totally down to Earth," William said earnestly, then laughed at his own choice of words. "So to speak. I mean, even though we're based on Minbar. He's the farthest thing you'll ever find from a cult leader."

"Well, I've read about your Ranger One, like everyone else. Isn't this the same Jeffrey Sinclair that was captured by the Minbari during the war? The same Jeffrey Sinclair that was sent to Minbar as a goodwill ambassador *at the Minbari's request*? And then tried to represent himself as having more authority than he really had? Sounds like he's gone native, if you ask me. Who knows what his motivations really are?"

"You shouldn't believe everything you read in the papers, Marcus, and very little of what you hear coming out of official EarthGov sources these days. I didn't think I'd have to remind someone raised on a colony of that. Some bad things are happening on Earth right now. I believe someday the Rangers may be necessary to help out there as well. Come back to Minbar with me, and see for yourself. I told Ranger One all about you and he has agreed to talk with you, to ask you to join us."

"I have a business to run," said Marcus, then paused. "Damn it, Will, I am glad to see you, even if you're right that we can't seem to say two words before we start yelling at each other. But believe it or not it's because you're my brother and I love you and I worry about you. You've spent your whole life jumping from this thing to that, never staying with anything for very long. Why should I believe this Ranger thing will last any longer than any of your other past pursuits?"

"Because this is different. This is important. Because I'm doing something important. It's what I was meant to do in this life, I can feel it. The Rangers represent something greater. If you'd only come to Minbar, meet with Jeffrey Sinclair—"

"Willie, you're a acting like a fool," Marcus said impatiently. "Chasing legends, playing the hero. Look at you in that ridiculous outfit, pretending to be a legendary Minbari soldier, probably risking your life, and for what? Well, little brother, if it makes you happy, fine. But don't try to drag me into it. I have a real life that needs attending to."

William sat back, sighed, looked at the ceiling, looked back at Marcus. "You know, you used to be fun," he said, catching Marcus off guard. "You were the fastest wit I ever knew, had the best sense of humor of anyone I ever met. Just being with you was enough to make me feel better when we were kids, no matter what else happened. Now look at you. A storm cloud hangs over you. You call this a real life? And you've done it to yourself. You say I'm a fool, risking my life for no good reason. But I'm happy. And I'm making a difference for the better. Can you say the same?''

Marcus didn't have an answer. The truth was there was something different about his little brother. He seemed more mature and more sure of himself than Marcus had ever really thought possible. And yet it was still William in the most important ways. He didn't act brainwashed, as Marcus had at first feared. He just acted like someone who had found himself. And yet it was all so ridiculous—Shadows and Rangers and all of that.

''I suppose you'll be leaving with the Minbari ship?'' Marcus said finally, with more than a touch of regret.

''No,'' said William, as if coming to a decision. ''I'll send them on. I'll catch the next ship. We still have a business deal to work out. You don't have to like the Rangers to sell them Q-40, do you?''

Marcus smiled for the first time. He didn't want to admit it, but it would be nice to have his brother around for a while.

CHAPTER 16

CATHERINE Sakai hit save and exited the database. The final planetary stop on her itinerary, UTC67-02C, code-name Mjollnir, was now just an entry on her flight log and a closed report awaiting delivery to the Ops ship that awaited her on the other side of a jump gate four days away.

She had never felt happier to be in hyperspace and this first day had been just as uneventful as her last two planetary stops had been. Uneventful, but not unsuccessful. Mjollnir had proved as bounteous as Glasir, more than offsetting her disappointing fourth stop at UTC59-02B, aka Skirnir. Two successes out of five tries was a very high percentage under any circumstances. *Skydancer* was bulging from the collected mass of rich soil and rock samples she was bringing back along with her detailed reports and data compilations, which she figured should make everyone happy.

And she had encountered absolutely nothing out of the ordinary at these last two planets, enabling her to set aside thoughts of mysterious destructive aliens in favor of geology, chemistry, and orbital mechanics, subjects she much preferred.

But best of all she was on the first leg of her journey back to Babylon 5 and Jeffrey Sinclair.

Her sensor panel sounded a low warning tone, and she immediately checked it out. Before entering hyperspace she had set her sensors to extreme sensitivity and had been rewarded all day long with frequent warnings. This one, like all the others, was just a hyperspace artifact, not a ship and not any kind of danger.

Hyperspace frequently "knotted" itself into little eddies, whirlpools, and temporary clumps that highly tuned sensor equipment could detect and would sometimes report as an object. This meant a pilot had a choice: keep the equipment highly tuned and put up with the many false warnings that resulted; or turn down the sensitivity for a little peace and quiet, knowing that any encounter with other ships or real objects would be at much closer range, occasionally closer than was comfortable.

Most pilots, including Sakai, usually chose the latter option, on the practical basis that such encounters in hyperspace were relatively rare; and even if they did occur, there would still be enough time to react; and in most cases the spatial displacement that formed around all objects in hyperspace actually helped to prevent collisions.

That's what she *usually* chose. Not this time. She had chosen instead to put up with the constant pings, bells, and buzzers that sounded as the sensor panel warned her of what it thought were various-size objects. She was too close to getting home to leave anything to chance. If she were to encounter any unknown aliens in hyperspace, she didn't know how, or even if, they would register on her sensors, so she was content to check out each and every little warning until she left hyperspace and reached the Ops ship. Just in case.

According to the chronometers, day one in hyperspace was just about over, and it was the scheduled time to go to bed. Sleep in hyperspace always seemed a little redundant. Most of the waking day felt like a dream, and her real dreams at night were almost always of piloting through hyperspace. It could sometimes become difficult, particularly at the end of a long flight, to differentiate between the two states of consciousness. Which made it all the more important to stick to the schedule, and put in those six hours in the bunk, whether sleepy or not. At least this time, she really was tired. Maybe she could actually get some decent sleep.

She made her way to the back of the cockpit and pulled herself into the bunk webbing. She drifted off to sleep almost immediately and in her dream was frantically trying to extricate *Skydancer* from a strangely entangled area of hyperspace. Though obviously very hazardous it was causing only the lowest level alarm to sound, a steady *ping-ping-ping* she only gradually became aware of . . .

Sakai abruptly jerked awake, hitting her head against the bulkhead in the process. She had somehow managed to wrap herself up in the webbing, and tussled with it sleepily to free herself. The alarm was real. Something had set off the most sensitive sensors. Probably another false alarm, but she was leaving nothing to chance this trip. With a sigh, she pulled out of the bunk and floated over to the console. She yawned as she turned off the alarms and called up the sensor readings, then forced herself to focus on the numbers.

What she saw brought her instantly to full alertness. This didn't look at all like a hyperspace artifact. The sensors seemed to indicate that she had just passed through an area where a jump point had opened, even though it somehow hadn't triggered the usual alarms. She had to go on the assumption, therefore, that these other readings indicated spaceships, but they certainly didn't match the configurations for any ships she was aware of. Still, there was no other reasonable explanation.

Suddenly, her computer sounded a new warning: "*Skydancer* is moving off course. Please advise as to course adjustment."

She checked the heading and was about to order the computer to put *Skydancer* back on its original course, when she decided it might be better to first determine what had moved her off course in the first place.

She strapped into her console chair, and studied her readouts.

"Okay," she muttered. "Who are you?"

Whatever was out there, there were at least twelve of them, all around her—including three that should be visible through her cockpit window and canopy. She leaned forward and peered out, trying to make sense of the perpetual chaotic dance of light and color that was hyperspace and somehow spot the anomalous objects.

Then she saw them. At first they seemed to be just more of the many small areas of darkness that formed in the folds of light and color, then quickly dissipated. But these stayed steady and unchanging, like three negative-image stars.

"Computer, maximum magnification on sensor-recorded object number one, straight ahead."

A moment later her monitors displayed a glistening black spider-shaped object that was definitely a ship of some kind, but like none she'd ever seen before. Jeff had been right—it wasn't at all similar in appearance to what she had encountered at Sigma 957, but it was every bit as disquieting. And she was dead center in the middle of a fleet of them.

Should she try to make contact with them? That

didn't seem wise, not given what she had seen at Ymir, and not given Jeff's warning to her.

Had they even detected her yet? Most likely, but it was *possible* they hadn't, given the conditions of hyperspace. They had apparently come out of normal space just as she passed by their jump point, and spatial displacement had put her right at the center of their formation. *Skydancer* was a much smaller ship than the alien ships, and they might have passed her off as a hyperspace artifact. She could hardly count on that, however, and certainly not for very long. They would have to detect her eventually.

She looked up again at the monitor, and shivered. Just having the image on the screen was too much like having it looking at her. And she didn't like the thought of that at all.

"Computer, normal view on all monitors."

At least they weren't shooting at her. In fact, she thought, she was probably right now in the one place where they wouldn't dare take a shot at her. Given the unpredictable properties of hyperspace, any missiles or even energy weapons fired at her could easily bend off course and strike one of their comrades rather than her.

But *Skydancer* was still gradually being moved off course and away from her targeted jump-gate coordinates. Any course correction would surely attract their attention, something she absolutely wanted to avoid. But she couldn't just let them carry her off course indefinitely.

She still had no proof, of course, that these strange alien ships meant her any harm. Perhaps she was overreacting. She had to be rational and consider that possibility. Which she did, for all of two seconds.

No. In her gut she was sure these had to be the things Jeff had been trying to warn her about. She wondered how he knew about them. What he knew about them. She wished he had been able to get just a little more information to her, although she also knew he would have if he'd been able to.

With no other information, it seemed best to wait for the moment, to see what they would do. She was still not that far off course yet, nothing that couldn't be made up to keep her scheduled rendezvous with the Ops ship. Perhaps she could find some way to ease away from the fleet—

Once again, the sensor alarms sounded.

"Now what?" She turned off the alarms, pulled up the new readings, and felt a flood of relief, hoping it was justified. The ships seemed to be leaving, peeling off from the formation one by one. She double-checked with a visual scan. The three dark ships that had been in front of her were gone. She had the computer do a full-grid visual check at maximum magnification even as she continued to scrutinize the sensor readings. She wanted an exact count. She had determined with a fair amount of certainty that there had been twelve ships. Now the readings indicated that nine ships had moved off on new headings. That left three ships that had simply vanished from her view and her sensors. But however they had done it, they all appeared to be gone.

Was it going to be that easy? she thought.

"Sakai," she said aloud, "when has it ever been that easy? Computer, do another sensor scan at maximum detection for any apparent anomalous objects, sensor shadows, or echoes."

She didn't have to wait long.

"Confirmation, at maximum sensor range, one eight zero by one eight zero."

Straight behind her. She checked the numbers on the screen. It might be a sensor anomaly or a hyperspace artifact, but it was the computer's judgment it was probably a ship. It was her judgment as well. Now to see if it was following her.

"Computer. Set course adjustment, original heading and increase speed to reach jump gate at scheduled rendezvous time." Then she watched the readings. Her new companion matched course and speed.

They had noticed her after all, and apparently now wanted to see where she was going. And then what would they do? Simply note it in their logbook? Or blast her ship into a cloud of dust before she could report what she had seen of them? She feared the last option was the most likely. She had no proof of that, just once again a gut reaction. And no pilot lived for long without learning how to trust her instincts.

She had to hope that the alien ship planned to follow her all the way to the jump gate. If it decided to attack her before then, that would be that. She would have no options. *Skydancer* carried no weaponry or defensive shielding, and Sakai felt sure her ship wouldn't be able to outrun or outmaneuver the alien ship.

But if it waited until she got to the jump gate—well, then she might have a chance. One of the other things she had learned as a pilot, was that even the slimmest of chances was better than none.

She was running across a devastated landscape, as massive ships, jagged and dark, thrummed low overhead, blasting everything in their path, their destructive weapons just missing her again and again. She had to keep going. There, just ahead, on the horizon, she saw Jeff caught in a glowing sphere of light, a terrifyingly easy target for the alien warships. She had to get to him, but she could not run fast enough, could not close the distance between them . . .

"Thirty minutes to jump-gate rendezvous."

The computer voice woke her up where she had drifted off to sleep in the console chair. That would not do at all. She was going to have to take another stim shot. She would pay hell for it later, but there wasn't any other choice.

As she put the hypo to her arm, fragments of the dream came back to her. *Talk about your psychological displacement,* she thought with grim amusement. She was the one who might have to gamble everything on one chance to save herself from destruction, and she was dreaming about trying to save Jeff.

She checked the sensors. Her alien companion was still with her, still at the same distance it had maintained for the last three days. Did it know they were approaching an Earth-built jump gate? Could they tune in to what was supposed to be a coded homing beacon usable only by authorized ships? How quickly could the alien ship cover the space between them? Did the alien ship really plan to do anything at all? It was amazing how thoroughly she could be convinced of one thing—that the alien was bent on keeping her from leaving hyperspace in one piece—and yet still keep hoping with all her heart that somehow she really might be wrong—that the alien was just observing her, and meant her no harm—and she wouldn't have to do what she was planning to do.

Right, Sakai. Don't be a sap, she thought. *Check the sample bay one more time and make sure everything's ready. And don't overthink the consequences on the other side. Just be ready to do it.*

It was very simple really. She had to shut down the jump gate after she went through it but before the alien ship could follow her. All she had to do was dump her entire sample bay, all the valuable material she had spent four months gathering, the very reason she had been sent out to the Rim, and she had to dump it at precisely the right moment. Too soon, and she wouldn't make it through the gate herself, leaving her to be destroyed by the alien, or by the malfunctioning of the gate itself. Too late, and the alien ship would still be able to get through before the gate shut down, leaving the alien free to destroy her, and quite possibly the Ops ship as well.

For good measure, she checked everything two more times. She finished just in time for the computer's announcement.

"Approaching jump gate Quadrant one hundred three zero, coordinates five four by eight zero two by six five in ten minutes."

This was it.

"Computer, initiate hyperspace departure sequence. Establish contact with the exit jump gate. And report on position of alien ship."

"Acknowledged. Alien ship increasing velocity, on collision trajectory, estimated intersection in nine minutes at present acceleration."

Would it fire before she went through the gate? It was a secure, coded gate. If it wanted to know where the gate opened into normal space, it *should* have to follow her through the gate. How much sooner would it be able to get an accurate fix on her for weapons fire? Perhaps it wanted to get at least one shot at her here, and would only follow through if it missed.

"Computer, load new instructions E-X four two into the hyperspace departure sequence and initiate. Increase speed to maximum and ignore safety override."

It was not a good idea to enter a jump gate at the speed she had just ordered her ship to attain—but by catching the alien off guard, she hoped to be through that gate before the other ship got within firing range.

"Approaching gate entry point," intoned the computer. "Prepare for jump to normal space."

"Acknowledged."

"Entering gate."

Skydancer flew through the jump-point opening. The cockpit started to spin around Sakai even as she gave the final order.

"Eject full contents of sample bay."

She felt *Skydancer* recoil as every last ton of radioactive soil and rock spewed out behind her, hit the folds of hyperspace, and carried forward with *Skydancer* toward the jump gate's transition point where she hoped it would foul the transition boosters, overload the energy exchange, and shut the gate down behind her.

Energy crackled around *Skydancer* like a lightning cocoon, and other massive discharges of energy flashed and thundered beyond the ship. Sakai held on as *Skydancer* pitched and rolled, then shuddered furiously. What should have taken no more than an instant, was taking long seconds. Why wasn't she moving through the transition point? Had the radioactive debris shut down the gate before she could pass through?

Finally, *Skydancer* stopped shaking and she felt the Universe elongate.

Only this didn't feel right, either. As always at the point of transition, physical reality seemed to stretch into an infinite, one-dimensional length of atoms. But this time it continued to stretch and extend far beyond anything she had ever experienced before during a jump. The distance between each individual atom was greater than the gulf between the galaxies. She felt reality itself evaporating away into an absolute nothingness from which she would never return.

The Universe snapped back into place with shocking suddenness. A last discharge of energy crackled over *Skydancer*'s hull and faded away, even as the ship continued to shudder for another five long seconds. Then Sakai saw the stars. *Skydancer* limped into normal space and slowly headed toward the UTC Ops ship ahead.

"Computer! Did anything follow us through the gate?"

"Negative. Jump gate is currently nonfunctional."

She hadn't expected such a violent reaction from dumping the material into the transition point. She had only meant to clog up the works, not set off a fireworks display that almost took her ship apart, and that may have done more damage to the jump gate then she had originally planned.

The electrical system in *Skydancer* failed, and the small emergency generator took over. Time to stop worrying about the jump gate, and see what she did to her own ship.

"Computer, display damage assessment."

A lengthy damage report scrolled by: life support systems at minimum functioning, electrical systems nonfunctional except for emergency systems, propulsion unit two damaged and nonfunctional, damage to the hull, including ruptures in bays 3, 5, 7, and 9. This much damage, coupled with the unexpected pyrotechnics in the gate, led Sakai to wonder . . .

"Computer. Was *Skydancer* fired upon by the ship that was following us?"

"Energy weapon discharge indicated."

She called up the readings on the screen, and began to analyze the data. Did she once say she hated hyperspace? Wonderful hyperspace with its twisted topography and unpredictable currents? Those properties of hyperspace, assisted in some small measure by the debris she had ejected and the turbulence of the jump transition itself, had apparently saved her life. The alien must have fired from practically point-blank range as she entered the gate, and just missed by a hair's width, scorching the outer hull in places and igniting the debris-filled hyperspace around her. But the force of it had actually propelled *Skydancer* forward and out of harm's way.

She decided she might even owe the mysterious alien a thank you—at least she now had some defense for her actions other than gut instinct. This gave her some small measure of comfort as *Skydancer*—damaged and empty of its valuable cargo—entered the docking bay of the massive Universal Terraform Operations ship.

CHAPTER 17

MARCUS didn't notice the startled looks on the faces of his employees as he said a cheerful good morning to everyone he passed by on his way to meet his brother. They were not used to seeing their boss in a good mood, and were careful to return the morning cheer—and move on quickly.

It had been a good couple of days. Marcus had shown William every aspect of the orbital side of the operation, top to bottom, both on the Refinery Platform and here on the Inhabitants' Platform. William had seemed eager to see everything, asking a lot of informed and perceptive questions, and not just because he was striking a business deal for the Rangers with Marcus. He appeared genuinely interested. For the first time in a long while, Marcus felt truly proud of what he had been able to build here—and William seemed to be proud of him for it.

William had also continued to talk about his time with the Rangers as Marcus had shown him around, but without saying it aloud they had struck a truce. Over these past few days, Marcus hadn't tried to convince William to leave the Rangers and join him in the business, and William hadn't tried to convince Marcus to leave the business and join him in the Rangers. They had gotten along better than they had since they were kids.

"Good morning, Marcus."

He had just a turned a corner to come upon Hasina. "Good morning to you. How are things in Planetary Forecasting?"

"Quiet so far in the mining areas," she said. "In fact, unusually quiet planetwide. Volcanic and earthquake activity are lower than normal for Arisia. It's as if the old girl is holding her breath."

Marcus laughed. "Is that your scientific appraisal?"

"No," said Hasina, also with a laugh. "My scientific appraisal is waiting on your computer for your inspection."

"Seen it," said Marcus. "Your usual fine job. Just thought I'd get your personal observations."

She smiled in return. For some reason, Marcus couldn't think of a thing to say, even though he really wanted to.

Hasina rescued them both. "How does your brother like our little operation here? He seems like a fine young man."

"He is, isn't he?" said Marcus, as a thought occurred to him. "Listen, would you like to join us for dinner tonight? We've got all our business talk out of the way. It would be nice just to have a social dinner." In fact, thought Marcus, it would be his first since coming to Arisia.

"I'd like that very much. And I have an idea. I still have that authentic African cuisine dinner my mother sent out to me," she said. "It'll be fresh in that stasis pack for another year at least. Anyway, she sent more than enough for three people . . ."

"Sounds great. I'm sure Will would love a break from commissary food."

"My quarters then? At seven?"

"We'll be there," said Marcus. "Now I have to roust my brother out of bed."

Marcus continued on his way. Maybe William had been right about one thing. Maybe it was time to expand his definition of a "real life."

Marcus reached his brother's small visitor's quarters and entered without knocking, intending on rudely and loudly waking him up. Instead, to his profound amazement, he found William sitting in the middle of the floor, fully dressed, apparently meditating. During the last few days Marcus had been too busy to see his brother before lunch, and had just assumed William would welcome the chance to sleep in as he always had.

William didn't open his eyes. "Good morning, brother. I heard you coming down the hall."

"Since when did you start getting up this early in the morning? And when did you start meditating, of all things?"

At that, William opened his eyes and gave his brother a you-figure-it-out look.

"Of course," said Marcus. "The Rangers. Though what meditation has to do with being a soldier . . ."

"You'd be surprised," William said, getting to his feet. "So what's up for today?"

"We're going planetside. You're going to get the grand tour, so I hope you didn't eat a heavy breakfast."

William gave him a curious look. "No. Why?"

Marcus just smiled. His little brother was going to get a close-up view of Perdition Bridge and his big brother's flying skills, but he wanted it to be a surprise.

Marcus carefully eased his XO-Sphere out of the IP docking bay, and set course on a leisurely arc that would first take them past the Orbital Refinery, then back past the Inhabitants' Platform, and finally toward the planet. William had seen the platforms from the Minbari ship when he first arrived, but Marcus wanted to give him another, all-around look.

William gave the appropriate reaction of approval, but was clearly eager to get to Arisia 3 itself. They were already in their pressurized excursion suits. "I never got to go planetside on a Class 4 world. Heck of a thing for a miner's son to say, but somehow it just never happened. I was always too young—"

"And then you left," Marcus said without thinking. No. He wasn't going to start that argument again. Not now. "You were a skinny little rugrat," he said in a lighter tone. "Father was afraid the 2-G's would collapse you like a cheap tent."

Marcus finished their turn around the ORP, and was taking a wide turn back toward the distant IP.

"Is it as hellish down there as they say?"

"Worse." Marcus was about to elaborate with as gruesome a word portrait as he could conjure up, when a warning alarm interrupted him.

"What's wrong?"

"I don't know," Marcus said, checking the control panel. "These readings don't make any sense. They indicate some sort of massive disturbance straight ahead."

Instinctively, both men looked up from the controls to see if they could spot the cause of the disturbance. The Inhabitants' Platform, still some distance in front of them, began to fade from view into total darkness. Marcus suddenly realized there was *something* between his ship and the platform, a large spidery shape of shimmering black. And beyond it, similar things were solidifying out of empty space. In his ears—or was it only in his head?—he heard a terrible shriek that cut through to his soul.

His brother's voice broke the horrifying spell. "Get us out of here! Now!"

Even as Marcus frantically brought his tiny XO-Sphere around, the first energy beams from the alien ships sliced into the Inhabitants' Platform.

"Oh God!" Marcus pointed the tiny ship away from the destruction behind them. "My people! We have to do something!"

"We have to get away—that's all we can do!" William shouted over the ghastly shrieking that seemed to fill the tiny cockpit.

Marcus realized he was right. The XO-Sphere had no weapons and no defensive shielding. It was just a short-range personal flyer. Had anyone else gotten away?

"What the hell is that?"

"The Shadows. They may not have seen us yet!" William shouted. "Do we have enough fuel to get to the jump gate?"

"No! Computer, set and maintain course for Site 13."

A blinding flash of light filled the cockpit. Without looking, Marcus knew: the Orbital Refinery with its full load of Quantium 40 had exploded.

"We have to get to Arisia!" Marcus shouted. "There's a fully fueled emergency shuttle down there. It can get us to the jump gate if we can get to it first!"

He could only hope the aliens had not yet gotten to the planet.

His computer sounded a warning. "Object on collision course, approaching starboard aft, one two four by one six three, distance—" Another flash of crackling light cut the computer off mid-sentence, as simultaneously the small craft shook violently. The smell of ozone overwhelmed the cockpit. The XO-Sphere spun out of control toward the upper atmosphere of Arisia.

Marcus struggled to regain some manual control of the craft as the computer came back on line.

"Port engine gone," it intoned calmly. "Compensating. Attempting to reestablish attitude control. Descending through planetary atmosphere. Outer skin temperature approaching critical."

The temperature inside the craft was rising steadily, the heat almost unbearable, as they plummeted through Arisia's atmosphere at too steep an angle. Marcus and the computer fought to bring the nose up.

"Emergency landing procedure in effect," the computer intoned again. "Approaching landing area Site 13." The surface of Arisia 3 was coming up at them far too fast.

"Hold on!" Marcus shouted over to William. "I've done this before."

Their approach glide was far steeper than Marcus wanted, and as the braking engines fired to slow them down, he tried to level the craft off.

One hundred feet. Seventy-five feet.

With only one engine and extensive damage, he didn't have the control or the fuel for a hover landing, or to pull up and try for a better glide angle. They were going to land in a few seconds, one way or the other.

Fifty feet. Twenty-five feet.

The XO-Sphere leveled off, but not soon enough. The landing gear lowered and the wheels hit the level patch of ground that served as Site 13's runway. The XO-Sphere bounced several times off the hard surface, then flipped over to skid toward the field of boulders at the end of the runway. The screech of metal against rock deafened them as the whole ship seemed to disintegrate around them. Then, all at once, it was over.

Marcus did not believe in miracles. But he was alive. He was on his side, still strapped into his seat, still in the cockpit—what was left of it. The other half, where William had been sitting, was simply gone, and Marcus was looking up at the open sky. His body was pressed under the planet's heavier gravity, and every movement he made was difficult and painful. He struggled to release himself from the safety harness.

"William," he said over his pressure suit's radio. "Can you hear me. Will!"

There was a burst of static in his ears, then, very faintly, "Marcus."

William was alive. Marcus freed himself from the harness and slowly pulled himself up. Had they been unconscious? He wasn't sure. The pressure only afforded them two hours of safety from the planet's naturally occurring high levels of radiation. They had to reach that shuttle.

"William. Hang on. I'm coming."

Marcus climbed out of the wreckage. It was nearing sundown at this site, and with the thick atmosphere and overcast skies, it was almost too dark to see. Did he dare turn on his pressure suit's beam lights? There was nothing else at the site to attract attention from the aliens above. There was no refinery or mining equipment here. This was a safe storage area and emergency shelter, built far from the mining areas in one of the region's most geologically stable areas, consisting solely of low-built storage buildings that were so covered with dust they were almost indistinguishable from the surrounding rock.

He took the chance and swept the area with the light, finally spotting his brother less than a hundred feet away. William had been thrown clear of the wreckage and was lying facedown on the rocky runway. When Marcus reached him, he turned him over as gently as he could in the punishing gravity, and saw that his brother's faceplate was smeared with blood.

"William," he said frantically. "Jesus! Talk to me. Come on!"

"Marcus." His brother's voice was even weaker now.

"I've got to get you to the shuttle," Marcus said. "It's just a couple hundred yards away. Can you sit up?" He helped his brother up as best he could, propping him against his own chest. But it was clear his brother wasn't going anywhere under his own power, and in the heavier gravity Marcus couldn't lift him, couldn't even drag him. It would be like trying to drag over three hundred pounds while carrying an additional hundred-and-seventy-pound weight on his own shoulders.

"Marcus. Go on. Leave me here. Take the shuttle. Warn—"

"I'm an idiot!" Marcus said suddenly. There was a surface rover in one of the buildings. "Listen, Will, I'm going to leave for just a little while, but I'll be back with a—"

"No," said William more forcefully. "Don't you see them?"

"What?" His brother was obviously hallucinating. "Come on. Stay with me, Will. Don't do this."

"Marcus, listen. We didn't think–the Shadows would attack–an Earth settlement. You have to go to Minbar . . ." His voice trailed off again.

"I'll take you there myself. Just don't die on me here. William!"

"Go to Minbar. Tell Sinclair. Take up the fight. Promise me, Marcus."

Tears stung Marcus's eyes, which he blinked back angrily. He tried to speak, but couldn't.

"Promise me," William said again insistently. "You were right. I never finished anything in my life. Help me finish this. Finish the job I started, Marcus. Please promise me."

"I promise."

"Then it's all right." William closed his eyes.

"Will!"

Marcus fumbled for the small panel covering the vital-signs monitor on the front of the pressure suit. The digital display lit up weakly: respiration, zero; heart rate, zero; brain wave function, zero . . .

It was pitch-dark when he heard a voice speak loudly and clearly: "Go!"

It startled him out of his fugue. William? No. His brother was dead. Lifeless in his arms. How long had he been sitting there? He checked the radiation monitor on his own suit. He was nearly at maximum safe exposure already. He had to get to that shuttle, get off this planet.

Abruptly, he was furious. He would go to Minbar, by God. He'd find a way to make these bastard Shadows pay for this. For all of it. For William. For Hasina. For all of them. He had to get to the shuttle. He could bring it back here, pick up his brother's body, then head for the jump gate. The Shadows must be gone by now.

Gently, he lowered his brother to the ground and, with a great effort, stood up. He couldn't see a thing, couldn't see his hand in front of his face. He turned on his helmet beam, but that only penetrated a few yards into the night. How would he find it? Location beacon. A low-powered location beacon was broadcasting at all times from the storage area. Turn on the pressure suit's location finder. Follow the sound.

Marcus stumbled slowly, painfully across the uneven, boulder-strewn landscape, adjusting his path whenever the steady beeping in his ears grew fainter, bringing it back to full level, focusing on that until he was aware of nothing else. The Universe consisted only of that sound and his forward motion.

He didn't know how long it took before he reached the first building, but when he did, time and space became real again. Exhausted and sick, he quickened his pace as much he could to get to the shuttle hangar. He pulled the wide doors open, entered the building, and climbed into the shuttle.

He powered up the controls, and they hummed to life with a satisfying sound. He engaged the engines, eased the shuttle off the ground and out the hangar doors, across the boulder field toward the runway. He would get his brother, then leave.

His head began to buzz. "Stay conscious, damn it!" he said, trying to shake it off.

He heard the energy beam slice through the night behind him, heard the explosions that destroyed the first building, and then the next. He felt the first shock wave shake his vehicle. The Shadows had found Site 13. What about his brother?

He heard the voice again.

"Go!"

The aft monitors showed the silhouette of a Shadow vessel against another explosion. Barely conscious of what he was doing, Marcus ordered full acceleration and sped away straight and low across the landscape.

He couldn't afford to waste any more fuel. He said a silent good-bye to his brother, and brought the shuttle into a climb through Arisia's atmosphere and out into space. His sensors detected no unusual energy readings. He saw no Shadow ships. There was nothing to see but the expanding cloud of debris that had been his mining colony.

"Computer, set course for jump gate. Engage and maintain. Emergency procedure three." Marcus took one last look at Arisia on the monitors. Strange red-and-orange lights glowed brightly in the lower atmosphere in various places on the surface.

He released himself from the console chair, floated up in the zero G, and pulled himself over to the medical station. He wrestled his pressure suit helmet off, pulled out a hypo of antiradiation serum, and injected it into his upper shoulder.

Then he lost consciousness.

CHAPTER 18

HE was being lifted onto a gurney and rushed down a corridor. Was this Arisia? Was he back at the IP? He would have to get word to Hasina, apologize for missing dinner. Where was his brother?

"Take him to Medlab 3," said a male voice.

Oh, God. Marcus remembered. He had left his brother behind in the fires of Hell itself.

"William!"

"You're going to be okay," said the voice. Who was it? Who was speaking to him when they were dead, all of them were dead? Where was he?

He couldn't focus his eyes—couldn't see anything but shadows moving in and out of his field of vision. Shadows. He started to struggle, tried to get away. Powerful hands held him down, then immobilized him. He heaved against the restraints, tried to break them, to get free.

"William!" he called out again. His brother was injured. Why weren't they helping him?

"Tranquilizer!"

He felt the hypo on his arm, the hiss and then the tingling as the medication penetrated the skin. He sank back, floating gently as the voices continued around him, fragments of meaning penetrating the haze, then skittering away.

A male voice. *Dr. Hobbs, over here.* A female voice. *What happened?* The voices mixed and overlapped. *We're not sure—ore freighter found him—alone on a shuttle—radiation poisoning—some kind of accident—Q-40 mining operation—only survivor . . .*

"Marcus." Unlike the others, the voice was clear and strong. It was Will.

He tried to open his eyes, but couldn't. Yet, then somehow, he saw his brother. Wearing that stupid outfit.

"They killed you," Marcus tried to shout. "If you hadn't joined them, you'd still be alive."

"And you'd be dead," William said softly.

"God, why didn't I listen to you! Maybe if I'd listened to you it would be different."

His brother smiled at him. "It's not your fault. I love you, big brother. Remember your promise . . . ."

Then Marcus was spiraling downward, as searing pain shot through his body. A wave of nausea overwhelmed him and he began to throw up, retching violently.

"Keep him under!"

A hypo. The pain receded under a blanket of warm darkness and Marcus gratefully gave himself up to it, remembering nothing more.

"*Skydancer,* you're cleared for departure."

Docking Bay 7 of the UTC Ops ship opened to space, revealing the welcome sight of the planet Epsilon 3.

"Roger that, control," Sakai said as she piloted her ship through the open space doors. "*Skydancer* is now clear. I'm proceeding to Babylon 5. Thanks for everything."

"Roger. We'll see you again."

It was good to see the stars again, to be in space even if only for the short time it would take to reach the station from where the Ops ship had taken up its position. She had been ten days in hyperspace aboard the Ops ship, which had its own jump-point generator, leaving behind the jump gate she had put out of commission to await repairs.

Her UTC employers had been amazingly forgiving about what she had done—once she had explained everything. Don't worry about the jump gate, they had said, their insurance would pay for it. What she had done was quite understandable under the circumstances, although they did wonder if it had really been necessary to dump the *entire* contents of her sample bay. But it was her call, they said just a little reluctantly. Her reports and the other data she brought back *almost* made up for it. Good job, they had said.

But remember, they stressed again and again, she had an oath of confidentiality about her missions, and that included this encounter with aliens. They'd report it to the proper authorities on Earth; that was their job. She could just relax now and spend her commission. She shouldn't worry about it. *It was probably just a one-time encounter with some aliens no one will ever see again,* they said. *Happens in hyperspace. Happened to her at Sigma 957, hadn't it?*

What about the devastation at Ymir? she had asked.

They would investigate that thoroughly. But her first thought had probably been right, the original probe had probably malfunctioned. Ymir had probably always been like that. But they'd look into it.

She didn't really know what to believe, but it was

their call. Let them talk to Earth Central about it. She had a life to get back to, and it was waiting for her on Babylon 5.

"Babylon control. This is Earth survey ship *Skydancer* requesting permission to dock."

She didn't recognize the voice that answered. "Roger, *Skydancer*. Proceed to Berth 27. And welcome aboard."

She hadn't called Jeff from the Ops ship. She hated the thought of their first contact after so many months being by vidscreen. She wanted to see him and hear his voice unfiltered by electronics and distance, to feel his touch.

She maneuvered *Skydancer* into its berth, then stepped out into the pleasantly familiar customs area of Babylon 5. As she waited in line to present her identification, she strained to look over the crowd, trying to see if Jeff was there waiting for her, growing more and more disappointed as she failed to spot him.

"Identicard? Ms. Sakai!"

A security guard was standing in front of her. She had met him a couple of times. Zack Allen.

"Zack. It's nice to see you again."

"Welcome back. You going to be here long?"

"That all depends," she said with a laugh. "Do you know where I could find the commander?"

"Ivanova? She's in C and C—"

"No," interrupted Sakai, puzzled. "Commander Sinclair."

It was now Zack's turn to look puzzled—then astonished. "You don't know?"

"Know what?"

"He was transferred. Promoted, I guess you could say."

"What?" Sakai said. "Where?"

Zack was clearly uncomfortable at being the one to tell her this. "To Minbar. He's Earth's ambassador there."

A disconcerting sense of unreality separated Sakai from what Zack was saying. This didn't make any sense. "When did this happen?"

"About a day after you left. Sorry. I thought you knew."

"That's okay," she said slowly, taking her card back from Zack. "Thanks."

She moved off, merging with the crowd, headed for—where? She had planned to stay with Jeff, as she always did. She would have to get a room. No, first she had to find Garibaldi or Ivanova. Jeff must have left a message for her. As she tried to move as quickly as she could through the throng of people, it suddenly struck her how oddly empty the station seemed to her now.

Marcus was sitting up in his Medlab bed, feeling very impatient.

"Well, you're looking much better today." Dr. Lillian Hobbs had entered his small room. "How are you feeling?"

"Fine," Marcus replied, more curtly than he had intended. He liked Dr. Hobbs. She had saved his life, after all. But he was ready to claw through the thick metal walls to get out of there. "When can I be released?"

"Very soon," she said, glancing over his chart. "You're doing remarkably well, but we don't want to take any chances. You were a very sick man when you came in here: severe radiation poisoning, concussion, internal bleeding. You're lucky. If they had found you even a day later than they did, you wouldn't be sitting here. The best thing for now is rest and quiet."

"Lucky is hardly the word I'd use," Marcus said bitterly. He gestured toward the bedside computer monitor. "Can I at least have access to the station's library and media system? I can't get anything but the most boring music on this thing."

Dr. Hobbs was silent for a moment. "Do you remember what happened to you, Mr. Cole?"

He looked away. "All too well." Then a thought occurred, and he turned back to her. "Have you been trying to protect me from something?"

"ISN has been running a report on what happened."

"I have to see it," he said. "They can't be saying anything I don't already know. It's important, please."

She nodded wordlessly and left. He switched on the monitor sound down so he wouldn't have to hear another note of that irritating music, and waited. Why was it so important to see an ISN report on what had happened? He had lived through it, hadn't he? Was he looking for confirmation of what he remembered? Or did he hope to find some answers to who and why?

The screen went blank, and then up came a Babcom menu.

"Search ISN files for all reports containing key word Arisia, latest date first."

Within seconds, he was seeing that morning's ISN daily report.

"The Energy and Natural Resources Department today released more information on the tragic Arisia Mining Colony accident that left one hundred and fifty people presumed dead," the news anchor said, "with only one known survivor. Department investigators report that a design flaw in the colony's Orbital Refinery was the probable cause of the catastrophic explosion that destroyed both the refinery and the nearby Inhabitants' Platform. The company that built the refinery for Cole Mining went out of business last year, but former company executives vigorously deny that their system could be responsible for such an explosion unless a series of human mistakes was also involved."

My God, they don't know, Marcus thought. He would have to tell them what happened. Warn them. He hit the bedside call button, then decided not to wait. He got up to find Dr. Hobbs.

It had been a frustrating day. The first thing Sakai had done was try to talk to Chief Garibaldi, but he was not available. Then she tried contacting Ivanova, but she was not available. As a last resort, she tried to make an appointment with the new station commander, John Sheridan, but he was not available. She then tried to get hold of Ambassador Delenn, only to find out she was not available, either.

The absence of so many members of the command staff indicated something big was going on, but other than hearing some talk about problems with a group of aliens called the Striebs, she couldn't find out what. All it meant to Sakai was that she couldn't get the information she needed about what had happened to Jeff. So her next step had been to get a room where she could sit and read through her mail in case he had left something for her. As the station was unusually full at the moment, she ended up in a cramped room in one of the less desirable areas of the station. She didn't care. She locked the door and started through the mail.

After five months away, there was a lot of mail waiting for her, both paper and electronic. Among the stack of real mail was one letter from Jeff, dated January

Second. It was a short letter, written hurriedly before he had boarded the ship for Earth. It said only that he had been recalled to Earth and didn't know why, but that he loved her and wanted to at least leave this message for her in case something unexpected happened. And that was it.

She turned to her computer mail, scanning the list of over two hundred messages, but again found only one message listed as being from J. Sinclair, that also dated January, less than two weeks after the other letter. It had been sent from Earth, right before Jeff had boarded the ship to Minbar, and had said essentially the same thing: that he had been assigned to Minbar as ambassador, that he would try to send her a longer message once there, and that he loved her.

That was it. No other contact from him once he reached Minbar. She didn't know what to make of it. If her long years as a surveyor had taught her anything, however, it was not to jump to conclusions without sufficient facts.

She left the other messages for later, and turned instead to search the news files. Certainly the first ambassador to Minbar was big news and would have created quite a stir. She began viewing the reports in chronological order, and at first was surprised at the relative paucity of information she found. It almost seemed as if Earth Central was deliberately playing down the importance of Sinclair's obviously historic appointment.

As she continued, the stories took on a more disturbing tone. Reports quoting government sources suggested some impropriety in what Ambassador Sinclair was doing on Minbar, building in fervor until one story quoted a senator calling Sinclair a traitor.

It was outrageous, all of it! She was furious at what she read, and deeply puzzled. What was going on? And why hadn't Jeff tried to leave word for her? There was a good explanation, and she would find it.

She opened every piece of real mail, but found nothing. Then she returned to her electronic mail to read every piece, no matter who it was listed as being from. It was late in the evening before she finally opened a short message, return address listed only as B5, dated from two months before, and unsigned.

> *No matter what anyone says, please come and I'll explain everything. Please don't decide anything until then.*

Marcus had been batted around like a badminton shuttlecock, from bureaucrat to bureaucrat to bureaucrat at the Department of Energy and Natural Resources, and was ready to go through the screen at whatever indifferent civil servant was next when Assistant Director Esperanza appeared.

This was somebody with at least some authority, Marcus knew. He launched into his story, growing more and more detailed as Esperanza listened with what seemed to be sympathetic interest. He told Esperanza everything he could remember and what little he knew about the Shadows; everything *except* the part about the Rangers, remembering at the last moment that his brother had requested that be kept secret. He wasn't sure why it had been so important to his brother, but he respected the wish.

When he finished, Esperanza nodded seriously, then asked: "Have you told anyone else about this, there at Babylon 5?"

"No. It didn't occur to me to do so. This is the Energy Department's jurisdiction."

"You made the right decision, Mr. Cole. Let me compliment you on how clearheaded you are about all this, especially after such a terrible tragedy. Nothing will ever compensate you for the losses you have suffered, but we can at least expedite your insurance payment. You must be strapped for funds right now."

"That's true," Marcus said. "But what about—"

"If you'll activate your printout, my office has already uploaded a form for you. Take a moment to read it over, then sign it and put it back in the scanner. An account will be created for you there on Babylon 5 with your full refund by tomorrow morning."

This was moving a little too fast and not at all in the direction Marcus had expected. But he got the printout and read it.

"This says Arisia Colony was lost to an industrial accident," Marcus said on finishing. "By signing this, I'm agreeing that's what happened. But I've just told you that's not what happened."

"Mr. Cole, your doctor on Babylon 5 says you arrived in a feverish, delirious state, suffering from severe radiation poisoning. Is it possible your memories of these aliens are only nightmares you suffered while you were ill? It would be perfectly understandable."

"No," said Marcus firmly. "My brother did not die from my fever-induced nightmares. I know the difference between nightmares and what I saw. And I know the government has been getting reports on these aliens from other people as well."

"Those reports haven't reached my desk, Mr. Cole," Esperanza said. "But perhaps you're right. You seem like a levelheaded man to me. I'll pass on what you've said to the investigators. But in the meantime, nothing is harmed by signing this insurance claim. You do need the money, do you not?"

"Yes, but—"

"If you're worried about liability, you'll see that the document assigns absolutely no blame or culpability to you."

It didn't feel right to Marcus. It had all the earmarks of a bribe to keep him quiet. But he did need the money.

"Do you have any idea when I can return to Arisia?" Marcus asked, partly to stall for time to think, and partly because to him it was a very important question.

"Not for some time, Mr. Cole. With the recent outbreak of the war between the Narns and the Centauri, the whole area has been placed under government jurisdiction. It's off-limits to all nonauthorized personnel."

"I need to bring back my brother's body. He died on the planet."

"Oh, I see," Esperanza said with great sympathy. "In that case, I assure you I'll report this to the investigators and insist they make recovering your brother's body a top priority. You will be notified immediately when that happens."

Marcus had hit a wall. The truth was, Will's body had probably been incinerated in the Shadow attack on Site 13. He had wanted to go back, just to be sure, but more and more he was realizing that wasn't what Will would have wanted him to do. The more he talked to Esperanza, the more he began to think that maybe Will had been right about everything. Marcus had to find out for himself—and keep his promise to his brother to go to Minbar. To do that, he would need a lot of money.

Under the smiling visage of the assistant director, Marcus took the forms and signed them.

"This Narn-Centauri war has everything in an uproar," said Sakai's UTC contact, who had unexpectedly contacted her early in the morning, "but it's going to be good for business, I'll tell you that."

Sakai took the cold-blooded statement in stride. She was no longer surprised at how the corporate men at UTC thought.

"So, it looks like we've got a job lined up for you much faster than we thought."

"I'm afraid I can't accept it," Sakai said. "In fact, I'll be unavailable for any work for a couple of months at least."

"Why?"

"I hope to be getting married."

The UTC man frowned. "I assumed that was off."

"Why would you assume that?" Sakai asked evenly.

"Well, because, Sinclair . . . I mean . . . isn't he on Minbar?"

"That's what the papers say."

"Listen, Sakai, I like you, and I think we've worked well together, so I hope you won't mind me saying something a little personal here. A continued association with Ambassador Sinclair might not be seen as a mark in your favor at corporate headquarters, if you know what I mean."

"No," she said coldly. "I don't know what you mean."

"UTC is a very image-conscious corporation, and Sinclair isn't exactly someone they would want associated with the corporate name right now, being so closely tied to the Minbari—"

"Thanks for the advice," she said curtly. "Don't expect to hear from me anytime soon." She cut the communication. Day two on Babylon 5 was starting out wonderfully, already burning one important bridge before breakfast.

Getting to Minbar was the only thing that mattered

right now. She would have preferred dealing with Delenn or Lennier, but they both seemed to be gone from the station at the moment. Perhaps someone at the offices of the Minbari Embassy could help.

The Minbari who appeared on her screen was not familiar to her. *Here goes nothing,* she thought.

"I'm glad I found somebody in," she said. "I'm Catherine Sakai, Ambassador Jeffrey Sinclair's fiancée. I need to obtain a travel permit to Minbar for my ship, as soon as possible."

"Yes, I am familiar with the name," said the Minbari, "And I have been instructed by the ambassador's office to tell you that the ambassador is not available, and that it would be best for you not to come to Minbar at this time. Good day to you."

The screen went blank.

"Like hell," she said angrily. There was nothing like a chorus of people she didn't trust telling her not to do something she wanted to do for strengthening her resolve to do that very thing.

Once again her comline buzzed. Who wanted to bring her more joy now?

"Yes?"

Chief Garibaldi appeared on the screen. "Catherine, hello. Sorry it took so long to get back to you. We're having a little trouble around here."

"Am I glad to see you," Sakai said.

"Listen, I don't have a lot of time," Garibaldi said, "but I bet you want to get to Minbar immediately. Come by my office and we'll get you on your way."

CHAPTER 19

THE City of Sorrows didn't have a spaceport, so Catherine Sakai landed at the port in Yedor. She left *Skydancer* in a hangar that had already been reserved for her by Ambassador Delenn. It seemed she and Garibaldi had been preparing for Sakai's return to Babylon 5 for some time, and when she had walked into Garibaldi's office, he handed her a waiting packet with everything she would need, including a filed flight plan to Minbar and special visitor documentation signed by Delenn that caused her to be whisked through customs without a pause. She then found that transportation to Tuzanor was waiting for her.

Now she stood outside the modest embassy building—if such a word could be used for dwellings carved out of large rock mounds and pillars—which was easily identifiable by the discreet Earth Alliance flag hanging flat against the front wall. She was unaccountably nervous. Garibaldi had assured her that Sinclair couldn't wait to see her, even though he had not actually spoken to Sinclair since his departure from Babylon 5. She'd had enough hard lessons in life not to count on anything, especially the things she wanted the most.

Just then a group of seven Humans and two Minbari

were ushered out of the embassy by two other Humans dressed in identical, very distinctive clothing.

It's now or never, she told herself, and entered the building. She found herself in a small antechamber facing a rather stern-looking religious-caste Minbari.

"I'm Catherine Sakai. I'm here to see the ambassador."

She knew a stunned look when she saw one, even on a Minbari trying to hide his reaction. She remembered what the Minbari on B5 had said about "the ambassador's *office*" not wanting her to come, and suddenly decided not to wait for this Minbari's reply. She headed immediately for the closed door behind him.

"I'll just let myself in, thanks." She was past him before he could stand. She opened the door and strode quickly into the room, the Minbari now behind her frantically trying to stop her.

Jeffrey Sinclair was sitting at a desk, wearing clothes similar to what she had seen on the two Humans outside, and was in the middle of dictating notes to his computer when the commotion caused him to look up. The Minbari behind her fell silent.

"Hi, Jeff. I got your message."

He rose to his feet, astonishment on his face. "My God! Catherine!" He looked past her to the Minbari. "It's all right, Venak. Thank you."

The Minbari departed silently as Sinclair came quickly around his desk. Smiling broadly, he took her in his arms and kissed her. For a moment, all her fears and doubts vanished.

He asked her a flurry of questions, and she told him in brief outline the path she had taken to get here. He reacted with dismay when she finished with a description of her alien encounter in hyperspace.

"You know about these aliens, don't you?" she asked.

"All too well."

He took her right hand in both of his hands and kissed it, then just gazed at her for a long moment, as if he didn't know what to say next, or was afraid to say it, the silence slowly becoming awkward.

"You look tired," she said.

"I've had trouble sleeping ever since I got here. And they keep me pretty busy."

"Is it still the dreams?" she asked with concern.

He nodded, then tried to laugh it off. "They've become quite—colorful since I arrived here. I've learned to live with them."

She squeezed his hand, then looked around the spartan office. "So this is where you spend most of your time, Ambassador?"

Sinclair laughed again, more genuinely this time. "No, no. I'm here only once or twice a week. Come on, I have so much to tell you. Let me show you everything."

In a torrent of words, like a man relieved to finally unburden himself, he told her of the Minbari, of the Shadows, of prophecy, of Valen, of the Rangers. Sakai asked an occasional question, but mostly she listened and watched, trying to take everything in and understand it. He piloted them in a small flyer from Tuzanor to the plateau that held the Ranger compound, taking a few turns first around the city, then probably one or two more turns than was necessary around the plateau before landing. He obviously enjoyed being in a pilot's seat even if only for a short distance in a low-powered craft.

He showed her every inch of the Ranger compound, and introduced her to everyone they came across, all of whom—Minbari and Human alike—bowed to him and treated him with great reverence, which he seemed barely to notice as he spoke to each of them with great openness.

They ended the tour at his quarters, a stone structure that he said was almost a thousand years old. She noted as they entered that Sinclair had somehow already managed to get her luggage delivered here from the Transport Center. He gave her a quick walk through the place, ending back in the front sitting room.

"The only person to live here before me was Valen himself. So it's almost like new," Sinclair said with a grin. "Not such a bad place to live, is it?"

"It's a lot more comfortable than I would've thought," she said.

There was another awkward silence.

"So what do you think of . . . everything?" He looked at her with such a mixture of hope and apprehension, she was almost afraid to reply.

"It's a little overwhelming," she said, sitting down. He sat in a chair opposite her. "I've never met a Second Coming before. The Second Coming of Valen."

She meant it as a joke, but he responded with intense seriousness. "And you haven't yet. I'm not even the official Entil'Zha yet. Just Ranger One. Just Jeffrey Sinclair."

"It must be kind of hard living in Valen's shadow, though," she said, but thought, *Damn it. Why am I avoiding the real issue?*

He looked at her for a moment, as if he were thinking the same thing himself, but answered her question instead.

"No, not really, not when you understand who

Valen really was. I've had a lot of time to read about his life, although there's a lot more legend than credible history. What's worse, the military caste and the religious caste have two separate sets of sometimes contradictory legends about his life. But the real Valen comes through if you read carefully, and I find I kind of empathize with him. He was just a military leader who was deified in the centuries afterward. He warned his people against doing that, but his life became so couched in legend, even during his lifetime, that it was almost inevitable."

"But most military leaders don't end up with that kind of legend," said Sakai. "He had to have been somebody extraordinary."

"True, he wasn't only a military leader," said Sinclair. "He was something of a social revolutionary, as well. That's where I feel sorry for the guy; much of what he advocated has simply been ignored or reinterpreted to serve individual prejudices."

"Wait a minute," Sakai said. "Is this the same Valen that created the Minbari caste system? I never thought that was a particularly noble act."

"No, Valen didn't create the caste system. That's another myth. It existed long before he came along. He just reorganized it, elevating the worker caste to full equality with the religious and military castes. And he said it was only to be a step toward abolishing the caste system altogether. Sometimes I wonder if he were alive today, if he would despair that so much of what he dedicated his life to was in vain. But I don't like to think of him as a man who would give in to despair. I'd like to think he'd just roll up his sleeves and try again. Maybe that's why the Minbari look for his return someday. They recognize that much of his work is still unfinished. They hope he'll come back and help them complete it.''

''But now they've got you.''

He stopped, shook his head as if irritated. He looked into her eyes intently. ''Why are we talking about the past? I want to talk about the future. Our future. That is, if we have one.'' He got up and walked across the room, came halfway back.

''When you agreed to marry me, you were agreeing to marry an Earthforce officer, based on a space station, with every expectation of eventually returning to Earth to live, maybe raise a family. You never agreed to all of this,'' he said with a gesture, indicating everything around him, inside the house and out, ''especially since I don't even know what this will lead to. I've made a commitment to see this through. It's important work. But I won't hold you to your commitment to marry me if this is not something you can live with. Everything has changed since we last saw each other, I know that. Everything but this: I still love you. I still need you. And I still want you to marry me, because I know we can still build a life together, here on Minbar, or wherever this thing takes us. But it's up to you.''

Sinclair was still standing in the middle of the room, with a look of uncertainty she knew was probably on her face as well. Sakai had arrived on Minbar to find her fiancé, a man who as far as she knew had simply been made an ambassador, and who she had worried might be having second thoughts about marrying her. She had found instead a clandestine military leader, dressed in Minbari clothes, treated like some kind of priest-king, being groomed by the Minbari apparently for the status of legend.

And suddenly she had been the one with the second thoughts as she tried to comprehend what she was seeing and hearing. Now she realized that her hesitation had come from only one thing: she needed to know that the overwhelming change in the life of the man she loved hadn't fundamentally changed him into someone she no longer knew.

Looking up into Sinclair's eyes, she saw that it hadn't. Whatever the Minbari and the Rangers thought of him, this was still the man she had known since the Academy and had left behind at Babylon 5.

She went to him. "No way I'm leaving you again, Jeffrey Sinclair." She reached up to kiss him, only the second time since she had gone into his office in Tuzanor. He took her into his arms, and it was a long moment before he let her go again.

"What kind of ceremony should we have?" she asked him. "Minbari?"

"Oh, no," he said, "the simpler the better, and *not* a Minbari ceremony. I've already been through their little rebirth/marriage ceremony, remember? No little red fruit for me this time. They taste horrible. Besides, I always had the uneasy feeling I'd gotten married somehow in that ceremony, but don't know to whom!"

She laughed. "I'd hate to think I was marrying a bigamist."

"Come on," he said. "Let's get your stuff into the bedroom."

"There's certainly plenty of room," she said as she helped him lug everything out of the sitting room. "It's pretty sparse in here."

Sinclair sighed. "You've no idea how hard I've tried to get at least some of my things sent here."

"Where is it all?"

"Some of it's apparently still tied up in a government warehouse somewhere, and the rest is with my brother."

"How is Malcolm?"

"Fine. I guess. I've only been able to get through to him once. I know he's tried, but he apparently hasn't been able to cut through the red tape to send me anything. It's not that I need a lot of stuff around me—"

"No," she said, kissing him again. "You've always put more emphasis on your life inside here." She tapped him lightly on the forehead.

"Comes from growing up as a military brat," he agreed. "When you've moved as much as I have, you learn to make do with fewer things, but those few things then have a greater value to you. And I would like to have some of them here. Besides, it has become the principle of the thing."

"Well, I can't help you with that, but I did bring a few things with me." She reached into one bag and drew out a brightly wrapped package. "I missed your birthday out on the Rim, so happy belated birthday!"

"What is it?" he said.

"Why do people always ask that?" She handed him the package. "Open it and find out."

He ripped through the paper and took out a commercially packaged AV data crystal and bound book. "*Frontiers of Laughter,*" he read off the package. "*A Twenty-four-Hour History of North American Comedy*. This is wonderful!" He immediately went to his office to look at it.

"I remember you said you'd sent your only copy to Malcolm and never got another one for yourself," Sakai said.

The opening credits came up on the console screen, but Sinclair quickly programmed it to jump to a specific sequence in a later episode. A scene from an old, black-and-white twentieth century television show flickered on the screen, then an older woman discussing it from an academic point of view. A line at the bottom of the screen identified her as ''Gemma Gildea Sinclair, Professor of North American Literature.''

''My mother really loved these shows,'' he said, intently watching as more scenes from twentieth and twenty-first-century television comedies came up. ''She wrote scholarly papers and books about them, but watched them for pure entertainment. As a boy, I just didn't get it. What could she possibly see in those antiquated old shows, I thought. I don't think I really understood until I was an adult and saw her on this documentary talking about it. God, I miss—''

He turned off the program, just staring at the blank screen for a moment. ''I miss a lot of things—and people,'' he said, rousing himself. ''But that's life, ever moving forward.''

''I'm sorry,'' she started to say.

''No,'' he said smiling. ''Thank you. It really is a wonderful gift. As you can see, I didn't bring much in the way of entertainment with me.''

Sakai walked over to his bookshelf, and pulled down the only two books she saw written in English. ''Marcus Aurelius? Don't you have this memorized by now?'' she asked, putting that volume back. She took the other book and let it fall naturally open, not surprised to see it opening to Tennyson's poem, ''Ulysses.''

''Honestly, Jeff,'' she teased, ''out of all the wonderful poetry in here, is this the only one you read?''

He took the book out of her hand in mock indignation and put it up on the shelf. ''I'll have you know I have almost every other poem in there committed to memory by now.''

''But somehow the book just happens to be creased

permanently open to 'Ulysses,' " she continued to tease him.

"I'll admit, since coming to Minbar I've been reading and listening to it just a little more than usual."

"I guess if we're going to get married, it's time I was brutally honest with you," she said jokingly. "I never much cared for that poem. I think it's rather insulting to Penelope—calling her 'the old wife' and implying that Ulysses is thinking of taking off with his mates and leaving her behind."

Sinclair took her in his arms again. "Oh, no. Not after everything they went through to get back together again. He left her behind once and made a vow he would never make that mistake again." He leaned down and kissed her gently, then continued. "When he takes off to 'sail beyond the sunset' to 'seek a newer world,' you can be sure this time Penelope will sail with him. That I promise you."

He drew her even closer and kissed her again, longer and with more urgency.

"I don't know if Tennyson would agree with you," she said between kisses.

Sinclair smiled. "To hell with Tennyson." He picked her up and carried her across the room toward the bedroom.

"You know I hate it when you do this," she said, only half kidding.

"I was afraid we were going to analyze poetry all night." He put her down on the bed. "I thought it would be better to make our own poetry."

"Oh, God!" she said laughing. "If only those Minbari who treat you with such awe and reverence knew how corny you can be."

"That's exactly why I need you here," he said, kissing her again. "It gets a little tedious being treated like some kind of saint in a religious pageant. It doesn't mean a damn if there's no one to talk to, if there's no one who knows you and loves you for who you really are.''

''Someone who will be excruciatingly honest with you,'' she said teasingly. ''Keep you from believing your own press releases.''

Sinclair laughed. ''God knows you've never had a problem doing that. One of the many reasons I love you.''

''Well, are we going to talk all night?'' she said. ''Or are we going to make some poetry here.''

Sinclair smiled and didn't say another word.

CHAPTER 20

"MITCHELL! Break off! Break off!"

"Not like this! Not like this! If I'm going out, I'm taking you bastards with me . . ."

"Who are you? Why are you doing this?"

"The council will render its verdict."

Delenn. Rathenn. Racine. Jenimer. Neroon. Turval. Venak.

Kosh. Ulkesh.

Valen.

The legendary Minbari stood alone in a circle of light.

How did he know it was Valen? He tried to focus on him, could not clearly see him. But he knew who it was.

Valen held up a Triluminary, its center stone glowing.

Valen held a mirror. Sinclair looked into the mirror—and the Human Jeffrey Sinclair peered back at him. He looked up to ask Valen—but the Minbari was gone.

He saw Ulkesh. And Kosh.

"You are what we say."

"Do not forget who you truly are."

"Jeff!"

It was Catherine's voice. He turned, saw her standing just outside the circle of light, half obscured in shadow. He went to her, wanted to hold her—but she shrank back from him, bewilderment in her face. What was wrong? He suddenly knew. He reached up, felt the Minbari bone crest growing out of his head.

"No!"

"Jeff! Jeff! It's all right. Jeff."

Sinclair thrashed out, struggled to come awake. He felt hands trying to hold him, a voice trying to calm him.

"Everything's all right. It's just a dream."

Catherine's voice. He opened his eyes to find her looking at him with great concern. He shivered, and pulled her close to him.

"I'm sorry," he said.

"Nothing to apologize for," she said, stroking his forehead to brush back a lock of tangled hair. "Must have been a hell of a dream."

"Oh, just the usual."

She wasn't buying the light tone. "They really have gotten worse, haven't they? Is it like this every night?"

"No, not every night. I'll go days without remembering any dreams at all."

"Do you want to talk about it?"

"No, I think I've had enough of it for one night." He kissed her. "Besides, it's almost time to get up."

"What do you mean?" She looked around at the darkened room. "It can't possibly be!"

"It's almost dawn."

"I just fell asleep," she protested.

"You've got to start getting used to these shorter Minbari days. Otherwise, it plays havoc with your sense of time."

As they got ready for the day, Sinclair reflected on how much he had missed this, simply performing the mundane tasks of daily life with the one he loved beside him. Sakai came out of the bathroom, and stopped short, sniffing the air. "Is that—bacon, I smell?"

Sinclair grinned. "We try to supplement the home-grown Minbari food with some Human food. Bacon is one of the harder things to get—don't have it more than once or twice a month, if we're lucky. But I made sure it was on the menu this morning."

When they got to the dining area, breakfast was already laid out, and the Minbari staff gone.

"Sorry the eggs are only *temshwee* eggs."

"That's fine." She poked at them a little dubiously. "I've always wanted to try them. They're considered real delicacies." She looked up and smiled at him. "It all looks great, really. Both the Minbari and Human food. Certainly better than the food I ate for five months on the Rim. Maybe even a little better than what I ate on Babylon 5."

"You know," he said, digging into his own food, "We never really got a chance to talk much about how things are on the station."

"It's hard to say. I wasn't there very long, but from what I could see, everything was in an uproar. Never could reach Ivanova, and I don't think Delenn was even on the station."

"Really? That's odd," Sinclair said. "What about Captain Sheridan. Did you get a chance to talk with him at all?"

"No. I got the impression he wasn't on the station, either. What do you think of Sheridan? I've heard conflicting things about him."

"He's a good officer. What have you heard that's bad?"

"Nothing specific," she said. "He's supposed to be something of a gung-ho superpatriot and jarhead, not really suited for a diplomatic post."

"Some have said the same about me."

"So you're saying it's not true about him either?"

"There's a lot more to the guy than you might think reading the propaganda that was written during and after the war."

"You were at the Academy at the same time, weren't you?"

"For one year," Sinclair laughed. "But I don't judge him by *that*."

Sakai looked at him quizzically.

"I never told you that story, did I?" he asked. "I met Sheridan during my first year at the Academy. He was an upperclassman. I made the unfortunate mistake of getting his attention by spilling a tray of food on him—don't ask. Since I was just a plebe, and it's every upperclassman's duty to haze plebes, he dedicated his last year at the Academy to making my life a living hell. When he finally graduated, and I was no longer a plebe, I got as drunk in celebration as I have ever been in my life, before or since.

"Well, we ran across each other a couple of times after that, during the war and right after, but only briefly each time. We were professional toward each other, two officers doing their jobs. I didn't really get to know him until the food riots on Mars. I hadn't been stationed there very long when the rioting broke out. I was trying to get back to my base without getting killed, but I was in an unfamiliar area of town, and with the power out and fire and smoke all around me, I wasn't sure which way to turn. So I picked the nearest alley, hoping to escape the rioters' attention, and ran right into four rioters and an Earthforce officer having a very spirited discussion, which the officer was losing. I didn't get a look at the man's face; I just saw a fellow officer in trouble, and jumped in to help. The two of us were able to win the argument and the four rioters hobbled away for reinforcements. It was only then I realized the officer was none other than my nemesis from the Academy, John Sheridan. Anyway, sticking around seemed like a poor idea, and Sheridan said he knew a bar that would be safe, where we could call to check in with our respective bases. So we made our way there, but then couldn't leave until things quieted down outside. We got to talking, finally got to know each other. I discovered he was a pretty decent guy. He even apologized, just a little, for the Academy. I haven't seen him since, but I'm confident he's not the martinet and puppet that President Clark probably hoped he would be."

"Just as you aren't the somber, serious mystic these Minbari think you are."

"Hey," Sinclair protested. "I possess gravitas. Father Raffelli told me that back in high school."

"Was that before or after you masterminded the disassembly of his speedboat and had it reassembled around the top spire of the church?"

"Before," Sinclair conceded.

A knock on the door interrupted further discussion. Sinclair found a bowing Minbari Ranger sent to summon him to a meeting.

"Anything wrong?" Sakai asked him when he returned to the dining area.

"Someone's called an early morning meeting. It could be anything. I'll be back soon." He kissed her and left.

* * *

When Sinclair entered the conference room, Rathenn was speaking in a low urgent tone with Jenimer. The Minbari leader looked drawn and in pain, and clearly should have been somewhere else resting. Ulkesh stood motionless at the back of the room.

"Chosen One," Sinclair said with a slight bow, "I wasn't informed you'd be here today."

"I have distressing news," Jenimer said. "Without my consultation or consent, the Grey Council has removed Delenn as Satai, and replaced her on the council with Neroon."

Sinclair was stunned. "Can they do that? Is that legal?"

"They have done it, and apparently care nothing for the finer points of custom, precedent, or law."

"But Neroon is military caste," said Sinclair. "That will give the military four seats and the religious caste only two. Valen himself decreed that each caste must have three members on the council."

"The military caste," Rathenn said bitterly, "no longer heeds any voice but that of their own ambition and hatred."

"The consequences of this action," Jenimer continued, sounding more and more tired, "will be far-ranging and unpredictable. I do not know how it will affect our work here, but I promise you, I will do everything within my power to protect you and your Rangers."

"I've never had any doubt of that, Chosen One," said Sinclair. Jenimer's ailing appearance had suddenly made Sinclair want to express his appreciation toward this kind and remarkable Minbari, even as he tried to shake off the feeling he might never have another chance. "You've been a good friend. Not only to the Rangers as a whole, but to me, personally. For that I want to thank you."

Sinclair had wanted to say more, but it seemed to be enough for Jenimer who smiled, obviously very pleased.

In the short silence that followed, Sinclair wondered if the meeting was over until Ulkesh, who had stood motionless until then, turned slightly toward the Minbari leader. Jenimer's smile faded.

''I fear there is another matter to discuss,'' Jenimer said unhappily. ''The presence of Ms. Sakai . . .''

''It is not acceptable,'' said Ulkesh in his harsh, synthesized voice.

Sinclair folded his arms and his eyes narrowed in anger, but otherwise he kept his cool. ''The Vorlon ambassador is a valuable ally,'' he said evenly. ''But my personal life is none of his concern.''

''You are the arrow and must not be deflected.''

''Get this straight, Ambassador,'' Sinclair said in a dangerously calm voice. ''I'm not just some unthinking tool for you to use any way you want.''

''There is concern,'' Jenimer said carefully, ''that your ability to concentrate fully on the task—''

''Will not be in the least bit compromised by the presence of Ms. Sakai,'' Sinclair said. He looked back at Ulkesh. ''After all this time, do you really have so little faith in me? If so, you'd better tell me now.''

The Vorlon turned and glided out of the room.

CHAPTER 21

I'M here, Will, thought Marcus Cole, *just as I promised. But understand, little brother, if this Sinclair and the Rangers aren't what you assumed them to be . . .*

He let the thought trail off, and looked around the small windowless room instead. Three other men and two women sat as he did on three stone benches, while one Minbari male and one woman, both dressed in Ranger uniforms, stood near the only door. The woman would occasionally leave, then reappear to speak in a low voice to her Minbari comrade. They had been waiting about forty minutes in the room, which had become uncomfortably warm and stuffy. Marcus shifted impatiently and wondered again if he wasn't making the mistake of his life by being here.

He had arrived on Minbar two days before, sure that he would feel more than just a little uneasy being on the homeworld of Earth's former enemies, surrounded by Minbari. To his great surprise, he found himself quite taken by the physical beauty of the place and charmed by the polite Minbari he had encountered, though he had quickly learned to steer clear of the military caste.

Immediately upon arrival, he'd wasted no time in seeking out the Earth Embassy office in Tuzanor, which helpful Minbari on the ancient stone streets were more than happy to direct him toward. He had asked for an appointment with Ambassador Sinclair, said he wanted to inquire about the Rangers, and had given his name. He was given an appointment for the next day. It was only then that he had realized he hadn't bothered to arrange for a place to stay the night. When he inquired about hotels, the Minbari Embassy aide wrote down an address for him.

He found it was a small private residence. Sure a mistake had been made, he went to the front door to make another inquiry about hotels, but was immediately welcomed inside by the Minbari family and told he could stay the night in a small guest room.

He did not sleep well, and morning came unexpectedly soon. The breakfast they offered him was mostly inedible. Nevertheless, he was grateful for their generosity and had tried to pay them, which they refused.

Now here he sat, hot, tired, and growing a little cranky.

"Is it going to be much longer?" he said suddenly, his voice sounding startlingly loud in the oppressive silence.

The Human Ranger looked at him blandly, but the Minbari Ranger seemed almost amused. Neither one of them replied.

After a moment, Marcus tried again. "Then I have another question for you." Now his benchmates reacted a bit nervously. The Human Ranger whispered something to the Minbari Ranger and left.

"Do we know in what order we will be seeing the ambassador?" Marcus continued. "Because if I'm at the end of the group, I'll take a walk and come back later."

"You will not be seeing the ambassador individually," the Minbari said in unaccented English.

Marcus found this more irritating than he knew he should. "I was told to expect an individual appointment, not some kind of cattle call."

"And who told you that?" asked the Minbari.

Marcus hesitated briefly. Was he supposed to say? "My brother," he said finally.

The Minbari looked at him intently. "What is your name?"

"Marcus Cole."

Surprise flickered in the Ranger's eyes.

"Was your brother William?"

"Yes."

The Minbari started to say something, then seemed to change his mind. "The ambassador used to conduct individual meetings, but regretfully no longer has the time. If you are with us long enough, you will eventually have the honor to meet with him individually."

Marcus was on the verge of responding sarcastically, but was interrupted by the reappearance of the woman Ranger.

"Ambassador Sinclair has been delayed," she said, "and sends his apologies. You may leave to walk about the city, if you wish. Please return in an hour, when you hear the central tower bells ringing."

Marcus stood with the others, and started to leave. But as the others filed out, the Minbari Ranger stopped him.

"I am Inesval," he said. "It is a great pleasure to meet you. William was a good friend. I am deeply sorry for your loss. William is very much missed by all of us."

Marcus felt some of his earlier pique drain away. "Thank you," he said quietly.

"William spoke of you often," Inesval continued. "He proposed his mission to see you on the basis of providing us with Q-40, but I knew that equally important to him was the chance to ask you to join us. I am very happy you have come.''

Marcus was caught unprepared for the wave of grief that overcame him. He had managed to repress it for so long in his focus to get to Minbar. He had not counted on how difficult it would be to meet these people who had been Will's friends, or to hear how his brother had talked about him.

''Perhaps, I might walk with you,'' said Inesval gently, ''while we wait.''

''Why not?'' was all Marcus could manage to say.

The fresh air helped steady Marcus's mood. He realized Inesval was waiting for him to speak. ''You know, you're nothing like the other warrior-caste Minbari I've met. No offense,'' Marcus added quickly.

''No offense taken,'' Inesval said with a laugh. ''I'm worker caste. Or I was. Now I'm a Ranger.''

''Sorry, I just assumed—''

''You'll find very few military caste among the Rangers. Mainly religious and worker. Most military would not pledge themselves to a Human.''

''And you would?''

''I like Humans. Some of your people who come to Minbar seem to want to drop their Human ways, and act only Minbari. I don't understand that. There is much to admire in your ways of doing things. But I'm not typical of most Minbari, I should warn you of that. Maybe I have a Human soul that got lost somehow, and ended up on Minbar.''

Marcus couldn't tell if he was joking or not, with that last remark. ''How did you end up joining the Rangers?''

''I had the honor of meeting Ambassador Sinclair shortly after he arrived. I perceived immediately that what was whispered about him was true—he possesses an extraordinary soul."

"And you Minbari can tell that by just looking at a man?" said Marcus skeptically.

"Can't you?"

"I don't believe there is such a thing as a soul," said Marcus.

"Then how do you judge a person?"

"By his actions."

"Then we are not that different," nodded Inesval. "So judge for yourself what kind of person our Anla'shok Na is. You say you have met members of our warrior caste. Would you say they appear to be a fearful group?"

"It's my impression they don't fear much of anything."

"They fear Jeffrey Sinclair," said Inesval. "It is said he is the only Human they have ever feared."

"Why?"

"Many reasons. He was one of your most successful fighter pilots during the war, killing many Minbari in one-to-one combat. The military entered the war believing that was impossible, and ended the war unable to explain away such losses except as Human treachery or luck."

"But there were a few other successful fighter pilots," said Marcus. "Why fixate on Sinclair?"

"There is more. We Minbari are much stronger than Humans. No Minbari warrior was ever defeated during the war by a Human in any physical confrontation. I do not say this to boast. It is a simple physiological fact."

"No argument from me," said Marcus. "Go on."

"But it is said that Jeffrey Sinclair has twice defeated Minbari warriors during direct, physical confrontations, no weapons involved. The first time, it is said a member of the military caste tried to frame Sinclair for an attack on the new Vorlon ambassador to Babylon 5, and when that failed, the warrior attacked Sinclair, only to be defeated by him.''

''They sure don't tell you everything in the news, do they?'' Marcus said with surprise. He had never heard of the incident involving a Vorlon, even though he was fascinated with the mysterious aliens, like most Humans, and read as much as he could find about them—which admittedly wasn't much.

''The second incident is even more troubling and embarrassing to the military caste, because the warrior he defeated is one of our greatest warriors, Neroon himself. It is said that Neroon ambushed Sinclair in the dark and from behind, an act which in itself might be called dishonorable by some, but which should have assured Neroon of victory. Yet Sinclair, as William liked to say, kicked Neroon's ass. Without any training in Minbari fighting techniques.''

''So what you're saying is that the military caste are sore losers.''

''That is an excellent way of putting it,'' Inesval agreed. ''So you might imagine how upset the military were when the religious caste and our Chosen One insisted over their strenuous objection that Sinclair, and only Sinclair, was worthy of following in Valen's footsteps as the one and true leader of the Anla'shok. Their fury only increased when Sinclair's first act was to open the ranks of the Rangers to the worker caste to whom it had been closed for a thousand years.''

Marcus had to admit to himself that this last act spoke well for Sinclair. But he wasn't convinced yet.

''It was Valen who first elevated my caste from near slavery into equality with the military and religious castes,'' Inesval continued, ''and when Sinclair reaffirmed that equality with his bold act, the whispered speculation about him increased: some believe that Sinclair, a Human, may possess at least part of Valen's soul. And that possibility frightens the military caste most of all."

Marcus was worried again. He decided not to ask how someone could have only part of someone else's soul. It was all superstitious nonsense to him anyway. Only one thing mattered: if Sinclair turned out to be just another egomaniacal, would-be messiah and the Rangers just another pathetic cult of deluded losers, he would be on the first ship back to Earth.

Marcus noted that the Minbari sun had reached its zenith, and suggested to Inesval that they head back immediately. The Minbari spent the walk back telling him stories about his brother, but that didn't help Marcus feel much better. All he could think of was that maybe Will had thrown his life away for nothing after all.

Once they had arrived back at the embassy, Marcus and the others did not have to wait long before being ushered into Sinclair's office. Marcus noted that he wore a slightly fancier version of the basic Ranger uniform, and that he was a very tall and dignified man with a pleasant, sonorous voice. The others bowed to Sinclair as they had been instructed to do. Marcus did not, and it caught the eye of Sinclair, who smiled just a little before turning away.

"You are here," Sinclair began, "because you have expressed an interest in joining the Rangers, and because we believe you are qualified candidates to do so. But first, you should know the essential facts about us. To explain who we are, I must first tell you who we are not. We are not a religious order. Those looking for eternal truths or a spiritual path would do best to look elsewhere. What you believe or don't believe regarding religion, God, the soul, or the meaning of life is your own business, and no one will try to evangelize you to another belief. You will find, however, that Ranger tradition is steeped in Minbari religious tradition, so if that bothers you, if you are not open-minded enough or secure enough in your own beliefs to be able to honor their traditions while keeping faith with your own, again, you'd be better off elsewhere.

"Second, and even more important, understand this: we are not a hate group, not a vigilante group, not an army of vengeance. Those looking for a license to commit violence or to pursue an individual path of revenge against the Shadows are not welcome here. We are dedicated to preventing destruction, not wreaking it. The enemy slaughters wholesale, we do not.

"The Rangers are a military group dedicated to nothing less then preserving the future and all life. Even our enemy's life, if possible. This is by the word of our founder, Valen. We are not looking to annihilate our enemy, only to defeat his aims of destruction. Never forget they are living beings also, however distorted their motives and actions appear to be.

"You will be taught as soldiers how to fight and how to kill. You will be taught to be the best at it because we must prepare for a war we do not want. That is the tragedy of war: that good people must take up those activities in self-defense. But teaching you those skills is not our sole mission. You will also be taught many ways of achieving our aims without violence, and where possible that will take precedence, even at the risk of your own life. If you are uncomfortable with so strict a code of conduct, you may leave now."

Sinclair paused to allow them to absorb what he had said, and to leave if any had the mind to do so. No one moved. Marcus didn't know what the others were thinking, but he was far more impressed than he had expected to be. With a sense of relief, he allowed himself to believe that maybe Will had been right about everything. At the very least he now believed it was worth sticking around to find out.

"All right," Sinclair said at last, with a smile. "These Rangers will accompany you to the compound and get you settled in to begin training. Welcome aboard."

Inesval and the other Ranger began ushering the new recruits out.

"Mr. Cole."

Marcus turned back around. Maybe his little breach of protocol at the beginning of the session was going to get him in trouble now. Sinclair waited until they were alone.

"Marcus, isn't it?"

"Yessir," said Marcus, instantly reverting to his old Earthforce days as a very young recruit.

"Please sit down. I apologize for not being able to see you yesterday when you arrived. I want to express how very sorry I am at the death of your brother. Can you tell me how it happened? Exactly what you saw?"

Marcus related the events in as much detail as he could remember, including Earth Central's unconcerned reaction, and the insurance forms he had signed. Sinclair watched him carefully while he spoke, but when he finished Sinclair looked past him for a moment, deep in thought.

Finally, he looked back at Marcus. "I saw great potential in your brother, from the moment I met him. William was among those I first contacted to join the Rangers. He turned out to be one of our very best. I can tell you he is sorely missed. I hope you'll find a home with us as William did.''

''Thank you,'' Marcus said, deeply moved. He was beginning to hope so, as well.

CHAPTER 22

"THERE'S a part of me," Sinclair said, looking up at the stars as he walked with Sakai across the compound, "that would still like to have the marriage ceremony on Babylon 5." He brought his gaze down from the stars and smiled. "But maybe that's only because I get a little anxious when I've been away from space this long. I've been on Minbar for what seems like an eternity already. Maybe I'm just looking for an excuse to get in the pilot's seat of a ship and go. What do you think?"

"We did ask Garibaldi and Ivanova to be our best man and maid of honor," Sakai said.

"And so many of our other friends are there. But unfortunately it would mean waiting at least a few more months."

"As far as I'm concerned, I've already signed the papers," she said. "It doesn't matter that much which day the ink dries."

He laughed. "You sound like a Vorlon."

"I only mean, if it's that important to you, I can wait for the formalities. Besides, it might be better to wait until . . ." She hesitated mid-sentence, apparently unsure what she wanted to say.

Sinclair gave her a questioning look, but continued to

walk in silence, letting her find whatever words she was looking for. Finally, she stopped and turned toward him.

For a moment all he could think was how beautiful she looked standing there in the light from Minbar's two moons, framed by Valen's temple behind her.

"Your work here is as consuming as it is important," she began. "And it rightly takes up most of your time. I haven't had any trouble keeping busy when I've been alone, reading up on Minbar and the Rangers, and studying the language. But it's not enough."

His heart sank. "I know how much you love your work, love being up there," he said, his eyes going briefly once again to the swarm of stars above. "And believe me I know how you feel. But I guess I was hoping we wouldn't be having this talk for at least another couple of months, not after just a couple of weeks. After what you went through on your last assignment—"

"I'm not talking about returning to work as a surveyor," she said. "Jeff, I want to go through Ranger training."

"No! Absolutely not!" Sinclair's vehemence surprised even himself, and he regretted it instantly when he saw Sakai's hurt and puzzled look. "It's just that . . ." He was floundering for an explanation that would sound reasonable to himself as well as to her. "It's too dangerous."

"What?" Now she was angry. "Damn it, Jeff, I was an Earthforce officer in the war. I'm a deep-space surveyor. I know how to handle myself in dangerous situations."

"That's the point," he tried to explain. "I don't want you to have to. I worry enough about you."

"You worry too much."

"You don't worry enough."

It was an old argument that had become almost a joke between them. It didn't seem very amusing at the moment.

"Why is it so wrong to want to protect you?" he asked.

"Protect me from what? Life?"

Their voices were rising, no doubt carrying in the clear, night air. He saw two Rangers walking near the temple.

"Come on," he said quietly, taking her arm. "I don't think it's appropriate for the Anla'shok Na to be having an argument in the middle of the compound."

She pulled her arm away, but walked with him. After a moment, she spoke, her voice a bit calmer. "Jeff, what is this really about?"

"I just got you back into my life again. I don't want you risking your life on this. It's something I have to do, but—"

"But it's okay for me to sit at home, worrying about you, while you risk your life? I know you love me and want to protect me, but I want to do this because I feel exactly the same way toward you. If I wasn't qualified, that'd be different. But you know I am. Jeff, if I'm going to be a part of your life, let me be part of all of it."

Sinclair didn't answer, trying to understand for himself why he felt this way. Up ahead he saw Valen's house—his house—and a chill went through him.

"Come on, Jeff," she said gently, "I know you too well. There's more to this than you're telling me."

Sinclair took a deep breath, let it out slowly. "In spite of everything, I have grown over the years to admire much about the Minbari. I find I genuinely like many of them, and consider a few of them as my friends. But they want me to believe as they do that I have a Minbari soul, that I am the fulfillment of Minbari prophecy. When I do something they approve of, they tell me I act like a Minbari. When I express appreciation for any part of their culture or world, they smile and nod knowingly. They have the unshakable certainty of true believers, and are backed up in their beliefs by the power and approval of the Vorlons.

"I don't know what motivates the Vorlons, but I do believe the Minbari mean well. Nevertheless, it's been difficult because at times it feels like they're trying to chip away at my Humanity, at my very identity. And then you arrived, a central and very Human part of my life untouched by the Minbari. This had made them rather unhappy, and where the Vorlons are concerned in particular, that's not a good thing."

Sakai reached out, took his hand in hers. "But all their efforts haven't changed you, Jeff. And they're not going to change me."

They had arrived back at the house. Once inside the door, he stopped and kissed her. When he spoke, he deliberately took a much lighter tone than before. "Being the fulfillment of prophecy is not all it's cracked up to be. No matter what I do, I can't get them to stop treating me like I was the Pope or the Dalai Lama."

"Well, you've always acted like a man on a mission from God," said Sakai, adopting the same light tone. "Maybe that's what they're seeing."

"Father Raffelli used to say that every living being—Human and alien alike—is on some kind of mission from God. The trick is to figure out what it is."

Sakai immediately seized upon that. "Mine is to be with you. To help you all I can. Let me help you to the full extent of my talents, Jeff."

He hesitated again, but knew she was right.

"You're going to be one hell of a good Ranger," he said at last, managing to smile.

"I always aim to be the *best,*" she said, leading him into the bedroom.

CHAPTER 23

MARCUS felt his left leg going numb. Perhaps he could move it just a little to relieve the pressure without attracting the attention of the meditation teacher Sech Turval and his reed cane. On the other hand, the whack across the shoulders he'd receive for such a slight movement might sting enough to keep him awake and save him from a far more painful thwack upside the head he'd receive for drifting off to sleep. It was amazing how Sech Turval could apply that lightweight reed in such a way as to not do any physical damage or injury, yet still have it sting as much as it did.

Marcus hated meditation class. It was the one part of Ranger training so far that he disliked the most. Most of the rest of it was bearable, some of it even enjoyable. He'd never had a problem with rising early, hard work, physical exercise, or learning new things. There was none of the depersonalization or pointless drudgery in this training that he had found so unbearable in Earthforce training. And it wasn't too bad being at the bottom of a chain of command, since no one seemed to abuse it. He was still having trouble getting acclimated to the shorter Minbari day, but that was only a problem in meditation class where he had a tendency to doze off.

What exactly was the point of this, anyway? How did

it fit into becoming a Ranger? None of Sech Turval's convoluted, indecipherable religious-dialect lectures had done anything yet to enlighten him.

On the very first day of orientation, Sinclair himself had told the new recruits, "The Minbari believe that every individual should learn delight, respect, and compassion. Of the Ranger, however, more is expected. He or she must *embody* those qualities. So everything you do here, everything you learn here, will be taught to you through these attributes. Understand this, and that which might otherwise puzzle you, will be made clear."

That didn't seem too far out in left field, and Marcus had been willing to give it a shot, but so far it had done nothing to explain meditation. "Respect" and "compassion" had definitely been stressed, right from that first speech Sinclair had given at the embassy office. And as Sinclair had promised, those qualities permeated every part of their training.

"Delight," too, was expected in everything they did—delight in effort, in learning, in accomplishment—but it was also taught in a special course, for one hour a day, right between the introductory courses to hand-to-hand combat and intelligence-gathering techniques.

The first two classes had been all right: they had simply spent time outside to discover delight in all the processes of nature. But this, unfortunately, had been followed by four classes to introduce them to a lot of tedious, incredibly complicated ceremonies for meals, for special Minbari holidays, for greeting the day, for going to bed at night, for giving gifts, for just about everything, it seemed, short of blowing one's nose and going to the bathroom. And at the end, they were told each ceremony would be revisited at a later time for a more thorough examination. Suddenly, "delight" no longer seemed like much of a delight to Marcus.

Things didn't improve with the next two classes, spent listening to long, pointless, and mostly incomprehensible stories by their Minbari instructor, Sech Nelier. Perhaps the stories might have been somewhat amusing had they been related at about one quarter the length and in English instead of the discursive, highly formal religious-caste dialect.

Marcus had been just about ready to give up on the very notion of ever being delighted again, when at the very next class, Nelier had announced that each trainee would get up and tell a story he or she found delightful, particularly one that made him or her laugh. The first few trainees, not really sure what was expected of them, hesitantly told rather pallid stories from their life, or from some book or movie they knew, that they clearly hoped would demonstrate an elevated, spiritual understanding of delight. Though not awful, the stories had elicited little laughter from the class and stern looks of apparent disapproval from Sech Nelier. This prompted the next few trainees to try a few jokes and some more colorful stories, and were soon drawing real laughter from the class.

Then trainee Catherine Sakai got up. Of course, Marcus and the others knew who she was, and he had wondered just what kind of story the Anla'shok Na's fiancée would tell. When it turned out to be a raucous, truly funny story from her Earthforce Academy days—involving a hated instructor, a visiting senator, an "exotic" dancer from a nearby nightspot, the Academy's goat mascot, a keg of beer, and a series of mistaken identities—the floodgates opened. The jokes and stories got more and more hilarious, and considerably more vulgar. Soon all the Human trainees were laughing so hard that tears were rolling down their faces and some could hardly breathe. Even the Minbari students were laughing and enjoying themselves.

Then it was time for Marcus to stand up. He had glanced over at Sech Nelier, expecting to see a scandalized look on the Minbari's face. Instead he saw the Minbari instructor smiling broadly with satisfaction, and Marcus realized this was what Nelier had hoped to achieve. At that moment, Marcus gained a much greater appreciation for the Minbari notion of delight.

Without planning to, Marcus had found himself telling a couple of stories about William and himself as kids, and as he sat down with the class's laughter ringing in his ears, he had wondered if maybe his brother had told those same stories to his class.

Marcus had to move, even just a little, or his leg might never recover. He adjusted his position slightly, moving his left leg just a fraction of an inch. He waited a few seconds, then flickered his eyelids open to take a quick look for Sech Turval. The Minbari was standing at the front of the room, staring right at him. Marcus squeezed his eyes shut and tried to look more meditative.

Marcus did not see how meditation would ever help him develop a sense of delight, respect, or compassion. It was merely boring. At least pilot training was next. That he absolutely loved, and not only because he was the best in the class, if he did say so himself. Sinclair was one of the teachers. And Sakai, though still a trainee, had been called upon to work as an assistant teacher because of her experience. The two of them were the best pilots he'd ever seen. The class trained on a motley collection of real flyers and shuttles, as well as on sophisticated computer simulations that included some amazingly advanced craft of Minbari design Marcus wasn't really sure existed for real, but which gave them all quite a workout.

Marcus had the uncomfortable feeling that Sech Turval had moved closer to where he was sitting. He didn't dare open his eyes to check, so he tried to sit even more still and hoped the Minbari would move on to someone else.

Just stay awake, thought Marcus. *It's almost over.*

What was after pilot training today? His other favorite class—the Minbari fighting pike known as *denn'bok.* That had proved to be an unexpected Minbari delight for Marcus. He remembered training briefly with similar weapons in Earthforce, but not liking it as much as this, or being as good at it. He was proving to be one of the best of all the recruits, including Minbari, and there was talk that he might qualify to be among the group to get personal training from Durhan himself.

Without warning, Marcus got a sharp whack across the back of his head from Sech Turval's reed cane, and he yelped before he could stop himself. He opened his eyes, resisting the urge to try and rub away the stinging pain, and found Turval circling him slowly, like a Minbari shark. Marcus sat very, very still, staring straight ahead.

"Everyone will please pay attention," said Turval, speaking in English for the first time since Marcus had been attending his training course. Now the entire class was staring at the Minbari instructor, and at Marcus. "Tell me, Mr. Cole. Do you find this daily practice of meditation to be a waste of your time?"

Marcus had still not moved. If he said no, he was likely to get another strike across the head for lying.

"May I speak freely, Sech Turval?"

"Of course."

Marcus looked up at Turval, who was still circling.

"Well, then frankly, yes I do. I think I'd benefit more from an hour of sleep. Sir."

"What about your other training courses, Mr. Cole? Do you find them equally useless?"

"No. Sir. Not for the most part."

"And how do you think you are doing, Mr. Cole? Please speak freely. No false modesty."

"Pretty well, sir."

"You're doing well in combat? Weapons? Surveillance? Minbari language? Cross-cultural studies? Weight training? Endurance training?"

Marcus answered yes to each in turn, but growing more and more uncomfortable.

"Pilot training? *Denn'bok* training?"

Again, Marcus answered yes, but grew even more uneasy at the Minbari's emphasis on the two subjects he had just been thinking about. Turval had the uncanny ability to seemingly read his students' thoughts, though there was nothing to indicate he was a genuine telepath.

"Quite the—what is the expression? Oh yes—quite the hotshot pilot, are you?"

"I think I'm pretty good, Sech Turval."

"And with the *denn'bok*? Are you 'pretty good' with that?"

"I think so."

"You *think,* do you?" Turval came to a stop right in front of Marcus. "Our Anla'shok Na has a different opinion. He tells me he fears you will one day plow an aircraft into a mountainside. You have great talent, he says, but you do not truly *think* at all. You are mentally undisciplined and unfocused. As for the *denn'bok* . . ." Turval pivoted and walked a little distance away, then turned around again. "Stand up, Mr. Cole."

When Marcus stood, Turval produced two folded

fighting pikes from his robe, and tossed one to Marcus. "Please clear a space for Mr. Cole and me."

The other trainees scrambled to the sides of the room.

"I am just an old religious-caste Minbari, Mr. Cole, perhaps not that far removed from the time I will go to the sea. But do not let that hold you back. Please show all of us your great skill with our fighting pike."

Turval twisted his hand just slightly, and the pike extended to full length. With a flourish Marcus followed suit, and then, grabbing the weapon with both hands, crouched in preparation for an attack. Turval stood easily, lightly handling the *denn'bok.*

"I give you the option, Mr. Cole. You may attack first, or defend my attack. I don't want it said I took you by surprise."

Marcus had begun to sweat nervously. It would be safer to defend. "You may begin," said Marcus with the proper ceremonial bow.

Turval returned the bow. They took the prescribed stance and distance from each other. Marcus tensed for the attack, trying to guess what attack movement the Minbari would use. But there was a blur of motion and before Marcus could react, his pike went sailing from his hands. Then he hit the ground, hard, Turval's *denn'bok* pressed just hard enough against his windpipe to make breathing very difficult, but not quite impossible. Yet.

"What is a Ranger, Mr. Cole?" Turval asked in a loud, clear voice. "The embodiment of what is best in an intelligent being, the embodiment of delight, respect, and compassion. What is a Ranger's mission? To observe and to fight in the service of the One for the preservation of the future and the protection and service of all life. Do you follow me so far, Mr. Cole?"

Marcus tried to say yes, but barely managed a grunt.

"Excellent. There is nothing you will learn here that is not based in what you will learn in meditation, Mr. Cole. Do I still have your attention?" Turval took the *denn'bok* from Marcus's throat and reached out a hand to help him up.

Marcus got up and, when he could speak again, said, "Yes, Sech Turval. You have my full attention."

"Good," said Turval, his attention still focused on Marcus, but his words aimed at the whole group. "A Ranger must know who he is, beneath opinion and conditioning and the constant prattle of his thoughts. He needs to know what he truly is at the level beyond thoughts and words, at the level of absolute silence out of which comes all that is truly meaningful. Learn that and you learn delight, respect, and compassion for yourself and all other beings. That is what meditation will teach you.

"A Ranger must know how to truly see and to see things as they truly are in all situations, not what familiarity, conditioning, opinion, and prejudice tell you it might be or could be or should be. For a warrior, misperception, willful blindness, or wishful thinking can lead to death for himself and others. Meditation teaches you how to see, by teaching you how to simply be.

"Finally, a Ranger must learn to act from his true mind, the center of his being, not from his thoughts or ego or pride or external effort and force. This should be true whether preparing a meal or defending oneself in battle. Meditation teaches you how."

Then, Turval softened his tone, speaking now for Marcus alone. "Learn this, and I believe you might one day become as good a Ranger as your brother was."

Marcus saw a kindness in the old Minbari's eyes he had never noticed before. Thoroughly chastened, he bowed to his teacher. "Thank you, sir."

CHAPTER 24

ONE difference between Earthforce training and Ranger training that Marcus most appreciated was that here they had no bed check, no confinement to barracks at night. A Ranger trainee was expected to learn discipline and how to apply it for himself. So if Marcus wanted to trade a little bit of sleep or study time for a short walk at night, that was up to him. Until now, he had not been actually able to do that—there was simply too much to study at night—but it comforted him to know the option was there. Tonight he felt the need to exercise that option, to have a little time to himself, the one thing that was in short supply during the rest of the day.

He found himself heading in the direction of The Chapel, the colored windows beautifully glowing from lights within. He wondered what the inside of the beautiful little temple looked like at night. He walked in and was surprised to see Sinclair sitting near the statue of Valen, facing toward Marcus but head down, reading. Marcus froze for a moment, not sure what to do, then started to back out quietly.

"Hello, Marcus." Sinclair closed the book and looked up.

"Sorry, Ambassador. I didn't mean to disturb your prayers."

Sinclair smiled. "I wasn't praying. I come here to read or just sit sometimes. Just to be alone. It's the one place I know no Minbari will disturb me. I don't know whether or not they think I'm praying in here, but since they themselves will admit Valen wasn't a god, I figure I'm not committing any sort of sacrilege by using this as a quiet reading room."

"I'll leave you then, Ambassador."

"No, it's quite all right, Marcus. Actually, I'd like to know how you feel you're getting along so far."

Marcus assumed Sinclair had already heard about the upbraiding he had received from Turval earlier that day, but wasn't going to bring it up.

"Doing my best, Ambassador. I'd like to think I'm learning."

"I believe you are, Marcus," Sinclair said warmly.

"Although there are times when I can't figure out what the heck the Minbari are saying," Marcus heard himself saying. He was nervous talking to the Anla'shok Na, and out of habit he had jumped in without thinking, to prevent an awkward silence. "I mean, they can be quite clear and precise when they choose to be, but other times they'll speak reams of words without making any apparent sense. This can be a bit of a problem when it's one of our teachers and he expects to be understood."

"Do most of the trainees feel that way?"

"I'd say so. There's a joke among us that the only way to understand anything Sech Turval says is to look at it in a mirror while hanging upside down from the ceiling." Marcus stopped, sure he was talking too much.

But Sinclair laughed. "I'll have to remember that.

There's a few others I know that could be said of. It'll be easier as you get more familiar with the religious dialect. But it's also wise to remember that the Minbari have learned that a good way to avoid answering a question or talking about an issue they don't want to get into is to reply with a non sequitur, or say something inscrutable or downright incomprehensible. It can bring the conversation to a halt so they don't have to say anything else."

Now it was Marcus's turn to laugh. "I'll have to remember that," he said. "Perhaps I should let you get back to your reading. A racy novel?" Marcus couldn't believe he said that last bit. What was it about Sinclair that had him blurting out things he shouldn't be saying? He desperately wanted to leave before he embarrassed himself again.

But Sinclair was smiling, obviously enjoying the conversation. "Left all of those back in my quarters. This is *The Meditations of Marcus Aurelius*. Are you familiar with it?"

"Oh, yes. I read that in a philosophy class back in college. Gloomy guy. And not the most readily accessible prose ever written. Barely got through it."

Sinclair held the book out to him. "Then it's time you try again. When you're finished, we'll discuss it. I've been considering making it required reading. I think you'll find it's one of the best books ever written on leadership."

"Thank you, Ambassador."

Marcus decided he would have to learn to keep his mouth shut. Still, he was also beginning to enjoy this conversation. How many other opportunities would he have like this, to just talk informally with the Anla'shok Na? And under the watchful gaze of Valen himself. Suddenly it occurred to Marcus, why not ask Sinclair, who might know if anyone did, the one question that still had him puzzled.

"You said earlier that Valen isn't a god to the Minbari, but there are times I wonder. We hear a lot about Valen from our instructors, and most of it sounds like religious awe to me. That was one of my biggest fears before coming here, that the Rangers would turn out to be just some kind of religious cult."

"You're not a religious man, are you, Marcus?"

"An atheist, actually. I stopped believing in God and miracles a long time ago."

"I suppose I've also had reason during my life to stop believing in God," Sinclair said slowly. "But somehow I haven't. I'm still working out the details, though."

"They say the Devil is in the details."

"God, too," Sinclair reminded him.

"The way I see it, no God, no Devil, no problem. You still have the details, but they're of our own making, no supernatural forces needed. I'm glad you warned us from the beginning how much around here is steeped in Minbari metaphysics. Made it easier to deal with."

"You don't have to believe it. Just respect it."

"As you said from the beginning, Ambassador. And I have tried. In fact, I learned today I'd do well to be a little more open-minded about some things."

Sinclair smiled knowingly at this. "Nevertheless, the work of the Rangers isn't dependent on Minbari religion—and must never be. That's from the word of our founder himself."

Sinclair looked up at the statue of Valen.

"But I thought he created a lot of the religion himself."

"Read for yourself, Marcus. The truth is there for

those who want to look for it. He didn't create any of it. Minbari religion existed long before his time, and it wasn't until years after his time that the Minbari started invoking his name in their rituals and daily life."

"Like Jesus," said Marcus.

"Well, maybe," said Sinclair. "Though I think of him more as King Arthur. He set up a sort of Round Table in the Grey Council; improved Minbari society rather like Camelot; fought off an invasion, like King Arthur; the circumstances of his death are unknown and there is no body or tomb, leading most to believe he didn't actually die but would return one day at the time of his people's greatest need to lead them to victory once again. The Minbari have even reported visions of him down through the centuries. Anyway, it's just another way we're like the Minbari. We've taken more than a few Humans and layered them with myth until we've nearly deified them."

"Like Elvis," said Marcus. Then thought, oh, damn. Maybe he shouldn't have said that. Sinclair had seemed so serious. He tried to explain. "I have a distant cousin who belongs to a sect that prays to Elvis as one of the saints. Black sheep of the family."

Sinclair's expression was absolutely unreadable until he burst into laughter, a deep, unselfconscious laughter that seemed to rumble out of the silent temple, and must have carried across the compound. It was contagious, and Marcus joined in, just a little.

"I never thought of it quite that way before," said Sinclair finally.

Marcus smiled and shrugged, not knowing what else to say.

Sinclair stood up. "I've enjoyed our conversation, Marcus. But we both need to get some sleep."

"You're right, of course, Ambassador." Marcus

held up the book Sinclair had given him. "I'll start reading this immediately." He started to back out—and backed right into somebody. Turning around, Marcus was appalled to see it was Rathenn. A member of the Grey Council himself. Though he did not interact with the trainees, Rathenn was a frequent visitor to the compound, often seen conferring with Sinclair.

"My apologies, Satai Rathenn."

Rathenn, a grave expression on his face, barely looked at Marcus, instead hurrying over to Sinclair.

Marcus bowed and left, and though he did not mean to eavesdrop, the Minbari's words carried out of the chapel into the night where Marcus heard them.

"Ambassador. I have distressing news. The Chosen One is dying."

CHAPTER 25

As they hurried to the flyer waiting to take them from the Ranger Compound to the Chosen One's palace, Rathenn explained to Sinclair what had happened. Jenimer had collapsed in the late afternoon, while in conference with the Grey Council itself whom he had summoned back to Minbar. "Perhaps he knew his time was short," Rathenn said.

The doctors had determined quickly nothing more could be done. It was feared the Chosen One would die without a last word to his people. But, after several hours of moving in and out of consciousness, murmuring incoherently, Jenimer had somehow revived just enough to speak, and sent Rathenn personally to bring Sinclair. Once he finished relating all this to Sinclair, Rathenn fell silent for the rest of the journey to the Chosen One's palace.

The great structure loomed before them in the dark, moonless night, dark except for a flashing beacon at the very top, and a soft glow of lights at the landing area. There was no light at all shining from inside the palace, and Sinclair assumed that all the windows had been turned from clear to opaque, to prevent any light from escaping.

The first thing Sinclair noticed on landing was how

many guards were about. During his only other visit to the palace, when he had agreed to become Ranger One, he had seen fewer Minbari throughout the entire building than he now saw on the landing strip, and near the palace entrance. The next thing he noticed was how utterly quiet it was. When the sound of the flyer's engine died away, Sinclair heard nothing else but the muffled sound of his and Rathenn's footsteps.

The guards were Minbari military caste, heavily armed, and gave Sinclair the uneasy feeling he was about to run a gauntlet when they quickly and silently formed two facing lines. Rathenn lead Sinclair through the line into the building.

Guards also stood at attention everywhere Sinclair looked within the palace, which was also filled with a nearly tangible hush, and even more dimly lit than during his last visit. But as before, Rathenn led him quickly and effortlessly through the maze of halls and stairs, and brought him at last to a wide hallway that ended in a massive set of doors, guarded by nine Minbari warriors, four on either side, and one standing front and center. The guards moved quickly to open the doors before Rathenn and Sinclair. As on his first visit, Sinclair found himself standing in a small antechamber, which became pitch-dark when the double doors closed behind them. Then a smaller door in front of them parted and slid open, letting in a faint glow of light.

Sinclair entered a cavernous room. At the far end, near the back wall, Jenimer lay in a bed tilted at a forty-five-degree angle and set high enough off the floor so that the Minbari leader's head was nearly at the level of those standing nearby. Tall, flickering candles set in elaborate floor stands were just behind the bed and provided the room's only light. At the foot of the bed was a single tall staff, set into the floor, holding a Triluminary.

On one side of the bed stood three doctors, looking on with grave concern, but doing nothing else. On the other side of the bed was an elderly female Minbari, who had noticed Sinclair's and Rathenn's entrance. Sinclair saw her gently touch the Chosen One's arm, and whisper to him. Who was she? She showed an intimacy with the Chosen One Sinclair had never seen anyone else take. It must be Jenimer's wife? Jenimer had never discussed his personal life with him, and Sinclair had believed it impolite by Minbari standards to ask.

Jenimer turned his head just a little, but nothing more. From where Sinclair was standing at the other end of the large room, it seemed as if Jenimer's eyes were closed. No one else in the room moved, and nothing else happened. In the heavy stillness, he thought it unwise to ask any questions of Rathenn, standing nearby, so Sinclair took a moment to look more carefully around the dimly lit room.

There were a great many other Minbari in the room, more than he had first assumed, most half hidden in the shadows at the room's edges, all silent and motionless. He tried to get a better look at who was there.

The first one he recognized was Neroon as their gazes locked briefly, the Minbari warrior having taken his eyes off Jenimer for one moment to observe Sinclair. Neroon managed to convey disdain as he turned his head away from Sinclair and back toward his leader. Neroon stood with his head covered by the hooded cape the Grey Council members wore, and Sinclair assumed that the other hooded figures around Neroon comprised the rest of the council.

Elsewhere in the room, Sinclair recognized a handful of representatives from the Council of Caste Elders, and wondered if the entire council was present. There were many more Minbari he did not recognize at all, from the very old to the very young. He even saw one young Minbari with a sleeping infant in her arms.

He did not see Ulkesh, but something told Sinclair he was somewhere nearby, maybe even standing in one of the darkened areas his vision could not penetrate.

Out of the corner of his eye, Sinclair saw Jenimer's wife move. As he turned his focus back to the bed, he saw her bending toward her husband, listening. The Chosen One's hand gestured slightly. Jenimer's wife straightened, looked in Sinclair's direction, and gestured for him to come forward.

Sinclair glanced around to make sure he was indeed the one being summoned, then crossed the empty center of the large room to Jenimer's side. As he did, Jenimer's wife moved a discreet distance away.

The Minbari leader's eyes were closed, leaving Sinclair unsure what to do. Should he say something or wait? Finally, he decided he should say something, and in a soft voice said: "Chosen One?"

Jenimer's eyes flickered open, and the hint of a smile crossed his features. He reached out to Sinclair, who took Jenimer's hand between his own hands, and bent down a little closer.

After another moment, in which Jenimer seemed to be gathering his strength, he spoke in English, in a barely audible whisper. "Remember me kindly."

Sinclair found himself fighting back unexpected tears. "With the greatest affection," he said, his voice thick with emotion. "And friendship."

That seemed to please Jenimer. Sinclair went to release his hand, assuming that was all the Minbari had the strength to say, but was surprised when Jenimer tightened his grip on Sinclair's hand, and spoke again, this time in the religious-caste dialect. "Continue to dream. You dream for us all." Then he closed his eyes and released Sinclair's hand.

When Jenimer's wife returned to the bedside, Sinclair backed away slowly, then turned and walked back to his original place by the door.

What did Jenimer mean? Sinclair wondered. Was it a reference to the proverb the Chosen One had told him when they first went to Tuzanor, that to dream in the City of Sorrows was to dream of a better future? It seemed likely that's all Jenimer meant, with the added implication that his work with the Rangers was the way toward that better future. And yet if Jenimer had simply wanted to reinforce his wish that Sinclair continue to function as Ranger One, he could have said so more directly.

But perhaps it was simply the Minbari penchant for poetic ambiguity. He had never told Jenimer of the nightmares that regularly tormented him, so the Minbari leader could not have known what a conflicting image the word dream summoned up for Sinclair.

Once again, Jenimer's wife motioned for someone to come forward. Sinclair saw a moment of silent confusion among the members of the Grey Council until it became clear that Neroon alone was being summoned to Jenimer's side.

Neroon hid his surprise with a posture of dignity, then briskly walked over. Jenimer's wife moved away to give them privacy. As with Sinclair, Jenimer reached out to take Neroon's hand in his clasp. The stiff-backed warrior bent closer to Jenimer, his stern expression softening just a little. Jenimer whispered to him and released his hand. Jenimer's wife returned to the bedside. Neroon straightened, and walked much more slowly back to his place, an unreadable expression on his face.

As the old Minbari bent down to talk to her husband, Sinclair continued to study Neroon, who stood stiffly alone, keeping what Jenimer had said to himself.

Then Sinclair realized there was a flurry of activity around Jenimer. All three doctors were at his side, checking him, conferring in soft, urgent tones. Jenimer's wife stood just a little behind them, and Sinclair recognized the rigid control of grief he saw in her face and posture.

One of the doctors went to the back wall, opened a hidden panel, and a previously unseen door slid open. Instantly nine guards entered, each carrying a folded section of a dark fabric screen that they quickly set up around Jenimer's bed, cutting it off from view.

Rathenn was at Sinclair's elbow, speaking quietly. "Follow me, please."

The entire wall behind them, which contained the small door through which they had entered, now parted at the center and moved aside to reveal the large main doors. These were opened by the guards. Rathenn and Sinclair were the first to leave, followed by a long single-file line of silent mourners. In his quick glance back, Sinclair did not see any Grey Council members among them.

Sinclair was too stunned by the sudden loss of his friend to ask where they were going or for what purpose. As ill as Jenimer had been from the first moment Sinclair had met him, it was hard to believe that such a powerful personality was simply gone.

Rathenn led Sinclair into a dark room illuminated only by faintly glowing crystals set flush into the floor, which he used to find his way through the room. Sinclair followed after him, and found himself growing irritated.

Why the hell don't they just turn the lights on? he thought. *What is going on now?*

He heard the room fill with people, though no one spoke. After a few moments, absolute silence descended. Sinclair stood there, waiting with the rest, but growing more and more angry. He knew it arose from his tremendous sense of loss, but damn it, why couldn't the Minbari do anything in a straightforward fashion?

A faint beam of light grew slowly to dazzling brightness in what Sinclair now assumed was the middle of the room, not too far from where he was standing. Overhead, he now saw a huge multipart mechanism, like a massive abstract mobile, rotating silently. Sinclair had been in a room like this once before, as prisoner on the Minbari warship. The Minbari were far too fond of the motif to suit Sinclair.

Neroon, his hood thrown back, stepped into the light, and spoke in the warrior-caste dialect. "The Chosen One's soul has returned to the great void from which we all arise, and to which we will all someday return," he said in a loud, clear voice, devoid of emotion. From the assembled Minbari in the darkness arose a rhythmic murmur, as if in unison they were chanting a prayer. Sinclair tried, but could not make out the words. He turned to where Rathenn had been, but Sinclair found he was now standing alone, with no one other than Neroon in sight.

Neroon waited, his head down, motionless, silent, as if lost in thought, until finally the voices died away. He raised his head and began to pace slowly away from Sinclair and around the outer edge of the circle of light. "Our leader has at last gone to the sea, but he left us with his final edict, which he entrusted to my safekeeping with his last breath.''

Neroon stopped in front of Sinclair, and regarded him with a contemptuous look that his carefully neutral voice did not convey. ''It was our Chosen One's sole last wish that Jeffrey David Sinclair of Earth be ordained, in the proper ceremony, before a quarter lunar cycle concludes, as Entil'Zha to follow in the sacred way of Valen. And thus it shall be done.''

Neroon bowed his head slightly to Sinclair. A second later, the room was plunged into total darkness, causing Sinclair to involuntarily tense against a possible attack in the dark. He willed himself to relax—not even Neroon would do such a thing at this time, in this place—and waited for whatever was next.

Light filtered into the room from above, as skylights slowly turned from dark gray to clear glass, letting in the early morning sun. Neroon was still standing square in front of him, and Rathenn was once again at Sinclair's side.

Sinclair started to ask Rathenn for an explanation, but the Minbari held up a hand, indicating Sinclair should wait. When the room had emptied of everyone but Sinclair, Rathenn, and Neroon, and the last door was closed, Rathenn spoke.

''As a Satai of the religious caste I will prepare you for the ceremony, Anla'shok Na, as our departed leader has decreed.''

''And I am Satai of the warrior caste,'' Neroon said, all the contempt now back in his voice. ''I do not know why our departed leader chose me for this unhappy task, but I will carry out my duty and oversee the preparations for the ceremony.''

''But you'd rather not,'' Sinclair said.

"The Chosen One's last decree is sacred," Neroon said bitterly, then turned to leave. Sinclair stopped him.

"Satai Neroon, no one heard that decree but you. Jenimer did not say anything of it to me."

Neroon regarded Sinclair intently.

"So, I'm curious," Sinclair continued. "Why did you go ahead and make public an edict that you so obviously disagree with, when you could just as easily have said nothing at all?"

Rathenn looked scandalized at just the idea.

Neroon was scornful. "Only a Human could ask such a question!"

"Maybe," Sinclair said, not at all insulted. "But I don't believe that only a Human would *think* it. If you can tell me with absolute truthfulness, Satai Neroon, that the thought never even crossed your mind, you don't have to answer my question."

Neroon glared angrily at Sinclair but did not answer right away. Finally, he said: "I will answer your question, but only because I have no reason not to. I honor our leader's last request because it is my duty to do so. Because I had come to respect the Chosen One as a person of will and strength, all the more impressive because of his physical frailty.

"And because I am told, whatever else you may be or represent, that you do not believe this outrageous falsehood about the transference of our souls to your Human species any more than I do. Yes, I was told the story when I joined the Grey Council. Had I been told at the Battle of the Line that this was the reason we were surrendering, I would never have stopped fighting."

"And you're proud to say that?" Sinclair asked. "Proud to admit you would have carried on with genocide? Even now?"

Sinclair wondered if he didn't see just a trace of uncertainty in Neroon's eyes.

"The past is dead. What concerns me is the present and the future. And if the *Rangers,*" Neroon emphasized the English word disparagingly, "are to be mostly Human, I see little harm in a Human Entil'Zha. As long as he does not fancy himself to be Minbari, or covet any position of power among my people. But know that we will be watching carefully."

"See," Sinclair said, "we have more in common than you want to admit."

Neroon grunted in angry disapproval and left.

By the time Sinclair returned to the Ranger compound, it was already noon. He found Catherine pacing anxiously as he walked through the door of their quarters.

"When I was awakened in the early hours of the morning by a knock on the door and you weren't in bed or anywhere to be found, I was more than just a little worried," she said, before he could get in a word. "A Minbari I've never seen before told me Jenimer has died, so all activity is suspended for the day. He didn't say so, but I just assumed you must have gone to wherever Jenimer was."

"I'm sorry I couldn't get word to you. Everything happened so suddenly." He sat down tiredly. He hadn't slept in twenty-four hours. Sakai sat next to him, and he put his arm around her. "I'm really going to miss him, Catherine. I hadn't realized just how much. In just a short time I really came to see Jenimer as my friend, as much as Delenn. As much as *anyone* I've ever known. A truly good person. Damn!"

They sat silently for a moment, Sinclair staring off into space, Sakai waiting patiently. After a long while, he looked down at her and smiled. "It makes me all the more glad you're here."

"Me, too." She kissed him. "So what happens now. Will they select another leader right away?"

Sinclair shook his head slowly. "I don't think so. It's the Grey Council's choice as to when a new Chosen One is selected, and I don't think they will make that choice until they have to. They don't have to until ten Minbari cycles have passed." He paused. "They did make one choice this morning, though. I'm to be made Entil'Zha, in about a week and a half."

"Well," she said, clearly not knowing what to say. "Are you happy about it?"

"As Neroon pointed out to me this morning, what harm could there be in a Human Entil'Zha for a group of mostly Human Rangers?"

"Then congratulations."

"Yeah," he said. "But I'd trade it all for a couple hours sleep."

"I don't think the Minbari would approve," she said as she helped him up and guided him into the bedroom.

CHAPTER 26

"THE ceremony protocols must be followed *exactly*!" Neroon said adamantly to Rathenn, from across the wide conference table.

Rathenn was every bit as determined. "We have presented you with the medical facts. A provision must be made for this unique situation. His Human physiology makes it impossible—"

"Nothing in our tradition justifies changing such an important part of the ceremony for the sake of *any* person. Besides," Neroon finished with great sarcasm, "none of this should be a problem for a 'Minbari not born of Minbari.' "

The two Satai glared at each other. The argument, the latest in a series of arguments, had been raging for the past fifteen minutes in Sinclair's presence, without either one of them asking for his opinion. He let them continue while he listened carefully. As the day of the ceremony to install Sinclair as Entil'Zha had approached, the two Grey Council members had been clashing repeatedly over the finer points of religious and political protocol, and Sinclair had let them work out their own compromises without interfering.

But now, with the ceremony only two days away, they had taken up the first issue to concern him in any real way, and it seemed more and more likely that only he would be able to resolve it.

"But you have already agreed to this," Rathenn said.

"I agreed only to help prepare for a *traditional* ceremony," Neroon countered. "And part of the ceremony is drinking a cup of *sha'neyat*. Just how much of our sacred tradition are you willing to discard for the sake of this Human?"

Sha'neyat translated loosely as *death destroyer*. Sinclair knew it was a potent liquid, of great symbolic significance, distilled from a combination of flowers, fruits, and grains. The drink was used only in certain religious ceremonies where it was considered an essential ceremonial element. Until now, only Minbari had been allowed to partake of it. Sinclair was to be the first, but the Ranger doctors had discovered one small problem: *sha'neyat* was deadly poison to Humans.

"So you would have us follow the ceremony to the letter," Rathenn said, "even if it kills the Entil'Zha?"

Sinclair decided he had heard enough. "I don't think you should present that as an option to Satai Neroon," he told Rathenn in a good-humored voice. "He seems a little too eager to take you up on it."

Neroon and Rathenn both looked surprised at the interruption. They were aware Sinclair had deliberately kept out of all previous disagreements over ceremonial details, and seemed to have momentarily forgotten that he had a personal stake in this one.

"I've participated in other Minbari ceremonies, and I've read a lot about this one in particular. As far as I can determine, there is no requirement to drink a full cup of the stuff. I'm sure you'll correct me if I'm wrong, but I believe the relevant phrase is 'taste of it.' I only need to take a sip to satisfy tradition."

"But Ambassador," Rathenn immediately protested, "the doctors say even that could make you deathly ill."

"They say it depends on how large a sip I take. It can be done." Sinclair turned to Neroon. "Will that satisfy your protocols?"

Neroon regarded Sinclair a little suspiciously. "You are willing to actually swallow some of the liquid? Not just raise the chalice to your lips?"

"I give you my word."

Neroon studied Sinclair for a moment more. "That should suffice," he said with a small bow of his head, showing maybe just a touch of respect, the first Sinclair had seen from Neroon since coming to Minbar.

It didn't last long. "Now for this contemptible notion that the ceremonial meal afterward will not feature the *Se n'kai* fruit," Neroon said. "This is an insult to the military caste."

"The Satai is quite aware that is not an essential part of the ceremony," Rathenn immediately countered. "*Se n'kai* trees were far more prevalent in Valen's time than now . . ."

Sinclair sighed and sat back to let them argue.

"Are you sure this is safe?" Sakai asked for what must have been the twentieth time. She and Sinclair were leaving Valen's house in the predawn darkness, headed for the center of the compound where a stand had been erected and everyone had been assembled for the ordination of the new Entil'Zha. She couldn't help asking one more time. If he displayed even the smallest doubt, she would do everything in her power to dissuade him from drinking the noxious potion and Neroon could go straight to hell.

But Sinclair just laughed it off. "The doctors assure me I'll survive. Just one small sip."

"There's a lot of things that can kill you with just one small sip," she replied, still not convinced.

"Come on," he said, putting his arm around her. "We have other things to worry about. Like not screwing up this ceremony."

"After all of Rathenn's tutoring? I could do it in my sleep. In fact I have been. When you woke me up I was dreaming about it."

"Was it like those dreams where you show up at school or work without your clothes on?"

"Yeah," she said, "only in my dream you were the one who wasn't dressed."

"Oh, did I forget to tell you about that part of the ceremony?"

She laughed. She knew he was trying to ease her apprehension over what was coming up. It was working. Sort of. Actually Sinclair did look somewhat underdressed without the brown hooded cowl he was usually required to wear over the basic Ranger uniform. That was because he'd be presented with another one at the ceremony, and one of her responsibilities would be to help him don it with as much dignity and as little effort as possible.

They had reached the administrative and classroom complex, and made their way between the darkened buildings so they could approach the platform from behind.

As they neared the area, though not yet in view of it, he gave her one final squeeze, then released her, and pulled himself up just a little straighter. He might joke with her, but he understood the seriousness of the event and would comport himself from now until it was over with the solemn dignity befitting a Ranger One and Entil'Zha. She fell into step a pace behind him, as Rathenn had tutored her to do.

Her function was as his second at the ceremony. They had worried that Neroon might fight Sinclair on his selection, but apparently the stiff-necked warrior hadn't objected at all. So here she was in her freshly pressed Ranger-in-training uniform, suddenly worried she'd forget what she was supposed to do, even after what she had just told Jeff.

C'mon, she thought. *It's not that hard.* The ceremony was relatively simple, and her responsibilities easy.

They turned the corner of the last building and saw the simple wooden platform, illuminated by two torches, one on either side, each attended by a Minbari Ranger. The stand had been built high enough to afford a good view of the event for all those out front. The participants would climb to the top by way of a long, wide ramp in the back. The idea, Rathenn had explained, was to allow the new Entil'Zha to rise into view slowly, like the sun coming over the horizon at dawn—which was now only minutes away.

Rathenn and Neroon were waiting for them at the bottom of the ramp. Sinclair bowed his head to them in greeting. No one spoke.

After a few moments, a gentle breeze kicked up and Sakai heard the distinctive sound of the *temshwee* and other Minbari birds greeting the first light. Dawn was breaking behind them on a beautiful, clear morning. Rathenn gestured, and the two Rangers doused the torches. Rathenn bowed his head to Sinclair, indicating the ceremony was beginning, then went up the ramp. As soon as he reached the top, Neroon and Sakai followed, he on the left, she on the right. An audience of several hundred people was standing at solemn attention: Rangers in the front row, then teachers and staff, Ranger trainees, and selected citizens from Tuzanor and Yedor, including some members of the Council of Caste Elders, and members of Jenimer's family. Sakai also knew who wasn't out there—other members of the Grey Council. As part of some sort of compromise, only Rathenn and Neroon were present. Delenn had also been invited, but regrettably could not attend.

While Rathenn watched from the left front of the stand, beaming with satisfaction, Neroon took his place in the back, a few steps from his counterpart, looking very stern, observing everything carefully through narrowed eyes. Sakai took her place to the right, near a small table at the back that held the items she was responsible for: an ancient religious book and a clear crystal chalice filled with deep purple liquid she wished she could "accidentally" dash to the floor.

Then they turned to watch Sinclair walk slowly up the ramp, coming into the audience's view with the brilliant morning sun low on the horizon behind him. He had a carefully composed expression on his face as he walked with measured steps to the center of the platform, and nodded subtly to Rathenn. Rathenn looked to Sakai, who picked up the crumbling book and solemnly handed it to him.

Rathenn began to read in a loud, rhythmic voice page after page from the ancient texts, all in a language so old, only a few Minbari still understood it. It was to the modern Minbari dialects what Latin was to English and the European Romance languages. Jeff had already taught himself to read it, but he had a natural gift for languages she lacked. She had her hands full just learning what she needed of the modern religious- and military-caste dialects.

Rathenn's reading had a hypnotic cadence that was

beginning to put Sakai to sleep, even though she was standing. To stay awake, she focused on Sinclair's profile, and wondered what he was thinking at that precise moment. Or was he, like her, just doing his best not to doze off? How much sleep had they gotten? Two hours at best.

Suddenly, she began recognizing some of the words and phrases Rathenn was reading, and realized he was nearing the conclusion. Rathenn carefully closed the book, then raised it in a gesture toward the audience. It was show time again. Sakai quickly came forward, bowed to Rathenn, took the book, bowed again, and returned to her place, setting the book back down.

The part she'd been worrying about most was almost upon them. She cast a sidelong glance at the deceptively pleasant-looking goblet of *sha'neyat*. She didn't trust any drink that had the word "death" in its name. But first the most amazing part of the ceremony.

Down the center aisle, from the very back of the audience, a young acolyte approached, a look of true awe on her face, carrying a brown hooded robe that looked very much like the one Sinclair had been wearing all along as Ranger One. But this garment, carried so gingerly in the hands of the young Minbari, was unique. It was Valen's original robe, preserved for a thousand years for Sinclair now to wear, at least for the duration of the ceremony. The acolyte ascended a small staircase at the front of the platform, bowed, placed the robe at Sinclair's feet, bowed again, and backed away as quickly as she could to hasten back down the staircase.

Sakai took a deep breath, having dreaded this moment ever since the Minbari doctors had made their discovery about the effect *sha'neyat* had on Human physiology. She picked up the goblet with the liquid that looked so innocently like wine, and brought it to Sinclair, handed it to him.

He gave her the subtlest of smiles, and she knew that look in his eyes. *Don't worry,* he was trying to convey to her one more time. She backed away, unable to take her eyes off that chalice. Rathenn was reciting a blessing in the religious dialect, which she barely heard until he came to *the* words.

"Taste of it," he said. "Taste of the future. Of Death. And of Life. And of the Great Void that lies between. Through this act, may Death be destroyed."

Transfixed, Sakai saw Sinclair raise the chalice for all to see, then put it to his lips. He took some in his mouth—how much she couldn't determine—and swallowed. His shoulders jerked back slightly and his spine stiffened, while his eyes squeezed shut for a moment.

Rathenn, his back to the audience, appeared to be as concerned as Sakai was. Neroon looked on only with suspicion.

She was about to go to him, protocols be damned, when with an obvious effort, he relaxed his stance and opened his eyes. He nodded to Rathenn, who then nodded to Sakai. She sprinted forward, far more quickly than she had been drilled to move in the rehearsals, and picked up Valen's garment.

Sinclair's face was ashen, his expression a taut mask of controlled agony. His hands were clenched tight and he was trembling faintly. As she helped him on with the robe, she could feel that his clothes were soaked through with sweat.

"Are you all right?" She whispered to him when she had the chance, knowing it was a stupid question, but what else could she say?

"Tasted—like—molten lava," he managed to whisper back.

Finished, Sakai stepped back, only a half-step away, determined to be right there if he collapsed. But he stayed solidly straight and motionless, his head up, his eyes looking out over the audience, somehow maintaining the noble bearing he knew was expected of him. Fortunately, there was only a little more to go.

Rathenn turned back to the assemblage. "As it was done long ago, so now we name him who will lead us. Among the Rangers let Jeffrey David Sinclair be known as Entil'Zha."

Immediately, the Rangers down front shouted out in unison: "Entil'Zha! We live for the One. We die for the One!"

"Entil'Zha," Rathenn continued. "He is the light in darkness. He is the bridge between worlds."

At that, a roar of approval went up from the whole crowd. The ceremony was over. They were to leave in reverse order. Sinclair turned and walked steadily to the ramp. Sakai did not wait for him to get halfway down as she had been instructed, but went immediately to his side as he took the first step down, staying a step behind, but prepared for anything.

Neroon waited until they were well down the ramp before leaving; Rathenn followed a little more quickly than protocol required. When she was sure they were out of sight of the crowd, Sakai put a steadying hand on Sinclair's elbow. His steps were beginning to falter, and he was now shaking visibly.

"My God," she said as they reached the bottom of the ramp and headed for the nearby buildings where the doctors were waiting for him. "What the hell did they make you drink?"

"My own damn fault," he whispered. "So nervous—swallowed—more than I meant to."

Rathenn was beside them now, looking on with concern, but before he could say anything, Neroon had joined them.

"Entil'Zha," Neroon said in a cool voice. "Feeling a little ill?"

Sakai wanted to go for him, wanted to knock the contemptuous smirk off his face, and a lot more, but she wasn't about to let go of Sinclair, even if she thought she had a chance to do Neroon some damage, which she knew only too well she didn't.

Her anger quickly turned to astonishment, however, when she heard Sinclair manage a weak laugh.

"A sense—of humor, Neroon?" he said hoarsely. "Didn't think—you had one."

Neroon halted, perhaps out of his own surprise, leaving Sakai and Rathenn, who now had Sinclair's other arm, to hurry the new Entil'Zha into the nearest building.

Sinclair did not lose consciousness until they entered the room where the doctors were waiting. He was hurried onto a gurney and hooked up to a nightmarish-looking collection of IV tubes, electrodes, and monitoring patches. They administered what they claimed was an antidote, explaining that pumping his stomach would make matters worse, not better. After an hour, they placed him in a medical transport, and sent him home with Sakai.

They had done everything they could. All that remained now was to wait and let him recover.

For three days and three nights, a fever burned through him. Sakai stayed with him, doing what she could to calm him when he thrashed about and called out in his delirium, sleeping there at the bedside only when exhaustion forced her to. The Minbari doctors checked in regularly, assured her everything was proceeding properly, then left again.

On the morning of the fourth day, she had fallen asleep leaning forward on the bed. She was brought out of a hazy dream by the touch of a hand on her face. She opened her eyes to see Sinclair sitting up a little, smiling a little weakly, the fever broken.

"Hi," was all he said.

"Good to have you back." She took his hand and pressed it against her cheek.

"It's good to be back. I took quite a ride. Some wild dreams."

"I gathered as much," she admitted. "You did a little talking in your sleep."

"I imagine you heard your name a few times," he said.

"A few times."

"You were in almost all my dreams, sometimes just as a silent observer. Even on the Line. I spent an eternity on the Line. And on the Minbari ship. It was odd, but everywhere I saw death and destruction I kept seeing Ulkesh as well. Made him something of a demonic figure, I'm afraid. What do you think about that?"

"I don't know," she said.

"My subconscious was probably being very unfair to him."

"Maybe. Did you see Kosh, as well?"

"Yes," he said, as if suddenly remembering something. "It seems to me he was trying to tell me something, but I could never quite make it out." He thought about it for a moment, then shrugged. "But do you know, I also dreamed a lot about Father Raffelli and his wife. I haven't dreamed about them in years."

Sakai knew they were the husband and wife priests who had run the high school Sinclair had attended after his father had been killed in the Dilgar War. They had become lifelong friends until their deaths several years back.

"Went back to school again, did you?"

She wondered if she shouldn't be contacting the Minbari doctors, or maybe just letting him sleep. But though he looked tired, his color was returning as clearly was his energy. And he seemed to want to talk.

"Sometimes. I went back a couple of times to the day I first arrived there. I can still feel how angry I was at God and the Universe at large for taking my father away. My poor mother hadn't known what else to do but send me there. There he was, this decrepit-looking old priest, and me wondering what kind of a prig he was—only to have him invite me for a spin on that speedboat of his. I was sure we were both going to die the way he hurled that boat around."

Sakai smiled. She'd of course heard all this before, but he hadn't spoken of it in some time.

"But what I dreamt about more was when I went back to see them after the war. You remember how I was, so enraged with the Minbari that I shut out everything else in my life. I wouldn't let myself express it, and I couldn't let it go."

"I remember," she said softly.

"So here I am in these dreams, going back again and again to that retreat I took with the Raffellis after the war. Kept hearing them talk to me about forgiveness and love, urging me to learn as much as I could about the Minbari. Study their languages, read their history, examine their culture. Because, they said, through knowledge comes understanding, and through understanding comes forgiveness. And without forgiveness, they said, we lose what is best in our Humanity."

He closed his eyes, as if suddenly running out of the little energy that had come back to him. She wondered if he had gone to sleep, when he sighed and opened his eyes again. "I also remember that at times it wasn't the Raffellis talking, but Jenimer." He smiled. "I have a feeling they would have liked each other."

"I'm sure you're right," she said.

"I think I'll sleep for a while," he said, drifting off almost before finishing the sentence.

She left quietly to call the doctors from the other room, but she knew he was going to be fine.

CHAPTER 27

"I AM a Ranger. We walk in the dark places no others will enter. We stand on the bridge and no one may pass. We live for the One. We die for the One."

Sinclair felt a surge of conflicting feelings to hear Catherine Sakai's voice among those of all the other newly initiated Rangers saying those words and making that pledge contained in the last two sentences. He was very proud of her, of course. But he had certainly never asked her to live or die for Jeff Sinclair, and he wasn't comfortable having her do so for the Entil'Zha.

It was just Minbari tradition, he reminded himself. He no more expected her to take that pledge literally than he did the other new Rangers assembled before him in the chapel. He knew that all his Rangers would accomplish their work and do their duty to the best of their abilities regardless of personal risk. More than that he could—and would—ask of no one.

He tried to concentrate on his feelings of delight and pride at what this group of Humans and Minbari had already accomplished, and the enthusiasm with which they were embarking on the future, Catherine among them.

Sech Turval dismissed the new Rangers and they filed out. Sinclair allowed himself one brief moment in the temple by himself—not counting Valen, of course—to collect his thoughts. Lately, these ceremonies had been raising other emotions in him. Looking into the eager faces of new Rangers waiting for him to send them off on their first missions, off Minbar and out among the stars, he found himself feeling a familiar restlessness that was getting harder and harder to push down.

Sinclair left the temple and stood by the entrance to look on as the excited Humans and Minbari congratulated each other, shaking hands, bowing, hugging—depending on who was congratulating whom—laughing, and in a few cases crying. A typical graduation. It might be the last typical thing any of them did for a long time. With Shadow activity expanding rapidly, tensions growing between Earth and Minbar, tensions growing between the Minbari military and religious castes, and the Narn-Centauri war escalating in ferocity while going ever more badly for the Narns, there was plenty for every Ranger to do.

Sinclair saw Catherine and Marcus congratulating each other, each with huge grins. Marcus had turned out to be as fine a prospective Ranger as Sinclair had hoped. Intelligent, resourceful, quick to learn, quick to admit a mistake, a holy terror with the *denn'bok,* and one hell of a pilot. A Ranger didn't necessarily have to be a good pilot, but Sinclair admittedly had a certain prejudice in this area.

Sakai finally made her way over to where Sinclair was standing. Everyone knew of their relationship, of course, but he didn't think public displays of that kind of affection were proper for his position. So he just smiled broadly and said: "Congratulations. I'm very proud of you."

"Thank you," she said with an equally decorous

bow of the head, but then couldn't contain her grin. "It feels pretty good."

They left the celebration behind and headed back to the house, walking in silence for a while.

"Well," Sakai said at last. "It's time to bring up *the* subject again. What now?"

Sinclair had been waiting for this question. "What you asked me to do three months ago. Put your talents to their fullest use to help with the work." That sounded more formal than he'd planned. "I'm going to assign you full-time to training pilots. The other teachers and your fellow students are united in—"

Sakai laughed. "I wasn't being very clear, was I? Although, that's an excellent idea, Entil'Zha, and I'd be most pleased to be assigned to that duty. But actually I was talking about our postponed wedding. We both agreed it was better to wait until after graduation—"

"Oh," Sinclair said with a grin. "That. Well, it doesn't look like a trip to Babylon 5 is in the cards anytime soon, and I don't think we should wait any longer. So, I guess we'll just have to have the ceremony right here. We have an ordained minister and a Buddhist priest among our Rangers."

"Now if the Entil'Zha can just find time in his schedule," she said, teasing.

He nodded. "Don't worry. He will."

As the Rangers continued to grow in both number and responsibilities, his duties kept him busier all the time. Perhaps just a little too busy, he had slowly come to believe. If they were trying to keep him so occupied he wouldn't have time to think about other things, it hadn't succeeded. The work, in the broader sense of what the Rangers were trying to do, was important, of course. But the work in the more narrow sense of his day-to-day responsibilities was sometimes frustrating.

And a raw, restless dissatisfaction had been building inside him lately. He wondered if sooner or later Catherine wouldn't feel the same thing. Lines from "Ulysses" came to mind . . .

"What are you thinking about?" Sakai asked.

"I don't know if I want to tell you," he said with a laugh. "Tennyson . . . again."

"Which verses are rattling around in your mind today?"

" 'How dull it is to pause, to make an end; To rust unburnished, not to shine in use!' "

Sakai was silent for a moment. "I know you well enough to know what that means. You're feeling planet-bound, aren't you?"

"I've been on Minbar for eight months now," he said. "I haven't been to space in all that time. On Babylon 5, I could just get in a Starfury when I started to feel like this. I can't do that here. I've been keeping my piloting skills sharp by flying the trainer craft and using the computer simulations. But it isn't the same. All my life I've tried to avoid flying a desk and pushing paper. But somehow, I keep having those jobs pushed on me. Giving it a Minbari name doesn't make it any better."

"I understand," she said.

"Listen, I'm sorry," he said as they came up to their quarters. "I shouldn't have brought it up, not today. Everyone feels a bit restless now and again. I'll deal with it."

"Jeff, don't do that—" she started to say, but stopped abruptly after she opened the door.

Rathenn and Ulkesh were waiting for them inside.

Sinclair had not seen the Vorlon as often as he had when Jenimer was alive. Whenever he did appear, Rathenn was usually with him.

"I do apologize, Entil'Zha, for this unavoidable invasion of your privacy,'' Rathenn said, ''but we have a matter of the greatest urgency to discuss with you. One that must be held in the strictest of confidence and there is no more secure place to talk than here.''

Sakai started to leave. ''I'll take another walk.''

Rathenn stopped her. ''No. It is better for you to stay.''

It appeared to Sinclair they were going to have this discussion standing in the middle of the room, which the Minbari seemed to find perfectly normal. Obviously, so did the Vorlons since he'd never actually seen one sit down. Sinclair had once seen just enough in Kosh's quarters on B5 to assume the Vorlons didn't have corporeal bodies in the same sense Humans and Minbari did, so the very concept of sitting was probably irrelevant to them. It wasn't to Sinclair, however. He'd been on his feet since dawn.

''Perhaps I should begin by asking a question,'' Rathenn said. ''Has the Entil'Zha told Anla'shok Sakai about his experiences with the time rift in Sector 14?''

There was very little that Rathenn could have said to him that would have astonished him more. ''I'm much more interested in what *you* know about it, Rathenn.''

''Less than one Earth year ago,'' Rathenn said, ''Babylon 5's sensors detected unusual tachyon emissions coming from the area in Sector 14 where the space station Babylon 4 had disappeared. You went to investigate personally and found that Babylon 4 had reappeared. On the day it vanished, it passed through a time rift, emerging four years into their future, although it seemed to them that only a few days had passed. You evacuated the crew just before the station again disappeared through the rift. After that, the time rift seemed to close down and Earth quarantined Sector 14 because of dangerous residual effects leaving time and space there in a turbulent state. Are those the essential facts?"

"More or less," Sinclair said carefully. Rathenn had left out the part about the alien Zathras and the mysterious figure in a blue spacesuit who seemed to be responsible for Babylon 4 going through the rift. "But I'm interested in your use of the phrase '*seemed* to close down.' Are you saying that rift is still open?"

"Is Anla'shok Sakai also aware of the presence of the Great Machine at the heart of Epsilon 3?" Rathenn asked, rather than answering Sinclair's question.

Now Sinclair was really puzzled. Babylon 5 had been built and placed in orbit around the planet Epsilon 3 under the assumption that it was uninhabited. But about a month before the appearance of the time rift, Sinclair had discovered that Epsilon 3 housed an immense and incredibly powerful alien apparatus controlled by a mysterious alien that lived as part of the machine. When that alien died, his place had been taken by a Minbari named Draal, an old friend of Delenn's. For the first time, Sinclair considered the possibility that there was more than coincidence at work here.

"She's aware of all of it," Sinclair said, glancing briefly at Sakai who was listening with great interest. "Are you saying there's a connection between the rift and the Great Machine?"

"The rift is a natural phenomenon the Vorlons believe to be unique," Rathenn said. "Only the power of the Great Machine can control it. After Babylon 4 went through the second time, Draal closed the rift so that no other ships could accidentally pass through. But he did not close it off entirely."

Sinclair didn't like the way this was beginning to sound. He looked at Ulkesh, looming silently as usual. "What do the Vorlons have to do with this?"

"They are aware of all these events," Rathenn said, "and have been cooperating with Draal and a very few selected Minbari to maintain the rift and keep it from being misused."

"Why?" Sinclair asked, still looking at Ulkesh. "What interest do the Vorlons have in the rift? Are you responsible for what happened to Babylon 4?"

Rathenn sounded uncomfortable. "I do not know the exact chronology of all these events."

Sinclair ignored this nonanswer and continued to train his attention on Ulkesh. When the Vorlon didn't answer, he tried again. "What's your interest in the rift, Ambassador?"

"It has value," Ulkesh replied.

"What kind of value?"

"Unique value."

"What do you know about what happened to Babylon 4?"

Again, Ulkesh did not answer.

"Entil'Zha," Rathenn said, almost pleading, "there are more immediate and urgent concerns to discuss."

"Like what?" Sinclair asked, his attention still on Ulkesh.

"The Shadows know about the rift, and are attempting to seize control of it for their own use."

That brought Sinclair's attention back to Rathenn. "Have the Shadows attacked Epsilon 3?"

"No, the Vorlons assure us the Shadows would never attack the Great Machine."

"Why not?"

Rathenn was appearing ever more discomfited by Sinclair's barrage of questions. "I do not know, Entil'Zha. I simply accept their word that it's so."

Sinclair hesitated, doubting he'd get an answer to

that question. He decided to press on. "Then how can the Shadows seize control of the rift from Draal?"

Rathenn was relieved to be on surer ground. "They have sent some of their allies to Sector 14 with a device to widen the rift far enough for ships to go through. Draal did not discover this until they were already beginning the process. He immediately countered their efforts, but he is expending enormous energy and using nearly all of his concentration just to offset the power of the Shadow device and keep the rift closed down enough to prevent entry. If he falters for a second, all will be lost: If the Shadows gain control of the rift, they will control history, and utter destruction will be the result. The Shadow apparatus must be destroyed."

Sinclair found himself once again caught in a very familiar dilemma. If what Rathenn said was true, it obviously would not be a good idea to hand over the rift to the Shadows. But Sinclair wasn't so sure he liked the idea of the Vorlons in control of that rift, either. What plans did they have for it?

Well, Sinclair thought, *first deal with the devil you know, and attend to the devil you don't know later.*

"Are they aware of this on Babylon 5? Have they already tried to do something?"

"No," Rathenn said. "The station's long-range scanners cannot detect the Shadow allies' presence. Their ships can amplify the time-space distortion in a way that renders the immediate area around them effectively invisible to all long-range scans. Only a nearby ship could detect them. Since the area is off-limits, that has not occurred."

"And you haven't warned anyone on the station about this?" Sinclair asked, already guessing the answer.

"No," Rathenn said. "It is best if the Shadows believe the station has no current involvement with the rift.''

''What about our Vorlon friends here?'' Sinclair asked, but not wanting to let the Vorlons off the hook too easily. ''Why haven't they gone in there and destroyed that apparatus? I'm sure they have the capability to do so.''

''The Shadows must not know of the Vorlons' involvement with the rift. The only way is to send in a small team of Rangers, who themselves must never discuss this mission or even acknowledge the existence of the rift.''

''But if we do that, then the Shadows will know about the Rangers. I thought you wanted to avoid that as well.''

''It can be done in such a way that the Shadows will believe the attack came from Epsilon 3. The Shadows do not know for sure what forces Draal has at his command.''

''It sounds good in theory,'' Sinclair said, ''but the reality is we simply don't have any ships that can match up to Shadow vessels.''

''There are no true Shadow vessels at the rift,'' said Rathenn. ''The Shadows themselves do not want to risk the unpredictable effects of the rift until everything is secure and ready. They have sent their allies instead, in small fighters. They are far less powerful than the larger Shadow vessels, and we believe there are only four of them guarding and maintaining the apparatus.''

''Four or four hundred, it doesn't matter. You know we don't have access to any fighters or warships suitable for a mission like this.''

''That is no longer true.''

''The Whitestar ships!'' Sinclair said suddenly as Rathenn nodded. ''They're finally ready?''

"Three small experimental prototypes are. These are single-pilot ships built to test the technology that is being used in the larger warships."

Sinclair's hopes plummeted as quickly as they had risen. "Then how does that help us?"

"They may only be small prototypes," Rathenn said, "but I am assured they are powerful fighter ships in their own right. Similar to your Starfuries but much more powerful and maneuverable."

"But only three of them? Against at least four Shadow ships of basically unknown capability?"

"The Vorlons assure us these prototypes are a match for their Shadow fighters. By attacking swiftly and with surprise, the mission should be easily accomplished—with the right pilots."

Sinclair exchanged looks with Catherine. Was that why Rathenn insisted she stay for this meeting? His worst fears were confirmed when Rathenn produced a list and handed it to him. "We have determined from the training records that these are the best Ranger pilots available at this time for this mission."

He saw her name at the top of the list, even as Rathenn said: "We believe Anla'shok Sakai is the best qualified of all those on the list. She has the most hours logged as a pilot, was rated the best by her teachers, has the highest scores on the computer simulators, and has real combat experience."

Sinclair hesitated while Sakai looked at him expectantly. Had she not been in the room, he might have simply vetoed the idea. Or he might have gone to her later and tried to find some way of presenting it to her while talking her out of it at the same time.

No. Most likely he would have said anyway what he was about to say now, both out of respect for her, and out of his duty as the leader of the Rangers. But he would rather have cut his tongue out than say it.

"Catherine." He kept his voice and expression neutral. "Do you want to volunteer for this mission? You're under no requirement to do so."

"You bet I do," she said.

Sinclair kept his emotions tightly under control and looked back down at the list. Marcus Cole was one of the names, far and away the best pilot among the other names, but . . .

"Nobody else here has combat experience. We have several Rangers currently away on missions with more experience."

"We cannot take the time to contact them and await their return. We must move immediately."

"How immediately?"

"The pilots must leave for the rift in two days."

Sinclair was incredulous. "That's impossible. You can't expect pilots to go into combat in unfamiliar ships."

"They will not be unfamiliar. All Ranger pilots have been training in these fighters through the computer simulators."

"That's not the same thing."

"The simulators were programmed to exactly duplicate the prototype fighters in every way. The pilots will have one day to familiarize themselves with the actual ships. The Vorlons and our own engineers assure us that's all they will need."

"Absolutely not. They must have more time—"

"I'm afraid there is no more time, Entil'Zha. The Vorlons tell us Draal cannot counter the Shadow device much longer. And we fear the Shadows may be preparing to send reinforcements, perhaps even a second apparatus to widen the rift. The device and its guards must be destroyed now. Once that is done, Draal will be able to reassert his control over the rift in such a way as to make sure this does not happen again. But we must move immediately. Any delay could mean the destruction of history itself.''

Sinclair didn't like this at all. He didn't like the feeling he wasn't being told everything. Didn't like being pushed into hasty action. Didn't like sending his Rangers, including Sakai, into combat without adequate preparation. Didn't like having to do *any* of this simply because the Vorlons were unwilling to take any action themselves.

But he had taken this job on the assumption he could at least trust the Minbari to try and do what was right. He wished Jenimer were here. All he could do was trust Rathenn—and Draal. He examined the list of pilots again.

''I'll ask Marcus Cole,'' Sinclair said finally, confident Marcus would jump at the chance. He handed the list back to Rathenn. ''And I'll be the third pilot.''

Sakai wasn't at all surprised. Rathenn, on the other hand, was thunderstruck.

''No.'' That was Ulkesh, as emphatic as Sinclair had ever heard him. ''The path is clear. Do not deviate.''

Sinclair took grim pleasure in how much he had upset the Vorlon.

''You said you want the three best pilots to go. I've trained extensively on the simulators myself. I've had the most combat experience of anyone on that list. And I'm the only person who's had experience with the time rift.''

''The Entil'Zha must not risk his life,'' Rathenn said, finding his voice. ''As leader, your life is too important. You must—''

''Hide behind the lines? Send men and women possibly to die, but take no risks myself? That's the philosophy of bureaucrats, Rathenn, not leaders. A leader has to take necessary risks. Simply put, I'm the best man for the job. Besides, there's an old saying on Earth: 'Nothing motivates a man more than to see his boss putting in an honest day's work.' "

Ulkesh moved toward Sinclair. Was the Vorlon hoping to intimidate him? Sinclair stood his ground.

"An electron follows its proper course," Ulkesh said. "So does a galaxy. You must follow yours."

"That's exactly what I *am* doing."

"Choose another pilot."

"No," Sinclair said. "But I'll give you a choice. Either I lead this mission, or you send Vorlon ships to do it."

CHAPTER 28

"WHAT do you think?" Sinclair asked over the com from the cockpit of Fighter 1.

"It's even better than the simulator!" Marcus said from Fighter 3, rolling his craft into a tight spin.

"Agreed," said Sakai from Fighter 2. "Handles better than anything I've ever seen."

The three new fighters were skimming low over the airless landscape of Minbar's smaller, uninhabited moon, the pilots already having tried every maneuver with the ships they could think of. They had been given only a few hours to get comfortable with these Minbari-Vorlon hybrid spaceships, and though Sinclair would have preferred at least a couple of days of practice for them all, he had to admit he already felt totally at ease in this fighter.

"Whatever else you might say about the Vorlons," he said over the com, "they know a thing or two about building spacecraft."

"Amen to that, Fighter 1," said Marcus. "Can I keep this one when we're done? As a souvenir?"

"I'll see what I can do," Sinclair said with a grin. He had not forgotten how serious and dangerous the task before them was, and had made a point of stressing that fact to both Catherine and Marcus when they saw the prototype fighters for the first time sitting in the empty docking bay of an orbiting Minbari freighter. But, at least for this moment, Marcus wasn't the only one having the time of his life.

"What about target practice?" Sakai asked.

"On schedule, Fighter 2," Sinclair replied. "We're coming up on it in Valerian's crater, straight ahead."

Some of the Ranger laser targets had been arranged in the wide, shallow crater to allow them to test the accuracy of their energy cannons and missiles. Sinclair was not surprised to find the weaponry systems to be as well engineered as the rest of the ship. There had been no surprises. Everything on the fighters performed exactly as with the simulators or better.

All too soon, it was time to return to the Minbari freighter. They entered the docking bay and the space doors closed behind them even as the lumbering freighter headed toward Minbar's jump gate to begin the three-and-a-half-day trip through hyperspace to the Babylon 5 jump gate.

Sinclair was surprised to see Rathenn waiting for them as they emerged from the docking bay still in their pressure suits, helmets under their arms, and right in the middle of a spirited evaluation of the ships.

"Entil'Zha," Rathenn bowed. "Do you approve?"

"Very much, Rathenn. I didn't know you'd come aboard. Shouldn't you be on a shuttle off of here before we hit that jump gate?"

"I will be accompanying you to Babylon 5, Entil'Zha."

"I see," Sinclair said. It struck him as more than a little unusual. Rathenn had already debriefed them thoroughly. Or so Sinclair had thought. "Catherine. Marcus. Go on ahead and change out of your pressure suits." As they left, Sinclair gestured for Rathenn to take a walk with him, then got right to the point. "Please don't take this wrong, Rathenn, but is there any particular reason you've chosen to come along?"

"To be of assistance where I can, Entil'Zha."

The Satai could do a passable imitation of the Vorlon when he wanted to. "Do you have more information for us?"

"Nothing at this time, Entil'Zha."

Sinclair stopped walking. "Rathenn, if you have anything more to tell me, anything of importance, I'm asking you, don't leave it for the last minute."

Rathenn gave him a quizzical look. "Information is always given at the proper time, Entil'Zha," he said.

Sinclair tried not to sigh. That did not particularly reassure him, but there didn't seem to be much he could do about the Minbari penchant for parceling out information as they deemed best.

"Then if you'll excuse me, I want to catch up with my fellow pilots."

Rathenn would make his purpose known soon enough, Sinclair knew. In the meantime, he, Catherine, and Marcus would have plenty to keep them occupied during the time in hyperspace, going over every inch of their ships to make sure all was in order, studying what information they had been given about the Shadow fighters and the device they were to destroy, and planning an attack strategy.

Rathenn had said the mission should be easy to accomplish. Sinclair wasn't willing to give that assurance any credence at all. Nothing concerning the Shadows—or the Vorlons—had ever been easy.

Sinclair caught up with Catherine and Marcus, and as they continued toward their bunk area to get out of their pressure suits, he resumed their discussion of the fighters, pushing doubt out of his mind for now.

* * *

''Do you think this is the only time rift in existence?'' Sakai asked.

As they ate their dinner in the mess area set up for them, Sinclair had been doing his best to answer whatever questions Marcus and Catherine had about his experiences with the time rift.

''I don't know,'' Sinclair replied. ''Rathenn said that the rift was a unique natural phenomenon. But it seems to me, if the laws of physics and nature can cause it to happen once, it's possible for it to happen more than once, in more than one place. Maybe Rathenn only meant it's an extremely rare phenomenon.''

''Or maybe it's unique,'' Sakai said, ''because nature got a little help in its creation, say from the Vorlons.''

''Which would imply they could do it again, if they wanted to,'' Sinclair agreed. ''But we just don't know. All we know for sure is that they are very concerned about keeping control of this one.''

''Well, that's not the part I have a problem with,'' Marcus said. ''I have a problem with the notion of this rift being some kind of a time machine.''

''Then how do you explain what happened to Babylon 4?'' Sakai asked.

''That's easy,'' Marcus said. ''Let's say the rift does distort space-time in some previously unknown way. B4 had the bad luck to get caught up in it and was accelerated by the effect enough to experience relativistic effects. When they slow down, presto, they think it's a couple of weeks later, but find out four years have passed. Nothing too mysterious about that. And a heck of a lot easier to accomplish than going back in time.''

''I don't know,'' Sinclair said. ''That doesn't explain

the time flashes we experienced while near the rift. I had the feeling I had been propelled forward in time, but Garibaldi relived something from his past.''

''You experienced *something,* but I thought you said you never physically ever left B4.''

''I'm not sure. There'd be a blinding flash of light, and afterward someone would report having experienced a time flash. Now, did the person physically go backward or forward in time and then return to the present, all within the time frame of that flash of light? Or did we only experience it in our minds, and not physically travel in time at all? I don't know, except that it *felt* real.''

''Whatever you experienced happened outside the rift. You never actually went through the rift itself,'' Sakai added. ''But Marcus has a point. If this rift really is a time machine, why haven't the Vorlons used it? Why don't they just take a quick trip to the past and change things so that the Shadows are no longer a threat to anybody. It's the sort of thing they're afraid the Shadows will do if given the chance.''

''I've asked those same questions,'' Sinclair said ruefully, ''and haven't yet gotten a satisfactory answer. I know this: persons claiming to be from the future came aboard B4 and took it through the rift because they said it was needed to fight a great war. And I believe the Vorlons know something about that incident, and are now very concerned about maintaining control of the rift. But that's all I can say for sure.''

''Well, people can *claim* anything they want,'' Marcus said skeptically. ''All we really know for sure, Entil'Zha, is that *somebody* came aboard and took B4 through the rift for some purpose. But I have a hard time believing they were from the future without some proof, like a future edition of *Universe Today.*''

Sakai laughed. ''Do you have a personal grudge against the idea of time travel, Marcus?''

''Only traveling *backward* in time,'' he explained. ''We all travel forward. I put traveling backward in time in the same category as superstition and myth. It violates too many laws of physics, logic, and causality to be possible. It's just a romantic notion, a form of unhealthy nostalgia. I mean, who wouldn't like to be able to travel into the past, knowing everything that's going to happen, so that you can correct old mistakes? But let's face it, if you want to rectify your mistakes, you have to do so in the present—the past is done and gone. If you spend all your time wishing you could change the past, you miss your opportunities to change things right here and now.''

''You make a persuasive argument,'' Sinclair said. ''And the truth is, I tend to agree with you. Nevertheless, I experienced things near that rift that I still can't explain. You'll just have to see for yourself.''

''That's one of my mottoes, Entil'Zha,'' Marcus said.

When they finished dinner, they said good night and went to their assigned sleeping quarters. The Minbari freighter had not been designed to accommodate passengers—or Humans—and the small area set aside for Sinclair and Sakai offered few amenities other than privacy. It was a rectangular room with bare metal walls and a ceiling so low Sinclair's head brushed against it if he stood up too straight. It was just barely large enough to contain the usual Minbari bed, set at a forty-five-degree angle.

Sakai started laughing when she saw the bed.

''You wouldn't think it was so funny,'' Sinclair said with mock indignation, ''if you'd had your hand caught in the gears of these things as many times as I have.''

"Come on, I'll help you fix it."

She held the bed straight while he grabbed an extra blanket and crouched down to reach the gear mechanism. "And here I thought we wouldn't have time for a honeymoon trip," he said, as he shoved the blanket into what he hoped was the right place in the mechanism. He stood up to test it. The bed held firmly in the horizontal.

"You can't have a honeymoon before the wedding, Sinclair," Sakai said, testing the steadiness of the bed for herself.

"Who says?" he replied, smiling.

The Minbari freighter left hyperspace through the jump gate at Babylon 5 exactly on schedule. To Command and Control on the station, it was just one of many Minbari commercial ships that used the gate and so it was given little more than a cursory glance as it made its way to take up an orbit around the planet Epsilon 3. Many ships took similar orbits, then used small shuttles to travel to and from the space station. That this freighter's orbit would take it to the other side of the planet away from Babylon 5 would hardly be noticed by anyone.

The three-and-half-day trip had been uneventful but productive. Sinclair felt sure that they were ready to do the job. They were comfortable with their fighters, and confident they had the firepower and the maneuverability to face the Shadow fighters, who would be hampered by their need to stay close to their apparatus at the rift to protect it.

The plan was simple. As soon as the freighter was on the other side of Epsilon 3, out of sight of Babylon 5 and any other ships, Sinclair, Sakai, and Marcus would leave for Sector 14 in their fighters. The trip in normal space would take three hours, and their trajectory, if traced back by the Shadows, would show them as having come from Epsilon 3, as the Vorlons wanted.

Sinclair had been assured that the distortion effect used by the Shadow fighters to hide their activities from Babylon 5's sensors would also make it difficult for the Shadow fighters to detect them as they approached from the other side of the rift, away from the Shadow apparatus.

As Rathenn had said, it all appeared straightforward, almost easy. And that's what worried Sinclair the most.

The three of them suited up in the docking bay, and checked out their pressure-suit systems while they waited for word they could launch. Pressure suits were customarily used by Earthforce pilots as backup protection, and although the cockpits of the prototype fighters had full life-support systems, Sinclair had decided wearing the suits would be a wise precaution.

"Entil'Zha?"

Sinclair hadn't noticed Rathenn's arrival. They hadn't seen much of Rathenn during the trip, and he still didn't have any idea what purpose had brought the Grey Council member along with them. Maybe they were finally going to find out.

"We have reached the desired position in orbit," Rathenn said, "but there will be a short delay before your launch. I must ask you and your Rangers to please accompany me out of the bay. A shuttle from the planet will be docking within minutes."

Even as he spoke, an alarm sounded, and a warning was broadcast in worker-caste Minbari to clear the docking bay. They followed Rathenn out to the holding area and then watched through the observation window as the space doors opened and a small shuttle landed. The odd craft was of a design unfamiliar to Sinclair, and he wondered who was in it. Draal was literally part of the machine below, and couldn't have left the planet even if he hadn't been completely preoccupied with the Shadow threat. Beyond that, Sinclair had not been aware anyone else lived on the planet.

When the bay repressurized, Rathenn asked them to please continue waiting, and went alone to the alien ship. A hatch opened and Rathenn went aboard, to emerge only a minute later, carrying three small boxes. He returned to the holding area, and the space doors in the bay opened once again to allow the tiny shuttle to leave without ever having revealed its pilot to the others.

Sinclair inspected the small boxes, each marked with a different glyph in an unknown alien script. Rathenn examined those glyphs carefully before handing one box each to Sinclair, Catherine, and Marcus. Each box contained a round metallic object, somewhat bigger than a belt buckle, with a clasp on one side.

"These are time stabilizers," Rathenn explained. "They will keep you anchored in the present and protect you from the effects of the time distortion caused by the rift. You must attach them to your suits and not remove them for as long as you are near the rift. This is imperative. The effects of the time distortion are unpredictable and can be fatal without these stabilizers."

It seemed hard to believe such a small, almost featureless device could have such a protective effect, but Sinclair had seen firsthand how dangerous the rift could be and would take any help he could get.

"We'll use them, don't worry," he said.

"Then it is time for you to depart. May Valen light your way." Rathenn bowed and left.

"Do you really think these things will do us any

good?'' Marcus asked as they walked back to their fighters.

''Don't take the chance that they won't,'' Sinclair replied.

Marcus shrugged and attached the stabilizer to his suit. ''See you in space,'' he said and climbed aboard his ship.

Sinclair stopped Sakai. ''Let me see your stabilizer for a minute,'' he said.

''Why?'' she asked, handing it over to him.

''Didn't you notice each box had a different glyph?'' he asked, examining her stabilizer and comparing it to his own. ''I just wanted to see if I could find any difference between them.''

''And?''

''They look exactly the same to me. Here.'' Sinclair handed her a stabilizer, hoping she wouldn't notice he was giving her his, and keeping hers for himself. ''See you in space,'' he said, and gave her a quick kiss.

''See you in space.''

Sinclair walked to his fighter, still examining the stabilizer. They *looked* exactly the same, but it also looked as if some distinction had been made. The way Sinclair saw it, the only one of the three of them that he could be absolutely sure would be given a device that would have a protective effect was himself. The Vorlon and the Minbari both seemed to have a vested interest in his safety. He'd take his chances with the stabilizer meant for her. It might have been an unnecessary thing to do, but after eight months around Ulkesh, it didn't seem unwarranted.

He climbed aboard his fighter and prepared to launch.

CHAPTER 29

SINCLAIR made visual sighting first. They had already begun deceleration when he saw the tiny blue dot that his ship's sensors confirmed was the time-rift area. That there was anything to see at all was a change from Sinclair's first visit to Sector 14 the year before; the area, while emitting high levels of tachyons and other radiation, had looked normal from the outside, showing a visible distortion only as his shuttle had passed from normal space into the rift area itself.

But as they continued toward the rift, Sinclair could see it now appeared as a bright blue disk with a small black area at its center, surrounded for a few hundred miles by a visual distortion that caused the light of the stars beyond to undulate like so much phosphorescent foam upon an ocean.

"You're sure it's safe for us to go through this stuff?" Marcus said from Fighter 3 as they approached the outer edge of the distortion.

"The Vorlons and Minbari think so," Sinclair said. "Besides, this distortion will hide our approach until the last possible moment."

As they passed through, an energy discharge momentarily surged around each of the fighters.

"Remember," Sinclair said, "the closer we are to

the rim of the disk, the better. But try not to come in contact with it.''

''But it isn't the opening itself?'' Sakai asked.

''No, that seems to be an outer boundary where the energy levels and distortion are highest,'' Sinclair said. ''The actual rift opening is that dark area in the middle. That's what the Shadows are trying to open up, and that's what we want to keep closed down.''

The nearer they got, the more the phenomenon in front of them resembled a mile-wide wheel of blue fire, with a much smaller dark area in the middle that was constantly changing shape and size, opening and closing in an unpredictable pattern. Occasionally the center would open just enough to reveal a field of slowly spinning stars. A closer look revealed those stars were not shining through from the other side of the disk, but rather from some distant time or place within the rift.

For the moment, their trajectory was taking them straight toward that opening, on line with its axis, in their attempt to stay hidden from the Shadow fighters as long as possible. So far, it seemed to be working.

''The Shadow apparatus is on the other side,'' Sinclair said. ''The minute we crest the rim, we should see at least four Shadow fighters, but there may be more than that. Engage at will. We have to get all of the enemy fighters before we can blow the apparatus from a safe distance away. All right, let's do it.''

''Entil'Zha veni!'' Marcus said.

''Entil'Zha veni,'' agreed Sakai.

''God help us,'' Sinclair said, and pitched his fighter up and away from the rift opening into a vector toward the rim, followed on his left by Marcus and on his right by Sakai.

Before they'd even reached the top, Sinclair saw the first enemy fighter. It was coming over the rim, a strange spiky ship, just slightly smaller than his own fighter. It seemed to have a stubbornly indeterminate shape and an indistinct gray mottled surface, making it difficult to look at closely. It had no discernible features other than a front maw from which the alien immediately fired at Sinclair.

"Go!" he yelled as he went into a steep dive under both the enemy fire and ship. Sakai rolled right and disappeared over the disk edge, Marcus rolled left and did the same. Sinclair headed straight at the disk, then pulled up sharply to skim along the tops of the radiant energy flares and surging time-space distortion fields. The cockpit around him seemed to shimmer and shift with the distortion, and he climbed away as soon as he could and headed back for the rim. The Shadow fighter was on his tail. Sinclair slipped left and spun his fighter on its vertical axis to face his opponent and avoid another incoming energy burst. Still hurtling—backward—toward the rim, Sinclair fired and scored a direct hit on the Shadow fighter's own weapons port, exploding the alien ship from within.

He was finally on the other side of the rift. He turned his fighter around again as his com suddenly crackled to life. He had apparently been cut off from communication while on the other side of the rift. "—you okay? Fighter One, respond!" It was Catherine.

"I'm fine, Fighter Two."

He saw her in pursuit of a Shadow fighter, firing once just under it, then again, hitting one of the craft's spiked projections, wounding but not destroying it.

Another ship was zeroing in on her.

"Fighter Two, ten o'clock starboard, enemy in pursuit."

He set course to intercept as Sakai went into a turn, but Marcus was already in pursuit of the enemy fighter.

"I'm on it," Marcus said as he came in from above. The enemy ship was about to fire as Marcus fired once, grazing the Shadow fighter and jarring it just enough to knock the enemy's shot at Sakai off course. Sakai came around and finished the Shadow fighter off.

Sinclair turned toward the remaining wounded Shadow fighter, which was coming around again with renewed vigor. He pulled up to evade an incoming shot, brought his ship into a tight loop up and over, then dove down on the fighter from above, firing two shots that shattered the enemy ship.

"All right," Sinclair said, bringing his ship to join the others. "We seem to be clear of bogeys out here. Let's take a look at the main target."

The three fighters fell into line and headed for the rift opening. For the first time, Sinclair got a quick look at the Shadow device they'd been sent to destroy, and it was nothing like he'd expected.

A single jet-black sphere, about the size of a Starfury, floated over the center of the constantly changing rift opening. It was so dark it was difficult to see at all, and was visible only as it occasionally cut off the light of the stars behind it in the rift. Emanating from the sphere were eight pulsing tendrils that seemed too long and fluid to be metal or any other hard material, and yet were clearly solid. The tendrils seemed to be sunk right into the rolling substance of the disk around the rift opening, as if they were pumping something in or out.

And it was guarded by two more Shadow fighters.

"You know the drill," Sinclair said. "We have to take out those fighters without hitting that contraption. Which from this angle, won't be easy."

"They don't look like they're going *anywhere,*" Sakai said.

"Get the feeling they're more afraid of their bosses than us?" Marcus asked.

"Safe assumption, Fighter Three," Sinclair said. "No way we're going to draw them out into the open. So here's what we'll do. All three of us will go in just close enough to get their attention and draw their fire. Fighter Two you'll roll off to the right and up, Fighter Three you'll roll off to the left and down. I'll stick around in front to keep their attention while you two loop back and catch them in a pincer, Fighter Two shooting from directly above the one on the right, Fighter Three from directly below the one on the left, so that you're never shooting in the direction of the apparatus itself."

"Fighter One," Sakai protested immediately. "You're the better shot. I'll take decoy out front."

"I'm pretty good at dodging," Sinclair replied. "Besides, it'll be like shooting fish in a barrel."

"For them or us?" Sakai asked.

"Entil'Zha," Marcus said. "Perhaps you should let me take decoy. After all, you're—"

"That's an order," Sinclair said firmly, cutting off the discussion. "We're approaching the targets. Get ready."

As soon as they were in maximum range, the Shadow fighters opened fire at them. They avoided the first few rounds easily enough, but as they drew closer and the barrage increased, it became increasingly more risky for three ships than just one. Now was the time.

"Go!" Sinclair ordered. As Marcus and Sakai peeled off, Sinclair put his own fighter into a highly erratic evasive pattern. On closest approach, his fighter shook from a volley that stripped the top covering of metal from his port engine nacelle with a shower of sparks, but without doing serious damage.

"Fighter One. Get out of there now!" Sakai shouted over his com.

Sinclair immediately turned and accelerated straight down the center away from the rift opening, as behind him Marcus and Sakai came in for the attack.

"Got 'em!" Marcus yelled, after firing a shot that spun the Shadow fighter away from the apparatus and into the rift's energy disk where it exploded.

A second later, Sakai scored a direct hit on the final Shadow fighter, blowing it apart instantly.

"Zero bogeys," she said.

His sensors—though not working perfectly within the time rift's distortion field—indicated that was so.

"Five Shadow fighters accounted for," he said. "One more than they told us to expect."

"But who's counting?" Marcus chimed in.

"The area seems to be clean," Sinclair continued, "so let's get to the main event."

"A pleasure." Sakai sighed. "I don't like the look of that thing."

"I'm sure that makes three of us," Sinclair agreed. "We're supposed to be outside the distortion field to be absolutely safe when we blow that thing."

"At that distance, we won't be able to see it," Marcus protested.

"We can rely on the computer targeting to do the job. We'll fire three missiles each. I'm sure we'll know right away if we've hit or missed."

"I hope so," Marcus said. "The least we deserve after all of this is a decent fireworks display."

"I'm just happy to get away from here," Sakai said. "I haven't experienced any time flashes, or anything like that, but the area still gives me the weirdest feeling. I don't like it here at all."

"These time stabilizers do seem to be working as

advertised,'' Sinclair said. ''But I agree with you, Fighter Two. This is one area of space I'd just as soon never have to visit again.''

They reached the area demarcating the time rift's extended distortion field from normal space. Sinclair felt a surge of relief as the brief energy discharge around their ships marked their passage out of the time-rift area. He brought his fighter back around, followed by Marcus and Sakai.

''Computer, target object at rift according to sensor readings. Ready missiles for preset detonation at minimum range, and wait for my command. Fighter Two?''

''Ready.''

''Fighter Three?''

''All set.''

''Fire missiles.''

The missiles launched, and Sinclair began a silent countdown: nine, eight, seven, six, five, four, three, two, one . . .

Sinclair saw a small burst of light in the middle of the rift. *That should do it,* he thought, as he watched the fireball expand rapidly.

Without warning, there was a blinding flash of light, as disorienting as those that had preceded the time flashes Sinclair had experienced once before.

Suddenly, the Universe exploded around them.

Sinclair felt his ship tumbling wildly out of control, tried desperately to stay conscious. As darkness threatened to swallow him, he fought to bring his ship back under control, struggled to speak.

''Computer. Emergency override. All systems to stabilizers.''

The ship slowed its tumble, but he still didn't have full control. It was enough, however, so he could check on Catherine and Marcus.

"Fighter Two, are you okay? Fighter Two?"

There was an agonizing pause, then: "I'm all right. What the hell happened?"

Sinclair breathed a whole lot easier, even as he continued to work his console to reestablish full control over his ship. "I don't know yet. Fighter Three? Come in. Are you all right? Fighter Three? Fighter Two, can you see him—"

"I'm okay, Fighter One," Marcus said finally, sounding shaken. "Sort of."

"Full attitude control reestablished," intoned the onboard computer. Sinclair looked up and was puzzled. Then why was the star field outside his canopy still rotating?

"Oh, my God!" That was Sakai's voice. "Look at the rift. We're right on top of it."

Sinclair realized what he was looking at: the rotating star field in front of him was the one in the rift. Somehow, the explosion of the Shadow device had done a lot more than anyone had anticipated. It had altered the time rift. The disk of blue energy was now only a thin ring surrounding a mile-wide, open and obviously passable portal. And they were being drawn into it, Sakai straight ahead of him, Marcus right behind him. By all the laws of physics he could think of, they should have been hurled clear of the rift by the force of that explosion, but he had come to accept that the laws of physics just didn't seem to work the way they should near the rift, and instead they were being pulled rapidly toward it.

"We're going to hit the portal within five minutes if we don't get out of here," Sinclair said. "Let's go back the way we came. Formation turn to starboard."

Sinclair tried to turn his fighter to the right, but it

didn't respond to manual control. "Computer, bring fighter around to starboard, formation turn."

"Unable to carry out command," the computer intoned. "The ship is locked into present course, will not respond to directional controls. Please advise—"

Sinclair was already giving his order. "Computer. Emergency procedures. Engines in reverse. Back away from the rift. Full priority. Fighter Two, Fighter Three—"

"Engines in reverse," Marcus and Sakai said almost simultaneously.

Sinclair's fighter shuddered as his reverse engines kicked in, full power. His forward motion began to slow, then stopped. The ship groaned and shuddered again, then slowly, very slowly began backing away from the rift, inch by inch.

"It's working," Marcus said.

"Yeah, but how long can these ships keep this up?" Sakai asked. "We're pouring everything we got into this. The engines can't tolerate this kind of strain forever."

"They shouldn't have to for long," Sinclair said, trying to sound more hopeful than he felt. "Draal should be working right now to close that portal down."

But Sinclair wondered if the explosion had put the rift out of Draal's control somehow. There were just too many unknown factors at work, and Sinclair didn't like it at all. That explosion, for instance, was nothing like he'd been told to expect. Perhaps the Vorlons knew less about Shadow technology than they thought. Or was it that the Vorlons knew less about this rift than they pretended to know?

"Fighter Two, Fighter Three. How's your progress?"

''Slow but steady,'' Sakai answered.

''I'm picking up just a little bit of speed,'' Marcus said.

Sinclair checked his console again. Nothing, then—yes—he was beginning to pick up just a little speed.

''I'm reading it, too,'' said Sakai. ''A small increase in speed. Looks like we're doing it.''

''Roger that, Fighter Two,'' Sinclair said. ''Perhaps—''

Suddenly weapons fire slammed into Sakai's starboard engine nacelle from above, shearing it off completely from Sakai's fighter, and sending her ship spinning to the right. Then it began tumbling rapidly toward the time rift.

A Shadow fighter swooped down into view, and came straight at Sinclair. Their sensors hadn't detected its presence. It had come over the top of the rim, just as they had, hiding in the distortion the rift created, undetectable until it was too late.

''Marcus, keep going! Get out of here!'' Sinclair yelled. Sinclair fired a split second before the alien ship pulled up to go over Sinclair's ship. The burst hit and took off two of the spiked projections and a good chunk of the lower back portion of the hull, but did not destroy the enemy ship. Like Sakai's fighter, it veered suddenly and uncontrollably toward the rift.

''Computer. Cut reverse engines! Full power ahead! Take us into the rift!''

He was thrown backward into his seat as his fighter jumped forward and hurtled toward the spinning star field ahead.

''Entil'Zha—'' Sinclair heard Marcus say before everything on the com was lost to static.

''Catherine! Do you read me!'' He tried but couldn't get through the interference. He couldn't talk to her, but he could see her ship up ahead, past the tumbling alien ship. They were all on the same trajectory toward—what? Sinclair didn't know. But he was certain that Catherine could have survived—*must* have survived—the attack. These prototype fighters could lose an engine nacelle without damage being done to the cockpit or life-support systems. In fact, because of the Vorlon technology, the ship had the capability of repairing some of the damage automatically. She still had one good engine nacelle with which she could maneuver. He just had to get to her.

Light flooded the cockpit as the star field disappeared and a flowing river of light and energy rushed past his ship. He strained to see ahead, to see past the alien ship, itself almost completely obscured by the moving currents of multicolored light, to find Catherine's ship. He just caught a glimpse of it before it was covered in the fog of light and color.

There was no way to increase his speed; he was already at full power. They were still in the middle of the rift, still had time to go back the way they came, if she could reassert control of her ship and reverse her course . . .

He suddenly realized he had been so focused on going forward to get to her, he didn't even know if it was possible to reverse course inside the rift. Well, if not, he would just keep his course straight ahead and hope he would emerge from the rift at the same place and time that she did. Together, they could figure out what to do next.

The atmosphere around his ship grew less murky. He could see the alien ship clearly now, and just ahead Sakai's ship came back into view.

Then he saw the darkness ahead of them. It looked like a wall of solid obsidian surrounded by blue fire.

"Catherine," he tried again. "If you can hear me, I'm coming through after you. Just hang on. Catherine! Can you hear me? I'll be there. I promise!"

He saw her ship hit the wall of darkness and go through, disappearing section by section until it was gone. The alien ship was next.

The atmosphere began to change once again. Flashes like sheet lightning flared suddenly, increasing rapidly in number and intensity all around him. The alien ship hit the wall, and began to disappear through it, the nose, the middle . . . and stopped, halfway in, with Sinclair's ship headed straight at it on a collision course.

Sinclair tried to pull the nose of his fighter up, tried to veer left or right, but as before, he was frozen into his trajectory and could not alter its course.

"Computer. Collision avoidance. Engines in reverse. Full stop."

His ship began to slow down, but Sinclair realized grimly it wasn't going to be enough. The only question now was would his ship slow down enough to make it possible for him to survive the impact? He braced himself, and concentrated on willing himself to survive, to make it through somehow . . .

He was still a couple of hundred yards out when the alien ship burst apart, as if the wall had closed in on it and crushed it, spewing shrapnel that clanged and clattered off his ship's hull and hard crystalline cockpit canopy like a hailstorm. One piece damaged the port engine intake cone, another larger piece sheared off a sensor array beneath the cockpit, and one small pellet punctured the cockpit canopy, punctured Sinclair's helmet faceplate, snapping his head back and tearing through his left cheek to lodge under his cheekbone.

In front of him, the wall of darkness shattered into a million pieces, revealing an intense, blinding light that swallowed Sinclair and his ship as he clenched his eyes shut and put his arms over his face in a futile attempt to block the painful light.

Then darkness.

"Fighter One! Are you all right?"

It was a moment more before Sinclair's eyes could focus, but then he saw the stars through the canopy, and straight ahead he saw a barely visible circle of translucent energy glowing dimly, slightly distorting the light of the stars behind it, but with no opening to the revolving star field of some other century. The rift was closed.

He heard another voice: his computer was giving a damage report. He must have asked for one, his training having taken over automatically, but he didn't remember doing so.

"Sensor array three completely disabled. Engine two at three-quarters power. Damage to cockpit canopy automatically repaired, life-support systems at nominal."

A part of his mind marveled at how the Vorlon-Minbari-made cockpit windshield had instantly and seamlessly repaired itself, covering the hole caused by the shrapnel, almost like a living creature growing new skin over a wound. The same could not be said for his more conventionally manufactured suit helmet, which was cracked and punctured.

Sinclair pulled the now useless helmet off and hooked it to his chair. He felt a searing pain through the entire left side of his head, felt blood trickling down his cheek, but beyond that—nothing. He was numb, as if his entire being, his body, his mind, his heart, were encased in ice.

"Fighter One! Are you okay? Entil'Zha!"

From a long distance away, he heard himself answer Marcus. "I'm here. Fighter Two is gone."

CHAPTER 30

IT took the damaged fighters five hours to limp back to Epsilon 3. As the freighter made way immediately for the jump gate, Rathenn met Sinclair and Marcus in the docking bay, expressing his regret and sorrow. Sinclair was rushed to the freighter's small infirmary. Along the way, Marcus gave Rathenn a quick report, but the Minbari already seemed to know much of it, apparently having received some word from Draal.

After treating Sinclair for shock and removing the piece of shrapnel from his face, the Minbari doctor told Sinclair he would be fine, but that he would need further treatment on Minbar to completely heal the wound on his face and remove the scar.

Sinclair shook his head, saying nothing. He got up in spite of the doctor's protest that he needed rest.

"I'll rest in my quarters," he said and left.

Leaving Rathenn behind to confer with the doctor, a concerned Marcus went with Sinclair. They walked silently through corridors of the old freighter. Sinclair had said little during the flight back from the rift, and Marcus, then, as now, had not wanted to intrude, trying to help just by his presence. Marcus understood what it meant to lose someone so close, knew what feelings were overwhelming Sinclair. There were no words that could help right now.

When they got to the bunk area, Sinclair paused at the door to his small cabin.

"Thank you, Marcus," he said without looking at him, then disappeared behind the door.

The cramped narrow room seemed like a coffin. He stood just inside the door, unable to move. He had been somehow going through the motions now for seven hours, and it seemed as if he had watched someone else being stitched up by the doctor, someone else being spoken to in sad, hushed tones.

He found he was shaking, realized he could no longer stand, but couldn't bring himself to go over to the bed. His knees buckled and he let himself slide to the floor. He sat in front of the door for what seemed like a long time. Gradually he noticed he was staring at Catherine's duffel bag, leaned up against his own.

"God damn it!" he said, pounding the hard metal floor with his fist. He wanted to cry, but couldn't and that made him angrier.

So much time wasted. So much time they had spent apart over the years, far too often for stupid, avoidable reasons, for stubbornness and for hurt pride and for pointless arguments and for conflicting demands of work . . . and for what? And now when they had finally put all the pieces together, saw that they fit and were always meant to fit together, she was taken away from him again.

And this time it was his fault. He should have refused to let her go on the mission. He should have found a way to reach her ship before it went through the barrier and made the jump into the past. He should have done *something* that he didn't do, something that would have saved her. Something.

He had no idea how long he had been sitting there, staring, unmoving, before he heard a knock on his door.

"Are you all right, Entil'Zha?" It was Marcus, concern evident in his voice.

He almost laughed at the question. *No,* he wanted to shout. *I'm not all right. What the hell do you think? Go away and leave me alone.* But all he could say was: "Yes."

The rest of the trip back to Minbar passed in a fog of pain and anger. He did not eat, did not lie down on the bed or truly sleep, and spoke only a few words to Marcus. Still he could not cry.

Instead he thought about the rift. And that Catherine's fighter had been intact when it made the time jump.

Upon arriving back at the Ranger compound, the doctors insisted Sinclair stay overnight in the Ranger medical facility for observation. He agreed without protest, and slept for the first time in four days. The next morning he demanded an immediate meeting with Rathenn and Ulkesh. He continued to resist any effort to further treat the sutured wound on his face.

This seemed to be a matter of great concern to Rathenn, as Sinclair met with the Grey Council member and the Vorlon in one of the small conference rooms.

"Entil'Zha, the doctors say if you do not let them treat the injury, it will result in a permanent scar that will be much more difficult to remove later."

"The wound will heal on its own," Sinclair said. "We have more important things to discuss."

"But Entil'Zha," Rathenn persisted, "it is not considered befitting for a leader of your rank to have such a visible physical flaw, not when it can be treated as easily as this one. You are a symbol of—"

"Things change," Sinclair snapped. "I don't wish to

discuss it further, and I would appreciate it if you'd also tell the doctors as much."

Rathenn started to protest further, but on seeing Sinclair's expression, thought better of it.

"I want a full report on what happened to the time rift," Sinclair said.

"The explosion did much more damage to the rift than had been anticipated," Rathenn said. "And the backlash of energy caused some small injury to Draal as well, through his connection to the Great Machine."

"When will the rift be open again?"

Rathenn glanced over at the silent Ulkesh. "It will take several months at least for Draal to repair the damage."

"As soon as it's repaired, I'm going after Catherine—"

"No," Ulkesh said.

"—there's a good chance," Sinclair said over his protest, "that she survived both the attack and her passage through the rift."

"She is gone," Ulkesh said. "And can never return."

"You don't know that!" Sinclair said. "I'm sure she was alive when she went through the barrier—"

"Entil'Zha," Rathenn said. "It cannot be done."

"I don't accept that."

"I am told it is almost certain she could not have survived the time jump. You underestimate the difficulties and dangers of traveling through the rift. I am told that it requires far more than just the time stabilizers. No trip through the rift is without considerable risk, even with careful preparation, which she did not have. But even if she had survived, where would you look for her?" Rathenn asked quietly. "The rift was not under Draal's control when she passed through it. Even he cannot say where in the past she went. How would you find her among the millions upon millions of years past?''

''Draal must have *some* idea where she went.''

''He does not.''

''We have to at least try.''

''Would you ask others to risk their lives on so risky a mission with so little chance of success?'' Rathenn asked.

''No. But I will.''

''For you it would not just be a risk, Entil'Zha. The Vorlons say it would be a death sentence.''

''What are you talking about?''

''With the proper precautions, you might jump through the rift to the past without harm, but you could not jump forward again without aging, or even dying, if the span of years was great enough.''

''I don't understand, I thought the time stabilizer prevented that.''

''But you were without a time stabilizer when you first visited the rift a year ago. You were unprotected when you were exposed to the burst of tachyon radiation released as Babylon 4 jumped through the rift. One such exposure without a time stabilizer makes any time jump thereafter potentially lethal, with or without a stabilizer. Even if she somehow survived the time jump, which is unlikely, and you were able against what are surely insurmountable odds to find which era she went to, you could not return with her.''

''Why didn't you tell me this before?'' Sinclair asked angrily.

Rathenn seemed to think the answer was obvious. ''We had no reason to think you would make a time jump during this mission.''

Sinclair didn't want to believe it. ''There has to be a

way. Just how much more haven't you told me? What about it, Ambassador Ulkesh? Maybe Draal doesn't know, but what about the Vorlons? Do you know where she went? What year, what century?''

''It is irrelevant,'' Ulkesh said.

''Irrelevant?'' Sinclair instantly was on his feet and around the table. ''You son of a bitch bastard!''

Rathenn quickly put himself between the Vorlon and the enraged Entil'Zha.

''Please! Entil'Zha. Your grief is understandable, but do not let it cloud your reason. I have told you the truth in this matter.''

Sinclair tried to bring his anger under control. ''I'm sure you have, Rathenn. At least as much as you've been told.''

''Then Entil'Zha, let me say again how very sorry I am for your loss. Anla'shok Sakai was liked and respected by all, and we grieve with you. But the work we do here—''

''Is all important to you, isn't it?'' Sinclair took a deep breath. ''Don't worry. The work of the Rangers will continue. But there's going to be a few changes around here. From now on, I deal only with you, Rathenn. I don't want to even see the ambassador from Vorlon unless it is absolutely necessary.''

Rathenn glanced hesitantly at Ulkesh, but then bowed his head in compliance. Sinclair turned and left.

He walked, not knowing where he was going. He couldn't bear returning to the house he had shared with Catherine for such a brief time. Everything there was now a reminder of his loss.

For once, was he being told the whole truth? Was the Vorlon right? Was there no chance, no hope at all? Was Catherine truly gone forever? Over and over, he asked himself these questions as he walked blindly. He didn't care about the risk to himself, but Rathenn was right—even if he could somehow persuade the Vorlons and Draal to grant access to the rift, he couldn't ask others to risk their lives without even a small hope of success. And with no way of determining even to which millennia she had gone, he didn't even have that much.

God, why? he asked again, as he had innumerable times. *Why?*

He found himself in front of The Chapel. Not knowing where else to go, he entered. Marcus was sitting in the temple, meditating, but quickly scrambled to his feet.

"Forgive me, Entil'Zha. I'll leave."

"No, Marcus. Stay where you are. I didn't mean to disturb you."

Silence fell between them.

"I never really had a chance before now to tell you how truly sorry I am," Marcus said. "Anla'shok Sakai was the best. All of us, all the Rangers—we're going to miss her."

Unexpectedly, Sinclair felt tears stinging his eyes. *This is not the place to start crying,* he thought almost angrily. He was the Entil'Zha. There wasn't a Ranger under his command who hadn't experienced a loss. He was a symbol, Rathenn had said.

To keep the tears from falling he looked up—at the statue of Valen, at the *temshwee* birds nesting in the upper reaches of the temple, at the afternoon light streaming through from above. What was he doing here? He found himself thinking about the last time he had been here, pinning the badge of the Rangers on Catherine, seeing the delight in her face . . .

"Delight, respect, and compassion," he said, almost in a whisper.

"I beg your pardon, Entil'Zha?"

It was easier to keep his emotions under control if kept his gaze focused upward. He concentrated on the serene features of the statue. He found that he wanted to talk. "Delight, respect, and compassion. Valen insisted that be central to the Rangers. There's a lot written about Valen's compassion, and about his sense of respect for others. But not about what delighted him, what gave him joy. Not a lot said about that. Maybe he didn't know any happiness in his life. Maybe that's why Valen stressed the need for delight, because he knew how transitory it is. How difficult happiness is to find and then to hold on to once you've found it. Enjoy the few moments of happiness while you can because all things pass away."

"Maybe Valen," Marcus said quietly, "was also trying to tell us to remember that while the pain never goes away, there's always the chance of finding delight and joy again somewhere down the road. And that it's worth holding on for."

Sinclair looked back at Marcus, a little surprised. This was a man who had also endured too much tragedy in his life. "Maybe so, Marcus. But it's extremely difficult to believe sometimes."

Marcus nodded with understanding.

It was time to return to the house. Sinclair said goodbye to Marcus, and made his way back across the compound. Everything looked different to him now, starker somehow, harsher. But nothing more so than the house. Even from the outside, it looked unbearably empty and cold. He entered, hardly able to see anything, lost in a flood of memories as he closed the door. All the times it had fallen apart, Catherine had been the one to help him pick up the pieces. Now, he had to do it without her. He knew that she would want him to, but that was little consolation.

He went into the bedroom and sat down on her side of the bed, picked up the picture of the two of them she had carried with her since it had been taken shortly before the war. It was in a frame he had given her, black lacquered wood decorated with tiny golden stars. It had been taken when they had visited her aunt in Hong Kong . . .

He realized with a tight feeling in his chest that he would have to contact the elderly woman and tell her, and that suddenly made it all the more real that she was gone. The tears started down his face. This time he let them fall, didn't try to stop them, even though it did nothing to stop the pain.

It was several minutes before he realized he was not alone.

He turned around, and was stunned to see Kosh. He stood up, still holding the photograph. He had recognized the Vorlon ambassador to Babylon 5 immediately, not only from the different encounter suit Kosh wore, but from the different sense this Vorlon somehow gave to Sinclair. "What are you doing here?"

The Vorlon glided forward, seemed to be scrutinizing Sinclair for a long moment. "To give condolences."

That was the last thing Sinclair had expected, especially after his encounter with Ulkesh.

"Thank you."

"It was not anticipated. But you must continue."

This was too much for Sinclair. Were they never going to leave him a moment to himself, never stop pushing, interfering, manipulating, not even to allow him to grieve?

And what the hell was Kosh saying, anyway. Sinclair knew enough about the Vorlons not to assume he understood what Kosh was talking about. Exactly *what* had not been anticipated? *Who* had not anticipated it? And what exactly must he continue? Long association with the Vorlons had taught him to automatically consider those kinds of questions about every statement they made, and never jump to the easy conclusion.

To ask a Vorlon to explain a statement was to get a "clarification" that only made matters more confusing. But he was angry again.

"Why? Why should I 'continue'? Why am I so important to the Vorlons, Kosh? And don't give me any stuff about my having a Minbari soul and fulfilling prophecy. That doesn't play with me the way it does with the Minbari. Why me?"

"You have a role to play."

"And I'm the only one who can play it? I find that hard to believe. I've always gotten the impression we mere mortal Humans and Minbari are pretty much interchangeable to you Vorlons."

"Only you can play the role as needed. Only you will see the difference."

"I don't suppose you want to explain that a little further?"

Kosh didn't answer.

"I didn't think so," Sinclair said finally. "If even a fraction of what you Vorlons say is true—and I have no confidence that more than a fraction of it is the absolute truth"—he paused, hoping for some kind of reaction to that, but not really surprised when none was forthcoming—"then I will 'continue,' as you put it. I will see the work of the Rangers through. Because it means saving lives, and that's what's important to me. As for what's important to you and the rest of the Vorlons—I really don't know. But I sometimes get the feeling that what's important to you, Ambassador Kosh, is not the same as what's important to Ambassador Ulkesh."

Again, Kosh did not reply. But neither did he turn to leave. He stood there, as if waiting for Sinclair to say more.

Sinclair looked down at the picture he was still holding, and felt a sudden twinge of hope. He had never gotten what he considered a straight answer out of Ulkesh. Would it be any different with Kosh?

Or am I just grasping at straws? he thought. *At any hope, no matter how improbable?*

There was nothing to lose by asking. And everything to gain.

''Kosh, do you know where the rift sent Catherine and whether or not she survived the time jump?''

The Vorlon didn't answer, although even that was an improvement over what Ulkesh had said. Maybe he hadn't asked the right question.

''All right. Just answer me one question. I'll believe what you tell me, because I think we respect each other enough for that. And no matter what your answer, I promise I won't just abandon my responsibilities here. But tell me this: do you know if there is any hope at all of my finding her again?''

With a surge of bitter disappointment—all the more painful for the hope he had allowed himself—Sinclair saw Kosh turn and leave without responding. He followed the Vorlon out to the front, watched him go out the door. He had been a fool to think even for a moment he would get an answer.

But as the door closed beind the Vorlon, Sinclair heard a reply, whether spoken aloud or directly to his thoughts, he was not sure.

''Perhaps.''

CHAPTER 31

MARCUS paused outside the Earth Embassy in Tuzanor, and looked around. He was a little early for his appointment. It was his last day on Minbar—for how long he didn't know—and he had taken a couple of hours to walk along the streets of the City of Sorrows one more time. Now he was back at the beginning of it all, the embassy. He hadn't been here since the day he had first met Ambassador Sinclair and been accepted into Ranger training. It seemed appropriate that this was his last stop before heading to Yedor, and from there to his new assignment on Zagros 7, a Drazi colony where Marcus was to help establish a Ranger training camp.

He had received his official orders and instructions already, but the Entil'Zha had requested he stop in just before leaving so they might talk unofficially and say good-bye, a request that had pleased Marcus very much. He hadn't seen much of Sinclair in the month since Catherine Sakai had been lost to the time rift, and he had worried that the Entil'Zha associated him too much with that painful memory.

Certainly, from what Marcus had seen of Sinclair, the event had changed him. He was more somber now, and when he did smile, it was too often tinged with sadness. He was still involved in every aspect of the

Ranger operation, continued to teach classes, and remained open to any Ranger who wished to speak to him, keeping the same concerned interest in each of them that he always had. But there were times when it was clear he needed to be alone; he had even taken to wearing the hood of his cowl when he took his walks, something he had never done before. Those Rangers who had been with him since before the incident understood and respected this need; those Rangers who joined after the incident simply accepted this intriguing aloofness as part of the Entil'Zha's mystique.

Marcus decided it was close enough to the appointed time, and entered the building. He was waved through by Sinclair's ever-efficient assistant Venak, and Marcus walked into the ambassador's office feeling a little nervous.

"Hello, Marcus. Please have a seat."

Marcus was put at ease by the warm smile with which Sinclair greeted him, but he could still see the sadness beneath it.

"Entil'Zha," Marcus said, with a small bow, before taking the offered seat. It was still a shock to see the pronounced scar on Sinclair's face. All the Rangers knew that he had refused treatment to remove it, even though such surgery was a simple matter. And all of them understood why. It had also added to the mystique, though that had never been Sinclair's intention.

"I wanted to wish you good luck on your mission to Zagros 7," Sinclair said. "You'll find the Drazi a very interesting people, but occasionally infuriating. With them, be sure to remember the first lesson I taught in reconnaissance class—"

"Watch out for the half truth that is told to mislead from the real truth," Marcus quoted to him, "A half truth can be worse than a lie."

Sinclair smiled again. "Glad to see you were paying attention."

"I think I've learned that lesson in spades, Entil'Zha," Marcus said, deliberately taking a light tone. He had already been fully briefed on the Drazi, as Sinclair well knew. It seemed the Entil'Zha just wanted to talk, and as Marcus had come to think of Sinclair as a friend, as much as any Ranger and the Entil'Zha could be friends, he was happy to oblige. "It seems to be a favorite saying of the Minbari, though for the life of me I can't figure out why, since they seem to love their own occasional half truth. I still haven't figured out how a people who claim they haven't killed one of their own in centuries, can still have a ritual fight to the death."

"The *denn'sha,*" Sinclair said with some surprise. "That's not part of Ranger training. How did you learn about that?"

"The Minbari Rangers mention it from time to time. It seems to be pretty important to them."

"But rare," Sinclair said. "The way I understand it, when a Minbari agrees to the *denn'sha,* he is agreeing to take responsibility for his own death should he lose, thereby removing any responsibility for his death from his opponent."

"A very neat word trick," Marcus said. "The Minbari can twist words with the best of them."

"They've learned just a little too much from the Vorlons in this area," Sinclair said, suddenly very serious again. "Don't ever forget that, about either of them." He leaned back in his chair, still looking at Marcus, but with a distant expression, as if trying to decide what to say. "You're an excellent Ranger, Marcus. One of our very best. I hope you know that."

"Thank you, Entil'Zha," Marcus said, pleased at the words, but not forgetting the lesson on hubris he had learned from Sech Turval and Sinclair the last time he had gotten too pleased with himself.

"I'm confident that your position with the Rangers will continue to grow in importance and responsibility. Where it will take you, I don't know yet." He paused again.

Marcus wondered just how many people there were on Minbar now with whom Sinclair could just sit and talk, muse out loud, work out his thoughts. He doubted there really was anyone. Though not a close friend, Marcus at least shared some experiences with Sinclair that made talking with him apparently easier than with most. And now Marcus was about to leave, too.

"The Minbari and the Vorlons talk sometimes about 'the arrow of destiny,'" Sinclair said. "That a life is like an arrow shot from a bow, directed to a predestined target, and all our misery comes from failing to realize this and conform to that path."

Marcus nodded. "We heard a little of that in some of our classes. But you always said we didn't have to accept all their metaphysics to be a Ranger. So, if it wasn't going to be on the test, I just didn't pay much attention to it."

Marcus was gratified when Sinclair laughed at this. He hadn't heard Sinclair laugh in some time.

"You'll hear more about it, believe me," Sinclair said. "But beware of the false analogy, Marcus. Like the half truth, it's one of the greatest enemies of reason. A conscious, rational being is different from an arrow in one very important way: an arrow doesn't have free will. A Human being does. With free will, an arrow can change its flight and select among many different targets, regardless of where the bow was initially aimed. Always remember that. A man must determine his own destiny, and never give up his responsibility for choice. I don't believe anything is absolutely predestined."

"I've always believed that myself, Entil'Zha," Marcus replied. "I guess I'm just stubborn that way. I refuse to accept that everything's already been written and said. Seems kind of boring to me. There'd be no surprises."

"Well, there may come a time in your life as a Ranger where you'll be asked to do something because *others* have decided that it's your destiny. If it appears to be the right thing to do, then go ahead with it, but for your reasons, not theirs. They may think they have released an arrow toward a predetermined target, but they may be surprised where the arrow actually hits."

Marcus looked at Sinclair curiously. He seemed to be trying to work something out for himself. As excited as Marcus had been about his assignment, he now found himself wanting to stay. A Ranger pledged to live for the One and Marcus took that pledge very seriously. Perhaps his duty would be better served by staying on Minbar.

"Entil'Zha," Marcus said, then stopped. What could he say? He couldn't second-guess his orders. This was his superior officer. Sinclair had his reasons for sending him, and not someone else, to Zagros 7. But he had to say something, especially as Sinclair was looking at him expectantly, waiting for him to speak.

"Are you going to be all right?" Marcus instantly wanted to recall the words. Was he being presumptuous?

"Thank you, Marcus," Sinclair said. "I appreciate your asking, as I've appreciated your friendship. I'll be fine. Our job as Rangers is to help create a better future. In spite of everything, that's still a pretty good job to have."

Sinclair got up and Marcus quickly stood as well. ''Before you go,'' Sinclair said. ''I'd like to give you a small gift. I know you'll make good use of it.''

He handed Marcus a Minbari fighting pike. From the look of it, it was a very old one. Marcus couldn't resist snapping it open, and was amazed at how smoothly it sprung into place, how beautifully balanced it felt in his hands. It was without doubt the finest *denn'bok* he'd ever seen.

''Thank you,'' he said. ''I've never seen one like it.''

''I was going to give it to Catherine,'' Sinclair said very quietly. ''I think she'd appreciate you having it.''

Marcus was overwhelmed and didn't know what to say, but for the first time in a long time, he felt tears stinging at his eyes. He straightened to attention and saluted, hand to chest. ''Entil'Zha veni!''

''Until we see each other again, Marcus.''

EPILOGUE

MARCUS realized he'd been sitting too long. As he healed from the injuries he had sustained in his fight with Neroon, he found he couldn't stay in any one position for too long. He decided he'd be more comfortable standing up again.

He looked around and wondered once more where Sech Turval was. He had been told his old meditation teacher spent a lot of time in the chapel now as there were certain very involved rituals that had to be performed on a regular schedule for several months following the loss of a Ranger One and the installation of a new one.

Loss. An interesting choice of word, Marcus decided. He thought about the conversation he had had with Sinclair before leaving on the mission that took him to Zagros 7 and eventually Babylon 5, when they had talked about how words could be used to hide the truth. Was he trying to hide an unpleasant truth from himself now? Sinclair had traveled to the distant past to become Valen. Every Minbari who had lived in Valen's time was now dead. But Marcus simply couldn't think of Sinclair in those terms. When he thought of the Entil'Zha, it was always in the present tense. It was impossible for Marcus to think of him in any other way. A week after Sinclair had taken Babylon 4 into the rift, a package had arrived for Marcus from Minbar. It had contained Sinclair's copy of *The Meditations of Marcus Aurelius*. For several days thereafter, Marcus had to keep reminding himself he couldn't send the Entil'Zha a thank you—not unless he could send it a thousand years into the past.

Maybe it was because Sinclair always talked about the future. He taught every Ranger class the Minbari proverb about Tuzanor: that to dream in the City of Sorrows, was to dream of a better future. It seemed to have special significance for Sinclair.

Perhaps that was why Marcus had been so shocked when Sinclair had told them he would be taking Babylon 4 into the past on a one-way trip. Marcus had even volunteered to go in Sinclair's place. The Entil'Zha had always seemed so concerned with the future.

It was only much later that it occurred to Marcus that Sinclair had an equally strong connection to the past. That's where Catherine Sakai had gone. And though Marcus had thought of her as gone forever, he realized that Sinclair must have held her in the present tense, just as Marcus still did when thinking of Sinclair.

He had been told that no rescue attempt could be made to try and find Catherine, because there was no way to determine where in the past she had gone, and Marcus had accepted that. But of course he realized now that Sinclair most certainly never did. Had he gone into the past carrying some hope of finding her? Or had Sinclair gone to do what he thought he had to do, carrying only the consolation that he could at least share a similar fate with her, marooned in the past?

Marcus didn't know.

He couldn't stop looking at the statue. Didn't look a thing like the man he knew.

The Minbari had decided it was not wise to make it generally known that the great Valen was actually a Human. Marcus was one of the few people, even among the Rangers, who knew the truth.

"Anla'shok Cole!"

Marcus turned around, pleased to see the familiar face of Sech Turval. "It's good to see you again."

"I am always pleased to see one of my students who has done well," the old Minbari said with a slight bow, which Marcus returned. "I am sorry I was not here to greet you, but I was only just informed you had arrived."

"It's all right. I enjoy sitting here. Or, at the moment, standing."

Sech Turval looked at the statue of Valen. He was one of the few others who also knew the truth about Sinclair. "It would be pleasant to talk with you a while, Marcus, before you return to Babylon 5. But first I must give you something, and I will leave you alone to examine it. This was found only last week. I do not know what it means."

He handed Marcus an envelope and left.

Marcus saw that his name was written on the envelope in a familiar script. He also recognized that the envelope was made from a kind of Minbari paper that was only used for important occasions. The paper was made to last for thousands of years, and the older the unused paper was, the more valuable it was. The more important the occasion, the more care was taken to find the oldest sheet of paper possible. Someone had apparently thought this letter very important, since the paper seemed to be very old.

He opened it carefully. Inside was an unsigned note that read: "From both of us, our thanks and friendship.

Continue to dream that better future . . . where perhaps we'll meet again.''

Marcus sat back down, unsure what to think. It seemed to be Sinclair's handwriting. But when had it been written? The age of the paper told him nothing. The letter itself could have been written a month ago—or a thousand years ago. He looked back up at the statue of Valen, and wondered.

And he couldn't help remember what the Minbari always said.

That Valen would return someday.